THE PLACE WE ALL GO

M. DYLAN BLAIR

MOODYCATMEDIA LLC.

This novel is dedicated to any person who's ever stared into the Darkness and felt it stare back.

Also, to the real Jackson who inspired this novel:

Go fuck yourself.

"Whoever fights monsters should see to it
that in the process he does not become a monster.
And if you gaze long enough into an abyss,
the abyss will gaze back into you."
~ Friedrich Nietzsche

SENSITIVE TOPIC WARNING

If you are someone who needs a trigger warning, here it is. However, by reading this, you will spoil parts of the plot for yourself. Please be safe, whoever you are.

This novel explores some of the best and worst parts of our humanity. It includes topics such as mental illness, institutionalization, suicide, domestic violence, substance use, misogyny, and murder.

Oh, and needles. Really big needles.

PART I

THEN

SOMEWHERE IN DALLAS

RED LIGHTS, ONLY RED lights.

The river of stopped traffic snaking along the Central Expressway should serve as a warning to the hours-long delay. But for those unfortunate souls who missed the detour sign five miles back, the swarm of emergency vehicles parked along the median drives the point home.

Midnight will be long gone before the motorists escape this gridlock and return to their families—to their lives. With no viable alternative, those remaining are committed to the long haul, trapped between the torrential rain and flashing emergency lights.

Farther down the roadway, two men lean against a nearby guardrail while a third paces the asphalt, each captivated by the chaos unfolding. To their relief, this world is too absorbed in its own mundane troubles to notice their presence.

Not yet anyway.

Unlike those stuck in traffic, the angry rain does not bother the three men. It's a refreshing distraction from what comes next.

The tallest of the three rubs his face. His tired, pale

complexion is an ever-present reminder of what's on the line tonight. His calloused hands slide across his scalp, brushing his wavy brown hair out of his eyes. He glances at his watch. *It's late.*

"You really think this'll work, Kenji?" he asks the man next to him, a broad-chested middle-aged Asian whose only visible emotion is how tightly his lips are pressed together. "What if you're wrong?"

Kenji draws a long sip from his half-melted cherry Slurpee. "Let me worry about that, Kane. You shouldn't bother yourself with such things. You'll get wrinkles like me."

Kane sighs. Both know the younger man's nature won't let things go; being careful is what's kept him alive this long.

Kenji points to their third companion wandering in the roadway. "You sure about that one? He seems a little . . . *unsteady.*"

Kane studies their newest recruit. Based on how the man paces in circles on the black asphalt, probably not. "Zaire?"

Their bewildered third glances over, his tawny complexion unable to hide the blood coating his brow. Nearly a head shorter than Kane, Zaire's sable curls, lush beard, and hooked Middle Eastern nose don't take away from his everyday human attire. If anything, he appears normal in his black leather jacket, white cotton T-shirt, and faded denim jeans. Aside from the deep gash running vertically down his right eye and cheek, he *was* normal until moments ago.

Now he's like his newest companions—caught between two bad choices where the likelihood of getting what they want is extremely slim. Kane slides off the railing and shoots Kenji a cross look. "Last time and then it's over? We have a deal?"

The man nods and takes another slurp. Death always was a thirsty business.

☥

Kane walks toward Zaire and then stops, turning back. "It's never been done this way. Not in two thousand years."

Kenji smiles. "Times be a changin', Kane. You'll see."

Kane thrusts his hands into his pockets. "Fine. Which one are you taking?"

Glancing down the stretch of road toward the flashing lights, Kenji draws silent. After a beat, he clicks his tongue. "Well now, I've got my pick of the litter and this night's only getting started. I'll let you know."

"Don't do what you did last time, Kenji, and screw us all," Kane says, grimacing. "Remember the rules. No meddling."

Kenji waves a hand in the air. "Always were such a fun killer."

Shouts from the accident echo back up the roadway; the rescue team has found the next body.

"Fantastic," Kenji announces. "Thanks for the drink, by the way. These are pretty good."

They watch as the firefighters use the Jaws of Life to extract the next corpse, ripping the poor soul free from the machination that was once a vehicle. A birdlike female with hair the color of straw, a difficult thing to distinguish given all the blood and viscera.

Zaire teeters, and Kane is quick to steady him.

"Kenji, maybe we should discuss this first. He's not ready—" Kane looks back at the guardrail, their companion gone. It's only the melted Slurpee now.

"That's decided," Kane says, turning toward Zaire. "Listen, are you positive you want to do this? There are no redoes."

"What choice do I have? I've lost her."

"Try some other way," Kane says. "Not this."

It's not long before the first ambulance howls along the gravel median, the vehicle's piercing sirens a dire warning to those still trapped in traffic. Eventually, Zaire ambles down the roadway toward the city, forcing Kane to give chase.

"Wait up," Kane hollers.

Zaire stops. "You act like you don't have skin in this too. I'm just willing to do something about it."

"What if you fail?" Kane asks. "What then?"

"It won't happen. Not if we've got you." The shorter man wipes the blood from his eyes on his jacket sleeve and clasps his new companion by the shoulder. If he doesn't get to a hospital soon, there's no doubt he's headed for a nasty-looking scar. "Don't forget you're our ticket out of this."

A pang of nausea hits Kane in the gut. *This was wrong. All of it.*

He'd seen countless other zealots fight the system and lose miserably. With Kenji now involved, Zaire will simply become the next fool in a long line of individuals willing to watch the world burn if they can reign over the ashes.

Like a disjointed version of The Three Musketeers, each man has their own reasons for pursuing this descent into madness.

Kane tosses his head back and stares at the darkened firmament now that the rain has finally tapered. Keeping those two in line will surely be a Herculean task, one that might kill him in the process. Seeing this through is the only option he has.

Find her and it's over. Find her and he's home scot-free. Once and for all. That's the deal.

Kane buries his hands in his jacket pockets and waits as the remaining ambulances pull out like the hounds of Hell are on them, their quarries in tow.

Whether he likes it or not, Kenji's right.

It's going to be a long night.

☥

A FEW DAYS LATER
SOMEWHERE ELSE IN DALLAS

I ALWAYS KNEW OUR story would end like this—one of us getting lowered into a fresh grave. Too bad I guessed the wrong person.

Apologizing to the dead won't do any good. Not anymore.

I tighten my grip on the oversized umbrella until all feeling disappears, half from the freezing rain, the other from the terrible fear paralyzing me in place. It's the only thing stalling the panic attack looming in my chest.

You showed. Of course you did, you sonuvabitch. No decency, no tact. Our client deserved better than this.

Avoiding the angry rain is a gargantuan endeavor, a task my chosen attire—a black pencil dress and matching blazer—isn't too pleased with. My dry cleaner is going to love me. My thick medium-length black curls are tied back, exposing the simple drop earrings I pull out for occasions outside of court. No makeup, simple kitten heels.

Honestly, I should've chosen something warmer; I'm small enough the brisk October air pierces through me. But today isn't about us, even though it should be.

☥

We're the reason this nice family's child is dead. After all, we're the ones who killed her.

If we're lucky, these heartbroken folks don't know that and never will. This family is too busy mourning to stop the funeral, so we play these games instead.

My head lowers as the priest starts his eulogy on loss and God. Though I'm not a faith-bearing woman, I am respectful all the same. I have enough common sense to keep from showing up at a place of grief and show my ass.

You, sir, however, do not.

Jackson Alders, the Golden boy of Dallas prosecutors and my narcissistic ex. Unfortunately, also my law partner.

Today Jackson's not dressed to the nines in his favorite bespoke suit like he usually is. A symbol of my love, the damn thing finally went into my trash last week. In its absence, he's donned a simple cashmere button-down and slacks instead.

Dressed like a commoner, it's amazing the man left the new penthouse. With his wavy surfer-blond locks slicked back, he spots me from across the cemetery, his bleached smile lighting up like the Fourth of July. His square jaw, perfect sun-kissed tan, and all-American frame drive home that Jackson's not a threat.

To these people, he's a hero.

To the city, Jackson is the gorgeous, young city prosecutor who's never lost a case. Not even this one. One phone call was all it took to convince Judge Abbott to strike the case from the docket. All charges were dismissed one day before the trial.

Eight hours later, our client was dead, and the police didn't glance at the firm. Not a single whiff. A simple coincidence.

The bastard's *untouchable.*

I try to ignore Jackson's strides and the way his thigh-length trench coat stretches over his muscular frame. Katie, our legal assistant, trails behind with an umbrella in her manicured hand, fighting to keep them both dry. By the way the storm has soaked her burgundy mini dress, it's clear the woman's losing.

But it doesn't matter. Not since those two began sleeping together. Give their relationship a few months and it won't be long before he ditches Katie too. The poor girl's low-hanging fruit. The shiny, new object on Jackson's top shelf. *Women are replaceable,* he had told me once.

The other half of Alders & Allbrook Law reaches where I hang back from the main crowd, caught between the towering live oaks and the snaking cobbled sidewalk. "This is a private function, you know," I whisper, not bothering to look over.

"Of course." Jackson nods. "Invitation only."

The priest notices the commotion but ignores it; he's got a eulogy to finish.

My heels sink into the wet grass, reminding me how much I hate funerals. "I see you brought a date."

While Katie isn't aware their tryst is public information, Jackson doesn't hesitate at the chance to parade her here on purpose.

"Katie is my assistant," he corrects.

Don't get me wrong. She's a great aide, thorough and kind to the firm's clients in their time of need, but she's a pawn in Jackson's schemes, like I was. The poor girl catches up, scrambling to find partial shelter under the mossy live oaks. Her dress is a lost cause, and she looks like she's been crying enough that no amount of waterproof makeup can save her in the rain.

"Sorry, I'm late. Morning, Jesly," she greets me. "How you holding up?"

I don't bother answering her. I'm too ruffled by the fact that Jackson's even here in the first place. With his wholesome appearance, he appears unfazed, as if he's got all the time in the world. Katie, on the other hand, just stands there awkwardly. She looks like I feel.

I run my tongue over my teeth and turn to Jackson. "You've got balls showing up. What if someone recognizes you?"

His brow crunches, scorn angling down his Roman nose. "Everyone recognizes me. I'm the face of the city, Jesly."

Sighing, I know better than to start an argument that there's no chance of winning. Six months of therapy for narcissistic victim abuse and codependency has gotten me here. Living alone in an oversized apartment and trapped in business with a psychopath. *Healthy boundaries,* my therapist keeps reminding me.

Jackson digs into his trench coat and pulls out a sealed legal envelope with the word *Discovery* stamped all over the front. He thrusts the goldenrod envelope in my direction. "I brought you a present, Love."

"Stop calling me that."

The words no sooner escape my lips than his bleached grin falls, tearing away the mask he so carefully wears. Before Katie can even notice, Jackson's cheerful demeanor returns.

Poor girl. She won't even see it coming. Hell, she's too busy staring down the casket to do anything anyways.

He sucks in a breath. "I figured you'd enjoy it."

I stare at the envelope like it's a snake. Our schedule is clear this week. I made sure of it. Today's docket is blank; there's not one case. "What is it?"

The illusion intact, Jackson's smile doesn't drop. "You know."

I do. *Damnit.* I snatch the envelope from him; it's too late.

☥

"Leaving the scene of a crime with injury, DUI, and reckless homicide," Jackson rattles off, grinning like the Cheshire Cat. "You really did it this time, Jesly."

"I hate you."

"I bet you do. The holy trifecta might get you life in prison," he croons. "See what breaking up gets you? It's a good thing the cops were able to track down witnesses."

My jaw tightens. People are beginning to listen—something the bastard was counting on. Celebrating that evening wasn't even my idea; it was his. But it doesn't matter. Not to him or the throng of family and friends attending our dead client's funeral.

He's playing you for the ignorant fool you are.

"What did you just say?" I hiss at Katie, horrified.

Her eyes widen, and she looks to Jackson for reassurance. "Nobody said a word, Jesly."

He narrows his gaze, pretending to act concerned. After all, the crowd is watching. "Haven't these nice folks gone through enough without you here?"

"You're blaming me?" I ask.

"If the shoe fits."

I suck in a breath and count to ten. *Don't take the bait.* As I squirrel the envelope from the downpour, my free hand bumps the Ativan bottle stashed in my blazer pocket. Six months of working with a therapist has left me with a crappy sleep schedule and these fucking anxiety meds.

Rushing from the apartment this morning, I didn't stop to take a dose. A few hours later, the cramp in my chest is horrible. But I won't reach for the bottle here, not in front of everyone.

After six years together, Jackson knows every one of my triggers. Causing pain is sport for him, provoking a breakdown is

☥

a bonus. No one leaves Jackson Alders. Not alive anyway.

A flash goes off somewhere in my peripheral vision, and I almost wrench my neck trying to find the culprit. "What are cameras doing here?"

"All press is good press," he says.

Another flash.

Fucking scavengers, even in the rain. Reporters would chase after a dead body if it paid. *Literally.* "You called the news?"

His shit-eating grin is back. "No need."

The rain's gotten worse, pelting the remaining attendees like tears from Heaven. Those who aren't immediate family have trickled toward the reception hall, leaving only a few to steward as the first shovels of dirt hit the casket. Each drop echoes in the pit of my stomach.

Plop, plop, plop.

Another flash. *Goddamnit.*

Before the human vultures draw any closer, an unruly-looking guy with an unkempt beard and a bottle tucked in a corner store bag chases them off the sidewalk. Even with the disheveled jacket and tattered cargo pants, he can't be much older than us. That same bottle buries itself four inches deep into the glass windshield of the closest news van parked along the trailing drive. The camera crew and reporters are caught between filming the chaos and protecting their equipment.

They choose the former.

Although the funeral is held on public property, it doesn't account for lack of human decency. Anybody can show up, including Jackson and his paparazzi.

My small hands shake as I clutch the rain-battered umbrella tighter. Coming here was a mistake. It's likely seconds before I become the axis of a carnival's merry-go-round. Vertigo makes walking a bitch. I bite my lip to distract myself from the pain bolting down the right side of my cheek. *Breathe in, breathe out. No tears. Do not give him the satisfaction.*

Jackson follows along, matching my stride. "Jesly, you really should secure an attorney before the arraignment." He beams like I'm going to pick him for kickball. The bastard planned this whole thing under the assumption I'd run back and beg for his help.

Well, not anymore. "Jackson?" I stop in the middle of the sludgy grass.

"Yes, Love?" he says hopefully.

"Fuck off."

People often say the road to Hell is paved with good intentions, but that's a warped version of the truth. Some idealistic bullshit, which only exists in fairy tales and college lecture halls. The road is actually lined with blood that Jackson and I spilled the night that we walked away and left everyone else for dead.

The Universe's sense of irony was on full display that evening; the opposite car housing our own client. Now the woman's dead, and we're standing at her funeral acting like we didn't murder the goddamned woman.

I look over at Jackson, his emotions like a steel cage. Whatever witnesses he's trumped up, my checkbook has likely paid for it. Slapping the pending charges on me is a win in his book. Collateral damage is expected, especially when we've broken up for the third time.

A few more flashes go off, the press eating up tomorrow's morning headline. Whoever they are, they're willing to risk vehicle damage if it gets them a byline. Every single media outlet believes no jury could convict the man of any wrongdoing—the beloved prodigal son of Dallas' underbelly. In an over-incarcerated America, fighting against the machine is free publicity.

To them, he's a god fighting the good fight. Working tirelessly to end corruption and clean up our streets.

The truth is that Dallas is full of fools hungry for a sensation. Not a soul in this entire cemetery knows what he's capable of. Not yet. But they soon will.

There's no one Jackson wouldn't use to get what he wants, even me, and we were engaged for over half a decade. Like with any narcissist's trap, victims don't see the monster until it's too late. It was that same hold that convinced me to drive.

It never should've happened, but not every mistake gets erased. Not even when you want them to. A reality staring back at me now that I've made it under the nearest overhang. Beneath a massive stone mausoleum with a faded name I can't make out, I dig the envelope out of my blazer.

Most people don't climb out of bed and decide this is the day to fuck up their life, but it happens to the best of us. That's the piece the world's just now figuring out—the part where I killed someone.

SOMETHING WICKED
NOW

I DIDN'T DESERVE THIS. You knew that, but you did it to me anyway.

"Happy Thursday morning, Dallas-Fort Worth. As we bleed into the third week of the investigation, the heat is turning up for Alders and Allbrook Law, a once-shining star in our city," a woman's voice blasts from the wall-mounted TV as I fidget in the morning Starbucks line. "Minutes ago, WFAA News learned the attorney general's office has named firm partner Jesly Allbrook as an official person of interest in the criminal investigation. What will this do to DFW's favorite power couple?"

The door chimes and a rush of teenagers burst into the café. It's not long before the cacophony of youth drowns out the news anchor with the ubiquitous bob cut. The legal envelope burns a hole in my hand as I clutch it tighter than my tote bag. The paperwork hasn't left my sight since the funeral days ago.

The damn thing's like Pandora's box. There's no point in opening it—I already know what happens when I do. The end of everything, including me.

"Small half-caff hazelnut?" a female voice calls from behind the service counter.

My eyes stay glued to the screen above our heads. *I can't do this.*

"Miss?"

"Hey." One of the teenagers nudges my arm and I suck in a breath. "That you?"

My eyes lock with the flustered barista holding out the cup. "Oh, sorry." I grab it and scurry to the closest empty table. My leather tote thumps on the wooden surface as I scramble to shove the envelope inside.

Reminding me how much the universe hates me, the news station flashes a picture of Jackson and me from last year's Christmas party. We're arm-in-arm; a beautiful young couple in love. Even then, happiness was an act. Not mine, but his. *Always.*

Now I get nauseated just looking.

If I don't get out before someone recognizes Dallas' soon-to-be most wanted, my lunch break will go from bad to worse. Barreling through the checkout line, I bolt out the door, only for the crisp fall air to snap at my face. My tote tumbles onto the sidewalk and with it the envelope.

"Shit," I yelp.

"Oh, let me help." An older man stops to gather my belongings from the concrete.

"No, it's okay." I drop to my knees and scramble to shove everything back in my purse. All but one.

"Here," he says, handing over the envelope.

Foolish woman. Now he knows too. They all will.

"Miss, you alright?"

Forcing a smile, I latch onto the paperwork. "Thanks."

I glance in his direction and stumble backward. The right side of his face has morphed into a bad Salvador Dali painting, his features drooping exponentially worse than any possible stroke. His eyes no longer sit affixed in place; rather one lingers above his brow while the other sits in the crevice of his right cheekbone.

My gasp is audible.

It's not real.

It's not real.

It's not real.

I close my eyes and count to three. When I open them, only the man's bewildered look remains.

Don't let him see. Don't let any of them see. They'll lock you up again. Just like last time.

"I've got it. Thank you," I manage.

He left you to clean up this mess, like you wanted. Pathetic.

I swallow my unease and glance at my watch. *11:11*. The dial's been stuck for a while, something I haven't gotten around to fixing. Yet another broken thing in my life, which means I'm already late.

Racing down the sidewalk into the heart of downtown, I can't shake the feeling I'm being watched. This malaise has been rolling in since the funeral, but now it's off the charts. *Something's wrong.*

Traffic is crap in Dallas, and those of us crossing downtown on foot are subjected to its unyielding wrath. I pull my peacoat tighter to block what cold I can. The weather hasn't been above 52° in weeks.

If I'm quick, I can make it in less than fifteen minutes. Thankfully, I know the building like the back of my hand. With my caseload cleared, I've had ample time to consider this.

My plan will work. The Renaissance Tower.

The birth of philosophy, literature, and art, and precursor to the Enlightenment. My favorite era in history. *'Man is born free, but everywhere is in chains.'* Rousseau's greatest line. Today I'm making it my epitaph.

The executive buildings sit less than a mile from the café, but I've parked far enough away that each step hammers this afternoon trip home.

After today, I won't have to do it anymore.

After today, it's over.

Minutes pass before I drag open the massive glass door and slip into the building. Unlike other downtown Dallas high-rises, this skyscraper has a food court attached, but I prefer grabbing my coffee a few streets away. The long walk grounds and centers me before I plunge into the first rung of Hell.

The emergency stairwell lives near the bathrooms, and with everyone rushing to grab their overpriced lunches before returning to corporate purgatory, no one notices the emergency exit click closed behind me. *Good.* It grants enough time for what comes next.

For the past six months, eighteen days, seven hours, and forty-nine minutes, my goal has been to find the emergency stairs of each client's building and climb to the roof. A crazy habit, I know, but I'm not some nut.

Yes, you are, Jesly. Stop lying.

Reaching the roof is damn near impossible. Downtown high-rise buildings typically have secured roof access. Of the hundred or so buildings I've checked, less than five have been accessible.

With no sun in sight, the sky has turned an abysmal gray. The bitter wind stings as it whips past again. It's not like the movies. No one even knows you're out here. This is the only promising roof so far.

The Renaissance Tower. My eyes roll.

☥

A new life? Not for me.

At seven hundred and ten feet, the Renaissance Tower is the quintessential all-American high-rise. An amalgamation of postmodernism and decorative spires, its peak beckons photographers and thrill chasers alike.

My goal is simple: to end this madness once and for all.

You won't do it. You're a coward, Jesly.

Shaking the thoughts away, I carefully lift the metal tabs off the legal envelope, though it won't make a difference. I avoid looking directly at the paper and stare out at the cityscape before the afternoon sun peeks through the dismal sky. Digging my phone out of my pocket, I mash the combination to unlock it. The phone log opens, with my last five calls going unanswered.

My chest tightens, suffocating me. *I didn't deserve this.*

Everyone thinks ending a life, or more colloquially, 'taking a life,' is such a sin. It's not. There are times it's the only answer— an opportunity of sorts. Dying solves a problem with no other viable solution.

Sometimes you're too far gone to become someone new, and it's only through a reset—a real life-altering, ground-shaking moment that things change. But I'm not trying to erase my past. I'm here to make amends to whoever's in charge because Jackson sure as shit won't.

A life for a life.

A burst of cold air rushes past, forcing me to clutch my jacket tighter. The meteorologist lied when he said to expect warmer weather. Or perhaps I'm high enough the windchill counteracts any chance of warmth from this miserable day. A high of 41°. *No, thank you.*

I should call Jackson again and tell him off one last time. *Not that he'll care.* My thumb trembles over the little green phone icon. I know there's no point, but self-control isn't my strong suit.

I lose the battle.

He won't answer. *Ring.* We haven't spoken since the funeral. Not really. *Ring.* I drop my stuff on a concrete outcrop nearby and take one last swig of hazelnut coffee. A dying woman's dream; there's nothing better. In college, I tried to drink cold coffee, but it didn't stick. *Ring.*

"Hi, you've reached Jackson Alders. I am—" I hit **END** and chuck my cell across the rooftop slabs. Fighting the tears is useless.

Sometimes when I hold my breath, I pretend time stops, and with it everything else. Even if it's for a few moments. *Tabula Rasa,* a clean slate. An idealist's dream, perhaps.

After law school, I poured everything into the firm and built it from the ground up. With the last remaining bit of scholarship funds and a sizable chunk of my trust advanced to me, Alders and Allbrook Law was born. I even put Jackson's name first to show him how dedicated I was to our future—a terrible mistake looking back at it.

The man had found his meal ticket up the social ladder. It only added tinder to a voracious spark, making an already emboldened man even bolder.

It's the same hunger that made us walk away that night.

You bastard.

Up here, there's no barbed wire. No fencing. Nothing more than a flimsy metal guardrail no wider than my wrist. Once you get this far, there's only God to stop you, and I doubt he gives a shit about me now.

Not after what I've done.

I glance at my watch. *It's time.*

With zero chance that I'm going to read the documents, I toss them over the edge. I won't give Jackson the satisfaction, not after he's taken everything from me.

One last deep breath rattles the cage I've boxed myself in, but it's too late to change my mind. Though my hands are still damaged from the accident, they're strong enough for this.

Climb over and let go. Easy.

"You shouldn't stand so close to the edge," a calm male voice startles me from behind, and I'm forced to catch myself preemptively. "You could fall, you know."

Less than a dozen feet away is a light-skinned guy about my age, looking no less exhausted than I'm sure I do. He's at least a whole head taller, with a headful of medium-length chestnut brown waves and a square jaw hidden beneath a short boxed beard. Casually dressed; a tan canvas jacket, olive Henley, and faded jeans cling to his muscular frame, making it hard to discern which floor he works on. At any rate, he's dressed warmer than me.

I clutch onto the weak excuse for a railing. One small impact and it'll break. "How did you get up here?"

"I could ask you the same thing."

"Is it any of your business?"

"No, probably not," he agrees and steps in my direction. "But it's a nice morning. Thought I'd get my steps in."

"On the roof?"

"Yeah, why not?" He shrugs. "You're here."

"Excuse me?"

"You're here," he repeats. "Can't be all bad. I mean, attracting tourists and all."

I stare at him blankly. *Is he serious right now?*

"I never took rooftops for such hotspots," he says as his boots crunch across the portion of the roof that's strictly pea gravel.

A pang of fear rushes through me. My phone's too far away to use—near the edge of the concrete slabs—the cracked device closer to him than me.

His eyes follow mine. "Need me to grab that?"

I blink, caught. "Uh, no . . ."

"Alright . . ." Heading farther along the railing's edge, he tries to keep his distance.

Maybe he's not a total creep, but I'm running low on time. "Raincheck on getting murdered if that's okay."

He stifles a laugh and leans against the railing. "Wasn't planning on it? I'm going to go out on a limb and guess you don't talk to strangers."

I watch him warily, my white-knuckled grip unrelenting. "Guilty. I'm a lawyer. Call it a professional hazard."

"Maybe." His gaze drops to the city below. "Maybe it's something else."

I smile politely.

His grip tightens on the railing, even more than mine. "We all have our demons."

A faint icy breeze washes over the rooftop, a stark reminder of how horrible this day really is. The weather sucks, I'm one police call away from ending up arrested, and now not even killing myself is going to plan. *How do you reschedule your own suicide? Does the universe grant rainchecks for that type of thing?*

"Look. I'm just here to . . . sort things out," I explain.

"I get it," he says. "Getting away from the chaos can help clear your mind. But sometimes, being alone with your thoughts is worse."

Who is this guy?

"I can stay until the top of the hour, if you'd like. I'm not really one to eat lunch. More of a snacker, anyway." Reaching into his jacket, he pulls out a pen and a small brown leather notebook. The pages are flooded with indiscernible scribbles to which he adds more.

"Taking notes?" I point to the notebook.

"Something like that." After a few moments, he clicks the pen and stuffs both items back in his jacket pocket. "Do you want to talk about what's bothering you? I promise I won't judge."

I spin the broken watch on my wrist. As much as I'd like a neutral party's advice, I can't risk him being an undercover—

"I'm not a cop, by the way. If that's what you're wondering," he offers randomly.

The wind turns on us again. I clutch my jacket around me tighter. "That's a common misconception."

His smile fades. "Oh?"

"Sorry," I say, flinching. "I'm sure you're trying to help. I'm not good at this kind of stuff."

"Talking?"

"Being human."

He snorts. "Yeah, me too sometimes."

"Are you religious?" I ask, pointing to the small gold cross around his neck.

"Excuse me?"

"You know, fire 'n brimstone kind of person?"

He digs into the concrete with his boot. "If I say not exactly, would that be bad?" The corner of his lip curls; it's a sloppy-cute smile as he runs a hand through his waves.

I shake the thought away faster than I can blink. Jesus Christ, I'm here to kill myself, not pick up men. "No, just figured. I was curious what God thinks."

"Why don't you ask him?" When he sees my face, he adds, "I

mean, when you have questions, don't people always say go to the source? Why not talk to a priest?"

I shake my head and scour the rooftop again. That feeling from earlier, like I'm being followed, surges back to life. Jackson could have easily had a tail on me since before the funeral. Plenty of investigators in DFW would love a bite at a salaried position with the firm, even if it means taking me out.

But I can't talk to anyone. It just puts them in danger too.

"Priests can't say anything," he adds. "It's in their vow."

The shock on my face hits him like a bullet. *Did he—*

The man glances over the edge again. "Weather's about to turn. I'm glad I decided to take lunch outside."

"Shit," I say, remembering the time. I've been out here too long.

There's no turning back now that Jackson made sure the entire city knows what I've done. He's left me no choice.

"Maybe it's not about fixing anything."

"Come again?" I ask.

"Survivor's guilt is a heavy burden."

I snort under my breath. "What makes you think I have survivor's guilt?"

"I'm familiar with it myself," he says. "I made peace a long time ago, otherwise it would have eaten me alive. We all have our purpose here. It's what grounds us, even if we don't understand why."

I snort. "I thought you weren't religious."

"I'm not. I didn't say it wasn't real."

"So what? There's some divine plan at work?" I say, leaning into the railing. "Sorry to tell you, it's just us. Nobody else."

He pulls himself against the railing. "A rather lonely way of looking at it, don't you think?"

"Some mistakes you can't take back." Tears prick at the

corners of my eyes, and I blink them away.

"You couldn't be more right, Jesly Allbrook," a different male voice announces from behind us, this one cutting like a knife and filled with rage.

A medium-sized man emerges from the roof exit, a subcompact pistol in his gloved hand. Dressed in baggy jeans, a gray sweatshirt with the hood pulled up, and a black fabric mask covering his nose and mouth, he steps toward us.

"Sometimes, it's not about forgiveness," the man says. "It's about revenge."

A gunshot rings out, and it takes a second to realize he's fired a shot in my direction. Not my new companion's. Something made immediately clear when the bullet strikes me in my chest, right below my collarbone. Pain sears my nerve endings, its claws cutting through me like lightning from Heaven.

For a moment, I blink wildly, gaping like a fish out of water. Blood coats my hands as I grapple for air. My grip on the railing fails, and with it the metal itself, sending me stumbling backward.

My new companion launches after me, but it's too late.

I plummet over the rooftop's edge, my body too shocked to even scream as I career toward the unforgiving pavement below. The last thing I make out before the ground swallows me whole is a sudden cloudless sky, and I know my fate is sealed.

Again.

FAMILY TIES

THE STERILE ASTRINGENT SMELL piercing my nostrils is the first thing to greet me back to the world of the living. The second is that my eyes won't open. Something glues them shut. *Shit.*

Panic floods my veins until the cacophony of buzzing alarms and whirring machines surrounding me breaks my thoughts. This much noise can only mean one thing—I'm not dead after all.

Of course not. Dying would be too easy. One would think I'd be used to getting fucked over by the Universe.

I take a quick inventory. Sitting up is useless. There's a stiffness I can't shake—like everything is too heavy and I'm too sluggish to even try. My hands work well enough to rip the tape from my eyelids, letting my dark brown eyes adjust to my new surroundings.

Geometric patterns line the tiles on the ceiling above me. *God, let it be a hospital*—something I never thought I'd live to say.

My nose itches and my fingers shoot up to find a cannula inserted into my nostrils. The burning sensation in my hand is quick to tell me I've stretched the IVs too far.

"Hello?" I say, my voice cracking.

Nobody.

"Hello?" I call again, this time a little stronger. It takes a second to drag myself into an upright position, with only hints of discomfort plaguing me. God forbid this IV drip ever stops; it's going to feel like Death rolled through.

There's commotion in the hallway, the sounds of staff bustling about. No one's noticed I'm awake yet. Simply another day for them—one in a million for me. On the day I decide to throw myself off a Dallas high-rise, someone beats me to the punch and shoots me instead.

Looking around the room, my eyes ache from the LED lights beaming down. The violent brightness is a stark contrast to the weather outside. In the bleak world beyond, rain splatters against the glass. Fitting I'd wake up to another endless torrent.

Inside, a run-of-the-mill hospital room welcomes me. Light seafoam green walls, a wheeled side table, and a small dry-erase board hanging next to the door that tells me the names of the staff on duty. Nothing out of the ordinary. All the way down to cards from people I don't care about and enough flowers to build my own Garden of Eden.

It's not until I notice the tattered, military-grade rucksack perched beside the visitor's chair that my breath seizes in my chest. The whole room spins for a second and my hands latch onto the bed railing. I only knew one person to serve in the military.

Jackson.

Lightning crashes outside and I surge upright, sending the meters buzzing as my heart rate skyrockets. *What's he doing here? Not now.* I'm not dead, which means neither is the threat Jackson poses. *Fuck.*

"Nurse?" I snatch the handheld buzzer and mash it repeatedly.

Seconds later, a stout-looking older woman wobbles in, chart in hand. With her faded ginger curls, bright blue eyes, and a toothy grin spread ear to ear, she's more than prepared for her new patient.

"How are ya, Jesly?" she says in her thick Irish brogue. "I'm Ailbhe, your nurse. Dr. Hiribaldi will be relieved you're awake. He'll come round shortly."

"Excuse me, whose stuff is that?" I point to the rucksack.

She stops reading the monitors to scribble something on my chart. "Some fella. Been here nearly since you have."

I shake my head. *Please God, no.* "Where am I?"

"You're at Ashview Medical, downtown. Off Ridgeview?" She eyes me suspiciously and points to the row of flowerpots lining the windowsill. "Real sweet. Brought enough to start a garden."

Back in the hallway, laughter rings out at the nurse's station slathered in pink and red decorations, and we both look up.

"Speak of the devil." She smiles and shuffles out before I can stop her.

There's a brief conversation right outside the door I'm not a part of; I'm assuming Ailbhe is telling Jackson I'm awake. I choke back the urge to vomit. *How could they do this to me? Don't they know this man is certifiably crazy?*

This room has nowhere to hide. No exits other than the one Ailbhe and my uninvited guest are blocking. The only weapons are an empty bedpan and my IV tubes that I'm pretty sure won't strangle anyone. My only hope is the bathroom, but I'm strung up like a marionette, so it's out of the question.

My grip goes white on the bed rail, and I screw my eyes shut. *Please God.* This is not happening.

Not now. He wouldn't come.

☥

The tension in the room is palpable—charged like a hurricane on the horizon.

"Hey," a soft, male voice says, and I glance over. A guy not much older than me stands in the doorway, his brown hair and bushy beard doing little to hide his awkward smile.

It's not Jackson. *Thank fucking God.*

Nor is he the guy from the roof. While both are brunettes with medium builds, this guy's face is narrower and more oval. He wears his dark chestnut hair shorter and brushed back, even though it doesn't want to stay that way. His long nose and widow's peak cuts his face in two, only accentuating his dimpled chin. But it's not his rigid features which are so striking. It's the way his mismatched eye color haunts you, almost like staring into the bottom of a well.

"Do I know you?" I eke into a sitting position with the help of the bedside controls. Whoever this guy is, I've seen him somewhere before. I try to get a better glimpse.

An easy feat given the wicked concoction dripping from the IV. At least I can still move my back and everything I've attempted thus far. Slowly . . . painfully, but my body still works. Whoever my attacker was, the bastard could've been a better shot.

"Hi. I'm, uh, Dax," the guy introduces himself and awkwardly eases a small potted gladiolus onto the side table.

I don't say a word.

He nods toward the hallway. "I kind of told the staff we're dating."

"Excuse me?" I choke, my eyes widening. He *is* crazy.

"I only need five minutes of your time," Dax says in a rushed whisper and slips into the bedside chair. "I have some questions."

"Listen, buddy. I'm not speaking to the press," I snap. "So go away." My right hand reaches for the call button, but before I get the chance, he snatches it from the blankets. My heart lurches in my chest; this guy's fucking nuts.

"I'm not a reporter," he snaps, tears forming in his eyes. "I need your help."

"In case you missed where we are, I'm really not up for entertaining charity cases." I hold up my IVs. "You'll need to call my office and speak with someone not on their deathbed."

"No." He sucks in a breath. "No one else. It has to be you."

"Dude, are you deaf?" I say. "Give me that button right fucking now or I'm going to call Security."

He slingshots back around the bed and closes the door quietly. What little light there was gets cut in half. The LED lights overhead flicker for a second. "Please, I'm not going to hurt you."

I can't help but snort, my skepticism getting the best of me. "You know, I don't need another stalker. We're all filled up."

"Awesome. I wasn't looking for a job," he says and silence washes over us for a moment. Eventually he adds, "You knew my sister."

"Your sister?"

He nods. "Told me to find you if I ever needed help."

As I search his face, I can't shake this feeling. "I've seen you somewhere before," I blurt out. If Dax has the audacity to break into my hospital room and convince random strangers we're lovers, I'm going to know who the fuck he is. I wave my hand to keep him talking.

"We haven't met before *exactly*. Only in passing."

I place his face finally—the funeral. "You're Dagny's brother?"

"Twin brother, actually." Dax nods. "When I saw you at the service, I knew you could help."

☥

"Eh, I think you're grasping at straws. I was there on behalf of the firm."

"Granted, it didn't go the way I expected," he admits. "Between the rain and the reporters, nothing's gone right since I got back to Dallas." He thrusts a small torn slip of paper with his name and number on it.

Suddenly, it clicks. "You were the guy running across the green?"

"Not my finest hour, but yeah. Sure was," he says, his jaw tight. "I still don't know how those assholes even tracked us down."

"My ex-partner, Jackson Alders," I say. "He brought them."

"I'm not shocked. He's been a dick since the first day Dagny and I swung by your office."

That gets my attention. "You've met?"

"Yeah." He nods. "Dagny reached out to him months ago about something she'd gotten involved in. Two weeks later, she was dead."

A gust of wind rushes past the window, distracting us both as it snaps at the glass.

"How long have I been out?" I wince and clutch my ribs.

Dax checks his watch. "It's the twenty-eighth of January, maybe twelve weeks? You'd have to ask the staff to be sure."

"What?" I swallow hard, a wave of emotions washing over me as I search the doorway for any signs of the police. "That's impossible."

"*Impossible* is surviving after falling off a high-rise, but here you are," he admits. "Seems like you've got an angel on your side."

I shoot him a cross look and clutch my side. "There's no such thing as angels, God, or anything else supernatural. It's all bullshit."

"Not a believer, I see." Dax rushes to help, but I wave him off.

☥

"I can barely trust my own senses, let alone the unseen," I say. "I've got this."

He drops back into the chair. "You sure?"

I nod.

"So why did you do it? Jump, I mean." He leans against the chair's wooden frame.

"Honestly, I don't see how that's relevant," I tell him. "I didn't, if you must know."

He clicks his tongue and digs a small orange pill bottle from his pocket. Unscrewing the lid, he fishes out one or two large white pills, and tosses them into his mouth. "Well, that's not how your partner spun it. Told all of Dallas you tried to kill yourself."

"You said you had questions—you didn't say they were about me."

Ignoring the flickering LED lights above my head, I slide the gladiolus back across the side table, and we sit in silence. Combined with the harmonic beeps, it's futile to drown out my encroaching headache. I close my eyes hoping he's gone by the time I open them.

Nope.

"I'll answer whatever you want if you help me out of here."

"Can't do that." He digs through his rucksack to pull out a worn ID. Next to a terribly lit picture of his face is a Star of Life. "I'm also a paramedic."

"Fine." I rip the tape off the back of my hand and ease the needle out, snatching the now tangled cannula from my nose. "I'll do it myself."

Dax is on me in an instant, his hands barring me from going any further. "Jesly, stop. You could re-injure something and make it so that you never walk out of here."

I weakly shove him out of my way but find I'm still tied to another tangle of tubes, only this one heads under my nightgown. "The fuck?"

"We need somebody in here. Nurse!" Dax inches closer to the doorway, his eyes never lowering. "Jesly, don't pull that out. It's tied to your catheter."

Ailbhe storms in, the alarm in her eyes matching Dax's. "Hey there, Jesly. It's not time to leave yet."

"Don't care," I bark back. "I know my rights. You can't keep me here."

She nods at the doorway. "Go get Dr. Kenji."

Before I can argue, Dax bolts out of the room and Ailbhe blocks my way out. "It's just you and me now, chicken," she says, her shoulders straightening with a grin. "And I always catch my hens."

My bare feet dig into the bright linoleum. "Not gonna work for me. Take out this fucking junk out right now. I can't stay here—it's not safe."

Ailbhe says softly, "Jesly, AMC is perfectly safe. The only thing you need is rest," she says. "Where you tryin' to go?"

"Not your business."

"It is, actually," a patronizing male voice sounds from the entryway. This time, it's tied to a middle-aged Asian man in a crisp lab coat, heading straight for us. The nametag on his chest reads Dr. Kenji Hiribaldi, and by the no-nonsense look he gives and the way his short, dark hair grays at his temples, I can tell getting out of here got infinitely harder.

"Ms. Allbrook, I'm Dr. Hiribaldi," he says with a smile. "I hear that you've decided to check yourself out."

"Sure have," I say as Dax hovers outside the door. There's three of them, one of me, and I'm still tied to this damn bed like a puppet.

"Unfortunately, that's not going to happen." Dr. Hiribaldi pulls a stool from somewhere and sits, blocking my exit. He motions for Ailbhe to leave. Two down, one to go. "You fell from the Renaissance. That's fifty-six stories. Frankly, we don't even know how you survived."

"Sheer dumb luck," I say. "How long?"

"Well, first things first." He glosses over the chart in his lap. "This is the first time you've been conscious to speak with, let alone run any tests requiring you to be awake."

"Great. Let's run them."

"Hold on. You have a history of suicidality, and this isn't your first hospitalization. There was an attempt early last year too."

I wipe the blood from my hand onto my faded seafoam green nightgown. "I didn't try to *kill* myself. There was a man on the roof. He shot me; I fell. The end."

He flips a page. "Excluding the damage from the fall's impact, no bullet wounds were detailed in the surgery report. No fragments. No gun residue."

My hands clench at my side. "Are you saying I imagined it?"

He sets my chart at the foot of my bed. "I'm saying discharge involves more than a few scans, Ms. Allbrook. You went through something traumatic. With your medical history, it would border on negligence to release you."

This is why people hate doctors. "You all think I'm crazy. Did Jackson put you up to this?"

"Ms. Allbrook, let me be frank."

Foolish woman. He knows.

I suck in a breath as Dr. Hiribaldi leans toward me, his jaw shifting until it dislocates and snaps back into place. All I can do is blink. *Don't react. Don't even acknowledge it. It's not real. It's just your mind playing tricks.*

That's what he wants—what they all want—to keep you locked up forever.

I do my best to flash my winning smile.

You're never getting out of here.

Dr. Hiribaldi straightens the stiff white cuffs of his medical coat. "Let me break this down for you. Excluding your current psychological state, you suffered an epidural hematoma, four broken ribs, dislocated your shoulder, and ruptured your spleen. You should have died, but it seems someone out there likes you."

The sound of laughter breaks my focus. At the nurse's station, an armed security detail hangs around. "That for me?" I ask.

Dr. Hiribaldi ignores my question. "We'll need another MRI before talking about long-term plans," he says, his good doctor routine already fading. He's done trying. "A psych eval also."

Outside, the wind's picked up. It's gotten angry, violent even. The intercom behind the headboard clicks a few times, but nothing comes out.

"How long?" I ask again.

He eases to his feet and slides the stool back in the corner. "If you're as lucky as you seem to be, Ms. Allbrook, it might take a few months."

"Days," I choke, my voice breaking. "I need to get out of here in *days*."

"Well, sorry if we're interrupting any recently made plans," he says, shooting a condescending look at Dax. "Hell, be thankful you're in one piece; some people aren't so lucky. I'd get some rest while I can. Radiology will be down soon." Dr. Hiribaldi snatches up my chart and closes the door behind him, leaving only the storm pelting the large windowpane to drown out the cacophony in my head.

Stupid girl. You seriously thought you could help someone? You can't even help yourself. Maniacal laughter ping-pongs between my ears, and I pull the flimsy knitted blanket over my head.

Dax slips into the suite, his head lowered. "I'm sorry, Jesly."

"So am I." I turn away so he can't see my tears.

Ailbhe comes in with a fresh pitcher of water and a plastic cup and sets them both on the table. She reaches for the cannula I ripped out, a no-nonsense look on her weathered face. Holding it out expectantly, she states, "Here."

My stomach churns, and I clutch onto the bed railing as I wait for it to pass. *Breathe in, breathe out.*

It does, leaving Ailbhe's watchful gaze drilled on my face. "Don't you worry. Our care is right grand. Ain't nuttin' else in the world like it. You'll see."

I screw my jaw shut.

Won't be long now. Soon, Jesly. Soon. That same laughter echoes again, reminding me I'm not alone. But the voice isn't my biggest problem. Not anymore.

If anyone has the desire to keep me locked up, it's Jackson. With me trapped here, it plays straight into his hands—ones I used to long for. Now those hands want me dead.

The second time the nausea washes over me, I don't fight it. Instead, I hurl my stomach's empty contents into the closest bedpan and let the last bit of my dignity go with it.

Shame it's only morning.

☥

UNINTENDED CONSEQUENCES

Tɪᴍᴇ sᴛᴀɴᴅs sᴛɪʟʟ ᴀs Ailbhe drones on about hospital procedures and what expectations I should have for the next several days, if not weeks, of my regrettable life. Scans. Consent forms. Physical therapy. Obtaining a lawyer if I'd like to contest my hold. Understanding the policy for visiting hours.

"No more guests, please." I finish cleaning myself with a damp washcloth and hand it back to her.

"If you say so." Her misshapen brow furrows with concern, but she lets it go, realizing there's no point in arguing with me. *Good for her.* "I'll clean that mess there when you leave for Radiology. Your fella's gotta stay here, though."

I nod. "Sure thing." Informing dear ol' Ailbhe his only connection to me is one I'm trying to hide doesn't seem like the best thing for self-preservation. She can think what she wants. Dax, on the other hand, just needs to stay away from me.

"A shower and a change of clothes will help," Ailbhe says, grabbing a thin sweatshirt and matching pants from the wardrobe. "First, we're goin' take out your catheter while your meds are runnin' strong. Get comfortable."

"You mean right now?" I squirm backward on my bed.

"A small discomfort down there, but you'll be peein' free from then on." This time, she waits for my approval. She's picking her battles. We both are.

Dax comes flying into the room. Wherever he was, he looks flustered, which luckily provides the distraction she needs to rip the treacherous contraption out before I can stop her. Dropping the device into a nearby container with a satisfied grin, she says, "Miss Jesly is gettin' cleaned up. Want to help?"

Dax shakes his head and starts backing up. "Sorry, I can't. Something came up. Jesly, I, uh . . . I'll call you later." He storms over to his rucksack and snatches it as fast as he can.

"Sure," I say. He doesn't even look at me as he races out of the room. "Have a good night, Dax."

My bewildered look must show because Ailbhe doesn't hesitate to guide me to my feet on her own. "Ah, he's just bein' an eejit," she says. "Let's get cleaned up now."

I stare at the door.

She pats me on the arm. "Don't worry. Fine lass like you, he'll come around. These things always make people nervous."

"I'm not so sure."

"He go off to tell your fam you're finally awake?"

We inch toward the bathroom. "Fam?"

"Your mam? Dad?"

I quickly shake my head.

Thirty years of experience tells her something is amiss, her gaze questioning as she shoves back the cheap plastic curtain and flips down the bathing chair. "Did ya want us to?"

"No," I say too quickly. "We've got it."

She sets the toiletries along the mini shelf. "Need help?"

☥

"I'm good. Thanks," I say. "This is great."

"I'll start the water and leave you be," she says. "Once you go get dressed and ready, someone will come 'round from Radiology."

The door closes behind her. And while her motherly concern is endearing, right now I just want some hot water. Three months of hospital tubes and unflattering nightgowns, and my humanity is somewhat lacking. For the first time in forever, I'm alone. Left to my own destruction.

I twirl the hospital band around my wrist while the water heats. Suicide watch does little for privacy. There's no cheap plastic razor in the set and I don't blame them. I wouldn't trust me either.

A familiar ringing sound threatens to barrel me over, and I'm forced to clutch onto the PVC handrail.

You're failing them. You couldn't even die properly.

Shut up, I manage weakly.

Plunging into the cold, white stall does little to quiet my racing thoughts. The first proper shower I've had in months, I scrub as much of the hospital smell out of my skin and limp curls as I can. The summer tan I'd been nursing into fall is long gone, and all I'm left with is a sick version of pale olive.

A knock on the door interrupts my reprieve, followed by a southern drawl I don't recognize. "Ms. Allbrook? My name's Beau. I'm here to take you for scans."

Shit. I'd forgotten. "Sorry." I wrench the water off. "One second."

"Take your time," he says from the other side. "I just wanted to let you know I'm here."

Scrambling as best I can to pull on the gym sweats given four broken ribs and bleeding on the brain, I run a hand towel through my long, stringy curls. Thirty seconds later, I'm dragging open the heavy wooden door.

☥

"Evening." A portly male orderly grins from ear to ear. "Ms. Jesly, you up for a trip?"

I glance into the room. It's only him. This far into winter, the sun's long settled in. Faint light flickers from an overhead bedside lamp and most of the rooms on the floor are also out. *It's late.* Time's slipped again.

"Miss?"

"Oh, sorry."

"No prob." Beau fetches a wheelchair from the hallway and locks the wheels in place. "Your carriage, madam."

"Thank you, sir." I play along. Anything to distract me from having to see Dax tomorrow. I don't know how long I can lie to him. Forever would be nice, but I doubt it'll happen. "Stupid."

Beau looks down as I get settled in. "What is?"

I blink. "I'm sorry?"

He kicks up the latch and we set off. "You were talking to yourself."

Not this again. "Oh, sorry. I didn't realize."

God, don't you ever get sick of lying all the time?

I exhale slowly, pacing my breath as we move through the wing. Hopefully, he's seen weirder things.

Snatching my chart off the nurse's station, Beau asks, "Scared of elevators?"

"No," I answer him. "Just thinking."

"Good. Many people get the heebie-jeebies in this ol' place." He mashes the up arrow on the wall panel. It's a few seconds before the elevator chimes and a rush of hospital staff pour into the hallway.

All but one person leaves. "What floor?"

"Four," Beau replies, wheeling me around to face the exit doors. "Thanks."

The elevator starts whirring again, and soon the fifth-floor staff rush on, crowding around us. I glance at the safety sign above the buttons. Max weight is 5,000 pounds or 35 people. The door chimes again, telling us we've reached our destination.

"Great." Beau eases me out onto the fourth floor.

Light is even more sparse now that the night staff has clocked on, and my stomach cramps with uneasiness. We stop just before the next set of double doors.

He asks, "Hey, I need to grab the order for your chart. It'll just take a minute. Will you be okay?"

My cross look tells him everything he needs to know.

"Alright, alright." He steps back with a chuckle. "My mama raised a smart man. I know when a lady means business. Twenty seconds, Miss Jesly. Don't you worry."

I smile and raise my hands. "I'm not going anywhere."

He nods apologetically and shuffles back the way we came before turning down another hallway. I lean against the wall and close my eyes. It's not long before the wheelchair moves again, jolting me upright.

"That didn't take long," I note, adjusting in the chair.

I pull the pale blue cotton throw over me. This floor is much colder and my nerves struggle to keep up. Another set of doors buzz open, and we pass into the next wing.

"Honestly, I hate hospitals," I say. "Ever since I was little."

"Mmm."

We turn down the next hallway, this one even more sparse. One of the overhead LEDs flicker absentmindedly. Other than the towering meal cart stacked with half-eaten dinners and the miscellaneous empty beds stashed out here, the hall's empty.

"How long have you worked as a tech?" I ask.

"Not long," he responds.

But it's not Beau's voice—it's one I'd know anywhere.

Deeper than the orderly's. More callous.

Jackson.

My grip tightens on the wheelchair. *It's only a hallucination.* There's no way he's here. He doesn't even know where I am.

I should run, but if I'm wrong, it's a one-way ticket to the psych ward. Something I'd like to avoid at all costs.

I inhale deeply and steady my voice. "Did you find the chart?" I ask as I eye the meal cart for a weapon.

A fork. A butter knife will do. I know the stakes if I'm wrong; but if I'm right, there's no security in this facility that can stop me. At this point, I'm willing to take the risk. I just need to bide my time.

I freeze in the chair, even though every fiber of my body screams to run. One wrong move and my next breath could be my last.

"I need the restroom," I blurt out instinctively. "Gonna need a little help though."

"Of course," the man replies and swings around to the front. It's not his footsteps clipping against the hospital tile that confirms it—it's the cologne permeating the air. He could be ten-thousand miles away and it would still stop me dead. It's etched into my psyche. A permanent reminder.

That same scent floods my senses now.

"How did you find me?" I latch onto the meal cart and snatch the first knife I see.

My uninvited guest sighs and avoids my wild swings. "I'm disappointed in you, Jesly," he says, stepping closer.

Another light flickers at the end of the hall, but it's still enough to see him in all his glory. It's Jackson.

He's here—dressed in a uniform that doesn't belong to him. His muscled frame is tense, his body dwarfing mine. There's a slight odor lurking beneath all that cologne but it's hard to place.

"Where's Beau?"

He runs his tongue along his bleached teeth. "The kid? He's around somewhere."

I hardly recognize my ex in the stolen uniform, the malignance dripping off him. No place is safe. Not even here.

To him, I'm the last obstacle—the only one who knows what happened that night.

"You can't keep me from testifying, Jackson," I say. Lovers for ten years and partners for six, I never realized I was in bed with a psychopath. A narcissist, sure. But not a psychopath.

Not until it was too late.

"I don't need to," he answers. "You're not crazy enough to hang yourself. Or maybe you are."

My grip tightens on the knife. "I should have left the first night."

"You say that, but whores like you always come crawling back," he tells me.

He inches closer, easily dodging my second attempt to stab him. He's been with me long enough to know what I'm capable of. I'm no threat to him, not like this.

His grip wrenches the knife from my hand and strikes me in the jaw, knocking the wind out of me. I should have expected it, but I'm not ready when he slams me into the meal cart, sending plates and trays crashing.

The pain in my already injured back fades as his hands latch around my throat, the knife clattering to the floor forgotten. *He's too strong.* But then again, he always was.

☥

"Listen, you useless bitch," he snaps, the facade collapsing since there's no one but us. Shooting stars ricochet in my vision as I thrash against the wall. "Two weeks. I'm giving you two weeks to clean up your mess, or you'll never walk out of here freely again."

My head swirls, his image blurs, and clawing at his grasp does nothing, his body pressed against mine.

"Do you understand?" he seethes, ignoring my gasps for air. "Do you fucking *understand* me?"

"Please . . ." Tears cascade down my cheeks as I flounder in his grip. The last time this happened, my face became a spiderweb of broken blood vessels.

"Blink, Love," he says. "Show me what a good little bitch you are."

I don't want to, but he's going to kill me. My eyes wrench tight, only for the tears to pour harder.

"Good girl." Jackson presses his lips to my forehead before letting go.

I collapse to the ground, gasping. The man I loved never existed. It had always been a ruse and nothing more.

"Oh, and Love?" He watches as I scoot along the wall like a blubbering child.

My chest rattles as I struggle for air, but I look my would-be killer in the eye. The next thing I see is his foot smashing into my broken ribs.

"Take your fucking pills before they figure out who you really are." He chucks an orange prescription bottle at my feet. "See you around, Jes."

The hallway spins as I lie there, unable to move, unable to breathe. The most I can manage sounds like a mangled cat as I try to call for help.

"Blessed Mother Mary and Joseph." Beau rushes from the

☥

same direction as Jackson. "Lord, what happened? Are you alright?" He eyes me suspiciously as my stifled sobs break the wing's otherwise eerie calm.

The lights flicker again. "No. Where is he?" I sob.

"Who?" Beau scours the hallway. "There's no one here, Miss Jesly. It's okay. Somebody help!"

A radiologist rounds a different corner and kneels beside us both. "What happened?" he asks Beau.

"I left to get the paperwork and found her like this."

"There's someone here . . ." I clutch my throat as they ease me back into my wheelchair, my ribs screaming even more than they already were. "You just walked past them. Tall, White, clean-shaven. Wearing blue scrubs. Impossible to miss."

The radiologist's gaze darts from Beau to me. "This floor closed at 9 p.m. Nobody's been up here for hours."

VISIONS

"Alright, Jesly," the male radiologist says from the monitoring room. "The MRI scan will last about thirty to forty-five minutes. You okay in there?"

"Yeah, I'm fine," I lie into the two-way speaker connected to the machine.

"I know it's kind of hard, but try to relax as much as you can," he says. "Beau's near the door, just in case."

I nod to the camera and slip the headphones on. "Okay."

The machine whirs to life and begins its ear-rattling passes. It's been nearly five years since my last scan, back when they were searching for the root of my nerve damage. Just like before, the contrast agent echoes in my mouth. Its copper taste is a relentless reminder of this nightmare. I hate these things, but my options are limited. Especially if I ever want to see freedom.

The machine ticks away, buzzing as it coordinates its passes. I count them. Seven clicks. Each one hammering home the fact that I have to stay still. After a while, the endless white noise of the machine begs me to close my eyes. The panel above my head cycles through its motions. Its programming relays data back to where Beau and the radiologist wait in the other room.

Forty-five minutes of my life wasted. I readjust the headphones as the machine whirs and clicks again.

The overhead speaker clicks on. "Still doing okay?"

"Yeah," I say. "Just tired."

"Understood. We'll have you out of here in another twenty-five minutes. If you'd like to doze off, we'll wake you when we're done."

"I'm good, thanks." I simply stare at the off-white plastic frame less than a foot away. My chest tightens. It's not enclosed spaces that bother me; it's the fact that I can't escape. I fight to slow my breathing before the panic sets in.

"Twenty-five minutes," a male voice calls across the overhead again. This one is different, smooth like butter with hints of reverie. "That gives us plenty of time."

"I'm sorry?"

"How have you been, Jesly?" the voice asks casually over the speaker.

It's familiar, but I can't place it.

"Beau?" I ask doubtfully.

The guy clears his throat. "No, no. The staff stepped out for a Coke. It's just me."

"And you are?"

Before he can answer, the machine barrels into its next round of deafening beeps, cutting our conversation short.

"Hang on a second," he says into the headset. "I've got an idea."

The whirring grows louder, the overhead lights mirroring its intensity until everything bursts in a flash of white. My hands shoot up to block the light and I bolt upright. It's already too late. I stumble to the linoleum floor, falling out of the scanner.

"What the hell?" Where I should have gotten a faceful of heavy machinery, only the open air of the room greets me. I'm standing less than an arm's reach from the contraption. My hands race across my bare arms, my torso, my hair. I'm not dead.

I look over into the viewing lab. No one's there. "What's going on?" I ask him. "What happened?"

"Me."

The man standing inches behind me. His medium-length chestnut brown hair flops out of place as he pulls me to my feet. He's an entire head taller than me, his square jaw lurking beneath a short boxed beard. Dressed in a white T-shirt and faded blue jeans, he digs a small leather notebook out from his back pocket.

The tightness in my chest mirrors the growing MRI noises. "Do I know you from somewhere?"

He smiles. "You do. We met a few weeks ago."

I stare at him like a deer on a winding country road as he waits for it to click. And then it does, my mouth agape. "You're that guy—from the roof."

"I am."

I rub my palms on my sweats. "Am I dead?"

He looks up from writing something. "Do you want to be?"

"What kind of question is that?"

"An honest one. One minute you're about to jump off a roof, the next I find you here."

My eyes dart to the exit. "How do you know that?"

"It doesn't take a genius," he says. "Can you stay calm?"

"About?"

He points behind me.

I turn slowly. Like in that horror movie kind of way, where I'm expecting the serial killer to be standing there. No dice.

It's just me . . . *somehow.*

"—the fuck?" I glance at the body lying on the machine slab. It's mine, but I'm right here. Intact. "How is this possible?"

"Science, astral projection, God. Call it whatever you want." He waves me over as he heads for the monitoring room. "Come on. There's something you need to see."

I glance at the clock on the wall. 12:48 a.m. The second hand doesn't budge. "What did you do?"

"Bought us some time." He points to the radiologist and Beau stepping back into the room, both unaware anything has changed. Their focus is solely on me. Still in the machine.

"Did you just kill me?" I ask, struggling to keep up.

"No."

I quietly close the door and point to the body out there. "Then who the fuck is that?"

Ignoring me, he drops onto a stool at the workstation, now inches from the others. They don't seem to notice as he rolls the radiologist out of the way. Almost like we're invisible.

"What do you want?" I eye the door he's blocking. "It's been a busy day."

"I know. That's why I'm here."

"To stalk me like everyone else?"

"To help you if no one else will." He mashes some keys on the keyboard. Seconds later, the whirring of the machines grows louder as the digital scans generate on the monitors.

"Hey, wait." I race toward the screen, my body somehow not fighting this time. No searing headaches. No bleeding skull. No broken ribs. "Woah. No pain."

"That's because you're outside your body."

"Neat trick," I say. "How long's it last?"

"Long enough to show you something." He holds out a calloused hand, albeit a little sweaty. "Come on. We need to get on the road."

I glance at my body on the MRI table one last time. Something tells me not to question his motives. It's visceral, and I don't like it. "And go where?"

"Don't worry about it."

"For what?"

He mulls this over momentarily. His eyes dart to the clock on the wall again, his right leg bouncing as he talks.

"You seem nervous," I say.

His lip twitches. "I need you to trust me for a minute."

We stare at one another—me in my baggy sweatpants and sweatshirt and this strange man who's infiltrated the Radiology wing. "What happens after a minute?"

He pinches the bridge of his nose. "You know, we really don't have time for this." There's a large brown leather messenger bag on the counter, from which he pulls out a familiar pair of worn sneakers and tosses them at me. Bright neon colors and very much used. "Put these on."

I stare at him like he's sprouted a second head. "Where did you get those?"

"From your house. Where else?"

My eyes widen. "Why were you in my house?"

"Allbrook, we really don't have time for this . . ." he says. "I don't know how long this will hold. I've never done this before."

"Done what?"

"Broken someone out."

My heart leaps for a second. "Did Dax send you?"

"No, Jesly. I sent myself. Now let's go." He waits for me to slip the sneakers on. As soon as I do, he's headed toward the exit.

I shake my head. "The doctors are right. I've lost it."

"No," Kane snaps. He takes a breath and smiles in my direction. "I really need you to just trust me on this."

"What if you're an ax murderer?"

"Would you rather be here?"

I grab his shoulder. "Hey, what's your name?"

"Kane." He looks down at my hand still on his shoulder, and I immediately let go. "Some other time I'll tell you everything, but right now—" he says, glancing at the MRI machine. "We need to get you out of here. This isn't the place."

"How did—"

"That you wanted out?" he asks casually. "I already told you. I know a lot of things." He holds out a hand expectedly.

"This is insane."

"Maybe, but we'll figure it out together."

"Why the hell not?" I concede, finally taking his hand. "Like this day hasn't been crazy enough."

Relief floods his face, his long fingers latching around mine. "Okay. Here we go."

Silence falls over us much like the tightening of his grip. All at once, my stomach lurches like it's coming out of my colon. There's a sudden ringing in my ears that sends me crashing toward the ground. The radiology lab disappears into the periphery, leaving only blackened specks of a blurry brown and gray. Almost like we're caught in a centrifuge that broke and blended us instead.

"Easy . . ." he says, steadying me. "It won't last long."

"Wonderful," I croak.

He lets go before I'm ready, and I stumble into a large stone obelisk that wasn't there before. Even before the accident, I struggled with vertigo. The merry-go-round hasn't stopped, forcing me to clutch on for dear life.

"We're here," he says softly, pulling me back into the present.

My legs buckle like a baby fawn's. "Great. Where is *here?*"

"It can't be. Not again." He ignores my question and treks across the lush grass.

We've landed in the middle of a cemetery and not a small one, either. Vaguely familiar, I can't place it. Not yet.

The high sun is obscured by sweeping crepe myrtles and magnolias, the latter's scent filling the open air. This place is beautiful as cemeteries go, filled with colonnades befitting the dead.

"Hey, wait up," I yell after him, but Kane's on a mission. I struggle to catch up, my sneakers sliding on the damp grass. "Kane, wait."

Eventually, he stops, his eyes stuck on one grave in particular. "What are we doing?" I ask. "Why did you bring us here?"

He turns around, his chiseled features consumed by worry. "I didn't . . ."

"Then who?"

"I don't know." He pulls us out of sight, long enough for paranoia to start chipping away as I feel someone watching.

Kane senses it too. It takes a minute, but he finds something more alarming. His eyes lock on something on the far side of the cemetery—a group of people, scattered around a casket.

Families. Couples. Individuals. Behind them, a massive mausoleum fills the open space, its doors open and inviting. *Jesus.* We've stumbled into a funeral.

"Crap." He grabs my arm. "We need to go."

"What? Why?"

"It's not safe for you here." He tries leading us toward the sidewalk, but I fling him off.

"Kane, stop. I'm not going anywhere until you tell me what the hell's going on."

He freezes, his back straightening to match his rigid jaw. "Allbrook, there's no time. I've got to get you back before—"

"Before what?"

He sucks in a breath. "Listen, I'm not the only one with an interest in what happens to you. Some people would rather you not succeed." He walks away, back toward the mausoleum.

With the funeral broken up, attendees slowly stroll different sidewalks, having already paid their respects. Only two stay behind—one man waits as the cemetery attendants move the casket through the open mausoleum doors. The other lingers beneath a swarm of crepe myrtles, doing his best to avoid the piercing heat.

I chase Kane through the thick crowd, most of whom nodding their solemn hellos as we pass. *They can see me?* Kane's far enough ahead that his tousled hair has disappeared amongst the throng. I speed up, weaving in and out. I'm fast but clumsy, and it's only a matter of seconds before I collide into a passerby's shoulder.

"Sorry," I say. Out of the corner of my eye, they look familiar, but I don't stop to have a conversation. I've gotta catch up.

With my muscles finally working for once, I don't hesitate. It's been a while since I've run. It feels good. Another dozen or so yards down the sidewalk, my impatience backfires and I plow full-force into a guy in a suit.

He latches onto my arms as we both try to keep from toppling on the concrete. "Jes?"

I look up, embarrassed. Until I realize who it is.

"Jackson?" I hiss, his own shock mirroring mine. I step back and land on the ground. "What are you doing here?"

His dark navy suit clings to his toned frame, and every blond hair is perfectly in place. Traffic has died down, but that doesn't mean anything to Jackson.

Public image is everything. Even at the grave.

The remaining attendees have shifted into the grass to avoid the commotion. He smiles and waves to the passersby, his expression fading as he stares down at me. "I could say the same for you. You're supposed to be in treatment."

I clamber back to my feet without his help. "For once in your miserable life, stop mansplaining. How did you find me?"

"Jesly . . ." He gives me that look again—like he's the smartest person in the room, and it pisses me off.

"Don't *Jesly* me." I jab my index finger into his suited chest, a stupid move given how easily he could snatch it and break my hand. It wouldn't be the first time he put his hands on me. "I don't know what you're playing at but stop following me."

He blinks, a rush of air escaping through his teeth. "You escaped again, didn't you? I'm calling Dr. Yamini." He reaches into his suit, pulling his iPhone out of his ironed shirt pocket.

"You can't do that," I protest as he unlocks the screen and starts mashing numbers.

He looks up from the keypad. "What do you want from me?" He's angry. *Good for him.* He puts his hand over the speaker. "I'm not doing this again, Jesly. I'm sorry. We're about to go to trial against Miller. I don't have time for your crazy-ass bullshit."

"Miller? That was *months* ago." A tear burns my skin, and my fingers jump to wipe it away. I blink, frozen like a deer in headlights. "I-I don't understand."

He nods solemnly. "I know. That's the point. Yes, hello?" His attention shifts to the phone, turning his back to me.

I nearly wrench my neck trying to look around Jackson's taller frame to find Kane. Wherever he's run off to, he's left me here with this. *Did he know this would happen?*

Finally spotting Kane across the grounds deep in conversation with a man I've never seen before, I notice Kane's unease.

"Okay, great," Jackson says into the phone. "Thank you."

I stare at him, dumbfounded.

He covers the phone again. "They're getting Dr. Yamini." He looks over my appearance. "Besides your penchant for escape, have you been doing well? Taking your meds?"

I blink in disbelief. *He's unbelievable right now.* "Are you fucking serious?"

Emotion drains from his face and then lights back up. "Dr. Yamini, hello. This is Jackson Alders. How are you?"

I snatch the phone from his grasp and mash the end button on the call. Shoving Jackson's cell into my sweatpants' pocket, I bolt as fast as I can.

"Jesly, goddamnit," he yells after me.

With the guests all but disappeared, I make a break for Kane and his associate. I'm gonna kill him if I get that far.

With any luck, Jackson won't follow. He's no fool—not when one record button turns into a five o'clock headline. My ribs burn from lack of running, but I make it, panting and clutching my side.

Kane and a Middle Eastern man I've never seen before stand shoulder-to-shoulder beneath the pink and white crepe myrtles. A fresh pink scar cuts through the right side of his face over his right eye and cheek.

☥

"Good morning, Jesly," the other man says, his down-turned eyes full of joy. Taller than me but shorter than Kane, his tawny complexion, long thick curls, and hooked nose are a stark contrast to my escort beside him. "Glad to see you could make it."

I look behind me.

"Don't worry," he announces. "Mr. Alders won't bother us."

"How do you know my name?" I spin back around, my hands protecting the phone in my pocket. With any luck, Jackson will never see this thing again. I'll destroy it right after I unbury every lie that piece of shit has been gathering on me.

The man scratches his trimmed beard. "Kane here has been meaning to introduce us. Ain't that right, ol' boy?" He clasps Kane by the shoulder, whose jaw tightens as he smiles.

"Who are you?" I ask.

Another smile. "Call me Zaire."

"And how do you know Kane?"

"Oh, he and I go way back," Zaire says, holding out his hand. "I'm glad you could make it. It's a relief, honestly. I was getting worried."

I clear my throat. "Um, thanks?"

"Glad to have you on our side." He looks at his open hand and waits.

"I'm not?"

A flicker of a frown before that Cheshire grin returns. So he does have more than one emotion. *Good.* "Oh, I don't know, Jesly. You'll come around. They always do."

I lick my lips. *Jesus Christ. Is everyone around me crazy?* "What are you talking about?"

Zaire snorts. "You didn't tell her, did you, Kane?"

"Tell me what?" I ask.

He stifles a laugh. "Glad to know she's in good hands now. If Kane here can keep from any more sightseeing, we might actually get something accomplished." He tightens his grip on Kane's shoulder, draining the remaining color from Kane's face. "Let's get you home, Jesly. Thanks for stopping by."

The man snaps his fingers near my face, and my back presses against the soft fabric of a mattress I don't remember laying on.

I'm back in my hospital room. My stomach lurches. Dying flowers and all. The lullaby of the old AC hums like white noise. I sit up, this time my body screaming as I try. My fingers brush my pants pocket. The phone—

Told you you're never getting out of here. Ethereal laughter reverberates in my ears, ping-ponging in my head.

Fuck you. I have to find it.

Sliding off the bed, I tear apart the room end to end.

But it's no use. It's gone.

Each time I get close to catching Jackson in a lie, something snatches it right out from under me. Always has.

I lean onto the side rail for support. Several breaths later, I realize Kane's nowhere to be found either. Wherever he is, he can't help me now.

With any possible proof of Jackson's scheming gone, convincing Dr. Hiribaldi to let me go is a pipe dream. I have to find my own way out.

Whatever Zaire wants, his business can wait. I've got to settle my own score first.

DEAD REMAINS

"WELCOME BACK TO MONDAY morning, Dallas," the hospital room TV announces above my head. "This is Kevin Lang, and I've got your 8 a.m. morning roundup."

The burning in my head begs me to fall asleep, but it's useless. My old friend, hypervigilance, has returned, and it doesn't seem like it's letting up anytime soon. The hallway bustles with morning staff, their positivity palpable as they swap stories from the weekend. With any luck, they've forgotten about me. I curl up tighter and pull the blanket closer.

The news anchor drones on, "In the wake of recent events at Alders and Allbrook Law, WFAA News has just received a report that the firm has reached the next stage of negotiations regarding a potential merger with one of the city's oldest and largest criminal defense firms. This is fantastic news for the troubled firm, which has been embroiled in tragedy since earlier this spring."

"What? He can't do that," I holler at the TV. Newsman Kevin can't hear me, but I don't care.

Good job. Now everything you've worked for will go to someone else. You failed.

A rap on the door distracts me. It's Dax. "Thought I'd try breakfast this time." He holds up a coffee carrier with two throwaway cups and a small brown paper bag.

I feign a smile, too focused on still trying to make out what Kevin is saying, but it's suddenly muffled. "You came back."

Dax sets the drink carrier on the bedside table. "Was I not supposed to?"

"No, it's not that." I point at the TV. "Just a little distracted is all." They've moved onto some segment about the local hospitals running at unusually higher than normal capacity. *Fuck, I missed it.*

"You okay?" He hands over a coffee.

"Not at all."

Into the bag he goes. "All they had was carrot and apple cinnamon. I didn't know which you'd want, so you pick first." He flashes an awkward smile and tries not to trip over the wires connected to the monitors.

Don't trust him.

"Shut up," I snap.

His face contorts in confusion. "I didn't—I mean, I'll, uh, go."

Shit. Nothing comes out of my mouth for a moment. There's no explaining this away. "Sorry," I stammer. "You don't need to leave."

"You sure?" The corner of his mouth twitches.

"Yeah. I, uh, didn't sleep well."

"Well, a swig of caffeine can't hurt, right?" Dax opens the blinds far enough that the morning sunlight hits me like a vampire.

"Ugh," I shriek in mock agony and reach for the paper bag. My hand snatches the first fluffy muffin it lands on. "Carrot." I toss the bag in his direction.

"That alright?"

"Yeah," I say, already stuffing my face. "It's great."

☥

"And the latte?" he asks.

I look down at the cup in my grip. Even without the caffeine, my hands shake. My ability to hold a conversation like a normal human is sorely lacking, and I don't know which to say first: Hey, my ex tried to kill me after you left, or my spirit guide and I went on a magic carpet ride last night.

Either will make me sound out of my damned mind, so I take Option C: Keep my mouth shut.

I tear into the muffin top and take a bite. A commercial plays above our heads and drowns out the harmonic beeps of the room. The muffin has the perfect amount of cinnamon to pair with the vanilla latte. *God, I've missed coffee.* Ailbhe hasn't popped her head in yet, so the coast is clear.

As we eat, he digs a book out of his rucksack, the same one from yesterday, and tosses it onto the bed. "I brought you something you might find interesting. Keep you busy, at the very least."

There's a slight burgundy tinge to the cover that won't budge when my thumb passes over it. "Is that *blood?*" My eyes meet his. *Is he trying me?*

"I tried to clean it." He grimaces. "Dags left this for you."

"Excuse me?"

"In her will," he explains and takes another sip. "I don't know why, but my sister thought she was onto something. Took it with her wherever she went. Read it like thirty times."

"*The Place We All Go* by Angela Cromwell," I say, reading the dog-eared copy. "Never heard of it. Did she mention why I should have it?"

My head swirls with unease. A dead woman's book—the person *I* murdered—and her brother sits less than six feet away from me, unaware.

Or, at least, I hope. The alternative is more than I can handle. Dax seems like a decent person. I'd rather not cause more heartache than I already have.

"No, she didn't," he tells me.

A newsflash rings from the TV right as Ailbhe's morning cheer hobbles into the room. With no other excitement on the third floor, our eyes glue to the screen.

"Welcome back, Dallas," Kevin Lang greets the city again. "Before the break, we were bringing you the latest developments with Alders and Allbrook. For more on this fascinating story that's gripped DFW this year, reporter Cami Abrigado spoke with Jackson Alders himself for comment." He spins his chair to the side, letting the camera pan to his co-anchor across the city. "Here she is now."

A beautiful Hispanic woman with a tight ponytail fills the flatscreen. "Thanks, Kevin, for that introduction. This is Cami Abrigado standing off Commerce St., where a recent tragedy has rocked a once-rising law firm here in North Dallas.

"I had the luxury of speaking earlier with the owner of the firm, Jackson Alders, and here's what he had to say regarding the recent tragedy of his law partner, Jesly Allbrook, as well as the direction the firm hopes to take with their merger with Messinger Law."

"What?" I stop mid-swallow.

Messinger is one of the oldest firms in the city—and the most corrupt. They are where dark money goes to thrive and the honest go to die. My worst nightmare and my gorgeous ex knows it. Blood drains from my face the moment Jackson comes on the screen.

All smiles and charm for Cami, he's already got her stumbling for words as they joke about traffic. It's nauseating, the snake in the grass.

☥

I struggle to set down my latte as Ailbhe launches into her morning checks. She doesn't realize we're the same Allbrook, but by Dax's similar reaction to Jackson's presence on the screen, I'm surprised it's not obvious. He says nothing as Ailbhe takes my blood pressure, letting her go about her job of keeping me alive.

When she's satisfied, she pulls the stethoscope from her ears. "Dr. Hiribaldi comes in at nine." She notes my updated vitals on the dry-erase board before logging them on the door chart.

I don't dare take my gaze off the TV screen. The remote is close enough that I crank the volume up, drowning any chance of conversation. She takes the hint and leaves Dax and me to our own destruction.

My new paramedic pal walks over to the doorway and holds up his empty cup. "I'm gonna throw this away and take a stroll. Stretch my legs for a few."

"Okay," I reply nonchalantly.

One battle at a time, and the individual on the screen takes precedence. Standing in the middle of the sidewalk and sporting a change of clothes from last night, Jackson appears unperturbed by the beautiful anchor's banter.

"Cami," Jackson says, "I'm so grateful to the people of Dallas and everyone at WFAA for allowing us to set the record straight." He flashes his Broadway grin, with her buying every last drop.

"We understand how hard it must be. First with the trial and then with your partner," she tells the livestream. "We all extend our condolences for your loss and the family's."

Condolences? The bastard's milking them like a leech. This can't get any worse.

Oh, honey . . . It sure can.

"Have there been any updates on your partner's condition?"

His mood sobers, always the showman. "Unfortunately not. It's been three months like this. But as much as we are hurting, our clients are hurting more."

"Bullshit," I yell at the screen. "I'm wide awake, asshole."

The anchor shoves the microphone closer. "Your firm was on an upward trajectory before recent developments. Can you comment on the pending litigation your firm is facing?"

"I cannot since there's still an open investigation. But we're incredibly grateful to Messinger Law for taking a chance on us. It's our intention to serve the citizens of Dallas for what we hope is several generations."

"It certainly has been a tumultuous year for you both. Here's hoping your spring goes smoother."

"Agreed." He smooths his suit lapel.

"Can you comment on who will assume the backlogged cases if the merger passes?"

He nods. "I can. According to the managing partners at Messinger, their associate, Ms. Maggie Messinger, will handle Ms. Allbrook's caseload directly."

Maggie—another one of Jackson's former paramours.

Ha! It just got worse. Ringing floods my ears, sending delirious laughter ricocheting around the room.

Cami brushes a windswept strand of hair from her face. "So glad to hear there's some positivity to this tragedy. Well, congratulations and good luck."

"Thank you. We're survivors. It's why we always prevail," he replies, locking eyes with the camera.

The camera shakes, and it eventually centers back on Jackson. But he's no longer his normal self, overly kempt in his suit and tie. He looks tired, haggard even. Like he hasn't slept or bathed in days.

I can't remember the last time, if ever, I've seen him like this. I watch the screen, horrified. He looks sick—like *really* sick. His casual clothes seem out of place. Like they're a size too large.

He grabs the camera lens, ignoring someone shouting behind him. "Jesly, if you can hear me . . . Everything's going to be okay," he says in a rushed voice. "But you need to run, Love. They're coming. Run now!"

The ringing in my ears grows as Jackson and the news anchor disappear from the screen, leaving only the deafening sound behind.

I vainly clutch to the bed guardrail. Collapsing to the cold tile floor, I scramble for my ears. The piercing sound has taken on new life, its energy pouring into the overhead lights as they go from a flicker to a blinding strobe.

Unable to see the sturdy grip that latches onto my shoulder, I'm trapped. It rips my hands from my ears and takes away my only means of protection. It wastes no time in wrestling my hands behind my back.

"Let me go!" I latch onto the bed rail, pulling hard enough that my head slams into the metal frame. Everything goes topsy-turvy, long enough to give them time to try again.

I roll over slowly. This time, I get a glimpse.

Clammy and nearly translucent, my attacker looks like death warmed over. Whatever it is, it isn't human. A dampness clings to my right ear, and it takes all my body weight to loosen the massive creature's hold on me.

"Get off me!" I cry again and try to ignore the blood pooling down my temple.

The long-fingered hands reach again, but now I'm ready. I'm not going to die here. Not when Jackson stands to ruin everything by giving my half-decade's hard work to one of his sluts.

A wail erupts from the creature's throat as I drive all my hundred-and-twenty-eight pounds onto the bridge of its foot. Whatever it is, I'm banking on its ability to feel pain. I snatch the closest item—a ceramic vase with decaying flowers—and smash it over its gnarled head. Its beady black eyes blink at me as both vase and creature drop to the ground.

The strobing has subdued, like someone lowered the dimmer switch, rendering the entire floor a muted shade of gray and red. A rotten smell punches me in the nostrils, and I nearly throw up on the spot.

I've got to get out of here. My bare feet smack against the cold tile as I round the first corner, broken ribs or not.

I slip past the nurse's station. Everyone's gone.

"Jesly," a voice rasps, and I turn around to find a desiccated corpse in an orderly uniform blocking the next hall.

Slamming my elbow into the closest fire extinguisher cabinet, glass shatters all around me. I rip it from its resting place on the wall. "Back the fuck up or I'll fucking kill you!"

"Jesly . . ." The creature creeps in my direction, its voice oddly human.

The fire extinguisher smashes into the creature's outstretched arms, sending it howling as I do it again. It collapses against the blood-stained wall, my head throbbing as it gets harder to breathe. Thirty feet to the elevator.

"Grab her," a female nurse yells to the creatures.

Her face reminds me of a paint swirl video on social media, all deformed and shifting. The stethoscope around her neck moves, coiling and unwinding across her chest. The damned thing is made of snakes.

"Didn't you listen, Jesly?" She tightens her three-fingered grasp on a half-burnt clipboard. "You're safe now."

She nods behind me, and before I can figure out why, I'm tackled to the ground. Those same pale fingers from earlier wrestle the fire extinguisher from my grasp just as a sharp burning pinch bites my neck.

"Easy now . . ." a voice purrs in my ear.

I gasp like a fish out of water, crushed by the weight on top of me. One of the underlings passes her something small, and it takes a second to realize it's a needle. *Fuck.*

My wrists scream as they are contorted behind my back against my will, and I'm dragged back to my feet. Burning heat ricochets through my body, my vision fading as a new figure slips past the nurse.

"Ms. Allbrook," it says disapprovingly as it comes into view.

The last thing I see before delirium takes over is Dr. Hiribaldi and the staff crowded outside my room, their faces full of horror and Dax nowhere in sight.

UNWANTED VISITORS

I'M LOSING MY MIND.

Like the faint echo of waterdrops in a vacant room. It's tapping, always looking for a way in. My head throbs, pulsing with each sweep of the overhead fan. Metal clinks when I move, and the scent of decay is gone, leaving only the sterile hospital scent behind. I'm chained to my hospital bed, the padded straps doing little to keep my thrashing at bay.

Tears flood faster than I can bolt upright. "No, no, no . . ." Yanking at the cuffs does nothing and my gasps for oxygen fill the empty air. I can't breathe.

A male in scrubs notices and eases into the room, his hands raised in the air like I'm armed. "Ms. Jesly? It's Beau. 'member me?"

I yank at the cuffs chained to the bed rail. "What is this? Where's Dax?"

"Mr. Huxley had to leave, ma'am," Beau says, nice and slow. "Visitation's over for today."

I turn to the window. "It's broad daylight."

"It's just temporary. We want you to get better."

Thrashing does no good. They've tethered my ankles too.

"What the hell? You can't hold me like this."

"Ms. Jesly . . ."

"Fuck your Ms. Jesly." I writhe and tug on the straps. I won't let them do this to me. "This is illegal. I'm going to sue your fucking asses."

Not again. Goddamnit, Jackson.

"I'm sorry about this." Sighing, Beau steps into the hallway and pushes the intercom button. "Code White. Room 708. Code White. Room 708."

It only takes fifteen seconds for Dr. Hiribaldi and the security team to reach my room. Their emergency management director would give them five stars.

Irritation lines the doctor's square-shaped face as he buries his hands in his lab coat pockets. "Ms. Allbrook, other patients reside in this wing. You need to calm down before you scare people."

"Calm down?" I shriek and thrash again. "You're holding a law-abiding civilian against their will! They should be scared!"

"Ms. Allbrook, stop," he says, leaving only a tight grimace behind. "You've had a psychotic break. This is a *physical* trauma hospital. We're not equipped in this department—"

"I'm not crazy. Something's wrong with this place." I shake my head. "You weren't there. You didn't see what I did."

"What we saw was you punch a hole in a glass cabinet and beat some technicians with a fire extinguisher," he explains. "What you *saw* doesn't matter. It's what you *did*."

"You don't understand. My ex wants me here—he's doing this. You have to let me out."

"That's not going to happen." He steps closer toward the bed but stays just out of reach. Just like the rest of them. They're all staring at me like I'm insane.

You are, Jesly. You always have been.

"We've contacted your previous doctor, Dr. Yamini. He's currently out of the office, but his secretary forwarded us your medical records."

"How? Who signed those releases?" I balk. "You've had me chained here like a fucking animal."

"We have a durable power of attorney on file from your last hospitalization."

"Well, I'm awake now and I rescind it," I snap. "Do you hear me? I rescind it."

He nods at Beau before studying me for a moment. "Listen. You attacked two of my staff this morning, and you have a history of involuntary commitment. Legally, I have every right to hold you for forty-eight hours. Our resident psychiatrist will evaluate you further. Even *if* you could revoke your DPOA, your mental acuity is nowhere in the realm of making decisions. So, for now, you're stuck."

"This isn't over."

His lip curls. "No, Ms. Allbrook, I don't think it's anywhere close. You have . . ." He turns his wrist over to check the time. "Another twenty-five hours at the *earliest*, so I suggest you get comfortable. Dr. Caspar will see you first thing tomorrow morning. In the meantime, the right combo of meds will help stave off any more *urges*."

"And if I refuse?"

The doctor laughs. "You don't really get a choice."

"What about a phone call?"

"Of course. This isn't Hell," he reassures me. "We're reassigning you to our lead RN. He'll assist you moving forward."

I take a deep breath. *That's a tall ask.*

☥

"You sure?" Kane's voice echoes in my head.

Dressed in blue scrubs, a new pair of Nikes, and an ID badge dangling from his hip, my wayward-companion strolls in. His thick brown hair is brushed back, his beard neatly groomed, and he avoids Dr. Hiribaldi's gaze long enough to pat Beau on the shoulder. Kane whispers something to the young tech before they leave, letting the door swing shut behind them.

"Don't. Say. Anything." He grabs the corded phone, suddenly projecting his voice. "About that phone call. What number did you want to dial?"

Unfazed by my wide-eyed stare, Kane nestles the phone on the bed between us. The nightstand is close enough that he pushes the junk aside and sits on the edge, considerably closer than I'm expecting. He hands me a scratchpad and our eyes lock—he's serious. Seconds later, I've got two numbers jotted down.

He tries the first.

When we get out of here, a thousand questions are headed his way. I snatch the handset and place the cold receiver against my ear. *Ring.* "How many phone calls do I get?"

"As many as it takes, Allbrook."

Ring. They're not going to answer. They never do. *Ring.* No one ever answers me. *Ring.* I don't know why I even bother. *"Hi, you've reached Walter and Linda Allbrook—"*

I shake my head and he presses his thumb down on the base. "Next?"

I take a deep breath, trying to steady the wobbliness threatening me. Kane dials the next number.

Ring. "Hello?" a voice answers.

"It's me, Dax."

"Jesly?" he says. "What happened? They won't let me in."

"A lot."

"Obviously. There's a security guard stationed at every entrance to your wing," he reports. "What did you do?"

The hairs on the back of my neck bristle. "What makes you think *I* did something?"

"You're right. I'm sorry," he apologizes. "You okay?"

I shake my head even though Dax can't see it, but Kane can. He's here, watching my every move. I'm not sure whether I can trust either of them, but I've got to start somewhere. Dax deserves that much. "Yeah."

"How long will you stay under lock and key?"

"A few days if I'm lucky."

"Dang," he says through the phone. "I could really use your help out here."

I fall back into the pillows and stare at the drop ceiling. "It's not going to bring her back, Dax. She's gone."

"You don't think I know that?"

"I-I'm sorry," I tell him. "That was rude. I'm just tired."

"You worry about getting better," he says. "I've got all the time in the world." A woman's airy laughter cuts like glass as Dax clears his throat. "Hey, I've got some company over. Call me whenever you get released and we'll figure out what comes next." The phone clicks. "Jesly? You there?"

"Sorry . . ." I inhale, trying to refocus. "Yeah?"

"Get some rest," he tells me, "but don't think I'm letting you off the hook."

"Okay." I hand Kane back the phone, my veins filling with concrete until I can barely move. He nestles the receiver back into its cradle.

"Well? Was that better or worse than expected?" he asks, his hazel eyes evaluating everything.

"I have no idea."

He returns the phone to the nightstand behind him.

"What are you doing here, Kane?" I ask as he draws the knitted blanket over me. Motives aside, I could do worse.

He narrows his gaze. "Research."

"On?"

"Ways to keep you safe."

"Can't you just teleport us out of here?" I ask, clanging the chains of the cuff.

He shakes his head. "No, Allbrook. It doesn't work like that. I'm not permitted to interfere."

"Since when?"

"Since always," he says plainly. "I shouldn't have done what I did. I could get in real trouble."

"With who?"

He ignores my question. "We'll find another way out."

"Hey," I say, grabbing his arm. "What if we can't? What if I'm stuck?"

He looks down at my hand. "Then we both lose."

Thunder claps in the distance. Kane digs a set of keys from his pocket and undoes the straps tethering me, putting his index finger to his lips. "I'm going to scout around—make good use of this uniform."

"Sure, whatever." I roll onto my side and stare out the window. The rain's back, pelting the windows in angry waves. *Again.* This weather feels like I do today.

"Allbrook?" he calls from the doorway.

"Kane?"

"Trust me," he says softly. "Everything will work out."

☥

"I don't believe you."

"I know, and I'm sorry. I'll return as soon as I can." He takes a quick inventory to make sure no one's watching before turning down the lights, leaving me alone with the newfound darkness and the emptiness tearing at me, one second at a time.

"—SIR, YOU CAN'T GO in there," a female voice yells somewhere close-by, breaking my weak attempt at sleep.

I pull the blanket farther over my head. It's been less than two days and I'm more exhausted than ever.

"Jes . . ."

I roll over to find Jackson standing inches away. He's soaking wet, tattered umbrella in hand.

"I got here as fast as I could." His tapered gray suit looks just as disheveled. He rushes toward my bedside, his jaw tight. He was busy. *Poor him.*

"Sir, you can't be in here," the nurse repeats, trailing after him. "Ms. Allbrook's not permitted visitors."

"I'm not a visitor; I'm her lawyer," he snaps. "I need to speak with my client *alone.*"

The nurse blinks, then gathers herself. "I'm going to have to see some ID. You've entered a closed wing."

"Yeah? And I need to see your fucking boss, doll, so go get him." Jackson drops his leather bag and overcoat on the chair. "Now!" he barks when she doesn't move.

The RN jumps this time, obviously taken aback by Jackson's brazenness.

Unlike her, I'm used to it. I slink toward the far side of the bed. "You can't be here; they'll arrest you."

"They can try," he says bitterly. "I'm your attorney on file, remember?"

"What do you want, Jackson?"

"You tried to kill yourself again?" Jackson snatches my wrists, only to see the bandages covering both arms.

I don't remember doing it . . . I shrink away. "Just leave."

"Well, you don't get a choice." He sits on the bed. "Your parents aren't getting dragged into this. Walt's reelection campaign is picking up, and he can't afford any negative press right now."

"Negative press?" I balk. "Are you fucking kidding me? I nearly died, and he's worried about his goddamned primary?"

"You didn't nearly die, Jesly." Exhaustion lines his chiseled brow. He's still striking to look at, even after everything he's done. "You hurt yourself for attention; there's a difference."

"Go to Hell." I slide off the bed and head toward the window. Outside the rain has shifted sideways, leaving the entire city in a downpour.

When I spin back around, Jackson's standing behind me, his clothes different from moments before. His slacks are stained, his gray Oxford torn and bloody. He's filthy and bruised. Worse now.

I stare at him, horrified. "What the fuck?"

He blinks slowly, his face contorted in confusion. "Jes?"

"What the hell's wrong with you?"

His eyes widen, and he latches onto my forearm, his grip tight and harsh. "The charges. Do you have them?"

"What?" I ask. "What are you talking about?"

"The paperwork!" he says more insistently. "From the funeral. He—*I* gave it to you. Where is it?"

"I don't have it anymore. I threw it away."

"Are you serious?" he hisses. "Why would you do that?"

My eyes widen as I wrench my arm from him. "Jackson, you're acting crazy. Now let go. You're hurting me."

He snatches me again. "Damnit, Jesly, no! Listen to me. You've got to get out of here!"

"What?" I say. "It's your fault I'm stuck in the first place."

"Before they come back. You have to leave. Now," he hisses frantically.

I shake off his grip and clutch my sweater. "What are you talking about? They won't release me."

"Don't listen," he cuts me off, his voice breaking as he monitors the door. "Trust no one. Not a single one."

"And I should trust you?"

"Yes," he hisses.

"Now who's lost it, Jackson?"

"They're *lying* to you," he whispers, his normally cold and even voice catching on every word. Whatever he's worried about, he believes it. He glances around the room. "I'm gonna get us out of this."

"No one asked you to, Jackson. I don't need you anymore. What part don't you get?"

"Y-You don't mean that."

"I do," I say defiantly. "After what you pulled on the news today, what did you expect?"

He blinks, completely lost. "What are you talking about?"

I return my attention to the downpour. One would think I'd have gotten used to Jackson's tricks after all these years, but I'm not.

Each time he gaslights me, the wounds cut deeper.

Each time, the blade tears into my flesh.

"Jes—"

"Just leave."

I spin around to find Jackson like he was moments before—in his suit that he's dead set on wiping the dampness away from. *It's official. I'm losing my goddamn mind.*

He clears his throat. "Let's just get Dr. Yamini to adjust your meds and you can get some rest. Okay?"

His boyish good looks belie his mastery of keeping secrets—this is the same man who made my life a waking hell. The same one who also holds a 50-percent stake in our law partnership that we've both worked too hard to stop now.

There's only one way out. For either of us.

Death.

But it won't be me.

"Christ, you're like ice, Jes." He pulls me against him and rubs my shoulders. "Can't have you getting sick now. I'll send Katie to fetch more clothes from the house."

Lightning shoots down my spine and I pull away. We can finally stop playing these games. "When is she moving in?"

Silence engulfs the space between us for a moment before he finally announces, "She already did."

I say nothing.

"I would tell you I'm sorry, but I'd rather not lie," he admits. "Did they say when they're releasing you?"

"Maybe you should ask yourself."

His tongue clicks. "You know the next time you're starved for attention, just let me know and I'll get you an emotional support puppy. It'll look better on the tax write-offs."

"Get out."

"I heard this same thing at Fourth of July weekend. Is this your new shtick—threatening to kill yourself every three months?"

☥

Laughing at his own amusement, he digs out a pocketknife and sets it on the rollaway cart. "Maybe do it right next time. Save me the gas."

My hand slaps the knife away, sending it clattering to the ground. "You're disgusting."

"But that's how you like it." He's on me in an instant, his face in mine. I collapse into the closest chair and his hands slide up both armrests. "You and that fucked up little head of yours. Should I RSVP now to your next show, or do you think maybe you can stay out of trouble for a day or two?"

"Never come back."

"Gladly." He snatches his briefcase and overcoat. "I'll send over your release request sometime this week. Or maybe next."

If I could set him on fire, I would. "Say hi to Katie for me."

"Don't worry. I will."

"Get the fuck out." I fling my lunch tray at him, sending uneaten food everywhere. With a million-dollar company trapping us together, it's more like an arranged marriage than anything else.

He looks down at the mess and steps over it. "You're fucking nuts, you know that? Nothing is worth this much aggravation. Not even you."

KEEPING TIME

"Where were you just now, Jesly?" The psychiatrist searches my face from behind his oversized mahogany desk.

"I'm sorry?" I look up from the hospital wristband I spin absentmindedly to find myself in a large office lined with bookshelves and cabinets stretching floor to ceiling.

This place is a showcase of his technical and medical knowledge. A statement that he knows me better than I know myself. *Psychology Today* and *The American Journal of Psychiatry* sit on his stone coffee table. Photos of his two children and a beautiful, tawny-skinned wife bring the illusion home. Dr. Caspar's desk is organized to imply he has endless time for his patients.

The typical kind of mental health scenery all shrinks use to make us feel calm. The walls are painted a subtle shade of blue. *Cornflower, maybe?* But it doesn't work; I don't like blue.

"Did you hear my question?" His honey-brown eyes study me, his umber complexion a stark contrast to his bright, all-American smile.

Each word I utter, or lack thereof, is a sign to these people. A secret code with a meaning unto itself.

"When can I leave, Doctor?"

A flicker of a smile. "We'll get there. You've been through a lot in this past year, Jesly. More than any one person should." He unclicks his pen and sets it beside his padfolio.

This psychiatrist wants me to believe he's not a threat—it won't work though. *This ain't my first rodeo.*

Anyone who can lock you away is a threat. Don't be stupid.

"Jesly?"

Nobody needs to know I've had a voice riding shotgun since the accident. Ignoring it works just the same.

"Therapy is a two-way street. I can't help you if you don't let me." He reaches for the coffee mug with an illustration of a corgi butt on it.

"I'm just tired," I lie and scratch under the wristband. Stupid thing is irritating my skin.

"As you should be. Falling from fifty-plus-stories is no joke."

I crane my head around to see if Kane's still outside Dr. Caspar's office. They haven't caught on yet, and we're not about to tell them. Kane makes a good enough guard.

Dr. Caspar's phone notification goes off. He reads the message, types in something, and sends it on its way. "My wife will have my hide if I don't answer. We have plans later."

I nod politely but honestly couldn't care less if his wife blows his phone up all the way to Tibet. I've got enough problems of my own. "When can I go home?"

He sets the mug back on its corkboard coaster. "Do you have family in the area?"

"No," I admit. A mistake I regret immediately. But knowing he's read my file, we can skip a lot of the formalities. "I'm not from here."

☥

"Where's home?"

"Originally?" I pick at my cuticles. "Massachusetts."

"I take it your parents haven't called since you woke up?"

"No."

I know he's not trying to make me feel bad. He likes corgi butts after all.

He's got an angle. Just wait.

"Jesly?"

He's watching me again. "Do you know why you're here?"

"In the hospital or in your office?"

"Both."

"Because you think I tried to kill myself."

"Are you saying you didn't?"

I cross my arms and sink into the chair.

"Don't you think it's time to process it? Maybe find out why you've been slipping from reality lately?" He unwraps a green Jolly Rancher from the candy bowl on his desk and tosses it in his mouth. "Want one?"

Don't do it. He's baiting you.

I shake my head and study the ceiling fan only to find it surprisingly dusty. This is the part where I create some explanation that doesn't make me sound insane.

"You better think fast," Zaire's voice sounds from behind Dr. Caspar's chair, making my eyes widen.

Dressed in the same faded denim jeans and black leather jacket from the funeral, Zaire grins like the Cheshire Cat.

I force down the lump in my throat. *What the—*

"Don't worry. Doc can't see me. That takes time." When he notices me glance at the door, he adds, *"Don't worry. Kane's outside. This won't take long. Just keep the ol' doc busy."* Zaire looks at the folding picture

frame on Dr. Caspar's desk. *"Hot wife."*

He's fucking with you.

"I don't know how."

Both men gawk at me, albeit for two completely different reasons. Zaire's face flickers with worry. He heard it too.

Fuckkkk . . . So I'm not crazy after all.

Dr. Caspar, on the other hand, waits for me to elaborate. *Damnit.* Goddamned entrapment. All three of them.

"Sometimes, it feels like my mind is going to explode," I blurt, covering.

Zaire starts rifling through the filing cabinets. To my amazement, Dr. Caspar doesn't seem to notice. He's too busy writing something.

"What are you doing?" I ask.

"Taking notes. I'm assuming you don't mind," Dr. Caspar says, though he's not asking permission. "Did you feel this way before you jumped?"

I sigh. "I don't need a shrink; I need a restraining order."

"From whom?"

"My ex—Jackson Alders."

That gets him to glance up from his padfolio. "Is this because of your report stating you think he broke into a secured wing after-hours and assaulted you?"

"I don't think. I know," I rebuke. It's the same way I'm certain Zaire is scouring the filing cabinets. But that's not something I can explain—not to Dr. Caspar.

To a psychiatrist, I exist outside the norm. Something that his years of medical school and residency tell him to diagnose. It won't be long now.

He flips another page. "It also says you attacked two staff

members, one of whom has a broken nose. What do you remember?"

"I didn't break anything." My left leg bounces as Zaire rifles through another drawer. *"How much longer?"*

Zaire pulls out the third drawer.

"What are you looking for?" I ask aloud.

"I'm sorry?" Dr. Caspar looks up.

Damnit.

"Stop talking," Zaire yells, turning around long enough to send me a condescending look. *"Hasn't Kane taught you anything?"*

"Was he supposed to?" I ask confusedly.

"Jesly?" Dr. Caspar's staring at me staring at the filing cabinet.

"Yeah?"

He leans in, suspicious as fuck now. "Who are you talking to?"

"No one."

Zaire snorts. *"You're terrible at this."* The pull-down shelves to the left of the desk consume his attention, his search becoming more frantic.

"Alright then," Dr. Caspar announces and moves to my side of the room. Dragging the spare client chair backward, he drops into it. "Self-harm, hallucinations, agitation, delusions, erratic behavior, disorganized thinking, gaps in memory—"

"My memory's just fine."

He raises a brow, noting which symptom I argue with. "This is a textbook definition of schizophrenia. What that means, Jesly, is that you're either faking it, or you're really dealing with a serious mental health crisis. You tell me."

"I'm not the medical professional here," I say. "You are."

"How about this," he says. "I'm going to read a list of statements, and you tell me if they feel true to you."

☥

"I *feel* like no one's listening."

"I *am* listening," he pits back. "How often does this happen?"

"How often does *what* happen?"

"You seeing people who aren't there."

I slip out of my chair, trying to put some space between us. If Kane has noticed Zaire's presence, he hasn't come rushing in. And I don't know whether I should worry or not. I peek my head around the window to find Kane still in the waiting area, pretending to read some book. My chest starts to cramp, so I rub my knuckles over it and fight to breathe.

Dr. Caspar notices. "The tightness in your chest? That's your truth waiting to come out."

I choke back a laugh. *If he only knew.*

"How about some music?"

"Excuse me?" I ask.

Smacking his leg, Dr. Caspar gets up and mashes a small remote control from the shelf. The room is suddenly awash in airy jazz. "What do you think?"

"It's great," I say, trying not to focus on Zaire's destruction of the good doctor's fastidious paper trail.

Dr. Caspar drops back into the chair across from me, grabbing another candy as he does. The man's got a sweet tooth. "These offices are always too stuffy, no matter how much we try." He reaches over into his pseudo-vintage mini-fridge and pulls out a water bottle. "Want one?"

"Yeah, sure."

He hands me his sealed bottle and grabs another. Breakfast jazz fills the emptiness, and I crack open my water.

A cabinet door slams. Ten shelves and three rows of cabinets later, Zaire turns his eyes to Dr. Caspar's desk where a stack of manila files waits.

"*What are you looking for?*" I finally ask, silently.

"*Don't worry about it. Just keep him busy.*"

"*I thought he couldn't see you.*"

"*Doesn't mean I need him focused on anything but you,*" Zaire explains. "*Flirt with him or something.*"

"*Excuse me?*" I choke on my water. "*What's wrong with you?*"

He drops the searched files into a new stack once he's done with them.

"*Just hurry up, Zaire; I'd like to leave.*"

"*You're a ballsy bitch, you know that? Must be why Kane fancies you.*"

All the feeling drains from my face. The voice was right—he's messing with me. "*Why are you rifling through this man's office? What do you want?*"

"Something personal," he says aloud this time.

"*And that's my problem?*" I balk.

Another folder hits the desk. "*Not everything is about you, Jesly.*" He rips open one of the doctor's sliding drawers. There's something he's not telling me, but tight-lipped Alice won't tell me how far down this rabbit hole I'll have to go to find out.

Fingers snap in front of my face, forcing me backward. They're Dr. Caspar's.

I blink rapidly and my eyes refocus. "What the hell?"

"You're dissociating again," he says disappointedly. "Listen, Jesly." He sets down the padfolio on the coffee table. "Even before your suicide attempt, you endured a very serious accident and a 5150 hospitalization before that. I want you to make it to spring."

Stop him.

"What are you saying?"

"Before we do anything, I'm going to discuss your medical

history and MRI results with Dr. Hiribaldi to try to figure out what we're dealing with."

Maybe I should tell him. If I'm lucky he'll believe me.

"Eureka," Zaire exclaims, snatching a piece of paper from one of the hanging folders. He slides the drawer shut with satisfaction.

"Got what you came for?" I ask sourly.

"More or less." He folds the paper into fourths and stows it in his jacket pocket.

Dr. Caspar sets the water on the coffee table, distracting me. By the time I look back, Zaire's gone. "This person you were worried about being on hospital property . . ." Dr. Caspar reopens my chart. "Jackson Alders. This is your ex?"

I nod. "Yeah."

"Well, in a previous hospitalization, it appears he was your advanced directive representative and DPOA."

"Yeah, but I rescinded that today."

His head bounces in agreement. "Unfortunately, Dr. Hiribaldi is right. It wouldn't be due diligence if I were to release you now."

No . . .

"I understand this wasn't the opinion you were looking for." He sets the file back down on the desk, folding the padfolio shut. "We'll see what we can figure out after I speak with Dr. Hiribaldi."

"What are you saying?" The nerves on the back of my neck bristle. The air is so thick it's almost palpable. I slink back into the chair just as the door to the office swings open.

Kane finally enters with a dog-eared book at his side. By the way his shoulders are bowed up and the tightness of his jaw, he probably ran into Zaire.

Dr. Caspar heads back around his desk to find the files askew. "As it stands now," he says, straightening the paperwork, "unless

Mr. Alders is willing to serve as your in-home caregiver, our inpatient facility at Calgary Springs will likely come next."

"You can't do that," I argue.

Kane paces the office like a panther in a cage.

"You spent three months in a coma." Dr. Caspar struggles with his shuffled papers. "We don't know what kind of damage this did to your brain psychologically. Physically, your recovery is going unusually well."

"Doctor, with all due respect," I say, "I'm not staying here one second longer."

He nods at Kane before passing my file over. "Jesly, I'm saying you may not have a choice."

UNWELCOME TRUTH

THE HOSPITAL CAFETERIA IS awash with staff and patients as the lunch hour progresses. A small cup of coffee sits untouched in front of me. It's the second real one I've had since waking up, and I can't even bring myself to enjoy it. Kane makes it over to our table with two clear plastic takeaway containers—sandwiches, by the look of it.

"Turkey okay?" He slides me the top one.

I say nothing.

"You need to eat something." He pops his lid open and dives in, making sure to pick off the sprouts.

"I'm fine."

"You need your strength. We don't know what's next," he says between mouthfuls.

"Whose side are you on?" I slouch against the hard wooden chair. My body feels sluggish, its adrenaline finally wearing off. A bad sign if Security comes for me. *I've got to be ready.*

"Yours, *always.*" He rips open a bag of baked jalapeño chips, pops one in his mouth, and spins the bag in my direction.

I spin it back. "Why? You don't even know me."

He takes another bite of his sandwich and leans in. "I know you well enough," he says plainly. "Your favorite color is sunset on an early winter night, you'll fight anybody in the break room over the last gingersnap, and you feel like no matter how hard you try, nothing ever works out."

"Just who the fuck are you?" I ask, my voice sharper than intended.

His face twists into a grimace. "What I *am* is a friend. Now stop stressing until there's something to stress about." When I don't budge, he adds, "Come on. Today's Monday. Dr. Caspar still has to speak with Dr. Hiribaldi, who from what the nurses say, is off. So relax and *eat* something."

He's got an angle. They all do.

"Don't you ever get sick of voices telling you what to do?" Kane's voice breaks through my thoughts.

Our eyes lock immediately. *"You can hear them?"*

"Why do you think I'm with you?" He shoves another handful of chips in his mouth and cracks open a can of Coke to wash the spice down.

I mull it over. "Honestly, I don't know. Keep an eye on me like a good crony?"

"What makes you think I'm someone's crony?"

"So you and Zaire—" I stop and finally drink my coffee.

He crumples the empty bag on his tray and notes the closest camera before leaning in. "Let's just say, I work for a party interested in how this all turns out."

"Maybe," I say. "Or maybe you just like the long game."

"You're a difficult person, you know that?"

No point in answering—we both know he's right.

This far past noon, the cafeteria has mostly cleared out, leaving

♀

those taking late lunches scrambling to grab something half-way decent. The crew bustle as they break down some of the serving trays to get everything cleaned before dinner.

"This *interested* party," I repeat. "What do they want?"

"If you happen to meet them, ask."

"Mr. Kane?" a young woman's voice erupts from the sidelines.

Her badge reads *Admissions*. A lanky medical assistant with box braids pulled into a high ponytail, she looks either new or nervous. With the way she keeps tapping her paperwork on her leg, I'd wager both.

"How can I help?" Kane smiles as he closes the plastic container carefully.

"Dr. Hiribaldi would like to see you both upstairs as soon as you're done here."

"We'll be right up," he says and raises a hand before I can say a word.

Visibly relieved, she scurries back toward the elevator.

"Hey!" I slam my coffee cup. "I thought you said he was off." When he doesn't acknowledge, I yell, "Kane."

"What? Oh sorry. He should have been . . ." Blinking, he leans in, his breath sweet like caramel. "Allbrook, I thought we already talked about this. I'm just going to need you to trust me."

"Yeah, well, you're making it kind of hard."

A frown weaves its way deeper into his face. "We already talked about this. I'm not going to let anything bad happen."

"So why don't I believe you, then?"

"Trust issues, maybe?" He pushes in his chair and waits. "Come on. As long as I'm around, I'll do what I can."

"This is bullshit." I throw my trash in the large garbage can at the end of the aisle.

☥

Outside the cafeteria, some staff pass us in the hallway, doing their best to avoid eye contact. My reputation has spread.

Good. Less to deal with.

Pulling his badge free from the elastic string, Kane presses it against the little plastic box on the wall. The door latch clicks.

"I could just run, you know." I bury my hands under my armpits. The building is increasingly freezing to me.

"And go where?"

We turn down the next corridor. "I'll figure something out. I always do."

"You're missing the point."

There's no winning with this guy. The remainder of our trip is silent as he lets me stew. If he can hear my thoughts, he makes no indication.

With the dayturn staff back from lunch, the hallways are more crowded. The wing opens into a large foyer filled with plush, oversized chairs and stone coffee tables. There are a few individuals working, sleeping, chatting. Massive double-paned windows stretch from floor to ceiling, driving the afternoon sun into this side of the hospital.

"Elevators are over there." He points toward the epicenter of the foyer where sleek metal contrasts the bright glass and lush carpeting. It's not far. Kane presses the up button on the panel, calling down the next elevator.

"Hey, wait," I say, "what if they really commit me?"

"Not going to happen."

The elevator dings and the metal doors spring open. An older couple steps out, the wife pushing her husband in a manual wheelchair. Instinctively, I move out of their way, not wanting to be rude. While I can't find love, at least these nice folks can.

☥

Once inside, Kane selects the seventh floor. "All aboard."

I glare at him and fight to ignore the small curl of his lip as we settle in. It's smooth sailing with just the two of us.

Beep.

Beep.

Beep.

The elevator lurches to a halt.

Kane presses seven again. Nothing. "Odd."

I shoot him a glance as the lights flicker. "You think?"

"What? I didn't do it." He tries the entire panel of buttons. Still nothing.

"Here, let me." I pound the **Open-Door** button repeatedly. All I get is a flickering overhead halogen that ultimately dulls, leaving the elevator in a disgusting shade of muted goldenrod.

"Feel better?" He squats and reads over the emergency directions. Stay calm. Call the desk. Usual stuff.

"Do you have a phone on you?" I ask.

"No."

"Can we pry the doors?"

"Are you crazy?"

I flash him a condescending look. There's no emergency box in this elevator, so we're either staying put or getting out. My vote is on the latter; I mash the buttons once more. The elevator roars to life and we start moving again.

Beep. The halogen flickers, and the doors crawl open at a landing. Not entirely centered on the next floor, most of the opening is concrete.

Kane just stands there, unable to refute the win. "I don't know about this. Let's just wait."

"No way," I disagree, already moving towards the square opening on the wall. "Let's go before the damn thing changes its mind."

I know it's just my own paranoia, but God help me if this damn thing decides to move again. Getting chopped in half is no one's idea of a good time.

If I ever think that just for a moment the universe has forgiven me, it's times like these that put me in my place. Squeezing out of a square hole the size of a cardboard box is a terrible idea by any account. Even mine.

At least the elevator stopped where I can drag myself up and out without too much effort. It just has to stay still long enough not to kill me. I shoot a hazardous glance at Kane who hasn't moved, my eyes trailing down to the gold cross on his neck.

If ever there was a time to pray, now would probably be it.

But I'm not religious—I can do this on my own.

Taking a deep breath, I drag my knees up and over the concrete and squeeze out like a snake shedding its skin. My hands land on the linoleum tile of the next floor. I roll over onto my side to find the thick elevator doors are still caught between open and closed.

A low, mechanical groan echoes in the elevator shaft, its metal creaking as the machinery reawakens. The cables above Kane shudder back to life, clattering as they roar with idle chatter.

"Wait a second!" he says, rushing towards the button panel. It's too late.

The doors shut, sending Kane upward.

I'm alone, *again. Shit.*

I spin around and see where I've landed.

The fourth floor. Signs serve as waypoints to the uninitiated. *Radiology* to the left, *Surgery* to the right. I was just here with Beau, albeit less intact than I am now. The emergency stairs must be close.

I scan for the sign with the little man ascending and push the metal handle inward. Each footstep echoes in the empty corridor as I lumber floor by floor. My thighs hurt, even though it's only been one flight. My body has become my enemy, reminding me I can no longer trust it to keep me safe.

I hang onto the railing and ease onto the sixth floor. *One more.* I should be thankful for being alive, but I'm not. Dying would've at least simplified everything; then my nightmare would have ended. The next fifty feet drag like eternity.

Even in the stairwell, the lights flicker. A Trauma One hospital having power issues is the last thing the staff needs right now. It's been getting worse.

Being awake feels surreal, like my fall from the Renaissance was a different lifetime. But it's not that easy. Some things don't get forgiven. Whoever my assailant was, they agreed.

I push open the door to the seventh floor, and it feels like a birth of sorts. Like Plato's *Allegory of the Cave*, I'm the only one to understand the nightmare waiting for me at the nurse's desk.

Jackson. But it's no hallucination.

Back to his usual self in his freshly dry-cleaned suit, he speaks to a physician I don't recognize. His cufflinks are undone just enough to roll his sleeves up and his tie is loosened. Other than that, pristine to a T. *W-what is going on?* A sharp pain cuts at my temples, nearly doubling me over as I yelp in pain.

Before I can run, he spots me. "Jes." Jackson's buttery voice pierces through every inch of me.

I can't move; my body won't listen. I'm trapped, and wiping the tears on my sleeve doesn't keep them from falling.

"Kane? Kane!" I search for my new companion, foolishly hoping he got off at the next floor.

Nothing.

The light clip of patent leather loafers slinks down the hallway. I screw my eyes shut. *Please God, no.*

"Hello, Love," Jackson's voice rings out.

I won't give him the satisfaction of looking up. My eyes glue to the tile floor. It's dusty. Dirtier than last time.

"Glad to see you could make it." He offers his hand like we're headed to prom.

Maybe if I count to fifteen, he'll disappear. One . . . two . . . I wait.

Nope.

He's here; I'm here. Neither of us is going anywhere. Not with a million-dollar company on the line. The only difference between us is that I'm not after the money; I wanted to help the accused. I just never thought it would be me.

"What do you want, Jackson?"

Had that assassin not tracked me to the Renaissance, Jackson would've never known I was here. He would be running around with God-knows-who doing God-knows-what. Now we're both lost—angry at each other and our costly mistakes. Too many things we can't take back.

Not anymore.

There is no forgiving what I've done—what we've *both* done.

He itches his jawline, his five o'clock shadow bothering him. "Dr. Yamini's been looking for you for hours. Could you just take one thing seriously?"

"What are you talking about?" I look at the clock on a nearby wall. The face reads 2:22. "They said—"

"Come on." He waves for me to follow. "Court's in recess long enough to get this handled. You should be grateful that Judge Carn even let me leave."

"Grateful?" I scoff. "You think I should be grateful?"

"I think it'd be a start, Love."

"Maybe if you stopped choosing when it's convenient to show up. You're here one minute, gone the next."

"What deluded bullshit did you get into your head this time?" he says, pausing mid-step. "I haven't been here in weeks."

"You're lying," I say as I scratch beneath my wristband again. The damn thing is getting itchier. *Can you even be allergic to these things?*

Jackson pulls off his tie and shoves it in his slacks' pocket. "Let's just go." In recess, he doesn't have to act presentable. In recess, he can just be himself. As much as a monster can.

"Why are you doing this?"

"Jes, I want to move on with my life." He stops to give the vending machine a once-over. "I can't keep doing this forever."

"How can you even say that after everything you've done?" I whisper under my breath.

"After what I've done?" He snaps around so fast I stumble. "Your head shit is the reason I'm even having to meet with investors. The firm is bleeding because of you."

"I hope you choke and die. I really do."

It's a moment before he speaks. "You're making a huge mistake. Don't say I didn't warn you."

"Don't worry. I won't," I snap and head down the hallway, leaving him and the dusty terrain behind.

My footsteps drag as I walk toward the nurse's station, counting the black-and-white tile design on the floor. The farther I go, the cleaner the area becomes. The floor's got one of those weird abstract patterns where the accent color is scattered all hodgepodge.

One, I count.

When I was a kid, I was extremely superstitious. Way past

stepping on cracks, I convinced myself to only jump on the black tiles when my mom was sick, and we had to visit her in the local hospital. I foolishly believed playing by the rules would keep everyone safe. That was a long time ago.

Two.

Twenty years later, focusing on the black tiles calms me. *Three.* I don't dare skip. The staff already thinks I'm crazy enough. *Four.* Nor do I divert my focus. Rather, I steady myself with the line of tiles. *Seven by* the time I reach the nurse's desk.

Ding.

The elevator chimes and out bursts a flustered Kane. "Cheese and rice. You okay, Allbrook?" He latches onto my shoulders and looks me over until he's satisfied that I'm not injured.

Scouring the hallway, all we find are a perplexed Dr. Hiribaldi and Dr. Caspar waiting behind the nurse's desk. "What took so long?" Dr. Hiribaldi asks with an RBF that might honestly be worse than mine.

Dr. Caspar, on the other hand, looks altogether way too concerned. Terrified, even. Subtle, but it's there haunting him.

Kane props himself on the counter. "The elevator malfunctioned."

"Really?" Dr. Caspar cranes around us to stare at the beast in question. "It's been working all morning."

"*Where'd you go?*" I ask silently.

Kane doesn't look at me. "*Nowhere.*" When he realizes both doctors are waiting for an answer, he says, "Yeah, well, I spent the entire time trying to get the elevator to restart. Jesly had to crawl out."

"It was Jackson—Jackson Alders," I tell Dr. Caspar. "He was just here."

By their twisted-up faces, they don't believe me.

Dr. Hiribaldi drops my file on the counter. "Ms. Allbrook,

enough. Mr. Alders was never here."

"Yes, he was," I argue. "He literally walked from the stairwell with me." I glance down the hallway for any sign of him but find nothing save for the piercing bright overheads and freshly washed tile. *What the fuck?*

"Jesly," Dr. Caspar says.

"I don't *understand*," I whimper. "He was just here."

"Jesly . . ." he repeats. "You need to listen to Dr. Hiribaldi."

While it's only early afternoon, my attending physician looks exhausted. He's got the complexion of a person who's seen more than his fair share of horrors in one shift. Maybe even one lifetime. Unfortunately, it's his job. One he's likely currently regretting.

The middle-aged man grips the nurse's station long enough for him to lock eyes with me. "Other than two of my RNs, this hall's been empty. The rest of my staff are at a quarterly HIPAA training downstairs."

"No . . ." I whisper in disbelief. "You're mistaken."

Dr. Caspar offers, "How about we all head to my office to discuss this privately?"

"Unless it involves going home, I'm not going anywhere."

"That's okay. We can talk right here if you want." Dr. Caspar slides out from behind the nurse's station. "Jesly, we were finally able to reach your parents."

"What?" I ask. Nothing like them waiting until the eleventh hour. *Typical.* "That wasn't necessary. I can sign myself out."

Dr. Caspar takes a deep breath, forcing my nerves to bristle. Kane offers nothing. Having been babysitting me for hours, he's no more up to date than I am.

"Not to release you, Ms. Allbrook," he clarifies. "It was to sign the consent paperwork requesting long-term inpatient care."

♀

"You can't be serious."

My parents want me silenced just as much as Jackson. There's too much to lose. Being the "mentally ill" daughter of a politician in an election year isn't going to cut it. They can play the "*good parents*"; i.e., lock your daughter away to get her the help she needs.

What I *need* is a restraining order and a small semi-automatic pistol. Even then, it's likely not enough. I've seen the stats. I know the odds.

"It's not as bad as you think." Dr. Caspar tries to reassure me and grabs the chart from the counter. He flips it open to a document with a bunch of signatures and slides it to me. *Magistrate's Order and Warrant for Emergency Apprehension and Detention.*

"You're committing me?"

Dr. Hiribaldi shrugs. "Committing is an ugly term, but if you want to get technical, Ms. Allbrook . . . we are."

Dr. Caspar won't look me in the eye.

"You were supposed to fix this." I step back. *Not again.*

The good doctor's umber features writhe with guilt. He knows he fucked up. "I'm sorry, Jesly."

"I want Jackson," I say. It's his fault we're in this mess. "Get him back here. He can convince the judge to rescind it."

"Ms. Allbrook, no." Dr. Hiribaldi slams his palms on the counter.

"What the hell's your problem, asshole?" I yell. "Doctor or not, that doesn't entitle you to be a dick."

The doctors exchange a glance, but it's Hiribaldi who opens his mouth. "Ms. Allbrook, you cannot see Mr. Alders because he's dead—three months ago in your car accident in October."

"He's gone, Jesly. I'm sorry." Dr. Caspar drops his head in shame, and I know he's telling the truth.

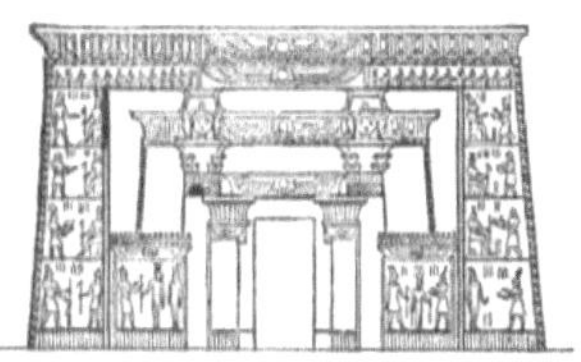

PART II

THE HOLE INSIDE

I DON'T PUT UP a fight as Kane escorts me back to my hospital room. Rather, I say nothing, the damage already done. It takes zero time to pack up, as anything I care about is already gone.

Dr. Caspar knocks from the entryway. "Hey."

"Why didn't you say something?" Between the tears I fight back, I stuff my spare clothes into a small drawstring bag. I'm shocked they've given me this, considering I could kill myself with it.

He unclips his maroon tie and stashes it in his slacks' pocket. "You nearly died, Jesly. Your brain's been through a lot—"

"That doesn't change what I saw."

"I know." He slips through the doorway and leans against the wardrobe. Deep lines crease his brow. "That's why I sent over my recommendation. You need to heal."

"What if I don't want to?"

"I'll pretend I didn't hear that." He points to the bag on the bed. "You all set?"

I nod. "Yeah, almost."

Dax's book is the last thing. *The Place We All Go* lies nestled in the folds of the disheveled comforter. It's the last item in a world where I no longer belong. I flip it open to a well-worn split where a battered silver coin serves as a bookmark. I palm the old thing and hold it up to the light. It's tarnished and pocked with age. On the off chance it's worth something, I stuff it in my pocket. If I'm lucky, Calgary won't search me.

A foolish sentiment, I know. Inpatient facilities aren't known for their decorum when it comes to patient comfort.

"And visitors? What about them?"

"After a processing period, yes," he answers. "I've sent over the intake forms as your designated psychiatrist, and Dr. Hiribaldi has signed off as your attending."

"That prick hates me."

"He doesn't hate you, Jesly. You're his patient."

I scoop the book from the comforter. Now the creepy thing is really the only possession I can call my own. There's just something about it. Like I've seen the cover somewhere before.

Dr. Caspar watches me, analyzing. "There's a car downstairs. Kane will escort you personally." He motions for us to follow.

"No paddy wagon this time?" I ask.

He doesn't grace me with a response. Our footsteps sync as we head toward the elevator. Kane opts for the stairs. After this afternoon's incident, I can't say I blame him. If it keeps me from climbing anything else, I'll gladly follow.

It's a laborious descent into darkness as we make our way to the lower floors. Some of the wall sconces are out on the landings we pass. My breath catches the farther down we go. If the others notice, they probably chalk it up to nerves.

It's not; it's something else . . .

A few minutes later, we hit the bottom floor. The scent of fresh paint with a classy hint of old urine greets us as we burst into the parking garage.

"This is where I leave you," Dr. Caspar announces when we finally reach the car. It's a plain black Toyota Camry. *Innocuous. Invisible.*

Perfect for hiding the bodies.

I take a deep breath and ignore Dr. Caspar's pensive focus. It's hard to forget that I may be the most interesting patient these doctors have seen in a while. Surviving a fall from a skyrise doesn't happen often. But I'm not going for attention; I'm going to disappear.

"Ladies first." Kane hits the remote start button. We hop in.

Dr. Caspar's cell chirps again and out comes the beast in question. It must be something unpleasant because he starts two-thumbing back a response almost instantly.

"Another patient?" I ask as I use the distraction to move the coin to a hidey-hole in my sneaker's tongue.

With the swoosh of his response sent, Dr. Caspar's grip lodges firmly on the passenger door. "My wife. We're celebrating our anniversary tonight. She'll kill me if I'm late."

"Congrats," I offer. "How long you two been married?"

"This year makes thirteen," he says with a lopsided grin. "Take care of yourself. Okay, Jesly? I'll see you tomorrow."

Surprised, I ask, "You're coming?"

He nods. "Of course. You didn't think I was just gonna send you to the wolves alone, did you?"

I squirm into the fabric seat. "I don't know what I thought."

He closes the passenger door and waits as I roll down the window. "It's okay that you have a hard time trusting people."

"That's where you're wrong, Doctor," I say. "It's not about trust. It's that they always betray me."

"I'll make a note."

"Don't bother," I tell him. "You'll see soon enough."

"It'll be okay, Jesly. I promise." He pats the driver's door and leaves me in Kane's care, giving my new companion a round of instructions a mile long. By the time Dr. Caspar is done, I feel like a gremlin.

The subtle lighting of the parking garage activates the headlights automatically. I try to take up the least amount of space as Kane backs out of the parking spot.

Dr. Caspar waves. I don't wave back.

"Not going to tell him goodbye?" Kane asks as he gets us out onto the open road.

At least one of us knows their way around here because I sure don't. It's another few minutes before he says anything else, undoubtedly leaving me alone in my head as I stare at the window. A dangerous place if he really knew. I mash the radio button to kill the silence, but all that comes out is static. I pick a second channel.

Still nothing. Kane either doesn't notice or doesn't care.

"What if we keep driving? Just you and me?" I ask, giving up on the broken radio.

He says nothing, flicks on the turn signal, and eases onto the freeway. Knowing it'll be a while; I pull out the novel Dax gave me.

The blood-stained cover makes me uneasy, and it's not the fact that I killed his sister. It's something else. The more I stare at the dark figure in the hallway, the worse the feeling gets. Whatever Dagny was meddling in can't have been good.

"How long before I get visitors?" I ask.

"Not long. A few days, perhaps." Kane doesn't take his eyes off the empty stretch of road. "Are you hungry? I'm hungry."

The clock on the dash reads 3:33 p.m. "We ate lunch two

hours ago."

"I'm aware," he acknowledges, "but there's some fantastic grub out here."

"Calgary isn't expecting us by a certain time?"

"Nah." He changes lanes, sending us closer to the next off-ramp. "They trust me—think I'm one of them."

Wherever we're going, he's been here before. The magnolias along the freeway slip by, and it's not long before the interstate hum causes my eyes to drag. A precarious situation on the off chance I'm wrong about him.

Each man wants something from me; I just don't know what yet. I can feel it, like a warning buried in the darkness. Beaten and broken, I don't fight the sleep that comes, knowing it might be my last chance for a while.

"HEY, WAKE UP." KANE nudges my shoulder.

We've stopped.

I jolt upright in my seat. "Where are we?"

Other vehicles surround us on three sides, and it takes a minute to realize we've parked.

"Somewhere off the freeway."

I wrench open the door handle and ease out of the car, slamming it shut. He locks it with a beep.

"For what?" I ask.

"Afternoon snack."

"I thought you were joking."

"About food? Never," he says plainly. "Come on. It's getting late." He heads toward the concrete building in the parking lot.

The gravel crunches beneath my sneakers. I'm glad for the sweatshirt now that the sun has already crested the sky. On a good winter's day, Texan temperatures border the upper fifties. On a bad one, well, it's about half that. Rare, but it happens.

Kane quickens his already frantic pace, and I struggle to catch up. "What's so important here?" I ask.

"You'll see."

"Cryptic much?"

He checks for traffic before jogging toward the entrance sidewalk.

Original Market Diner. "It's a restaurant," I note. "You *were* serious."

His shoulders pop into a shrug. "I told you. I'm hungry."

An old-fashioned bell chimes as we enter, and it's only seconds before a bubbly female swings around the corner. The hostess, apparently.

"Just the two of you?"

"No, there's one more coming." Kane scours the front windowpanes and doesn't entertain my shock.

She smiles. "Right this way."

We settle on a black wooden table smack in the center, forgoing any chance of privacy. Dropping three menus in front of us, she asks, "Do you know what you want to drink?"

"Diet Coke, please," I say.

He pulls his wallet from his back pocket and sets it on the table between us. "I'll take a hand-dipped shake, vanilla, and a coffee with cream. Thank you."

Her beaming grin returns. "Great. I'll go get your drinks while you look over the menu."

The Original Market Diner is a quaint little place. Hanging

☥

pendant lights match the homey feel, and most tables sit open. The staff doesn't seem too worried about the slow traffic. There's no revolving door of clientele. Everyone is just sitting, relaxing, talking.

Kane watches me curiously as the waitress sets down our drinks.

"I've never been here." I remove the paper tab from the end of my straw.

The doe-eyed waitress keeps staring at Kane. I can't blame her. With his wavy chestnut hair, finely trimmed scruff, and strong shoulders, he's easy on the eyes.

"Have you figured out what you want?" she asks.

Kane doesn't skip a beat. Not when it comes to food, apparently. "I'll take a Blue Plate Special."

I gawk. *Where does he put it?*

"Allbrook?"

"What?" I stop staring out the window. "Oh, sorry. Can I have a minute?"

The waitress clicks her tongue as Kane spoons some of the milkshake into his mouth. "You didn't eat earlier. Get something."

I flip over the menu. "Like what?"

He checks the time on his phone. "Like something edible. The food at Calgary isn't five stars."

"I take it you do this often."

Another spoonful. "Whenever I get assigned a new client."

"I take it I'm not your first patient."

He laughs into his milkshake. "No, not by a long shot."

"Been doing this a long time?"

"You could say that . . ."

He lets me sit with that information and waves the waitress back over. "Order something. I'd like to report you're cooperating."

"So lie."

"If I'm going to lie, I'd rather it be for the right reason," he says. "Not because you feel like acting like a child."

"Fine."

The waitress is all smiles, toothy and natural. She's probably used to small-town drama. "What'll it be?"

I order the first thing I see. "I'll take a grilled cheese with applesauce."

"Great." She reaches for the menu.

He stops me before I can hand it over. "That's the kids' menu."

"You said I had to eat. You didn't say how much."

Another smile at the girl. "Thank you," he tells her. Once she's gone, he leans in, his breath like vanilla. "Heavens, you're impossible, you know that?"

"Yeah, I do," I respond. "Thanks."

While we wait, the daily grind of the diner fills the silence. A couple in a back booth snuggle and giggle. A man next to the front window hacks away on his laptop keys. A group of rowdy college kids yell at a football game on the TV above the bar.

"Who are we waiting for?" I ask.

"Someone."

"How long?"

"As long as it takes."

I organize the condiments repeatedly to pass what time I can. **He's going to kill you. They both are.**

"Goddamnit," I cuss, loud enough to draw the attention of the entire room. I sink lower into my seat, the sound of the wooden feet scuffing the linoleum. "What's happening to me?"

"That's a complicated question," a familiar voice sounds from behind and sits beside Kane.

It's Zaire. "Hello again, Jesly."

My eyes widen at Kane as he slides Zaire the untouched coffee. "This is who we were waiting for?"

"He's got a job offer for you," Kane answers.

"What?" I jump up, sending the wooden chair careening backward into the next closest table. The stares return. "I don't want a job. I *want* to go home."

"Sit down." Zaire motions to my seat. "We don't have time."

"You lied to me."

"And we're in public," he says. "Please."

"Then tell me the truth. Both of you."

Zaire takes a nonchalant sip of his coffee. "What do you want to know?"

"Jackson . . ." I hiss, my voice breaking. "Did you know?"

Zaire rips open another cream container, stirring it in with a spoon. "Jesly, you are a lawyer, so I'm going to assume you understand discretion."

"Do you get what that feels like?" I yell. "Knowing people died because of you and there's nothing—*nothing*—you can do to fix it?"

Before I can storm off, Kane springs to his feet and grabs my arm. A bad decision. One that costs him a palm strike in the nose.

"Don't touch me," I say beneath my breath. "Not ever."

His back stiffens and he pulls away. "You are the most stubborn woman I have met, and I've met many."

Zaire laughs into his coffee as Kane drops into his chair like a sullen puppy. All the focus in the establishment has turned to me. Something I don't care for. I drop into my chair reluctantly.

"Thank you," Zaire says and wipes his beard with a napkin.

Before it can get any more awkward, the waitress scurries over and brings our food. Then slips us the check. *Oh, so subtle.*

Kane nudges it out of the way and shakes a good helping of salt and pepper on his meatloaf and mashed potatoes. "Eat."

I take a bite of the grilled cheese. The flavor hit me like a tank. It's been a minute since I've eaten anything this rich. He waits for me to swallow before shoveling his own food in his mouth. The man's like a garbage disposal. His metabolism must be off the charts.

Zaire stares out the glass windowpane, paying close attention to the sky. "A storm's coming."

Kane checks his watch between bites. "We'll make it."

I crane my head around. Not a cloud in the sky. Another average winter day in Texas. We eat for a few, saying nothing. Each bite feels like it's tethering me to this world. *How much further down the rabbit hole before I find a **Drink Me** vial?*

"Everything okay?" the waitress asks as she checks on us, keeping her distance from my side. *I don't blame her.*

I smile apologetically. "Yeah, it's great. Thanks." The applesauce is thick and homemade, with a hint of cinnamon in it. My spoon clangs against the side of the bowl. Once she leaves, I say, "Cut to the chase and tell me why you two brought me here."

Zaire reaches into his leather jacket and pulls out an old picture that's frayed around the edges. No, not frayed. *Burned.* Setting it between us, he points at the young woman in the picture.

"You remember the file I grabbed the other day?" he asks.

But he doesn't have to.

I know exactly who this is. Murdering someone really sticks with you.

Kane seems surprised. "Allbrook, you recognize her?"

I nod grimly. "She was a client before Jackson ran her off and withdrew as her lawyer the day before her court date."

"I need you to find her," Zaire blurts out, shoving the photo in my direction so I can get a closer look. "Please."

I peel the photo from the table. It's an old picture; Dagny's much younger than I remember. Her strawlike blonde hair falls around her dainty features, her body frail.

"That's impossible, Zaire," I finally say. "She's dead."

"No," he suddenly shouts and sucks in a breath. *Hell, now we're all getting stares.* "She's not dead. She's not."

"Listen, Zaire. I was at her funeral. She's gone."

"She's not dead, okay?" he says tersely. "You just need to believe me on this."

"Who is she to you?" I demand.

He slams the empty mug on the table. "My *fiancée.*"

Kane and I both choke for a second. Zaire doesn't meet Kane's look of horror. Apparently, I'm not the only one who didn't know.

"We were taking some time apart when this happened," Zaire tells us. "She can't be dead. Please."

The ice shifts in the soda in front of me. I shake the glass and contemplate my next move. It wouldn't be the first time someone faked their own death. "What makes you think she's alive?"

"I just do."

"What do you need me for?" I ask. "Why can't Kane do it?"

"He's tied up," Zaire explains. "But you—you can."

"If you separated, you seriously think she wants to see you?"

Kane clears his throat and buries himself in his milkshake, using his straw to reach the bottom of the malt cup. I've struck a cord. *Great.*

Zaire sighs. "Because they did to her what they're trying to do to you."

"They?" I ask.

"Please," he begs, ignoring my question. "It ended with her thinking I gave up on us . . . that I would let her die."

I stare at Zaire. He's sweating, his eye bags noticeable like he hasn't been sleeping. *He's right.* I can't have the woman thinking I let her die back there, either. Whether she wants to disappear or not, I can't spend the rest of eternity believing I killed someone. I have to see this for myself.

"What do I have to do?" I ask.

"Super simple," he says, visibly relieved. "Just get her out."

"I'm sorry? Out of where?"

Zaire finishes the last of his coffee and returns the cup to the saucer. Kane simply watches, his pensive gaze weighing us both.

"Calgary," Zaire finally says. "Once patients go inside, they don't come out. Not in one piece anyway."

"What can I do?"

"I already told you. Get her out of there. Anyway, anyhow," he says. "You do that, and I owe you one."

Kane leaves the two of us to banter while he goes off to pay the check. There's a twenty-dollar bill on the table for the tip. By the conversation he starts at the bar, it'll be a few minutes before we go anywhere.

"Zaire?" I say.

"Yes?"

"How long were you and her together?"

"As a couple?" he says, thinking. "I'm pretty terrible with dates. Dagny was always better with that stuff."

"And yet you kept tabs on her since you two broke up?"

He clarifies, "Time apart."

"And how long ago was that?"

"Not long. A few months, maybe," he notes.

"Did you know what your fiancée was involved in?"

His face searches mine, his thick brow furrowed. "You're a very curious person, aren't you?"

I don't trust him. *Not yet.* Still trying to kill time, I bus the plates and bowls into a neat pile. "From what I remember, she wasn't alone in the vehicle. There was a male with her. Medium build, dark hair, olive complexion. Word on the grapevine is that she was getting involved in something too heavy."

"You know," he says, leaning in, "Listening to idle chatter can get you killed." Satisfied, he leans back in his chair. "Dagny knows her way out of things. Always has. But sometimes, she's her own worst enemy."

Kane makes it back to our table; he's ready to go. Nervous. Flighty, almost.

"I can't lose her, Jesly," Zaire says, shifting my focus. "Not again."

"What's the plan?" I ask, my breath lurching in my chest, and I pray I'm wrong. Blood drips from my palms where my nails have pierced the skin.

Maybe one day I'll stop hurting myself. But for now, I can't. Not when I know what Zaire's about to ask of me, and I know I have no choice.

"You're going to help us kidnap her."

SWINGING VINES

KANE HASN'T SAID MUCH since we left the diner, and I don't press him. His white-knuckled grip on the steering wheel is enough. Having left civilization hours ago, we're in the middle of no-man's-land. The roads are farther apart now.

I'm left to tear at my fingernails. "How much longer?"

"Not long."

Sprawling old oak and ash trees stretch on either side, the stark quiet turning my stomach. This far outside city limits, it's a two-lane road. The city girl in me doesn't like it.

Farmland soon boxes us in, with fewer cars passing now. There's a Shell gas station up ahead on the right. He eases the car off the road and into the gravel parking lot, drawing it into a dilapidated gas pump.

Before the car comes to a halt, he's already heading to the gas tank. A knock sounds on the passenger window, and I pop open my door. "Do you want anything?"

I frown. "This over with."

"Let me know if you change your mind." He mashes some buttons on the gas pump and lifts the nozzle from the dispenser, setting it into the Camry's fuel tank. Seemingly satisfied with it locked in place, he heads inside the store.

Bored, I reach into the drawstring bag and pull out Dax's book. *Well, mine now.*

The Place We All Go.

Something about the cover nags at me and won't let go. I shove the book back in the bag just as the driver's door opens, making me nearly jump out of my skin. Kane plops into the driver's seat, dragging a white plastic bag full of Jiffy store delight.

"You really are a garbage disposal, you know that?" My eyes widen as he takes a sip from an oversized cup brimming with orange soda.

He shrugs and hits the button on the dash, letting the car whir into action. "I have my vices. Want any?" He holds open the plastic bag, offering me his spoils. Granola bars. Swiss rolls. Oatmeal creme pies. It's a diabetic nightmare.

I shake my head. "You didn't eat enough of this crap as a kid?"

"No." He wedges his drink into the cup holder. "Gotta get it while I can."

"What does that mean?"

"This might take a while." He jumps back out of the car and settles the gas pump.

I look at the book peeking out of my bag. It feels like a knife cuts through my temporal lobe, and I futilely try to shut my eyes. *If Dagny really is still alive, why and how?* But I don't get more time— Kane's back in the driver's seat, catapulting us toward my fate.

He notices my losing battle with the headrest. "You can lean the seat back if you need to, you know."

"No, thank you."

"Get some sleep. Nothing's gonna happen while I'm here."

"And last time?"

His white-knuckled grip is back, his restraint admirable. Silence falls in the car, leaving only the sound of the tires on the road.

"Sorry," I apologize quickly. "I just haven't had anyone in my corner in a long time. This isn't easy."

"Allbrook, it's alright," he says. "I understand what having the world against you feels like." He reaches for my hand but stops. Refocusing on the road, he slows down due to an old clunker going 55 mph in the fast lane.

I change topics. "Have you always had these abilities?"

"Abilities?"

"The stuff you did back at the lab . . . the traveling and telepathy. Are you some elite CIA super-spy?"

He nearly swerves into oncoming traffic. "What? No."

"Were you born with it, then? Like X-Men?"

"Jesus, Allbrook. What is going on in your brain?"

"Just curious." I tug at my wristband again. It won't budge. "Can you ever retire?"

"Retire?"

"Yeah. Like stop working and just relax or whatever."

"Not exactly," he stutters. "It's a lifelong commitment."

"Seriously?" I shift in the fabric seat. "Like never?"

He simply shakes his head.

"Don't you get tired? Want to see your family? Something?"

"I don't have a family," he admits. "Not anymore."

"I'm sorry."

"Don't be. It's been a long time now."

Stretches of farmland fade in an instant, turning into one ambiguous blur. "Why'd you do it?" I ask.

"I'm sorry?" His eyes dart between me and the road. "Do what?"

"Sign up for this job. What made you want this life?"

"Who said I wanted it? Maybe this is what we deserve," he spits back, harsher than I'm expecting.

He sees the color drain from my face and his own turns to horror. Decelerating the car rapidly, he hits the hazard lights and pulls the car onto the grassy shoulder. Now in Park, he turns to face me. He hasn't slept any more than I have.

"Allbrook, I didn't mean you," he breathes. "Nobody deserves what you're going through."

I clutch the loose fabric of my sweatshirt. "Am I gonna go to Hell?"

He inhales and grabs my hands. This time, I let him. His grip is firm, calloused. "Where did you get that idea?" He follows my gaze to the cross on his chest.

"What if Zaire's wrong?" I whisper. "What if she really is dead? What if I really did murder Dagny, and that's it? There are no second chances?"

"There's a chance she walked away," Kane reassures me. "If you did, maybe she did too. But I need to tell you something, and you need to listen."

I pull away slightly. "Okay . . ."

"Whatever Zaire says, do not trust him. He's not your friend."

"Then why are we doing this?"

"Because sometimes we don't get a choice," Kane replies.

"Did you know what Zaire was after?"

He doesn't say anything.

"Did you *know*?" I repeat, my voice breaking.

Eventually, his answer comes. "Yes."

"Jesus Christ, Kane."

"There are rules, Jesly, that people like me have to follow," he explains. "My job isn't like everyone else's. Some things we don't talk about."

"Why don't you break it down for me?"

"I can't . . ." He puts some distance between us and gets us back out on the open road. "It doesn't work that way. A Watcher cannot intervene."

"A Watcher?"

He nods slowly.

"That's your job title."

He looks around anxiously before nodding again.

"You don't think you have already?"

He goes tight-lipped again.

"Kane?" I say, my eyes widening. "What if you do?"

"Then this never ends," he says but doesn't elaborate further. "We're here." He points to a side road a few hundred yards to the right.

Had I not been searching, the turn would've been easy to miss. Gravel crunches beneath the car's tires, and I roll down the window as we follow our newfound path.

Live oaks tower over the car as if they've been the masters here for centuries. Wrought-iron lampposts serve as beacons in the fast-approaching darkness, and a mammoth-sized gate with end-to-end cameras greets us at the property's entrance.

"Here goes nothing." He slows the car and rolls down his window. Waving his badge at the camera, he waits for the gate to buzz. It does, and any option of escape dwindles.

Anxiously, I pull my bag into my lap. "Are you coming in?"

"I can't." He shifts the Camry into park at the end of the circular driveway.

The yard is massive, stretching for acres on either side of an ornate Victorian building that reminds me of something out of a 1930s horror movie. Parapets claw the length of the facility, all leading to a central clock tower. Rows of windows stretch the length of each floor. Medical staff donned in white scrubs pace the grounds, monitoring the patients outside.

"Just say the word and we'll leave." He notices my anxiety. "But understand there will be consequences—not just for you, but for others as well."

In the distance, another set of lampposts near the main building kick on, illuminating the sunbaked stone walkway. Even in the fading evening light, it's easy to tell the grounds are well-maintained with the plethora of variegated plants and rose bushes lining the circular driveway we've pulled into. Oak doors adorned with stained glass windows sit at the base of the building's entrance, where a beautiful tawny-skinned doctor hurries down the front stairs as a young technician yaps at her heels. Visibly stressed, she takes a deep breath and forces a welcoming smile.

I've seen her somewhere before.

Kane ambles out of the Camry and shakes hands with the fast-stepping doctor. He signals for me to follow, but I have no intention of moving. *Not yet.*

No one else is about to dive headfirst into the lion's den. It should be Jackson here, not me. He's the one who owes her, but he can't. *Not anymore.*

I killed him too.

The doctor and Kane exchange words after she hastily texts something on her phone and stuffs it back into her lab coat pocket. Heading over to my passenger door, she starts talking, knowing full well I can't hear her. She's banking on me opening it so they can drag my ass out. Not going to happen. She'll have to try harder.

Being pretty doesn't mean the universe bends to her will, medical license or not.

The clock on the Camry's dashboard reads 8:14 p.m. Getting here took longer than I thought it would. We're not that far from civilization, but surrounded by sprawling oaks and angry crickets, it sure feels like it.

The urge to run swells over me. Even with the car stopped, my vertigo makes a triumphant return. Latching onto the door handle, I wrench it open, collapsing to my knees in the sharp gravel.

The female doctor races to my side. "Jesly, can you hear me? I'm the medical director here, Doctor Kennedy. I'll be taking care of you tonight until Dr. Caspar can stop over." Her hand gently touches my back, and I recoil like a snake hitting the car door.

She exchanges glances with Kane, whose unforgiving grip latches onto my shoulders as we make it back to my feet. Under his breath, he whispers, "Jesly, tell me now . . ."

I refocus on Kane's steadiness. He doesn't let go as I sway, something I'm incredibly grateful for.

"I don't know if I can do this," I whisper, spotting the second nurse to arrive. It's been a while since they've had a springy one. They're ready.

Kane turns to Dr. Kennedy. "Can we have a second?"

She sizes him up, taking note of Kane's badge and professional attire. "Of course." While she walks back toward the entrance, the guards don't. They stay right there.

"Come on." He shuts the passenger door and leads me around the backside of the car.

I want to trust him. I *need* to trust him, but it's hard after Jackson. We stand where the staff can't make out our words.

He rubs his beard. "Just get inside, find Dagny, and get out safely. Zaire and I will be waiting."

"You really think she'll come willingly?"

"You can be awfully convincing if you want."

I have no idea why he has so much confidence in me. It's a bit unnerving.

"You've got this." He pulls me into a side hug, and I let him.

The physical touch feels good—makes me feel less like a piece of shit. This probably breaks some kind of patient-staff boundary, but right now, I don't care. A hollowness eats away at my soul that no amount of consoling can fix, but I lean in anyway. He pulls me into a full-on hug. We stay that way until my tears burst like a watershed.

By Dr. Kennedy's expression, she isn't certain what to make of this. After a beat, she climbs the stairs and takes the staff with her. *Good.* I don't need anyone else's judgment. I judge myself enough.

Kane's bearhug is tight enough that I can barely breathe. But right now, I need this. He lets me cry it out, something that I've been sorely lacking for so long. Our touch—it's platonic and visceral.

A reminder I still exist, even after everything.

It's a few minutes before he pulls me away, waiting until I've exhausted myself. Instantly, my world has gone cold. He's taken the warmth with him.

"It's going to be okay. I'll check on you in the morning," he announces, half to me and half to the staff.

Whatever Kane stands to gain from this, I just hope it's worth it. I force a smile. "Promise you won't leave me here."

He makes an X over his heart. "I promise."

Trudging toward the entrance, he leads me like a lost sheep. My steps echo in the evening air, the gravel crunching as we make our way toward the stone stairwell. At the top, the two staff members wait for Kane and me to say our goodbyes. Thankfully, they let me watch as he pulls the car back through the roundabout. Eventually, his headlights fade into the Texan evening, and I'm left to the mercy of these strangers.

It will be at least twelve hours before I see either Dr. Caspar or Kane again. Dr. Kennedy approaches me again. "Hey there, Jesly. Let's get you settled."

She grabs the wrought-iron handle and pushes the oversized wooden door ajar, welcoming me into the fold. We make it inside the rehabilitated Victorian manor, the sounds of the facility pulling me back to the present.

It's a rush of smells—from brown sugar all the way to the sterile smell mimicking a hospital. A frazzled, college-aged guy lingers behind the front desk, too busy fighting the ringing phones to acknowledge us. The foyer splits on either side with a grand stairwell opening up to the second floor.

Dr. Kennedy's phone goes off, and she checks it before shoving it back in her pocket. Wasting no time, she drones on about the sections of the facility, but I'm too busy scouring the patients to listen or care.

Passing her badge over a security panel on the nearby wall, she escorts me through a set of wooden double doors. Right into what I assume to be a dayroom. Patients all in matching gray sweats and red anti-skid socks fill the room, each engrossed in their social activities until the greenhorn appears. *Don't make eye contact.* It'll become a social hour—something I'm not here for. We move on to the area beyond, this time the cafeteria. Here the red and gray sweatsuits fly like fresh popcorn.

All but one.

Standing atop a lunch table with her back to us, a stringy-haired blonde with a makeshift noose made from white sheets is tethered to the ceiling rafters. By the way the staff swarms around her, de-escalation hasn't gone well. What chairs and tables that can get shoved aside have been. Patients who enter the dayroom get rapidly escorted out. This area is headed toward lockdown.

I latch onto the closest shoulder of a patient, an overweight girl who reeks of purging. It's faint, but I can tell. This is the one place we can't hide our demons. Not from each other.

"Who's that woman?" I ask, not taking my eyes off the blonde for an instant. A deep, unsettled feeling claws at my stomach and I pray I'm wrong.

"Some stupid chick named Dagny. Always asking for trouble."

Before I can say anything else, she scurries out of the dayroom, letting the door swing closed behind her. Unlike the bottleneckers trying to catch a view, this girl wants nothing to do with this. The commotion likely too much.

I'm inclined to say everything will be okay—that I can help. But I'm here also. The same as everyone else.

Someone that society believes is broken.

We're the ones who stand on tables with nooses around our necks, ready to end it all. Across the crowded dayroom, Zaire's fiancée locks eyes with mine, recognition crawling over her narrow features. And as that recognition shifts to horror, there are about twenty reasons why I can't get to her in time.

All I can do is pray to whatever god that has forsaken us as the sound of her neck snapping echoes throughout the cafeteria.

SPECTERS

"YOU'VE . . . GOT . . . TO BE . . . fucking kidding me," I announce to no one in particular, my mouth agape. There's no way. There's just . . . No. Fucking. Way.

"Get her down," someone orders as the staff floods from all directions, faster than flies on shit, all to save this woman who now hangs from the ward's cafeteria rafters. The remaining technicians lock down the room, ushering everyone non-essential out as fast as they can.

Dr. Kennedy has abandoned me for her other patient. Tight lines darken her beautiful features, her strained composure visible on her almond-shaped face.

Reviving Dagny wasn't on the agenda today, but suicide doesn't do appointments. Something the staff is forced to reckon with. That look of absolution.

I've been there myself. There's no going back.

"Vitals, now," Dr. Kennedy shouts to a technician in blue scrubs as they cut the knotted sheets, disentangling this woman as she drops. My stomach lurches, and I cling to the nearest wall.

"She's not breathing." A tech lays Dagny across the table

and starts resuscitation. They flood around her, the place consumed with bringing her back.

But it's pointless. She's already gone.

I've gotta get out. Backing up slowly, I bump into another tech zooming past with supplies.

"Sorry," he mouths before rushing toward the action. For a second, I stand there like a deer in headlights, useless and frozen.

Do the job right this time.

Every time, it's the same voice. It's been with me long enough that I can scarcely remember life without it. Like a shadow, it follows wherever I go. But one thing's certain— whatever it is, the voice doesn't want me to win.

I know that. I always have.

But giving doctors another excuse to lock me in a padded room is not an option, so I do the only thing I know how: *run.*

I'm already racing back the way we came. My Docs clap against the polished wooden floor, and I force myself to slow down. No reason to be even more suspicious, even if only for a second. Burying my hands in my sweatpants' pockets, I avoid eye contact with passersby. There's enough commotion that I reach the foyer before anyone realizes anything's wrong.

The front desk receptionist looks up since I'm the first to return from that wing. He rises from his desk, eager to please, his smile beaming across the entryway. Customer service, first and always. "Ms. Allbrook, welcome ba—"

He doesn't get to finish before I barrel through the double doors and race down the cobblestone stairwell. Tightening my grasp on my small drawstring bag, I make a break for the driveway. With the sun long gone, the moon's in charge, and she's not about to stop me.

I jog for what feels like forever, letting my body simply exist. Broken or not. I go slower than I'd like, but it's something.

A little farther down the road, a clearing cuts through the tall plumes of grass, and I duck between the openings. Only the fireflies and katydids are happy to see me. Not even the lone bullfrog that tries to drown out the sound of moving water. There's a river nearby.

My night vision is terrible with only the moon to guide me. Mother Nature, notwithstanding my needs, sends another cloud to dampen my progress. It's no use.

After a few, the clouds move on. I rush down a lightly trodden path to find a towering live oak nestled on an outcrop above the river. It takes nearly all my strength to pull myself over the large rocks. *This'll work.* No one will find me here.

My wrist itches again. I try to yank the stupid hospital band off. The little white clasps refuse to budge. *Fuck.*

Pulling my knees to my chest, I dig through my bag. No phone. No credit cards—nothing to call my own except Dagny's book, the bottle of meds Jackson threw at me, and the coin still stuck in my sneaker. With all the commotion, the staff at Calgary didn't search me.

The temperature cuts through me. It's colder than I would have expected this time of year, and I stretch the front of my sweatshirt over my legs.

I don't know how long it will take before they notice I'm gone. One is certain, though. I'm not going back. I did what I was supposed to do—Dagny is dead for real this time.

Maybe Jackson was right, and there's a way to spin it. Maybe she hit us, and it wasn't our fault in the first place.

☥

A slight rustle in the distance jolts me upright. A little creature chitters somewhere about its nighttime journey. The tremor in my hands has returned now that my meds have started wearing off.

I lean back against the tree, taking deep breaths to still my panic. Another branch snaps somewhere in the distance, this one much closer. I shift around to find myself blasted in the face with a 3,000-lumen flashlight.

"What are you doing out here?"

I wrench my eyes shut and pray to God I'm hallucinating again. For a moment, I naively think my prayers are answered. Then the light gets brighter, and the footsteps get louder.

It's Jackson.

He seems worse than the last time I saw him. How that's possible, I have no idea. Thinner, too. Like he hasn't been eating. No longer wearing his suit but instead jeans and a stained button-down. The same clothes I saw him wearing on the livestream. With his sleeves pushed back, his tattoos are visible—something that only happens in the after-hours of law.

He stands in front of me. *Alive.*

"You're not real," I say, my voice breaking.

"News to me." He lowers the flashlight. "We have to talk about this."

"Just leave me alone." With my back pressed against the sprawling trunk, there are only two places to go: up or down.

I choose up.

But my body is like a gear that won't catch; I keep turning over the engine, but it just won't move. Eventually, I catch a break. I scramble even higher in the sprawling tree, using what few climbing skills I obtained as a child.

"Come on, get down," Jackson yells from below. Something in the distance spooks him. He's afraid, but I'm not sure of what. "This conversation would be a thousand times easier if you would just come down. I'm trying to help you."

"Doubt it." I scoot myself along the old oak tree until I'm straddling a branch stretching over the river.

He's gonna have to wait a little longer. I'm not going anywhere near him—*I can't.* If I do, it just makes him that much more real.

Which he's not—the man's *dead.* The dearly departed don't come back, living or otherwise.

I pull myself across the wide branch and dangle my feet over the edge. Ignore him long enough and he'll disappear.

He has to.

Staring at the moon, I settle myself further. Even on a good day my balance is dodgy. One wrong move and I'm meeting that pitch-black river headfirst.

"Goddamnit, Jes, I'm coming up," he announces. The sound of him scraping against the bark assaults my ears.

You're not really here. This isn't happening. It's just the meds wearing off.

And what if it's not? Kill him, and this all ends here and now.

"You're lying . . ." Tears sting my cheeks as it suddenly gets harder to breathe, the air suddenly tightening around my throat.

It's the only way to make it stop.

"I can't . . ."

Not yet. But you will. You will.

The air loosens around my throat. My gasp is audible as I can breathe again. I look back at Jackson, who's now much closer.

But I'm not going back. With him or anyone else. Not ever.

In another ten feet or so, the branch becomes unmanageable. With no easy way across, diving into the river it is. I swing my right leg over the branch and push off before he can stop me.

For a second, I'm free. And then I plunge into the freezing black water. Beneath the surface, everything goes silent, even the katydids.

There's nothing.

Finally . . .

But it doesn't last. Human instinct kicks in. My leg muscles burn as I kick as fast as I can toward the far side of the river, using everything I have to make my strides count.

It's not easy with my body as weak as it is. The medicine alone leaves me sluggish. It's another twenty yards to the bank, but I manage. My lungs heave as I drag myself to shore.

I glance back across to the opposite bank. There's no one, save for the frogs serenading my descent into madness.

"Ms. Allbrook?" a voice bellows from afar. It's the staff. "Jesly!" another voice calls.

They haven't found me yet. Given my impromptu swim, I have a little time but not much.

"Why are you doing this?" I say in a rushed whisper.

"There's no time—you need to listen," he pleads, visibly exhausted and soaking wet as he stands on the bank beside me.

Fuck . . . I never even heard him cross the river. I stumble backward and nearly fall back in the water. "You know, for a hallucination, you're extremely annoying."

"I'm trying to save your life, you stubborn woman," he hisses.

"My life? You *ruined* my life." I vainly attempt to wring out my own mess of curls.

"What? No." He struggles to catch his breath, bracing himself on his knees. He was never an Olympic swimmer either. "These people aren't who they say they are. How many times do I have to tell you that you're in danger?"

"That's rich coming from you. For a figment of my imagination, you've really outdone yourself."

"Damnit, Jes," he says. "What part of *danger* do you not understand?"

I stomp into the brush. "If I am, it's because of you—no one else. Go bother someone who actually gives a fuck."

"I'm going to get us out of this." He reaches for my arm, but I pull away. Never again will he touch me. Hallucination or not, he's burned that bridge for the very last time.

"There is no *us*, Jackson," I balk. "That's what you wanted."

Before he can respond, I walk away, watching my footing as I go. With countless holes in the deep brush, there are bound to be a few nasties lurking.

"This isn't about us. It's about—" He's struggling to keep up, and I suddenly remember he's afraid of snakes.

Talented, gorgeous, and afraid of squiggly beasts with fangs. *Good.* It'll serve him right if a moccasin bites him.

"Please. I'm sorry. Okay?" he announces. "Is that what you want to hear? Just tell me, and I'll say it."

I do an about-face. He looks genuinely terrified, and I get the impression it's not the snakes. Even like this, he's a beautiful creature. But he's too damaged, too dangerous; anything that comes from his mouth is a pretty lie. I can't trust him.

"You know . . . It'd be one thing if you loved me or even

fucking cared. But you don't. You never did and never will."

"Jes, don't do this."

For a moment, I think I see his eyes redden. "Go save your crocodile tears for someone else," I say.

Stepping away from him takes everything I have—like each piece of me is being ripped out one cell at a time.

"Love, wait."

I turn back around. "Whatever it is, save it. Figure it out your fucking self. I won't help you."

I tear the drawstring bag off my back and rip it open to find my meds. One childproof cap later, I've got the rest of the waterproof bottle squarely in my palm. Choking them down is miserable but not as much as this reality. Like a cancer eroding me from the inside, he'll kill me If I stay any longer. I can feel it.

I leave him there and don't look back. A toxic vine that's grown into my spine; we've become one being. One hell I can't escape.

There is only one way to remove the cancer that is Jackson Alders: ripping him out at the core. But at this rate, I've got a 50/50 chance of surviving it. I've beaten worse odds. The problem is, I don't know if I really care to try.

FRIENDS IN LOW PLACES

IT'S A LONG WALK back to town.

One made worse by the number of meds coursing through my system. But there's no way I'm going anywhere near the facility or Jackson anytime soon. Walking it is.

I stay off the road and shift into the ditch, an even better place to meet lurking creepy crawlies in the dark of a Texan night. This close to midnight, even fewer cars exist in BFE. It's the perfect place to disappear.

We should never have gone out that night. Maybe then Jackson would still be alive, and I'd never been on that roof that morning. One single decision and everything changes, shattering across time and space.

Maybe I am a fool.

I rest for a moment in the grass, my eyes locking onto the night sky. Most of the clouds have moved on to greener pastures, leaving only me and the moon now. That and the katydids' melodic lullaby to keep me company.

What adrenaline I had has dwindled. I've been running on empty for so long that it's difficult to even know what I'm running from anymore. Maybe Jackson's right.

Whatever it is, I can feel it looming just out of sight. Just out of reach. It's watching—waiting for me to screw up and make a mistake.

Maybe I'm lucky and it's just Jackson's ghost haunting me after all. Or maybe all this running is for naught and it's something much worse. Whatever it is, I don't want to find out.

I drag myself along a hollowed-out path. Somebody's walked this before—often enough that the grass is worn in certain places, leaving a dirt trail in its wake.

It's another twenty minutes before a car engine hums in the distance. Faint at first, enough that I don't even notice it. But soon the car's purr is unmistakable. Headlights expand in the early morning fog.

I try not to pay them any mind. While the car should have passed, it hasn't. It's perched at the top of the hill I've just descended. Waiting. Bugs cut across the headlights, the fog engulfing us. Even with the faint moonlight, the car is too far away to make out the model. Could be navy blue or black. I can't tell.

It doesn't matter. The car starts creeping down the hill, keeping pace with me. The last thing I need right now is another spectator. My Docs squish against the rough Texan soil, the rocks and clay doing little to dissuade my path. For another five minutes, I do my best to ignore the car, but it doesn't change the fact that it's behind me every step.

When I stop, it stops.

When I walk, it follows.

We're gonna do this the old-fashioned way. I've got no choice. This time, I take off like my life depends on it. Because it does.

I had one chance to correct this. Now Dagny's dead. There's

no going back.

My feet strike the ground, my body forcing oxygen into my lungs to match my strides. It's no use.

There's no losing them. As I move faster, so does the car. Now at the hill's nadir, the vehicle gains on the open road. If anything, it's accelerating. Any chance it was a stranger went out the window five hundred yards back.

I've gotta lose them. Somehow.

The moment I head for the brush, something slams into me, sending me tumbling into the grass. It's seconds before I realize it's not a car but another human being that's swept me from my feet. A firm grip latches onto me as I thrash for control beneath its weight.

"Let go," I yell.

A calloused hand muffles my screams. "Come on, stop," the voice whispers shakily in the darkness.

We wrestle in the weeds, thrashing until we're both covered in mud.

Out of breath, the voice cracks, "Allbrook, goddamnit; it's me."

He's going to kill you.

I snatch a nearby rock, ready to bash the person's skull in. The dappled moonlight finally strikes Kane's face, and I realize who I've been fighting. The rock falls from my grasp.

"Kane, what the hell?" I use my body weight to shove him off me, and he goes willingly.

He clambers to his feet. One wrong move and the mud becomes a death trap. Scraping the muck from his face, he offers a hand to pull me out. I shake my head. Even with the half-flooded ditch, I make it to my feet.

"I came to find you," he explains, still trying to wipe the mud from his jeans and T-shirt.

"No shit? Well, you did. Good job." I leave him there.

"Hey, wait." He latches onto my bicep, but this time he's ready for my uppercut. Before I can land it, he's spun me around until I'm pushed against him, my back to his chest. Time stops for a moment, our bodies tight and out of breath.

Something we both realize at the same time. He releases me faster than being bitten by a snake. Taking several steps backward, he steadies his balance and lumbers out of the ditch.

"Dagny's dead . . ." I rasp between breaths.

"What? How?"

"She hung herself."

"No, that's impossible," he says in disbelief. "It doesn't work like that."

I throw my hands up. "I don't know what to tell you. The woman's dead, Kane."

We stare at each other for several minutes until he finally breaks. "You're headed the wrong way."

"Are you dense?" I ask. "Screw that place. I wasn't even there five minutes and she was dead."

"No," he repeats. "You're mistaken."

"Why would Zaire send us there? Did he know—" I stop mid-sentence. He looks horrified. "Kane ...? You okay?"

"We have to go back."

"What?" I balk. "Hell no."

"Hey, wait." He reaches for my forearm, but this time, I don't run. I don't fight. We don't go tumbling into the muck and mire. He simply holds on and I let him. We stare at each other, filthy and visibly stressed. "We have to get her out. There's no other way."

"What aren't you telling me?" I say softly.

He looks up at the moon for a moment and drops his shoulders. "Allbrook, just say the word, and I'll take you from here. No questions asked."

"And what if I do?" I pull my sweatshirt around me. The chill has finally set in, and we're both drenched in the dead of January. "What happens to you? What do you get out of this?"

"I'm sorry?"

"You told me you're doing a favor for him." Our eyes lock. Whatever it is, there's real fear. "What is he giving you in return that you're risking everything for a job?"

"It's not important. Let's just worry about you," he says and slips away. "Are you going back or not?"

"What if you're wrong? What if you both are?"

He shakes his head. "Zaire wouldn't have set you on this path for no reason."

"You told me not to trust him. Should I not trust you either?"

He says nothing.

"Kane?"

"I just need your help with this. Okay?" He holds out a hand, nodding at the car in the distance.

I close my eyes, my body writhing with exhaustion. "I'm just so tired."

"I know," he says softly. "But this isn't the end; it's only the beginning."

I latch onto his hand. "Fine."

He rubs his thumb over mine. "I'm not going anywhere. Promise."

Maybe it's my exhaustion creeping up but making our way

☥

back to the facility takes minutes instead of hours. But it's not the commanding presence of Dr. Kennedy waiting for us. It's someone I thought I'd never have to see again—Dr. Hiribaldi.

"Why is he here?" I ask Kane, who doesn't bother to answer.

We pull the car into the roundabout again, and he shifts it into Park, tossing the keys onto the dash. Stepping out onto the gravel, his muddy clothes are a reminder of the shadows surrounding us all.

"Where's Dr. Kennedy? Dr. Caspar?" I glance around the complex.

Hiribaldi grins. "Dr. Kennedy had a family emergency, and Dr. Caspar is otherwise . . . engaged at the moment."

Kane presses his lips into a grimace. "Alright, well—"

"We're so relieved you were able to find Ms. Allbrook," Dr. Hiribaldi announces as he descends the stairwell.

"It didn't take long. She was just down the hill."

"What?" I say.

"We'll take her out of your hands now," he says.

Kane nods. "Of course."

The bird flitting around my chest threatens to break out, and I'm forced to lean onto the car. This time, they've got the whole kit n' kaboodle, including the guy from the front desk. They all surround me like I'm the main attraction while Kane heads up the stairs. *Toward* them.

He was never helping me—never on my side.

"You *lied* to me," I breathe, horrified.

Out of options, I fight.

"Restrain her," Dr. Hiribaldi commands.

I'd like to say I win. But with more than enough milligrams of Haldol, all it takes is one good stick, and *it's* **Game Over***, folks*. As I collapse into the arms of the closest technician, I understand just how stacked the odds are against me.

But it isn't until I see Kane ending with his own venture into the darkness, a cloudy-looking syringe straight into his neck, that it's clear Wonderland isn't done with either of us yet.

Not by any stretch.

TRAPPED

THE SOUND OF SOMETHING scraping against stone is the first thing to beckon me back from the darkness. There's a metallic scent to the damp, mildewy air I cannot place, and a chill that claws at my bones.

Whatever concoction they injected me with has worn off enough that my senses come back like a rolling tide. My body cries as I move, slowly at first, and then like fire.

My hands don't want to cooperate; I have to stretch constantly and move my fingers like a puppeteer. It's a thing I've dealt with for years, and the doctors still haven't given me a concrete explanation. But the fact remains: whatever concoction they gave me has cleared my system, leaving only my failed nervous system behind.

A problem that the freezing temperature of this place makes worse. It's visceral, choking, and ever present, but it can't hide the fact that something's wrong. Very wrong.

My eyes bolt open. The iron smell—it's *blood*.

There's no telling how long I've been out. My mouth feels like sand, standing is futile, and something pins me to the ground.

Scouring the concrete floor, my hands find the shackles binding me to some iron contraption. *Great.*

I run my hands over my arms and body. Nothing to make me think the blood is coming from me. No matter where I touch, my hands come away dry.

Whoever's blood it is, it's not mine.

There's a nagging feeling I'm being watched. I know I'm not imagining it. Nor the blood.

Shit. Kane.

I don't want to be right. Not again. "Kane?" I whisper into the darkness, though I've seen enough horror movies to know I should keep my mouth shut.

The only answer is the constant drip that echoes softly wherever I am.

"Hello?" I pull myself to my feet slowly, my body crying as I do. It's about five feet before the iron shackle yanks me back violently. "Why are you doing this?" I say as I try to map out my new domain.

Nothing to give me any directions. No light seeping in. Maybe underground. The damp chill won't let up, leaving me to clutch my filthy sweatshirt tighter.

Silencing me solves everyone's problems. Especially for the merger to go through. "Jackson, this is the best you've got?" I scream.

Dr. Hiribaldi lied. Jackson isn't dead; they're working together. They have to be.

"This how you treat all your women?" I yell in case they're listening. Or more likely, watching. "Like the toxic piece of shit you are?"

Dropping to my knees, I run my hands along the concrete

floor. I'm almost at 180° when my fingertips brush the first bits of wetness. My hands recoil toward my nose. The iron smell is strong, but there's something else in it. Sweeter, almost.

"Kane?" I yell again, this time getting a scraping sound in the distance. Trying to piece together the direction of the noise, I ask, "Where are you?"

"I'm here," a voice rasps from behind me.

I shift my focus and crawl as close as I can. *It's so fucking dark.*

He's close enough that I can make out his shape but not much else. "What happened?" he asks, his voice straining and airy.

"You betrayed me," I pit at him. "Remember?"

He doesn't say anything. He doesn't need to.

"Where are we? What's going on?" I ask. Between the sea of blood and the sharp divots scratched in the cold concrete, it's nowhere good. "There's a lot of blood. Are you hurt?"

"I don't know." He lets out a grunt and shifts on the concrete. But without any light to assess the damage, it's anybody's guess.

"Don't move. I'll come to you."

"My shoulder hurts pretty bad. Might be dislocated." He inhales sharply as he scoots around on the floor, his own set of chains rattling.

"Is this what you wanted?" I push my matted curls out of my face and kneel as close as I can. "Is this some kind of sick game you're all playing at?"

"Please, I have nothing to do with this. . ." He shudders between breaths. Whatever happened to him, he's not lying about the pain. "I have nothing to do with this."

"You *work* for these people, Kane," I snap at him. "Ones who drug you and throw you in God-knows-where. What is this place?"

"It's a holding ground."

"For what?" I hiss.

"Nothing good."

I count to ten and pray that when my tears stop, I wake up from whatever hellish nightmare this is. "I should have listened to Jackson."

"Jackson? You saw him again?"

"He's not dead," I say, my emotions an unholy mess. "He warned me—he warned me, and I didn't listen."

"All—"

"Don't Allbrook me. You stopped me when I was getting away from this hellhole. If you aren't a rat, I don't know what the fuck is."

Silence consumes the gap between us. After a while, he opens his mouth again. "It's not what you think."

"Then tell me what it is," I yell, trying to pull myself back to my feet. "Because it seems like every time something goes wrong, you're right there. If you're not causing it, then what is it? Are you cursed? Damned to ruin the lives around you?"

He chokes for a second. "Jesly, it's not like that."

"But it is." My voice wavers a little. Each time I think I trust someone, betrayal isn't far behind.

My head is burning, pounding. Like I'm being pulled across the void, stretched a little too thin. I'm glad he can't see the tears pooling at the surface. I didn't believe I could cry after Jackson— that it was even possible.

I was wrong. I should never have dropped my guard.

The damp chill surrounding us distracts me from my sorrow. It seeps into our bones, worse than a Deep South winter.

"I thought you were going to fight," he says as I curl up into a ball against the wall and try to conserve what warmth I can.

☥

"I'm not doing shit."

"So you're just going to give up? Just like that?" he says dejectedly. "Zaire should've picked someone else to save Dagny."

"Fuck you, man," I say through a pounding headache. "You don't even know me."

This time, he says nothing.

"Just leave me alone," I tell him. "I don't want anything from you. If you see Zaire before I do, tell him that I'm done with this shit. I don't care what happens next."

EVERY NOW AND AGAIN, a dreamless sleep overtakes my willpower. At some point, metal scrapes against the concrete. This time much louder and with it comes a vertical beam of light. It takes a second to realize it's a door opening.

We're in a prison cell. Which means there's an exit. The yawning beam grows as someone pushes the door open and three bodies fill the space. One of them snatches me like a ragdoll and locks my arms behind my back.

Days in the darkness, my eyes recoil from the piercing light pouring in. It's exactly what they're counting on—to use those precious few seconds to immobilize us.

Two other guards head toward Kane, who's not in any shape to fight them and fails miserably.

I thrash in my captor's menacing grip. "Let him go!"

Whatever they want, they're not here to negotiate. The two guards use Kane for target practice until the only sound left is sheer defeat, one muffled cry at a time.

Wrestling my arms from the person holding them, I drop to

my knees, broken. This time, I don't try to escape. I don't fight back. Instead, my hands latch over my ears, and I succumb to the cold ground until the beating stops.

I'm so sorry, Kane.

IT'S HARD TO TELL the passage of time when trapped in darkness. After the first beating, hours passed before Kane regained consciousness. After the second, they dragged him out, leaving me to face my demons alone.

Whoever's leading this rodeo, they don't want me dead. Not yet. Food comes in, but I don't dare eat it. My stomach churns, but I'm not about to trust the generosity of people willing to kidnap us and turn Kane into a punching bag. One slip-up and a single forkful ends with me swallowing my own tongue. I'm not about to risk it for the biscuit.

Light deprivation makes it impossible to discern how long it's been. *Days, weeks, maybe?* Sleep chases me, but I won't let it win. *I can't.* My brain burns with anxiety.

I wait for Dr. Hiribaldi to rear his ugly head, but there's no sign of him or anyone else for that matter.

"This is a real shitty kidnapping," I shout into the darkness. "I don't know anything."

A faint electronic beep chirps and then is gone as quickly as it came. My eyes, now sharpened by the darkness, latch onto a faint red dot in the upper corner of the cell. They *are* watching. *Good, serves them right.*

Just give them a show. That's all they want. Kill whoever opens the door, and you'll be free.

"How? I'm tied down." I ask, my hand racing to clasp my mouth. *It's too late.*

Whoever sits on the other end of the camera heard. Admitting I hear a voice would be far easier. Speed things along even. Convincing them I'm not crazy is another thing altogether.

So tell the truth. Tell them how long I've been inside you.

I have no desire to give Jackson and whoever else is behind this even more reason to keep me locked up. Whoever they are, their bedside manner leaves much to be desired. I run through our list of current and former clients and staff. Anyone besides Jackson who would benefit from silencing me.

There's no one else.

More than a few folks would prefer me to disappear, but this is next-level shit. I didn't accept bribes from mob bosses or biotech firms desperate to hide their next pathogen. The most interesting fact about me was that my ex was a habitual cheater and a narcissist.

All I did was keep my head down and serve my clients by treating them like family and chasing the justice they deserved. Jackson was the one to get his hands dirty. Not me.

All until Dagny—the one where I was willing to lie over to keep Jackson safe. Now she's gone. Maybe this is what the Universe wants. My own form of justice—the one I deserve.

Time drags and my mind wanders. Back to Kane. I should've never trusted him. Trusting people gets you hurt.

Now we're both screwed.

Hiribaldi, on the other hand, is easy. Him, *I don't trust.*

Another tray comes in, a bowl filled with something resembling soup. *I'll pass.* There are far more urgent things. My ankle borders on a dog's chew toy, and my lungs burn when I breathe. This much mildew in the air and I'll be lucky not to end up with pneumonia.

I need to stop wasting energy and stay focused. My mind races, but that's what they want—to break me. Unfortunately, it's working. The few times I've accidentally dozed off, my brain has snapped me back to reality. *Not today, Satan.*

They're coming.

Shut up, I think, but we both know better. The voice won't leave that easily. Demons always come back.

Footsteps echo down the hallway toward us. It's another moment before the door latch unlocks and the vertical beam returns, flooding light into the cell. Guards drag in something resembling Kane and throw him in the corner. Like trash.

Kane's not a small guy, but whatever they did to him, he's not putting up a fight. Not anymore. This time, they don't latch the chains on before exiting.

And then it hits me—they're leaving us to die.

SHOUTING AND GUNSHOTS WAKE me. It's faint and muffled by the thick walls, but my senses lock onto even the smallest things. The latch unlocks and I sit up.

They're probably here to take Kane again. We have to get out. I steady myself, poised and ready for whatever comes through that door. I'm about five pounds lighter than when this started, but I'll give it a shot. I have to.

The beam of light returns, bursting into the cell like an explosion I'm not prepared for. Nor am I prepared to find Dr. Caspar standing in the doorway aiming a gun at a stout male guard.

"The fuck?" I shield my eyes from the light with my hand.

"Jesus, Jesly. I've been searching for you guys for weeks," he says, visibly shaken. He, too, looks a little worse for wear. His beard has grown out, his shirt is untucked, and a week's worth of dirt and grime line his skin. No longer do I see the friendly doctor with his two kids and beautiful wife.

Instead, he's unkempt and armed. Wide-eyed and ready.

"Dr. Caspar?" I ask in disbelief.

Run.

The warning bristles something at my core, but I don't heed it. *I can't.* Being chained doesn't allow a lot of options.

"Get them loose," he commands as he shoves the guard inside, his handgun drawn the entire time. "Are you okay?"

I nod at the corner. "Kane isn't."

Henry surveys the damage. We both do. My guardian's clothes are stained with so much blood that it's impossible to tell where he's injured.

An audible gasp tells me Dr. Caspar reaches the same conclusion. "Lord, have mercy," Henry breathes. Forcing the guard to the ground, he demands, "Where are the keys?"

The guard blinks repeatedly, gawking back and forth between us. "I have no idea. This wasn't me, man!"

Run . . .

"But you know who." Henry kneels beside the guard, never lowering the pistol. "Where are the keys? These aren't patients; they're prisoners."

Between the tightness in his jaw and the fresh sheen of sweat on his temples, this is far more than he signed up for. No honest doctor expects to see this. The gun's hammer locks into place.

The guard raises his arms. "Man, I don't know. I didn't do this!"

"You didn't do this?" I say, pointing to Kane's sunken form. "The man's dying, for Christ's sake."

Too late.

"I'll ask one last time. Where. Are. The. Keys?" Henry levels the gun at the guard's forehead.

"I-I—"

"Hey, I'm talking to you."

The guard backs against the concrete wall. His gaze keeps darting toward the doorway. It's hard to tell what he's more afraid of—what's inside the cell or what's outside. "Please, I'm begging you. I don't know!"

Henry levels the gun a little lower. "Then who does?"

"Me," Dr. Hiribaldi announces from the entryway, but he is immediately drowned out by the deafening blast of the shotgun he clutches.

His colleague crumbles to the floor in a shower of blood, the psychiatrist's body lifeless from the gaping hole where his head used to be.

☥

ALL YE WHO ENTER HERE

SOME DAYS, I THINK I'm the one who's cursed. That I must have done something so heinous in a past life to deserve this torment, since there's no way I could ever accrue enough karma to break whatever hold this hellish world has on me.

A notion that comes back swinging as I sit ankle-deep in a pool of blood, my hands drenched in something once human. My limbs stick as if my puppeteer has deserted me, leaving my movements languid and jerky. The only thing I'm certain of is the ringing in my ears.

Dr. Hiribaldi steps over Henry's corpse and tosses the keys and a pair of handcuffs to the cowering guard. "Get her up." Hiribaldi doesn't even have to raise the shotgun; the poor man is already scrambling to switch my chains.

The doctor watches as the guard's hands shake while he transfers my restraints from my feet to my hands. It takes two tries.

"Can you walk?" the guard asks.

Feeling empty inside, I just nod.

"Fantastic." Hiribaldi wipes blood splatter off his face with a rag before chucking it at his dead colleague's feet.

The handcuffs snap shut around my wrists, immobilizing my hands in front of me.

"This how you treat all your dates?" I ask Hiribaldi, staring straight at him. If he wants to kill me, he's going to have to look me in the eye when he does.

"Don't flatter yourself." He waves the shotgun, which the guard takes careful notice of. "Pahana, help Ms. Allbrook up before she stains the concrete."

"Why are you doing this?" I ask.

"You'll see soon enough." Hiribaldi props the cell door open with Henry's body, smearing the man's blood across the stone slab even more.

My stomach churns, and I retch nothing but bile, dry heaving until my skull throbs.

You should have run while you could. Now it's too late.

As much as I hate to agree, the voice is right. Wiping my mouth on my collar, I stare at Kane. He hasn't moved in God knows how long. He's breathing. Barely. We need help and fast.

Zaire? I think, hoping he'll hear me. *Zaire?* I try again but get nothing.

"Enough," Dr. Hiribaldi says. "Time's a tickin'."

Pahana helps me to my feet, and I don't know whether to be relieved or alarmed by the guard's kindness. At this point, anything's game. His own fear reflects back at me. *Now I see. We're both trapped.*

Dr. Hiribaldi heads toward the doorway, stepping over his colleague. "Five minutes. Pahana?"

The guard stammers, "Yes, sir."

"Don't worry, Ms. Allbrook. We're almost ready." Hiribaldi claps cheerfully, leaving us alone in this house of horrors. The clip of his loafers fades down the hallway.

The second guard lingers behind. "What about him?" He points at Kane.

Pahana shrugs. "Just leave him, I guess. He's not going anywhere, anyway."

"Fuck you," I snap, though it's evident my feelings are irrelevant to these psychopaths.

Pahana escorts me out of the cell, both of us taking care to step around Dr. Caspar's remains. I whisper a silent prayer for him; the man didn't deserve this. I say another one for Kane and a third for myself. Never having considered myself a God-fearing woman, maybe I should start.

Outside the cell, concrete walls line the dilapidated hallway. Time has eaten away at the faded burgundy paint, leaving only the crumbling stone beneath. As we walk down a sketchy set of metal stairs, Pahana and I duck to avoid the hanging pendant lights scraped together with bare wire. This building probably hasn't heard of OSHA.

"—esly—"

"Kane?" I ask silently.

Nothing.

We march past old bulletin boards lined with a map of a place I'm not familiar with. Its wings sectioned off; the area is divided into a maze of gargantuan proportions. Enough dirt and dust obscure the glass panels that it's impossible to make out where we are, but I rake my fingernails through the grime anyway.

"—sly . . . ge . . . ou—"

A buzzing halogen light pops above my head. *"Zaire?"*

Pahana eyes it suspiciously. "Keep moving."

We round the next corner and find ourselves staring at an

elevator shaft at the end of the hall. Other than our footsteps in the shallow puddles, it's silent. Every fiber in my body screams at me to run, but I can't. Not without answers.

Pahana presses the only button. *Down.*

"We're taking that?" I point.

"Yep."

"Where?"

The metal rust bucket looks like it's one collapse short of a tetanus party. Seconds later, the beast roars to life and the doors shake open.

"Ladies first." He motions toward the threshold.

I need to even these odds. With Pahana a whole head-and-a-half taller and about double my weight, he's out of my league. If Kane and I are going to escape, it won't be vis-à-vis.

I'm going to have to do this the old-fashioned way—fire, brimstone, and a whole lotta stealth. If we're lucky, maybe God, the Universe, or whatever will throw us a bone.

First things first though. We need to find the exit. *Any* exit. My ribs still aren't mended enough that if I move too fast, my head spins. Add that to malnutrition, dehydration, and my recent decline in muscle definition, and I'm ripe for the picking.

So the rust bucket it is.

With no telling how deep underground we are, this machine doesn't alleviate the fluttering in my chest. Scores of buttons line the elevator. One for each floor, I'm assuming. Pahana selects the lowest option and the doors clatter shut. Winding into motion, the elevator gears descend into what feels like Hell.

A smell grows in the air, one I cannot place. It's not like in our cell, where it was ripe with the scent of fresh blood. This is different. Dryer, older, and far more unsettling.

My throat hitches as I clear some stale air from it. Then the door chimes open and it's exactly what Dr. Hiribaldi promised.

The answer to everything.

"Where are we?" I ask incredulously.

Larger than any mass retailer I've ever seen, we stand in a massive, yawning void of a thing that ensnares us beneath the Earth's surface. It's a cavern. Across the rocky terrain, a lone figure hovers over a disheveled pile of clothes.

"Good luck," Pahana says, undoing my handcuffs long enough to push me off the elevator.

I spin around. "What?"

Ignoring me, he steps back inside and hits the up button.

Without Kane, there's a good chance I'm gonna need it. Each inch across the gravel echoes in my ears, my body heavier with my footsteps. It's not until I make it another hundred yards or so that the pile moves. *It's human.*

My steps quicken. I panic, searching for how I could've missed him. Maybe there's another way in. Which means there's another way *out*.

"So glad you could make it, Ms. Allbrook," Hiribaldi calls from across the wide expanse, a distraction from the paranoia welling inside my core.

It tugs and won't let go. The stale air clings to this place like a distant memory, a nightmare I'd long since forgotten. Maybe the doctors are right and I'm losing it.

Maybe I can't be trusted.

So I cling to what I know—what I *can* remember.

My name is Jesly Allbrook.

I'm twenty-seven years old and an assistant prosecutor for the city of Dallas. My ex and I were in a car accident this past April, one where we killed somebody. The doctors say my ex, Jackson, died there—that he never made it out alive.

But I know they're *wrong*. Because I can feel him.

Here . . . with me.

As much as I despise the man, we've always shared a connection stronger and more dangerous than any I've ever known.

Twin flames. People mix it up and call the connection soulmates, but they're wrong. This is a different beast entirely. Jackson isn't dead. I would know. Because if he were dead, I would be dead too.

But I knew that coming down here. I won't run, not without answers for both me and Kane, so I'll follow this rabbit hole as far as it goes. No matter the cost.

As I inch closer across the cavern floor, a massive chasm surrounds us on all sides, except for the one with the elevator. It's an odd place for a basement, but I don't have time to debate subterranean geography. That can wait until people's lives aren't in danger, including mine.

Zaire? I call one last time. Still nothing. Wherever he was, he's gone now. Or perhaps telepathy doesn't work this far underground. I have got no idea how it works.

Honestly, I don't even know if I care.

Hiribaldi waits on the other side, hovering over the sunken form. It's not until I get closer and recognize the ashen curls and rumpled gray button-down that my knees buckle.

In any world, at any time.

My heart skips and not in a friendly way, like it's fallen out of rhythm. Suddenly, it's nearly impossible to breathe; I'm left gasping, like all the oxygen has been sucked out of this vacuous space.

I stumble backward. "I-I don't understand . . ."

"You will." The sawed-off shotgun in Hiribaldi's grip beckons me over. But it's not the gun I'm worried about; it's his left hand that's spinning around something small and shiny.

A syringe.

I try to backpedal but Pahana's partner waits. He never even made a sound. The guard wastes no time in dragging me by the hair toward Hiribaldi.

No amount of weak punches and claw swipes stop him from dragging me like a garbage bag toward the dump, banging and crashing along the ground as we go. His vise-like grip scorches my scalp as we inch closer to where the not-so-good doctor waits with someone I had hoped I'd never see again.

A person Hiribaldi told me was dead.

But we're both here. Both alive. I screw my eyes shut and count to ten. No reality is as cruel as this.

This is a nightmare, another illusion of my insanity. I'll accept their diagnosis and swallow the rainbow of horse pills if it keeps this hallucination at bay.

I foolishly believed I could make this living hell stop. Yet here I am. *Trapped* with a deranged doctor and the madman of an ex he's managed to capture.

Jackson's expression twists in horror as he gazes up at me. "Jes? No . . ."

His lips mouth something else I can't make out, but it's not until Hiribaldi viciously slams the shotgun's barrel into Jackson's temple that I realize my nightmare has just begun.

A PRIME OPPORTUNITY

THE VISE TIGHTENING AROUND my chest makes it clear I'm not dreaming, but I don't feel fully awake either. It's almost like I've drunk one too many vials in Wonderland and there's only one way out—toward them both.

Hiribaldi stands between me and what's left of Jackson.

"Jackson?" I say.

"He can't hear you, Ms. Allbrook." Hiribaldi uses his boot to nudge Jackson's now unconscious body. I bolt toward them, only to get yanked back like a pitbull on a yard chain. Pahana's partner in crime is Hiribaldi's lackey through and through.

"What did you do to him?" I choke on the words.

Even after everything Jackson's done, he doesn't deserve this. No one does. Whatever Hiribaldi's done is inhuman—to both him and Kane. "How can you call yourself a doctor?"

He snorts. "Oh, easily."

"You told me he died," I say. "Made me think I was sick."

"No, Ms. Allbrook," Hiribaldi says. "I told you the *truth*."

"Bullshit."

He simply shrugs. "Denying reality doesn't change it."

"This isn't dead. This is *worse*." I signal in Jackson's direction.

Even now, there's no mistaking him for someone else. But he's not asleep; his breathing is too shallow. *I-I can't . . .*

My head whomps, the room spins, and everything is so out of whack. Like I'm staring into a funhouse mirror that's cracked with age, and I can't make a straight line out of all the pieces overlapped in my brain.

That shirt—it's the same button-down I bought Jackson last spring sale at Marshalls. But he's wearing it. *Here. Now.* I nearly fall over; the more I search, the more my memory blanks. "What have you done to us?"

The other guard reaches to help, but Hiribaldi stops him with a hand. "Don't. Let her figure it out."

All this time . . . Jackson was right. In the hospital. At the river.

So blinded by my hate, I didn't listen. His search for a way out. Foolishly, I thought he meant the trial. He had been trying to warn me—that we weren't safe—that something was wrong.

But I didn't listen.

Hiribaldi stares at the crumpled man at his feet and laughs. "Ms. Allbrook, I assure you, I haven't done a goddamned thing. This is all *you*."

"What the fuck does that mean?" I want to scour Jackson for any sign of foul play, to see if he's drugged, but the sawed-off shotgun in Hiribaldi's grip reminds me not to get any closer. Becoming a human colander isn't on today's bucket list.

"This is all for you," Hiribaldi explains, rolling Jackson's body over. My ex-life partner's features are sunken, darker than I remember, and the weight that made him strong is now a distant memory. If I thought Kane looked bad, Jackson is worse.

I wrestle from the guard's grasp and race to Jackson's side, dropping to my knees. Clutching him by the shoulder, I turn his body over to find his eyes rolled back into his head. The terrible odor emanating from his foam-filled lips forces me to fight back the vomit in my throat. "Undo whatever this is . . . whatever you did to him. Now."

He smiles. "I can't."

"Of course you can," I whisper and pull Jackson into my lap, clutching him tightly. *Not you too.* Wiping my tears on my shirt does little to stop them from falling. "Jackson, wake up."

"He can't," Hiribaldi says plainly. "Not anymore. The land of the living hasn't housed Mr. Alders for quite some time."

"What are you talking about? He was just with me."

"Ms. Allbrook, he's *dead.* His soul, however, that's another story."

"Jackson, please wake up . . . please," I cry.

Deep, angry veins line Jackson's face, enough to keep me from focusing on the man waving a shotgun around. Jackson's pallor is undeniable, like a clammy fishman who's spent more time on water than land. Cold to the touch, nearly lifeless.

I brush his wavy blond locks off his forehead. The likelihood that he's walking out in one piece seems slim. With the sickly aroma floating around him, time is short.

He can't be dead. Not like this. Not without me.

Hiribaldi squats in front of us. Pushing his lab coat out of the way, he draws something from his inside pocket. It's that same syringe from earlier. "Take this."

I don't dare breathe. "What do I want with that?"

He smiles, wide and threatening. "You're being presented with a way out."

"Are you high? This is a goddamned nightmare," I say,

steadying my footing.

Hiribaldi shrugs. "Only if you see it that way. Think of it as an opportunity."

"An opportunity?"

"You get to decide what happens with his soul."

"This is *insane*. You *people* are insane," I scream. "What do you want? Money? I'll pay whatever you want. I won't talk—just let Jackson and Kane go."

He snorts, shaking his head. "I don't want your money, Jesly Ann Allbrook."

My grip tightens around my ex. "Then what do you want? Is this some sick joke to you? People are dying."

"You don't get it, do you?"

Fuck it. I scream at the top of my lungs, blood-curdling and as loud as I can.

The guard lumbers toward me, but Hiribaldi stops him. Again. "Ms. Allbrook, anything we've done, it's only been in service to you. What you wanted."

I freeze. "I'm sorry?"

"You wanted Kane to pay, he has," Hiribaldi explains. "You wanted Jackson gone; well, that you have to do yourself. Here." He offers the syringe again. It's filled with a pale milky liquid that's likely not the life-giving nectar it claims to be. Something haunted clings to it, and to us along with it. "One vial and this goes away forever."

"Who are you?"

"Just a man doing a job. You can end this, Ms. Allbrook," he says. "Right here, right now. One vial and you can go back to your life without him in it. No more running, no more hiding."

"I-I don't . . . Jackson was *fine*. Now he looks worse than me.

You've done something to both of us. That's why I can't remember anything. You've drugged all of us."

"I don't need to." He holds out the syringe again. "It's simple. One injection, and it's over. No one will know."

I turn to Pahana's co-anchor, who idles nearby as if he's got no care in the world. It makes me wonder just how many messes he's had to clean up for his boss. "What about him?" I say, stalling. "He'll know."

Hiribaldi looks at the guard. "Who? Him? You're worried about Edik?" He levels the shotgun at the guard with his free hand. "I can handle that."

"Jesus fucking Christ. Hiribaldi, no!" I jump up, bolting between them, my hands outstretched. "What is wrong with you?"

"No, Ms. Allbrook, I've already told you what I am." He lowers the gun, much to the relief of both me and Edik. "I need to know your decision. What'll it be?"

Silence sinks over us until it fills the cavern, leaving only the sound of my pounding heart. I can't leave any of them. Not Kane. Not Pahana. Not Edik. And not Jackson.

Yes, you can.

My eyes widen in horror. "Wh-what?"

Hiribaldi grabs my hand and shoves the syringe into it. He wraps my fingers around it tightly and pushes it against my chest. ***This is the only way you'll ever be free.***

I suck in a breath. "It was you . . ."

The tightness in my throat grows. Nothing seems right. Even the stale air clings to my skin, clawing at me for an answer.

He stifles a laugh. "What'll it be? Time's a tickin'."

I kneel beside Jackson and latch onto him protectively. The entrance we came from is hundreds of yards away.

"If I say no? What then?"

Hiribaldi twirls the shotgun in his right hand. "For your sake, I'd hope you don't."

Looking back at Jackson, I'm no different. The gargantuan cavern borders almost a void, empty save for the palpable current caking the air like a poison choking us slowly.

Very slowly.

This feeling. I've felt it for weeks. Even before the Renaissance . . . the funeral. It's been here all along.

And then I realize—I'm already trapped.

We both are.

Hiribaldi's grin widens as he sees the realization dawn in my eyes, and I know it to be true. "We never survived that night, did we? This place—that's what it's for. Every single last one of us."

He doesn't say anything; he doesn't have to. Nausea floods my system, and I'm left retching on the cavern floor.

All this time . . .

After several minutes, he kneels beside me. "Enough stalling, Ms. Allbrook," he says. "This man took advantage of you— cheated you in every way possible."

My pulsing head threatens to bowl me over. "I-I can't . . ."

"He abused you, lied to you, cheated on you. He cheated and exploited others—innocent people—he broke every oath he made," Hiribaldi bellows, his pacing manic. "Why are you protecting him?"

I open my mouth but stop. *Hiribaldi's right.* Jackson has done all that and more. Some things I can't even bring myself to admit. "Even so, he doesn't deserve this."

"You asked for it, begged for it," he shrieks. "Even tried to jump off a goddamned roof for it. And now you get a free ticket to your prayers and you fucking turn it down?"

"Who are you really, Hiribaldi?"

With a reluctant sigh, he kneels beside me and touches my shoulder. It burns like ice, enough that I shrink away. "You died for this, Jesly," he says softly. "It's time you end this charade of a life once and for all. Start a new one somewhere else. No one will question a thing."

"You can do that—just send me back?"

"We can."

"What about the nightmares?"

"No more nightmares, no more hallucinations," he says softly. "Just quiet for once. Forever."

My hand tingles as I stare down at the syringe. I've clutched it so long I don't even feel it anymore. It can't be this simple. "What happens to his soul?"

"He'll go where we all do."

"Will it hurt?" I say.

"Do you want it to?"

Hiribaldi knows how much sits between Jackson and me— how tired I really am. I've spent so long running, hiding. Covering the bruises. Bribing and pleading with whoever was willing to bury the tracks. Playing the doting girlfriend, the all-American lawyer, the other half in everyone's favorite power couple.

I've spent so long fighting his demons that I forgot my own.

And my demons are a list unto themselves. I search Hiribaldi's empty gaze for a way out, but there isn't one. Not this time.

"I'll ask once more," he announces. "Can you bring justice to all the innocents his actions have wronged, or are you willing to let an unrepentant killer walk the streets for eternity?"

"I—" Death chokes this place. It's nearly suffocating, and I know what I must do. "If I do this, you release Kane."

☥

"Of course."

I'm so sorry, Jack. I inhale between tears and drive the needle deep into his neck, letting the liquid disappear. It's only a few seconds before his already weakened system seizes and his breathing stops.

For real this time.

The syringe clatters to the floor. It's done.

"I killed him," I say, horrified.

"Yes, you did. Well done." Hiribaldi grins, wide and menacing.

"What did you do?" I shriek.

"My job, Ms. Allbrook. It was so easy messing with you and your pathetic little memories." He nods at Jackson dispassionately. "So much trauma. So much to work with. But I'll give the man credit; he tried to fight it 'til the very end."

"You bastard—"

Before I can say anything else, what feels like fire scorches through my left wrist, sending me crashing to the ground. It takes everything I have not to claw my hand off. I watch in horror as faint blue lines snake their way around my wrist, carving their way into my skin until I'm left ragged and clutching at torn flesh.

"Think of it as insurance. Now you're going to hunt down the others," Hiribaldi says plainly.

Between my ugly tears and heaving chest, all I can do is wait until the pain stops. Soon only burnished lines remain. "What others?"

I don't get the chance to figure it out. The ground begins to tremble and shake beneath us, and I realize the terrible mistake I've made. For what I hoped to be an ending is the start of something else.

Something far worse.

☥

THE SCALES

WITH THE LINES FADING, my focus returns to the last bit of foam fleeing Jackson's lips, his pale blue eyes wide. He's dead. The stillness in the chamber shatters when I realize the air is electric. Choking and swirling like a current.

It's getting worse, not better.

I steady my breathing and blink through the pain. I focus on the syringe on the ground.

"Oh, Jesly, don't you remember your Bible studies? *'Thou shall not kill.'* " Hiribaldi's cackling drains the blood from my face. It's piercing, filled with vitriol, and centered on me. The doctor's persona is long gone. It's only the monster beneath.

"I'm not a murderer."

"'*Thou shall not lie*'," he says, his laughter growing more maniacal. "You really are fucked, aren't you?"

The ground shifts again, worse this time. Fighting the quaking rock beneath us, I scramble to my feet. Something terrible is coming.

"What's happening?" I ask.

Across from the cave entrance, a wide-mouthed tunnel looms.

Whatever's inside, it's gigantic. And fast. Another few seconds and a cacophony echoes from the chamber, discordant and angry.

Hiribaldi beams like the Cheshire cat. "It's your Judgment, Jesly."

BOOMMMM! The ground explodes with the scamper of claws, like a horde of beasts scurrying down the tunnel. Ringing assaults my eardrums. I fight the urge to cover my ears; doing so would leave Jackson unprotected.

The man's already dead, but he doesn't deserve whatever the fuck's coming down that tunnel. I'm not sure anyone does.

Pathetic. Hiribaldi interrupts my thoughts, leveling the shotgun back at me. "You codependent bitch. The man's dead and you're still trying to protect him."

"Fuck you," I snap back.

I need to try to get my bearings. With Jackson out of the picture, that leaves just Hiribaldi and Edik. Two against one. A decent enough outcrop looms about twenty yards away.

You won't escape. Not her.

I still can't believe I didn't recognize it at first. Now there's no doubt. Like a constant drip in my mind, ever-present and poised to break me. It's only ever been Hiribaldi's, plaguing me since the accident.

I never had a chance.

It's strange. I don't feel relieved—I feel *pissed.*

Pissed that Jackson made me drive because he was too drunk. *Angry* that we killed the person who needed our help most. And I'm fucking *belligerent* that I'm stuck here to clean up this mess.

As usual.

Another blast wipes out a massive portion of the rocky outcrop to my left. Luckily, the scattershot isn't so accurate at this range. If I can just keep this distance between the three of us, Edik included, I might make it. Whether I'm dead, alive, or somewhere in between, the fact remains—it hasn't been long since I was catapulted off a roof and my body is quick to remind me.

Weeks ago, all I wanted was to die. With my own afterlife hanging in the balance, survival has trumped anything else. Tears cloud my vision in this dusty terrain. The outcrop provides temporary cover, my chest heaving in complaint. *Just need a second to catch my—*

There you are.

Hiribaldi's hands latch around my throat and lift me from the ground. He's so much stronger than his slight frame suggests, and his lanky height puts me at enough of a disadvantage that thrashing doesn't get me very far. His sinewy muscles tense as he drags me from my safety, my own hands scratching and clawing at his grip.

"Enough wasting time," he says, lugging me back toward Jackson's lifeless remains.

Everything in this arid hell reeks of death. The scent of iron clings to the air, mirroring the rust-colored soil beneath our feet. He throws me to the ground, and I slide farther than any normal human should go. Jagged rocks tear up my forearms, this time baking them in blood of my own.

"This is a nightmare . . ." I whisper.

"Oh, no, my dear." He smirks and shoves the shotgun straight into my chest. "This place is very real. Very real, indeed. Ammit, come!"

The rattling in the tunnel grows louder until out bursts a creature the size of a Mack truck. The cavern quivers as it scampers toward us, my eyes widening as it gets closer.

"What the fuck is that?" I ask.

☥

"The last thing you'll ever see."

The creature looks like a child's nightmare—a grotesque assembly of mismatched toy parts. Large, beady eyes stare directly at me from the end of a long snout lined with multiple rows of teeth. Its head is covered in crocodile-like scales and its muscular chest is spotted like a cheetah's. A massive, cement-truck barrel waist gives it a lumbering gait as it advances toward us. The backside reminds me of something from a safari. Then it hits me.

I've seen something like this before. Middle school history class. *The Devourer of Souls*. "That thing's real?"

The corner of his mouth twitches. "She's not a *thing*. She's Ammit, and she's here for you, Ms. Allbrook."

"This isn't happening," I say. "Zaire?"

"He. Can't. Help. You." Hiribaldi slams the butt of the gun into my forehead, turning the cavern into a wonder of shooting stars. "This has been a most productive day. First Alders, now you. Lady Ammit, I offer them both."

I take a deep breath, hoping to slow down the spinning cavern, but it's precious seconds I can't afford. Hiribaldi yanks me across the cold stone, my nails catching on the deep grooves in the ground, tearing them as we go.

We stop on a large circular dais. I struggle to clear my lungs from the dust. The rumbling grows with each disjointed paw step Ammit takes toward us, blocking our only exit. Edik's sudden grip tightens on my arm to keep me from running, and we both watch as Hiribaldi lights an array of pillared sconces with a Zippo.

Jesus Christ, it's a fucking altar.

"Don't worry. It won't be long now." Hiribaldi looks up from the candles. "Lady Ammit will feast on the souls she's been given. Mr. Alders and then yours."

I bark out a laugh, even though it's not funny. Not at all. "This—this is crazy. I'm off my meds. I'm hallucinating."

"No, child," he says. "Every action, every choice has led you here."

Ammit lingers at the far end of the platform, waiting.

Leaving Jackson to whatever comes next seems wrong. All at once I've become the judge, jury, and the executioner. A thought that makes my stomach turn. We should've never driven that night. None of this would have ever happened and the others would still be alive.

Now it's just me—trapped in a nightmare I can't escape.

Then quit. Give up. "The Chasa don't like to be kept waiting." Hiribaldi says, lighting the last sconce. He drops from the platform, his five o'clock shadow noticeable in the flickering light. "They'll find their lost lamb soon."

"You tricked me," I tell him.

"I gave you an *opportunity*," he hisses. "You plowed through that door."

"Bullshit."

"This system isn't one to beat, Jesly Allbrook," he says.

Then it hits me. The roof . . . The hospital . . . "This whole time you were testing me, weren't you?"

Hiribaldi snorts. "Ding, ding, ding. Now you get it." He beams in delight. "You have no idea how long it took to bring you here. You would think a person like yourself would reach this place faster."

"Here?" I rasp, fighting down my nausea.

"The Duat, darling, and we've been waiting a long time." He outstretches his hands, beckoning me to take in the visage.

It's not until he does that I realize the outcrop is something more—a deteriorated obelisk, broken by the hands of time. The cavern walls bellow with symbols, etchings I hadn't noticed until now. Birds. Feathers. Strange, faded symbols. Reds, blues, golds. They encapsulate the walls, stretching until the ceiling disappears into the blackened stalactites.

I look back at the monstrosity chuffing calmly nearby, though I don't think it's friendly—not when fresh appetizers lie around. "And Kane?" I ask.

"What about him?"

"You said you'd release him."

"I lied," he says and heads toward the creature.

Better him than me. Wide as a living room and twice as tall, she's somehow the ugliest dog I've ever seen. A real live chimera of Death. One that's after me.

"Edik, get Pahana," he instructs. "Let's not keep her waiting."

"Yes, boss." Edik disappears across the closest outcrop.

And then it begins.

Hiribaldi snatches Jackson's body and drags it up the altar steps, dropping him into the center of the stone dais. With no telling the last time this thing ate, every second counts. If I remember my mythology correctly, souls don't pass over right away.

I can fix this. There's still time—

Cruunnnnnchhhh.

The sound ricochets off every nook and cranny of the massive chamber, reverberating until it feels like my own bones snapping. Grief knocks the wind out of me, creating a chasm I can't fill.

I'm not ready. Not for this.

But I have to steel my anger because anything more and I will break. I will crumple and die, and we will cease to exist. There will be nothing left—nothing left to stop my ugly sobs.

My hands shake harder.

I'm a stupid woman crying over spilled milk—over a man who didn't love me.

"It wasn't supposed to be like this," I breathe. Nausea washes over me until I'm left ragged and fighting not to vomit.

The cavern is massive, but it doesn't make the yawning chasm feel any less confining, sending the room spinning. My vertigo returns, consuming everything until it's impossible to focus. Like I'm stuck on a merry-go-round with no way off. My nails dig into the rocky soil, hoping to gain some traction but find something else instead. Left behind when I injected Jackson.

I can do this.

"We won't need this." Hiribaldi notes my slowing gait and sets the gun on the altar. "That feeling you got? That's Death, Jesly Allbrook." Kneeling beside me, he's oblivious to the syringe coiled in my right hand.

"And what about—?" I flinch with each bone Ammit snaps. "Wh-what will happen to him?"

"He's irrelevant." Hiribaldi's bloodied fingers brush my back, and I recoil from the singeing cold. "He got what was coming to him."

"I never asked you to."

"Yes, you did. He made your life a living hell and you know it."

"Bring him back," I blubber.

He shakes his head. "I can't do that. These aren't the same pedantic rules you humans have. You made your choice. Now only the scales of Justice and Balance remain."

"No." My grip tightens on the leftover syringe. *If a man can't see, a man can't fight. I have one shot.* "I make my own justice."

The needle jamming into his right eye takes him a second to

register. It's just long enough that I'm already bolting toward the gun, racing with all the energy my failing system has left. My hands latch onto the shotgun. Its heaviness threatens my grasp, costing me precious seconds I don't have. By the time I squeeze the trigger, he's already gone. And so is Edik. *Shit.*

I scramble beneath the next closest outcrop. If that thing—Ammit—sees me, I'm done. It's less than a hundred yards back to the elevator. Of the two ways into this chamber, meandering into Ammit's monster lair isn't on my bingo card.

"Everyone's story ends, Ms. Allbrook. Even yours." Hiribaldi rips the syringe from his eye socket.

Gouging his eye might not kill him, but it's enough to slow him. Seconds buy time; time buys me opportunities. Even if I manage to snatch the shotgun from where it fell, if I can't get a handle on the tremor in my hands, it's over.

If I listen to Ammit's crunching any longer, it'll destroy what's left of my soul. I foolishly thought it would be easier—enjoyable even to watch Jackson pay.

I was wrong.

It's only left me hollower than I already was. I have to make things right. For everyone. I pull the shotgun to my chest and wait for Ammit to finish the last bits of her meal.

Booommmmmm!

My left ear rings, the chamber turning smokey ash.

A distorted voice shouts in the distance, but I can't make it out. My hands lose touch with the gun, and it disappears into the cloud of debris consuming everything. Black lines snake through my vision and my left side is freezing. I fumble for Hiribaldi's weapon, but my eyes won't focus.

The voice returns, closer than before. "Je—Jesly?"

Pockets of fire rain down as a feminine figure fills my blurry vision. A face I don't recognize behind the respirator until she gets closer, my hands fumbling for the shotgun in the haze.

"Dr. Kennedy?" I balk. "What the hell are you doing here? Where's Hiribaldi?"

"I don't know," she tells me, "but I'm not about to wait and find out. Let's go."

She pulls me to my feet and steadies my footing long enough to let me retrieve the gun from where it's landed several yards in the opposite direction. Not taking no for an answer, she signals for me to follow. Flames stretch across the massive chamber. A caustic smell overtakes the air, mixing until only unholiness remains.

"What happened?"

"I blew up the place," she says.

"You what?" I ask. "I thought you were a doctor."

"I am. My GI Bill paid for med school. Stay low," she says, doing her best to keep us moving through the fog. "When Henry missed our anniversary dinner, I knew something was up. He's never even been late. Find My iPhone tracked him here."

And then it hits.

The phone call. The text messages back and forth. The wife in the photograph. One boy, one girl. The all-American family. "Dr. Caspar was your husband."

Even in this darkened hell, her eyes glisten. She already knows. "Thirteen years on the nineteenth."

Fuck. "I-I'm so sorry."

Her back stiffens. "Thanks, assuming I don't have you to blame."

I force a smile. She can't find out. *Not ever.* "No."

"Was it that bastard Hiribaldi?"

I nod solemnly.

There's not a lot to say. She could leave, but her oath as a doctor forbids her from abandoning a person in need. She's too good of a person. In the end, she stays.

I try to rub the exhaustion out of my face. "Did you see the technician who brought me to Calgary?"

"Yeah, he's—"

The crunching sound resumes, twice as loud as before.

"What is that?" she shrieks, jaw tightening.

"You don't want to know."

She yanks me around by the shoulder. "Is that what killed Henry?"

"No, it's after me. No one else," I answer truthfully. Elaborating is pointless. Divulging the truth won't allay her fears; it'll only make them worse.

That's how Hiribaldi works. Warping and twisting from the inside. Only with him, there's no respite.

Before the accident, running was the only way I could escape the cacophony in my head—now it's only Jackson's bones cracking between Ammit's massive fangs.

"Okay . . ." she replies. "This day just keeps on getting better. How much longer until it finishes that thing?"

I shake her grip loose. "That *thing* was Jackson Alders."

"It's eating a person?"

"Yeah."

"Then we get the hell outta here," she says. "Kane's upstairs."

"He's alive?"

"More or less . . ." she answers.

We limp across the sandstone archway separating the chamber and take refuge under a small overhang. A gurgling hiss echoes around us. Even in this smokey haze, I can tell Ammit is close.

The Devourer of Souls. The exactor of divine punishment, derived from the Scales of Ma'at. Hiribaldi knew I would fail. Even planned on it. But he didn't expect me to fight back. Me or Dr. Kennedy. Showing up after the husband he murdered. Neither did I. *#couplegoals* I guess.

"Ladies . . ." Edik calls out from the red sandstone bridge. Behind him, the elevator waits—our way out of this hellhole. Blood runs down the side of his temple and onto the collar of his once-starched uniform.

"Give me the gun," Dr. Kennedy tells me, and I oblige. "Is it loaded?" Before I can answer, she racks it. "Never mind."

"We just want to go home, Edik," I yell from behind the outcrop.

"I can't let you pass, Ms. Jesly," he says. "Doctor's orders."

Amy snorts.

I'm glad she's got the gun. The blood on my hands will never wash off. Not anymore. Dr. Kennedy, on the other hand, seems unfazed as she squares the shotgun. "Technician, get out of our way."

"I'm sorry, Dr. Kennedy, but that's not an option." He digs into his back pocket and pulls out a small-handled metal contraption with chains. It takes a second to realize it's a nunchaku. *Who the hell uses a nunchaku?*

She mumbles something under her breath, and I only catch the last bit. ". . . mercy shall follow me all the days of my life: and I will dwell in the house of the Lord forever."

It's not even a fair fight. The shotgun blasts a hole in Edik's abdomen, something that should slow him down if not kill him. But it doesn't. He staggers back to his feet, ignoring his ever-increasing blood loss.

☥

Dr. Kennedy digs into her blouse, pulls out her cross, and lets it fall over her heart. "We need to leave. This place wasn't meant for us. Can you run?"

"Not well, but yeah."

"Let's try then." Dr. Kennedy is fast, her lithe shape bolting out in front as we break for the elevator. Before my legs give out, I clutch onto the jagged rock face and rip the dilapidated lever downward.

"Where's Pahana?"

"Who?"

"The other guard."

"Big, stocky guy?" she says, aligning the shotgun higher on the bridge. Just in case someone comes. "He's unconscious. I knocked him out."

"Dr. Kennedy—"

"Amy is fine."

"Amy—" I echo, only to be interrupted by the clattering of the metal elevator and its familiar ding.

"Let's go." She wrenches open the metal gate not a moment too soon. We collapse into the elevator and drag the heavy gate closed. I breathe through the pain in my wrist.

If Amy notices, she says nothing. She presses the up button repeatedly. "What the hell is going on, Jesly? Kane won't say a word."

"Well . . ." I pop my lips. "It's complicated."

Her gaze narrows. "*Complicated* is scraping your husband's brains off the concrete. You'll need to do a little better."

"I-I—"

"Whatever you two have going on down there, it doesn't matter. It's not going to keep me from avenging Henry. If either of you have anything to do with it, I'd speak up. That way you both die with a clean conscience."

There's a fierceness in her eyes that underscores the gravitas of the situation. She's a tigress without her mate, dangerous and prone to strike.

I shake my head. "No, we didn't do it, Amy," I tell her. "But we didn't stop it either."

PART III

SWEET MEMORIES

THE ELEVATOR CLAWS ITS way back out of what feels like Hell. Amy says nothing, her body tense as she waxes and wanes between breaking down and holding it together. Did she have to clean up Henry's remains before rescuing me? *Do no harm*, they said. I bet she never imagined this when she took the Hippocratic Oath.

My ears pop as we crane out of the void, forcing me to lean against the wall. It's only silence around us now. What's been a few hours feels like eons. With every meter we gain, the earth vomits us back to freedom, out of a tarnished hell that knows only a blackened sky.

A familiar face appears when the elevator finally stops and the door yawns open.

"Kane, you're okay." I latch onto him for dear life. He's alive and miraculously in one piece. "How?"

"So are you, I see." He lumbers awkwardly out of the way.

Dr. Kennedy did what she could. His head is bandaged. His body has a tourniquet wrapped so tightly around his abdomen that it can't possibly feel good. The last time I saw him, he existed only in shades of bloodied black and blue. Now he stands in far better condition than I could've ever imagined.

He's still here. Thank God.

We both pay close attention to Dr. Kennedy—Amy—who stands an arm's throw away. Laying all the cards on the table when she's already overwhelmed seems cruel, so I step carefully down the hall.

"I killed Jackson," I say softly.

"I know." When he sees my confusion, he adds softly, "I always knew, Allbrook. You're my charge. It's my job to know."

"No, I mean like *dead*-dead. Just now."

He freezes mid-step. "What?"

"I killed him, Kane," I repeat. "Hiribaldi talked me into it."

Kane glances around, as if we'll invoke the doctor if not careful. "We need to talk." He leads me to a rundown office, and we duck inside its dilapidated walls. "Tell me you're kidding, Allbrook."

"What part sounds like a joke?" I whisper. "You think I enjoy being a murderer?"

His jaw tightens.

"The least you can do is tell me what you're thinking." I latch onto his shirtsleeve. "Please."

He sighs after a moment, his lips drawn into a tight grimace. "I think you just got your first glimpse of Hell, Allbrook, and the people who work for it. The Chasa don't give up their prey so easily. They never have."

"What do we do?"

"We?" He balks, never taking his eyes off Dr. Kennedy. "*We* are going to find Zaire. This is his mess."

"If you two are done huddling in a corner, we're not in the clear yet," Dr. Kennedy announces from the doorway, making me jump. "Come on." She kicks herself off the broken wooden doorframe and slips back down the hallway I came through earlier.

The buzzing of the halogen lights growls louder than before, the lights flickering as I struggle to keep up. A dampness clings in the air up here. Different from before. No longer arid. Now it's just a lover afraid of abandonment.

My wrist burns and itches in the worst way but checking it will have to wait. *"You belong to us now."* Whatever Hiribaldi's insurance is, I can't tell Kane. *Not ever.*

"Amy, did you tell somebody you were here?" I ask.

She stops dead, the kindness in her eyes gone. "And tell them what? Some giant monster is eating people in the basement of an abandoned facility?"

"Well, yeah."

"I'd rather not, if it's all the same to you," she says, avoiding touching the banister or the dilapidated walls.

Being quiet is nearly impossible. The hallways are drowning in puddles. Small divots in the time-worn concrete create grooves in the stone. Ones that carry on down the hall in nearly parallel lines—albeit a little sloppy. Scratch marks.

I try not to think about whatever could have made the deep scratches. With each length we gain, it gets easier to breathe. Like its power is waning, like we're leaving its domain. Something I could not be more thankful for.

A few dozen more yards, and the air finally loosens its unnatural grip on us. Amy's pace quickens after we slip through the first corridor. I know exactly where she's going.

Peering into the cell feels like a past life. No trace exists to show what happened here. The floor has been scraped clean of blood. Dr. Caspar's body has been carefully wrapped in some old, tattered sheets.

Amy rushes into the room and drops to her knees beside her fallen spouse. As she asks, "How long were you in here?", I can tell something dies inside her.

Kane shrugs. "Not sure. We—I lost track of time."

"Did you know Henry was following you?" she asks. "Did he say anything?"

I can't watch this. Filling in the details won't fix it.

"He told us he'd come check on me but never showed," I tell her. "Eventually, I figured no one was."

"He loved his patients." She fixes the wrappings, taking great care to keep his body from being exposed. After a minute, she finally looks up, tears in her eyes. "There's no signal—no phones anywhere. What is this place?"

Kane and I exchange a glance.

"I can't leave him. Not like this."

"I'm sorry, Amy, but we need to go," he says for the both of us. "It's not safe here."

Her jaw tightens. "And Henry? What about him? He's not becoming that *thing's* next meal."

"I understand. But Kane's right—we're sitting ducks here," I say empathetically. "If we don't get out of here, we're next."

"Don't you think I know that?"

"Hiribaldi could come back any minute," he tells her.

"That fucker's dead," she says. "I shot him myself."

For her sake, I hope she's right. But I know it's just a grieving woman's dream. We need a plan. Fast. Unable to deal with the fluttering bird in my chest, I use the flashlight I pulled from Kane's grip to search the hallway.

I've gotta stay busy—stay moving. Unlike me, Amy doesn't

have a death sentence over her head. With Dagny gone, I've gotta find another way out of this mess. *Somehow.*

Kane can tell from my face what I'm thinking. "Allbrook . . ." Kane trails me into the faintly lit hallway. "Her husband just passed. Give the woman a minute to grieve. Not forever, just a few."

"The Chasa don't give up that easily; you said it yourself," I say. "If I don't find a way outta this, I'm done."

"You don't think I know that?" he whispers under his breath. "Just give her a second."

I pace the room like a caged animal.

"We can't just leave her," he says. "She's part of this now."

"I've already got a large enough body count on my head. What's one mor—"

"You're a real bitch, you know that?" Amy interrupts from the doorway, her hands caked with dried blood. She shoves the shotgun into my chest and forces her way past. "Make yourself useful then."

Her determined footsteps echo down the hall as she swallows her grief. There's no antidote to finding the father of your children murdered at your feet. My grip turns ghostly white around the shotgun's stock.

I wish I weren't like this. *So scarred. Damaged.* So damn sure everyone's out to fuck me over that I'll hurt anyone who gets close. This is my mess and they're the ones paying for my mistakes.

Silence becomes our only company as we traverse the snake-like corridor to the outside world. Being alone would make this easier—at least then it would confirm that I deserve this forsaken life. But Kane and Amy don't abandon me, a kindness I don't deserve but am grateful for nonetheless. Nothing is familiar as we step outside of the winding maze that is this dilapidated prison.

☥

"You sure you know where you're going, Amy?" Kane asks, more for me than himself. Occasionally, he checks me for some sign of breaking, but I won't—I can't.

I owe him.

I don't know how Kane's not dead, but it gives me hope and terrifies me all the same. If he's intact, what does that mean for the man chasing us? Our best laid plan is to put distance between Hiribaldi and me and pray Amy's right. If she's wrong, it won't be long before my time runs out.

All because of the last person I loved—*No, not anymore.* It tugs like an angry tide, threatening to consume me if I let it. But this won't last. It can't.

Jackson deserved it. Hiribaldi was right. It didn't have to end this way, but Jackson chose his path. This time, he's not coming back.

I'm sorry, Jackson.

"Hey." Kane nudges my shoulder, and I look up from the broken concrete. "We're here."

Wherever *here* is.

There's no doubt I wasn't conscious the last time I entered this godforsaken place. I would have remembered the dilapidated lobby overgrown with flora and broken stained-glass everywhere. The shattered floor tiles make traversing it more treacherous. We push open the rusted metal doors.

The reprieve we hoped for gives us only another cage. A large courtyard long since turned into nothing more than a junkyard, it's complete with broken-down cars and overflowing scrap piles. Less than twenty yards away, a rusted chain-link fence overgrown with creeping fig stretches twice as tall as we are.

That same nagging feeling from the underground has

returned, like a tide rolling in. I glance down at my wrist. I can feel it there. Spreading beneath my skin. *Something's wrong.* One step closer and my wrist starts burning again.

"Amy, stop," I tell her. "We can't go this way."

"Not a chance," she counters, ignoring my warning. She snatches the shotgun back, slings the carrying strap over her shoulder, and vaults over a rusted car that's seen better days. Whoever Dr. Kennedy is, she's nothing like what I expected.

"No, wait," I shout before she can grab the fence. "What if that thing's hot?"

"The plants would be dead." Without a thought, she begins her ascension. Her body moves with the deftness of a lithe dancer on stage rather than traversing a twelve-foot fence.

Kane follows suit, latching onto the wrought-iron before turning back to me. "Come on," he says, noticing my hesitation. "First, we get out of here. Then we worry about what comes next."

My heels dig into the rocky soil littered with broken glass and waist-high foliage. My body feels sluggish, like I've stepped in wet concrete. The pain on my wrist is searing, and it takes everything I have not to claw my arm off. All I can do is grit my teeth and pray it will pass.

The slightest breeze rolls through. ***Jesly . . .***

No . . .

Amy's already crossed the peak and scrambled down the other side when Kane stops at the top, his watchful gaze distrustful. "Allbrook, what's wrong?"

"I-I can't . . ." I whisper.

Kane sees the horror wash over me. "Hey, it's okay. Come on. I'll pull you up," he says gently and holds out a hand. We both know I can't reach him, but he doesn't waver.

☥

"People, what's taking so long?" Amy's voice cuts from the opposite side.

Kane eyes me suspiciously before saying, "Allbrook just needs a second."

"Of course she does," she grouses. Her footsteps strike a path away from the border fence. It's just me and Kane again. Just like at the start.

He waits until the coast is clear. "Allbrook?"

"I think I should stay."

His terror mirrors mine. To my surprise, he slides down this side of the chain-link and lands inches away. Beneath the sweat, grime, and blood, there's a sweetness to his musk. It's hard to imagine anything in this place doesn't smell like death and decay.

"You're sweating and it's absolutely freezing out here."

"I just don't like heights," I lie.

"Nope, not going to work with me," he quips back. "You climbed to the top of the Renaissance."

Before I can make up a lie, he snatches my left arm and yanks my sleeve upward, exposing the branded coil of blue lines snaked around my wrist. They've grown since the last time I've seen it, and by the way Kane's eyes widen, that's not a good sign.

He inhales sharply. "What the fuck, Allbrook?"

"I-I—" I slink backward, clutching my arm.

He points at the mark. "When were you going to tell me?"

I lean against one of the broken-down cars. "Truthfully? Never."

"For Heaven's sake, that's not how this works and you know that," he says under his breath. "I can't keep you safe if I don't know what I'm keeping you safe from."

"Well, you've done a shit job so far."

☥

"I know," he says apologetically, digging his hands into what remains of his pockets. "And I'll be forever sorry for that."

"An apology? Seriously? You think that changes anything between us?" I say. "You betrayed me, Kane, and for what? What did you get from this? A nice little torture-fest?"

"Don't you think I know that?"

"Maybe."

Kane growls in frustration and throws his hands in the air before resuming his pacing back and forth across the courtyard. Running his hands through his mangled chestnut waves, he mumbles to himself, indistinguishable enough that I can't make out what he's saying. Eventually, his frantic pacing turns toward me. "If I could tell you everything, I would. But I can't."

"Can't or won't?"

"*Can't*," he says emphatically.

"Because of *rules*."

"Yes," he says, relieved that I get it.

I don't. "You think you're protecting me, but Hiribaldi isn't after you. He's after me."

"That's the point."

"How are you this naïve?" I grouse. "If you're with me, you're in danger. Not the other way around."

We stare at each other and wait to see who breaks first.

Unfortunately, it's me. My hand wipes the first stupid tear from my cheek. *Shit.* I'm getting too attached. I'll admit it—it's been that way my whole life. I've only known him for a few weeks, and I'm already catching feelings.

"I can't lose you too. You're all I've got left," I say so softly he has to lean in to hear it.

The hardness etched into his handsome face softens just a

little. Of course he would be as stubborn as me. He stops inches away and exhales, his breath miraculously sweet like mint. "Stop worrying, Allbrook. I'm not going anywhere. Not until we see this through."

I wipe another tear. "Why? Why not give up and let me die?"

"That's not the deal."

"But how can anyone forgive what I've done? What am I supposed to do?" The weight of my confession buries us for a moment before the dam can't hold any longer and it finally breaks. "I-I'm so sorry."

Unable to trap the tears, sobs overtake me. Crying for Jackson . . . Dr. Caspar . . . me.

A watershed somewhere inside me breaks open, and Kane does the only thing he can; he slips his hands around my back and pulls me into a hug, letting me cry into him from one human to another. Our bodies are exhausted and broken, but his protective grasp doesn't loosen as he watches the entrance of the building we've just escaped.

Amy's fast approaching footsteps pull us back to the present. "Hey," she calls, her voice breathy like she's been running. "There's a clearing up ahead that leads back to the main freeway."

"Okay," Kane shouts, his pensive face measuring me silently. "Did you find a different path around the fence?"

"No, I didn't get that far," she says from the other side.

"Okay, you go on ahead," he says. "We're right behind you."

"And here I thought I was the one holding us up." Amy doesn't waste any time running off.

As her footsteps disappear, Kane offers, "She's trying."

I nod and pull myself off him, realizing I've probably clung a little too long. If he agrees, he says nothing of it. It makes me wonder if having an enigmatic personality is a job requirement for folks like Kane.

"We need to leave before Hiribaldi takes another swing at you, or, worse, The Chasa."

"You keep saying that name," I tell him. "Who are they?"

"The Chasa?"

I nod.

"You're a lawyer, right? Think of them as judges for the Afterlife." Kane latches back onto the fence, this time reaching out for my hand.

"Is Hiribaldi one of them?"

Kane shakes his head. "He's something else . . . Something much older."

"Should I be worried?"

"Allbrook, if we don't find Zaire and figure out a solution fast, we should all be worried."

I've been around him long enough to know he's leaving something out. Whether that's for his benefit or mine, time will tell.

"We need to go." Skirting back over the fence, this time he doesn't wait. "Alright, you're next," he yells from the other side.

What takes them seconds takes me forever and all my focus to keep my footing. The sudden scuffling noises drown out any fears I have as I drag myself over the top of the iron death-trap.

It's not until my feet hit the sunbaked pavement that my brain can process the chaos unfolding in front of me.

Amy's got Zaire in a chokehold with the shotgun muzzle wedged beneath his chin. "Somebody's got explaining to do."

Kane steps between us. "Amy, it's okay . . . Just put the gun down."

"This guy says he knows you, Jesly," she says. "I've seen him before though. Skirting around the hospital."

"He's telling the truth," I say. "Zaire's with us."

She tightens her grip on the guy. "This is what I'm talking about! Either somebody talks or we're gonna have a real come-to-Jesus moment in a minute."

Strands of her relaxed hair shift in front of her face, and I'm reminded of the picture on Caspar's desk. That same photograph that had two young children in it, their joyful eyes bright and full of wonder. Kids who don't have any idea where their mother and father are right now or if they're ever coming home.

And I don't breathe a fucking word.

☥

MOVES AND COUNTERMOVES

"AMY, NO ONE ELSE needs to get hurt," Kane warns, his body still barring her path. "Put the gun down."

"Not going to happen," she says. "Less than forty-eight hours ago, I was dropping our children off at school. Now their father's dead. What am I supposed to tell Harlow, for Christ's sake? She's five." Amy's grimy leather jacket crinkles against Zaire's back, her vise-like grip unforgiving.

"I'm sorry," I offer.

"Are you high?" she scoffs. "*Sorry* doesn't bring their father back." Her boot heel slams into the back of Zaire's knees, dropping him execution-style in the overgrown weeds. The doctor gone, nothing but the soldier remains.

Kane steps toward her, his hands raised. "Amy, please don't do this. You don't want blood on your hands."

Her free hand draws a small black pistol from her waistband and the hammer clicks into place as it angles at Kane. "I'd say scraping my husband off the concrete saw to that," she says bitterly. "Please explain how you even ended up here and don't leave out any details."

Kane's jaw tightens. Zaire nods in agreement. We're drowning in too many secrets. But she's right; the woman needs something to go on. It takes longer than we'd like. By the time Kane's done, she seems to believe at least half of what we tell her.

"What does Hiribaldi want?" Amy demands. "More importantly, that creature—that *thing*—you said it was eating a human being. How is that possible?"

With an ache settling between my temples, I lie. "We're not sure."

"That so?"

"We have something he wants," I admit, this time closer to the truth.

"So give it to him."

I shake my head. "I can't. Things have gotten complicated."

"Then uncomplicate them."

"I'm trying."

Amy's frown weakens. "And him?" she asks, swinging the muzzle toward Kane.

"Me? What did *I* do?" he asks.

"Ever hear the expression, 'You're like a bad penny?'" she says bitterly. "One visit from you and my patient gets locked up in some macabre prison."

A grimace stitches across Kane's lips. Amy's not wrong.

"How do I know you aren't working with that fucker Hiribaldi?"

"You know me," he pleads. "I would never hurt you or your family."

"Two weeks!" she yells, her voice breaking. "When Henry didn't come home, I couldn't find him anywhere. When I finally did, he's dead."

"Amy, please," I say. "It's not Kane's fault."

☥

"Don't make excuses for them, Jesly," she snaps. "They're grown-ass men."

"I'm sorry."

"Enough. You're not a child." Her composure nears its limit. "Nothing's been right at Calgary for months. First the patients, now you. I don't understand any of this."

"*Patients?*" I freeze.

"*Steady,*" Kane warns silently.

"And this one? Can I trust him?" she says, quickly changing the topic as she glances at Zaire, the stiffness in her body loosening. In their leather jackets, they nearly match—both driven to chase after the ones they love. I can't help but envy their tenacity.

"Trust *me*," Kane says. "Hiribaldi is more resourceful than you think. This won't be the last time he rears his head."

Amy shoves Zaire into the grass, releasing him. "Fine."

"Appreciate it," he utters wryly.

"Don't thank me—thank him." Amy nods at Kane.

Relief floods my lungs now. One less thing to worry about. Explaining that Dagny is dead for real this time takes precedence. "That job . . ." I turn toward Zaire. "It didn't work out."

Zaire straightens his jacket. "Understood."

"That's it?" I say. "That's all you've got?"

Nothing escapes his lips. I turn to Kane for answers—a place that also gets me nowhere. The grave gives better results.

Amy eyes us suspiciously and stuffs the pistol back into her waistband. A force to be reckoned with, her anger is focused on the two men locked in a silent conversation, their bodies rigid like sentinels. Zaire hands a small red package over to Kane who tears it open at once. It's a bag of Skittles candy. *Jesus Christ.* The man has been tortured for weeks and the first thing he does is eat fucking Skittles.

Boys, I yell mentally, hoping it works. "You two have been acting weird for weeks. Out with it."

"Not important," Kane answers between mouthfuls. "Just ship talk."

"It's *shop* talk," Zaire corrects.

"It's *nothing.*"

"Come on, Kane," Zaire says. "Just tell her. Jesly's got a right to know."

"Tell me what?" I ask.

Foolishly, I'd like to believe this day couldn't get any worse, but when Kane avoids my gaze, my uneasiness returns. It could also be the faint scent of decay drifting from the abandoned complex.

Zaire steps in front of Amy, blocking her line of sight. Whatever it is, she's not included. "Fine, I'll do I t," he says, brushing off his pants. "My boy's the one who sent you back."

"Back where?" I ask.

Kane digs his boot into the soil. "Remember when we met at the top of the Renaissance?"

"Yeah?"

"It's not the first time."

"Excuse me?" I say.

Standing this close, I can make out the sweat beading along Kane's temples. Strange given the temperature outside is far from hot. In fact, it's freezing. Even outside the building, my body burns with an inescapable cold, undoubtedly the ramifications of my new tagalong tattoo. Which is surprisingly quiet now that it's had its way with me.

"You've . . . been with us . . . for a *while* . . ." Kane explains slowly, each word drawn like pulling teeth.

"Bullshit," I say. "I'd remember you."

"You're not meant to, Allbrook. It's against the—"

"Rules," Zaire finishes. Apparently, everyone knows about Kane's penchant for law and order.

I clutch my stomach, horrified. *Both men knew. This whole time.* "You had no intention of telling me, did you?"

Not a word.

"And you let me step out of that car? Why would you do that?" I fight the tears back as best I can.

"Jesly, wait. Please wait," Kane pleads, his professionalism slipping momentarily. He reaches for me, but I slap his hands away before he can.

Part of me is absolutely livid. The other contorts at the sound of my name on his lips. I shake the latter thoughts away. "Did you know this would happen?"

"Not exactly." Kane stuffs the Skittles wrapper into his pocket.

"This whole time I believed I was going mad." Driving my hands into his chest, he stumbles backward. "You sent me down here on this wild goose chase, and for what? To fucking die?"

"Down *where*?" Amy interrupts.

"Here." Zaire plops onto a nearby metal guardrail meant to further isolate this damned place. "On Earth."

"What the hell are you talking about?" Genuine anger burns in the doctor's eyes, unbridled and no longer teeming under the surface. This is probably the last way Amy would like to spend an afternoon, but I've got to give credit where it's due. Having taken an oath as a doctor, her morals override any other choice. No one can blame her if trust is in short supply.

That makes two of us.

A wave of dizziness crashes through my body as they argue back and forth. It's not long before pain snakes up my left forearm, leaving me breathless.

"Jesly died, Amy," Kane tells her.

The muzzle levels in my direction. "Bullshit. I read that chart myself. You're standing right fucking here," she says, her blue eyes weighing my soul. Convincing the grieving doctor we're not all clinically insane is a tall order, even for me.

"The patient records are wrong," I rasp between inhales. "I didn't survive the Renaissance. I never even survived my accident."

"That's impossible."

I shake my head.

"You're. Standing. Right. Here."

"I'm sorry," I offer.

"People don't just *come back*, Jesly. That's God's domain." Her furrowed brow collapses when she realizes she's the only one not up to speed. "Lord have mercy." Her fingers reach for her crucifix but come up empty.

"You saw that creature in the cave, Amy," I offer, but she's not listening. Not anymore. "What it was doing . . ."

"No, you're not dead. It's not possible." A frantic retracing of her steps around the fence line is futile.

"Amy?" I call out.

She backtracks toward the road. "This—this is something else. God's punishment, maybe? Whatever it is, I want no part." With her free hand, she digs into her back pocket, grabs her iPhone, and mashes a combination to dial emergency services.

Beep-beep. The call fails.

☥

She hoists it higher. It fails again. "I have no signal. Why do I have no signal?"

"Cell service might not work out here," Zaire posits.

"Amy, you need to listen," I say. "Hiribaldi could come back at any point."

She may have gotten us out of the building, but the longer we stay on the complex, we're sitting ducks. If Hiribaldi shows up, we're screwed.

But maybe she's right and he is dead. Doubtful.

Kane slinks closer with his hands raised. Further terrifying a distraught person with a gun is a terrible idea. "We need to get out of sight," he says gently like he's speaking with a child. "We can talk more about this later."

"No," she argues. "It's here or nothing."

"We can't." He points at the sky. It's been hours and the early afternoon sun hasn't moved from its zenith. "Something's wrong with this place. You can feel it. I know you can."

She looks up and sees it for herself; he's right. "Fine. But I'm going back in."

"What?" I balk.

"I need my crucifix," she says. "Then we can leave."

"I can't let you do that, doctor," Kane says and latches onto the gun's barrel, pulling it dead center onto his chest.

"Get out of my way, Kane."

"I'm afraid that's not possible."

"So help me if you don't move," she growls.

"Hiribaldi isn't who you think he is. I understand you're afraid, but he's going to come after Jesly. Then you. If you ever want to see your children again, we've got to leave. *Now*."

Fear contorts Amy's features as she digs the gun deeper into

Kane. "Henry's still down there."

"I know," Kane replies, his voice heavy. "But the best way to help him isn't going back in."

"If I live to regret this, you'll regret this." She finally lowers the gun. We both sigh in relief.

"Thank you," Kane says as he heads over to check on me.

A finely formed scowl has etched itself into the corners of Amy's mouth. Luckily, Zaire has distracted her with a conversation about the strange weather patterns lately.

"Why didn't you tell me?" I ask Kane.

His smile fades. *"You're not the only one with the odds stacked against you."*

"There are others?"

Kane's expression darkens. *"Really?"*

We stare at the horizon for what feels like centuries before anyone moves. The tightness of his jaw and the stress lining his shoulders belie the burden he carries. Whatever it is, Kane won't talk. Our trust is weak—fragile still.

What if you're wrong? I fold my arms around myself. *What more can I do if Dagny's already dead?*

"We'll find Dagny," he says a little too loud. "I promise you."

"Dagny? Like *Dagny Shepherd?*" Dr. Kennedy's brow furrows. "Age twenty-six, blonde, blue eyes? Why are you hunting my patients, Kane? What do you want with them?"

"You misunderstand," he says. "I'm just the escort."

She stares me down. ". . . Jesly?"

"I was supposed to get her out," I admit after a minute. "That's why I entered the facility in the first place. But I've failed— she's dead."

"News to me," Amy says plainly. "She's been back in solitary for the better part of two weeks."

"She's alive?" I whisper. "But I saw—"

"Her third suicide attempt this month."

"Third?"

"Yes." She nods.

"No matter what we do, she just keeps trying."

"Can't you do something?"

"As long as we keep her sedated, yeah. But there are laws. Ethics." Dr. Kennedy looks at us and sighs. "Given what she's told the staff, I doubt anything will stop her. Even us."

CIRCLES

IT'S BEEN A COUPLE of hours since any of us have spoken. Our hike back to the main road is now nothing more than a distant memory. We're a discombobulated group of wayfarers lost in the treeline, searching for something I'm not sure we'll even find. Having skirted the guardrail along the deserted freeway for hours, the absolute lack of traffic feels like a sign from the universe we're headed in the wrong direction.

Amy's attempts to stop the cars that do pass have failed. Zaire trails behind, his thoughts buried like his hands in his leather jacket pockets. Kane and I bring up the rear, with him keeping his distance. A cold steel wall drives deeper between us.

We say nothing to one another. But every few yards, he casts a glance in my direction. I can tell he wants to, but I'm not ready. Not yet.

We make our way steadily past the next mile-marker right as a muted gray fog settles in. The group is at least a hundred yards ahead of me. I collapse against the nearest thing I find—a rocky outcrop beside the solid white line. The red limestone rock face provides the only solace for miles. I'm too far out of my league.

No one stops until they realize I'm no longer trailing behind.

Kane asks, "You okay?"

"Yeah . . ." I say and yank the hair tie from my disheveled curls. Thick cumulonimbus clouds blacken the sky, bringing with them icy wind. The temperature continues to plummet. If it was cold before, it's five times worse now. I'm half-surprised it's not snowing somehow.

"I just need a minute."

"I'll wait with you," he yells over the increasing breeze and starts in my direction.

"No, no. You guys go on ahead." I wave him off and fight the urge to rub my left wrist. It burns and itches beneath my sleeve. Telling the others what Hiribaldi's put me up to isn't the best use of our time together. "I'll catch up."

Kane comes over and sits on the guardrail. "I can't do that."

By the rolling thunder echoing overhead, a storm can't be far behind. I race my fingers through my oily mane, suddenly aware of how terrible I must appear. I can't remember the last time I've eaten, or hell, bathed.

"Do you know how much farther a main road is?" I ask.

"Unfortunately, no," he laughs. "I'm just along for the ride."

"What are we going to do about Zaire?" I look down the road where he and Amy amble along the empty stretch.

He waves me over and I reluctantly oblige. "He's your best chance out of this."

"*You and me* are my best chance out of this."

"Listen. When I said I wanted nothing to happen to you, I meant it," he says and digs the tattered Skittles package out of his pocket. He offers me some.

"No thanks."

He shrugs contently. Two handfuls later, he tells me, "With The Chasa and Hiribaldi still out there, it's even more complicated."

"You could have told me everything from the beginning." I lean my head against the rocks and rest my eyes.

"Would you have believed me? Really?"

I shrug. "I might."

"Sometimes it's better to tell people what they want to hear. Easier that way."

"I'm an adult, Kane," I point out. "I can handle it."

He doesn't respond.

So I change the topic and dig the toe of my sneaker into the gravel. "What's going to happen to Zaire and Amy in the end?"

"That depends."

"On?"

"On whether you succeed," he says, his muscular frame vying to ease the tension in his shoulders. This trip is wearing him down too.

"Do they know?" I stare at the patterns I've drawn in the soil.

"They aren't my charges," he says slowly.

"But I am?"

He nods.

"Why me?"

"Why not you?" he asks.

I say nothing as we sit in silence for a moment.

Eventually, he breaks it, a haunted gaze poised in my direction. "You know I didn't set out with the goal of lying to you."

"No," I say. "But you did."

"I did," he agrees sadly. As he holds out a hand and helps me to my feet, his grip lingers a second too long.

"Kane?"

He blinks, lost in thought. "Sorry. Let's go." His hands slack to his sides. Crossing back over the guardrail, he waits for me to do the same.

The weather is deteriorating rapidly. Fog has settled in around us, making it harder to see passing traffic. Zaire and Amy wait at the large green road sign that splits the flow of traffic: Pineville to the east, Blue Ridge to the west. My ribs howl but Kane keeps pace, not willing to leave me behind.

Sugar maples and American beech trees line the deserted roadway, their scattered dead encroaching on our path. Between the leaf litter and the biting chill that's likely settled in for good, finding shelter takes precedence. But it's the sun still frozen in the sky that holds my attention as the first rumble echoes overhead.

"Where are we?" Amy asks when we finally catch up. "We've been walking for hours."

Zaire checks his watch. "Five hours, to be exact."

"That would drop us in the Gulf of Mexico, not the Blue Ridge Mountains," I say, trying to visualize a map of our state. "That sign? That's Tennessee."

"That's impossible," Kane hisses.

Amy throws her hands up, exhausted. "Anybody care to explain how we went from Dallas to the mountains in less than six hours?"

"Yeah, I do," Zaire announces. "Because someone's messing with us."

She storms over, her jaw tightening. "Messing how?"

"It's because we're trapped. All of us, including you, Dr. Kennedy."

Her eyes widen in shock.

"Kane, you explain," Zaire deflects.

We turn to him, looking for answers, and eventually Kane

confirms my fears. "We can't leave."

"Excuse me?" Dr. Kennedy says. "Leave where?"

Zaire smirks. This time it won't be him to break the news; it's Kane.

"Purgatory," the chestnut-haired man says. "We're in Purgatory."

And all at once, my worst fears are confirmed—Hiribaldi was telling the truth.

A lightning-hot wave of nausea crashes over me. I rush to the bushes, emptying my soul along with it. No amount of retching can shake the sudden cold consuming my limbs. My hair falls into the path of destruction, but I don't care. Not anymore.

My weeping distracts me from the fact that two hands pull my messy curls out of the way. Kane squats beside me, his grip gently present. "I'm sorry, Allbrook. I didn't want this to happen."

Wiping my dignity on my sleeve, I wrangle my hair into a haphazard bun. The heaviness in the air hasn't let up; rather, it's growing ever more present. It's in my bones now, chaining me to this place. "Hiribaldi was telling the truth, wasn't he? I never walked out of that accident."

He places a hand on my shoulder. "If I lie, will that change anything?"

"No," I grouse.

"Exactly. Your plans haven't changed. You get them out."

"Out?" I ask sharply. "How?"

He looks around for a moment. Getting answers is like pulling teeth. "There are ways," he finally says. "Complicated, Byzantine ways, but it's possible for you guys."

"And what about you?"

"Don't worry about me. I'll be fine," he says after a moment, watching as a distracted Zaire deals with Dr. Kennedy's own expulsions. She appears to be handling the truth as well as I am.

"How can you be certain?" I ask.

"This is not my first time doing this."

A sudden unsteadiness threatens my balance, like a newborn fawn learning to walk. Kane outstretches his arm and I link my own with his. As he steers me toward the others, thick ashen clouds finish snaking their way across the sky like charcoal smeared on a canvas. The storm is finally here. If the others notice, they say nothing. Even Kane.

After a while, he says, "When we found you on the roster of the newly departed, Zaire assumed you might be the key we've been looking for."

"The key to what?"

"Allbrook, I've already said too much. You shouldn't know half this stuff." He lets go, taking the warmth with him.

It's impossible to get warm anymore. *Jesus Christ, I am dead.*

"What about her?" I point at Dr. Kennedy, who's made it back upright herself. A visceral reaction, the nausea is unpleasant and seemingly unavoidable.

"Amy?" he asks. "She's a part of this now too."

We watch, Zaire included, as the woman gathers herself. But unlike Kane, Zaire's not emotionally invested in the outcome. He's only after one thing—Dagny. For what purpose I still don't know. Hopefully, it's love.

For Dr. Kennedy and Zaire, their pain is valid, their grief real. Dr. Kennedy lost Dr. Caspar; Zaire lost Dagny. But my loss . . . it's been a long time coming.

"Hey, Kane?" I call.

He turns around.

"Did you know what I'd done before you took my case? About Dagny?"

He nods. "Yeah."

"That didn't make you question helping me?"

"We've all done terrible things, Allbrook," he says. "Even me."

"Is Dr. Caspar really gone?" I ask, turning my attention to Dr. Kennedy who has shifted into the anger part of grief—she's cussing up a storm while throwing rocks into the treeline. Can't really blame the woman who usually dons a crucifix. Talk about disappointment.

"Yeah," Kane says. "But Dagny's not. She's trapped, just like you."

"Does she know Zaire's here too?"

His boots crunch the broken pavement as we slowly head in their direction. "No, he doesn't want to tell her."

"And you believe that bullshit?" I say under my breath.

"I do."

"Why?"

He mulls it over. "Because I do. You can see it in Zaire's eyes that his love for her is real. Shouldn't that be worth something?"

I grab him by the shoulder. "You think that hiding the truth from her is love?"

"Okay, Allbrook. Have it your way," he scoffs. "We tell Dagny that she's trapped. What good would that do? Don't you think the woman has already suffered enough?"

"Maybe it's the push they both need," I suggest. "The last time I saw her, Kane, she was hanging by the rafters. What if Dr. Kennedy is correct and she tries again?"

"That's why you have to go back," he says as Zaire notices we're discussing his fiancée like a football game. "You're the only one who can convince her to stop."

☥

I'M NOT SURE WHETHER to be relieved or disheartened knowing time has no meaning here. Amy hasn't said a word in hours. Miraculously, dusk has finally set in, the skyline a burnished rose as our pace slows.

"We need a strategy to get out," I announce after we pass another side road, this one diverging to some national forest. Every inch of my body screams and burns from abuse. If Purgatory looks like this, seeing the vacation package on Hell isn't really something I'm after.

"That's assuming we even can. We *need* shelter," Amy finally says. Her voice cracks from the weight on her shoulders. Unable to save herself or her family, let alone her patients.

Zaire suddenly spins around; his pensive gaze perks up. "There's a place up ahead." Without even waiting, he beelines along the abandoned roadway, unfazed.

Amy gives chase. "Wait, I'll come with."

"What if he's wrong?" I ask, signaling to the long stretch of road we've traversed. "We could be anywhere."

Blocking the setting sun with my hand, I find nothing but bramble as our only companion.

No birdsong.

No noise.

Our footsteps crunching in the leaves make the only sounds.

I exchange glances with Kane, his silent approval necessary for me to keep moving; he's the Virgil to my Dante. I have no choice but to trust him—I *want* to trust him.

No one wants to die alone.

Not even me. Not anymore.

He's just as exhausted but keeps going like he's got unlimited stamina. For now, I've stopped questioning his reasons for joining this escapade. Whatever hierarchy he's a part of, it's clear he's nothing but a cog in the machine. Something he's grossly aware of.

And as we follow Zaire and Amy, the feeling gnaws at me that whoever Kane's bosses are, they're close by. Always present, always watching. *"If you happen to meet them, ask."*

The more I ruminate, the more my vertigo races to meet me. So I focus on my footsteps. One after the other. *Inhale, exhale.*

If I don't, this will shift into a gargantuan merry-go-round with no exit. The minutes can't tick by fast enough. An ice pick drives its way behind my eye. I need sleep. *Desperately.*

Zaire and Amy are relentless in their pursuit of this place— wherever here is. "Zaire, what's back here?" I ask, scrambling to keep up.

"An old lodge," he tells us and dips onto a less-beaten path, one even more remote. He holds the branches back as we pass through the bramble and flora. "I still swing by periodically to check on the property."

Amy wipes sweat from her forehead. "You own the place?"

He doesn't stop. "My father and I vacationed here after my mother died. We'd go fishing and hunting to distract ourselves."

"You ever score any game?" Amy asks.

"Every now and again, but I wasn't the hunter my father was."

"Any chance there's a phone?" I blurt out, desperate for some Advil. Foolish I know. Even if I did find a working phone, who would I even call? The FBI? The Vatican?

"We're here," he announces. "Nothing fancy, but it'll do—"

We collide into one another as Zaire dead-stops at the trailhead.

☥

"What's wrong?" Amy echoes from behind, unable to peek over Zaire's taller frame.

He inhales sharply. "It can't be."

And then we see it too.

Looming not less than thirty yards away are the double-framed iron doors of the inpatient facility we left more than a day ago.

The ice pick wedged behind my left eye bowls me over. I latch onto Kane, who stifles his own shock, his jaw tightening as he holds onto me.

"They're not going to let us escape, are they?" I cry softly.

ONE WAY OUT

"I-I DON'T UNDERSTAND," I mumble beneath my breath. "How did we——?"

"Somebody's fucking with us," Amy says, already leveling the shotgun at the building. "Hiribaldi, you bastard! Come face me like a man!"

"Amy, stop," Kane yells. "This is crazy."

"Crazy?" she says. "We've been walking for a day straight and gone in a fucking circle. How is that even possible?"

And then I realize. "We never left."

"What?" Kane gasps.

Amy whimpers.

"We didn't go in a circle . . ." I explain. "We never left."

"That's impossible." Kane storms past me and yanks one of the door handles. The metal frame shakes but goes nowhere, leaving only the rattling of chains. "It doesn't work like that."

Zaire clicks his tongue. "It sure sounds like it does."

Before I can even blink, Kane is in his face, his calm demeanor suddenly unraveled. "Do you have a problem, Zaire? Something you want to say? Because the last time I checked, I'm the reason you're still here."

The darker-skinned man brushes his wavy locks from his eyes. His eyes slip their mask momentarily. Long enough to see the hatred brewing underneath as he storms off and Kane lets him.

"Lord, have mercy." Amy silently watches the chaos unfold. Her hand instinctively reaches for the missing crucifix.

Zaire's right.

We're all trapped. If anyone doubted it, we no longer do.

"How about we find something useful?" Amy searches the grounds, tearing through the cardboard boxes and garbage strewn across the lot.

"Your friend's got the right idea," Zaire says. "Time's a tickin'."

Amy perks up long enough to announce, "Not a friend."

I roll my eyes and scour the property. Long since abandoned, the yard has turned into a collection of misfit items, wooden barrels, and half-standing tables, filled with overgrown piles of semi tires and scrap metal. The wrought-iron fence doesn't extend to this side of the building; it stops at the edge of the long courtyard.

Russet-colored bricks line the towering walls, some of which are broken and found new homes amidst the knee-high grass. The ground's state leaves something to be desired. Odds and ends, trinkets and doodads all piled in a haphazard collection. The way Amy digs through the shrapnel tells me she's after one thing: ammunition. Not a bad idea considering the ineffable odds we're up against.

Unlike me, no one seems to tire other than Kane.

Taking advantage of our temporary reprieve, I pull my left sleeve up to find the dark blue-black design spreading like mascara after a good cry. Covering it back up, I drop in the dirt and start gutting out a divot.

☥

Kane notices my frantic digging. "What are you doing?"

"Making a fire so we can boil water and clean some of the grime off."

"Score." Amy collapses against a lean-to beside me, satisfied with her reward. A single box of buckshot.

Zaire cranes his neck around the stack of rubble. "A twelve gauge isn't gonna cut it. We need something stronger."

Amy yanks the grip of Hiribaldi's shotgun downward and stuffs in as many shells as possible. "It's better than nothing. What have you found?"

"Oh, I'm not too worried," Zaire tells her. "I've got a few things stashed for a rainy day."

"Let's hope it's enough." Kane scouts the entrance again. The handle rattles in his hands but won't budge. The door's locked from the inside. Something that bothers him and Zaire immensely as they encircle it.

"Now what?" I ask.

"This." Zaire yanks a jagged steel pipe from a nearby pile and slams it into the paned glass window. It takes a few tries, but the first chip eventually gives. The rest of the glass follows after. Either he's batshit crazy or immune to pain because he ignores the blood streaming down his arm. Reaching through the narrow opening, he only recoils when an audible click echoes in the crisp air.

The thick metal door scrapes against the painted concrete. Amy's newfound companion, her shotgun, takes point as she scours her former employer for any signs of life. There's none.

No patients.

No doctors.

Nothing explaining what's happened here.

All that's left are the tattered sheet-covers that drape over the facility's furniture. Thick layers of dust cover everything in sight. But it can't hide the pungent mildew smell clinging to everything in this place. The air tastes stale, like death itself, and there are enough cobwebs that I wish I had brought a machete.

Whatever happened here, this place has long been forgotten.

"Anybody else seeing this?" I ask incredulously.

"Sure am," Amy replies, much to my relief.

"How is this possible?"

Amy slips around the counter and reaches for the corded phone trapped beneath all the endless dust and decay. She puts the receiver to her ear. "Dead," she announces, as though we didn't already know.

"We'll find something," I say.

Nothing else has moved.

Almost like the building is frozen in time. The visitor log still sits on the top of the high counter. The wide-mouthed glass vase once full of vibrant flowers holds their desiccated corpses, long since abused from lack of light and life. I dump out the heavy vase and scoop it up for my own. *This'll do.*

"Zaire, what are we doing?" Kane follows him into the common area. "There's nobody here."

The sound of metal scraping against the linoleum fills the uneasiness welling between us. "No . . ." I say. "Something's here."

It's only been a day or so, but already my vision strains against the darkness. The stillness of the place weighs heavily as we move past the foyer entrance. Without a flashlight, it's difficult to make out. Plunged back into the black, our eyes finally adjust. A darkened form looms in the wisps of my peripheral, and I spin around to face it.

One I recognize.

☥

But not fast enough to keep from swinging the vase at it. I nearly strike a disheveled blonde woman in the head.

It's hard to distinguish her from the shadows. She's so frail, she reminds me of a porcelain doll. And then her stringy locks move out of her face, and I realize who I nearly killed.

Again.

"Dagny?" I gasp. "You're okay."

"What the hell are you doing here?" She lowers her arm once she's satisfied that I'm not going to attack.

"We came to find you—"

"You can't be here," she says angrily as she pushes past. Still in the same white sundress I'd last seen her in, Dagny rushes to the floor-length windows and peers around the moth-eaten curtains and cardboard taped to the broken windows. "Did you come alone?"

I point to the others. Dr. Kennedy and Kane are behind me. Zaire, however, is nowhere to be found.

"No, I mean anyone *else*. Were you followed?" Her head peaks like a meerkat. Waiting, watching. She knows.

"Should they have?"

"Yes . . ." She lets go of the dusty curtain. Between the cardboard and the long-since mildewed windowpanes, hardly any light remains. "And no."

The familiar picnic tables have been shoved aside, leaving a large opening in the dayroom's center. Smack dab on the Oriental rug, a massive pile of metal canisters sits like a mountain of pickup sticks. A terrible idea for containers labeled explosive.

"Dagny . . ." Dr. Kennedy inches into the room, lowering the gun. "We came to get you out."

A delirious laugh erupts from the bird-like woman. "Rescue

me? You guys just *killed* yourselves!"

Amy's trusty shotgun rears its ugly head, not willing to take any chances. "It's okay. We only want to help."

I wave Amy to put the shotgun away, something she's grossly opposed to. We're one domino from Doomsday, and for her, dropping her only protection doesn't seem like the best self-preservation tactic.

The doctor takes a second to connect the dots, lowering the gun lowers begrudgingly. I've got to give her props on how well she's holding it together. Being hunted by Hell isn't the highlight of anyone's holiday season. Neither is being trapped in Purgatory.

I know why I'm here. I just don't know about the others.

But I'm certain I soon will.

BETRAYALS

A SECOND PASSES BEFORE I realize what's happening since not every vapor has a scent. Some chemicals, like the one Dagny has staged around the former dayroom, are nearly undetectable. If it weren't for the faint hissing sound coming from a handful of canisters, we might not have had the five-second start.

It's nowhere near enough.

"Take this. Tell no one," she says quietly as she shoves something into my hand.

"What?" I look down.

It's an ancient ankh necklace, tarnished and pocked with age. It's heavier than it should be. Cold. There's something about it. Something . . . *alive.*

The ankh's electrum no longer gleams. At its heart, an embedded lapis lazuli pulses with an Eye of Horus, encircled by columns of hieroglyphics. Its deep, protective sable hue a stark contrast to the vibrant blue of the gems.

"What is this?" I ask.

"There's no time." She pulls a handkerchief out of her dress pocket. "Just keep it safe."

At first, I don't notice how dark the fabric is. How stained. Unlike the gas seeping out of the canisters, this one does have a scent. *Butane.*

Running is futile; Zaire's already face-to-face with Dagny.

"Zaire?" she hisses. "Get out of here."

He slips past me. "I'm taking you home."

"*No one leaves.*" She pulls an old fire striker from the serving table and checks to make sure it still works. To her relief, it does.

"Whatever you think you've gotta do, you don't," I try to reason.

Nobody moves; nobody breathes.

Dagny has rigged this entire facility into a ticking time bomb, and the others are just standing around like we've got options.

"You're wrong." She grabs another canister and drags it into position. Snatching a hammer from the same table, she busts the valves off the canister. One after the other.

The hissing becomes deafening.

"Dagny, don't do this." Zaire's face is littered with sweat and tears. "You're going to kill everyone."

"Zaire, just stop. No more games." She ignores him and moves the last canister into place.

Zaire rushes at her but is caught by Kane. "She's not ready . . ."

He shakes off the other man's grip. "Dagny, it's me. It's Zai," he pleads, moving closer to the stringy blonde in a dirty sundress. He searches her face for any sign of emotion but comes away with nothing.

"We can't drag her out." Kane tries to take Zaire with him. "This has to be her decision. Nobody else's. You know how this works."

"I don't care," Zaire argues. "We will if we have to."

"Zaire," Kane hisses.

"She doesn't even know what's happened."

"Liar," Dagny's voice cracks in the stale air. "You wouldn't know the truth if it bit you on the ass."

"Dagny, please . . ." Zaire reaches for her again, but she shrinks back toward the suffocating gas. "This place isn't safe."

Her icy gaze deadpans on me. "He's lying. He knows exactly what this place is—he built it." She kneels next to the pile. It takes a few tries to wedge the mottled cloth into one of the broken nozzles; she's shaking too bad.

I make it about six inches before the striker stops me cold. "Dagny, do you remember me?" I say hesitantly. One wrong move and it's over. "Please put the striker down. You could kill everyone in this room."

"No, not everyone," she laughs. "Just *him*."

"Kane, do something. She's delusional," Zaire warns.

"I'm. Not. Crazy."

We freeze as she drags the striker across the surface.

Nothing.

I breathe a sigh of relief.

She tries again.

"Christ, no!" Zaire lunges again, but it's too late.

The dry-rotted cloth ignites like dust in the wind. The hissing finally grows quiet. No amount of running can save us from the explosion that catapults us into the decaying walls. Any available oxygen gets sucked out of the room, forcing us to the ground.

Everything hurts.

I struggle to see—to breathe. My lungs rattle and burn. What little light there was is now gone, save for the golden embers of broken wood and charred curtains. Flames stretch in all directions.

☥

A thick wetness coats my right eye. My fingers instinctively shoot upward and come away with blood. "Kane?" I rasp as I drag myself across the tile.

Smoke fills the dayroom, making it nearly impossible to spot the entrance. A male voice grunts as the sound of metal scrapes against the linoleum. "Jesly, are you okay?"

"Yeah . . . Where are you?"

"Here. I'm here . . ." he calls out, loosening the vise in my chest just a little.

I can't lose anyone else. *Not this way.* Not on my watch. His voice disappears, the sound getting sucked into the crackling flames.

Fire has consumed the walls, chewing the facility's construction down to the concrete slabs. The dayroom's massive pillars have been reduced to violent stakes, exposing the angry sky above us. It's just rubble now.

Another explosion ricochets around us, shaking the crumbling foundation I'm crawling over. *Goddamnit, Dagny.*

My lungs rattle as I fight to clear the soot. "Dagny?" I drag myself to a sitting position, my clothes now covered in ash. "Anyone?"

"Over here!" Kane calls out amidst more scraping and rustling. "She's trapped."

My movements feel like I'm dragging concrete. Each breath is labored, and the smoldering clouds above our heads aren't lessening with the crackle of flame. The room spins again as I wipe my forehead on my shoulder. Getting the damned blood out of my eyes doesn't work. All it does is create a painful mess in my hairline.

I can barely focus. When I do, Kane has wrapped a steel bar in cloth to use as a wedge. One of the walls collapsed on Dagny, leaving her unconscious.

☥

Zaire shoves me out of the way. "Move."

Kane waits for him to grab ahold of Dagny's shoulders. "I'm going to lift this bar. Zaire, I need you to pull her out."

Her husband-to-be nods. The two men work steadily, and soon Dagny is free, her breath shallow. Her body limp, she shows no signs of waking.

"Where's Dr. Kennedy?" I search through the haze. Dr. Kennedy's nowhere to be found. It's not long before I stumble over one of the canister remnants. The scent of seared flesh is all-consuming.

"Goddamnit, Zaire," I say. "Why didn't you stop her?"

"Stop who?" Zaire asks between CPR breaths. "Look down, Jesly."

I do.

Maybe it's the head injury, but my brain fails to register the metal contraption coiled in my hand. It's not until I bring it close that I see it's the flint striker.

I drop it like a snake. "What the fuck?"

Kane swallows hard. "This was you, Jesly. You did this . . ."

My throat tightens. "What are you talking about? I was next to you the whole time."

He holds my gaze momentarily before looking away. "No, Jesly. You weren't."

My hands shake as I stare at the smoldering ashes. "This is a trick. A hallucination again. Where are my pills?"

I dig through my pockets, ignoring the bloody snot that chokes me. All I can find is the necklace Dagny gave me. *I can't breathe.* Racing toward the only entryway I can see in this burning hell, I pray it's the exit. I slip the pendant around my neck before I end up losing it.

☥

"Dagny, wake up," Zaire pleads from behind me.

Another groan erupts nearby.

It's Amy.

Kane tries to pull her to safety, but the pain slows her down. Eventually, she sits shakily in the lobby. Burns line both her cheeks and her jacket down to the skin. He brings her a disposable plastic water bottle scrounged from somewhere and opens it for her.

She downs the entire thing before asking, "Why did you do it, Jesly? What were you thinking?"

A sharp pain bites at my wrist. *Jesly . . .*

No . . . "I-I wasn't—"

"No shit you weren't," Amy snaps. "Do you have a death wish? You were supposed to save her, not kill her." For a person bound by the Hippocratic Oath, her anger is understandable. First Henry, now Dagny.

"I don't understand . . ."

"No?" she mocks, her tone cutting like a knife. "You had one job, but you attack the person you were sent to help. Were you born knowing how to destroy everything you touch, or is that something they taught you in law school?"

You're losing them . . .

My grip tightens around the necklace under my shirt. "I didn't know—" Pain shoots along my left arm again. I stifle a cry and clamp my mouth shut.

"You didn't know?" Zaire stands in the entryway between us, his hands drenched in blood. "My fiancée is dead because of you."

"It's some kind of trick. Kane, please tell them."

"I already did," he says. "You weren't listening. You're not yourself, Allbrook." He points to my left arm, where the design has begun to glow, a hard thing to miss even through the fabric.

Horrified, I stumble backward. "No."

No one leaves. Dagny was right.

My footsteps smack against the remnants of the linoleum as I escape into the great outdoors. Back to air and natural light.

Amy limps her way out of the smoldering building. Kane helps Zaire carry Dagny's body. Their boots scrape the gravel as Zaire struggles to make it to the grass before collapsing.

It's a trick. An illusion. Meant to drive me insane.

No trick . . . You see the damage you cause?

The moment Amy spots her patient, she futilely administers what help she can. I try to squeeze through, but it's no use.

"Just get back," Amy says, waving me away. "You cause enough problems."

"That's not true," I say. "I was right here."

Kane's jaw tightens. "Jesly, just stop."

"Kane . . ."

"The moment you saw Dagny, you went unhinged," he says with disappointment. "Just listen to Amy. We'll handle this."

Amy rips off the remnants of her jacket and stuffs it under Dagny's head, her body limp and unmoving.

"I've worked here for fifteen years—I know this place inside and out," she states. "You knew exactly what you were doing, where you were going . . . Tell us the truth. Was that your plan this whole time? To kill her?"

She doesn't give me time to answer. Instead, she rushes at me, fist clenched.

By the time I realize I've been hit, I'm on my knees, my hands thrust into the soil for support. If the first punch hurts, the second feels like a Mack truck plowing through my jaw. She's far stronger than she looks, something I don't have time to admire as we tumble to the ground.

Finish the job, Jesly. Three left.

Thrashing underneath her does no good. She pins me, her grip moving to my throat. "Amy . . ." I rasp. She's wholly focused on resolving the cause of her family's destruction.

And in her eyes, it's me.

Jackson's the only individual to have ever trapped me like this. While I was in therapy getting over my trauma, I should've been learning to fight. I've lived when so many other women have died in the same situation. I just didn't think I'd need it so soon. She straddles me, her hips trapping mine.

"Amy, stop," Kane yells, scrambling to get to us.

"You traitorous bitch," she growls. "What body count are you going for?"

Kane drags her off me. "Amy, stop. This won't solve anything. What's done is done."

"Fuck you," she snaps, shoving him too. Looking back at her patient on the ground, she storms toward the empty yard in search of something—*anything*—that can save the dying woman.

Or maybe kill me. I'm not sure which. Not anymore.

A quiet stillness falls over the grounds until only smoldering embers remain. Zaire doesn't look up from cleaning Dagny's body. He brushes aside strands of her bangs.

"I'm sorry," I offer foolishly.

"I warned you and you didn't listen," he says. "Now we have no way out. I was wrong to think you could help. All you've done is seal our fates."

He reaches into his jacket pocket and pulls out an ornate watch, more intricate than any I've ever seen. Its clock face stares back, its many dials all spinning in different directions. With

Dagny cradled in one arm and his fingers deftly twisting the dials with the other, he spins the gears backward.

Alarm floods Kane's face. "Zaire, what are you doing?"

"What I should have days ago."

A whooshing sound breaks the stillness, and I spin around to find the source. Across from us in the open courtyard, three towering figures stand dressed in black.

One has donned floor-length black robes, its face obscured by a plague mask popularized during Europe's Black Death. Its eyes are blocked by large obtuse goggles attached to an elongated bird-like beak. The second figure, wider set, shifts beneath a heavy set of red armor, its massive face blocked by an Oni mask. The third figure dresses similarly. But it's this figure that lurches my stomach; its close-fitted black suit and large skull for a mask are all that greet me.

"K-Kane?" My voice catches.

His body language shifts, ever my protector. "Meet The Chasa, the ones judging you."

"What?"

"Please don't do this," Kane pleads.

It doesn't work. Zaire staggers to his feet and gently carries Dagny over to the creatures. The large Oni in the center outstretches its fire-hydrant-sized arms and takes her from him.

"Get her home," Zaire directs, evoking a quick bow as the first figure disappears. Only two remain.

Kane realizes it first. "Where did you just send Dagny?"

Zaire doesn't turn around. "Doesn't concern you. Not anymore. I was mistaken, my friend. You can't come where I'm going."

The remaining creatures amble in our direction. Amy's missing too.

"Allbrook, get out of here," Kane warns.

"What? No."

"I'll hold them off as long as I can. Go."

"They're not here for her, you nit," Zaire chuckles slightly. "They're here for you."

Skullface and Birdbeak disappear and reappear next to us. Both grab Kane before I can blink. There's nothing I can do as he's ripped from me.

"Zaire, why are you doing this?" I lunge at the two figures. Pointless, granted they don't need to lift a finger to send me flying backward. "Did Hiribaldi put you up to this?"

"Sorry, Jesly. I thought you understood." He kneels beside me when I finally stop rolling in the dirt and gravel, his expression vacant. He leans in, his voice barely audible as he pins me down with his boot. "Hiribaldi works for *me*."

He drives the steel toe into my abdomen a few times, knocking the wind from me. I writhe on the ground as I'm forced to watch Skullface and Birdbeak subdue Kane.

Both of us overpowered again.

Another rush of wind erupts around me again. Time's moving again and I can finally breathe.

Kane and The Chasa are gone.

Zaire, however, remains, his hands buried in his leather jacket pockets. "Your boyfriend should've left well enough alone. Dagny is *mine*, and she's not going anywhere. Ever."

My face scrunches in confusion. "Boy? You mean Kane?"

He snorts. "Sure. Him too."

"Zaire, what have you done?"

"Nothing that wasn't meant to happen."

I choke back my ugly tears. "You were never helping us."

☥

He shakes his head. "No. And now, neither will anyone else. You see, Dagny has tried this dozens of times. When she tries to escape, I stop her. So thank you for saving me the trouble of finding her. This place can be a real maze when it feels like it. See you around, Jesly."

The last thing I see is Zaire's boot striking me in the face before everything goes dark.

YAMALOKA

EVEN WITH MY EYES closed, the world still spins like I'm stuck on a carnival's merry-go-round that won't let go. The sky is dark by the time I drag myself to a nearby rock. The yard's empty, the last of its fires nothing but smoldering embers now. My lungs still rattle. The smoke and ash have likely settled in for good, and there's a lingering weight I doubt I'll soon lose.

Layered in soot, I'm more akin to a nineteenth-century chimney sweep than a twenty-first-century lawyer. But there is no justice here; it abandoned me long ago. Zaire's nowhere to be found, Amy's gone, and Kane's missing.

I collapse against the rocky ground and stare into the sky, its fading essence obscured by drifting smoke trails. There is no moon peeking through the clouds. It's already waned, much like my life.

I can feel time running short somewhere deep in my bones. With the moon tucked away, all that's left is darkness. A new moon serves as a period for introspection. It's only fitting that it would find me alone and abandoned. *"Tell them I'm sorry,"* *Dagny said.* Did she mean Kane and Amy? Or someone else?

Sitting here won't help me figure it out. I've got to find her.

And Kane now. *"This was you, Jesly. You did this."*

Now he knows what Zaire really is, what he's capable of. Whatever the reason Kane agreed to work with him must have been something terrible. It was naïve to think that Kane wasn't looking out for my interests this whole time. I'm always so fucking scared of getting hurt that I put Kane at risk. Zaire's been playing us the whole time.

Maybe Amy was right. Maybe I am cursed.

Regardless, finding Dagny takes priority. I owe it to Kane to at least try. Perhaps in saving her, I'll save him along the way.

The same road that leads out of the facility stretches for miles. As the traffic moves along the freeway, motorists avoid the haggard figure hobbling along the shoulder.

Hours pass. No one stops.

The moon remains high in the night sky, hidden but there. Time, it seems, plays by its own rules here. And I don't know whether to be afraid or relieved. I settle for the latter.

Luna, the name I've called the moon since I was a kid, looms unnaturally large, beckoning any wayfarers lost in their travels.

I'm not lost. I know where I am.

I just don't know where I'm going.

Being dead does that.

Across the parking lot sits a rundown gas station. The kind that has snack packages sitting for months and drinking their coffee might mean gastroenteritis. A dilapidated overhead sign flickers and the gas pumps look like they haven't been used in a while. As the only store within several miles with the lights on, it's the hole-in-the-wall option.

This deep into winter, the temperature is non-existent. I cling to what warmth I can find amongst my burnt clothing and tattered appearance. The door chime rings as I slip into the much warmer space.

To my surprise, the store inside is far larger than expected. Brighter, too. Fresh fruits and vegetables in small teakwood baskets flood the aisles. Sandalwood agarbatti fills the air, and everything from nuts and fresh tea leaves to various shades of dyed fabrics lines the shelves. On the opposite wall, a large golden shrine adorned with marigold garlands stares back at me, the statue of a man with an elephant-head and rotund belly.

Behind the thick plastic divider at the counter, an elderly Indian man sits on a wooden stool. Our eyes lock, but he says nothing as he goes back to completing a transaction for a young group of guys.

The cacophony washes away as the door chimes again, leaving only the quiet buzzing of the slushie machines and hot dog rollers. A petite woman about the man's age wipes down the coffee counter, her beautiful braid dangling over her shoulder while she works.

I must look like absolute hell to these people because she freezes when she notices me. They exchange a look, and he nods, sending her scurrying down the aisle. Toward the rear of the store sits a lonely water fountain, its mouthpiece covered in a bluish-green corrosion that makes me second-guess my thirst.

"Here," a woman's voice says behind me.

She holds a Styrofoam cup in one hand and fresh clothing in the other. She shoves them into my chest without asking, and I nearly spill the orangey liquid in the cup she has brought from somewhere.

Too thirsty to refuse, I down the beverage in seconds. It's hot and pungent, its earthy taste both unfamiliar and sweet.

She smiles as I bring it to my lips again, her watchful gaze instructing me to drink it all. "Haldi doodh. It will heal whatever ails you."

I grimace at its strong flavor. "Thank you."

"Thank Asim, my husband. I'm Chandni." She cranes her neck around the drink coolers, pointing toward the door at the back. "There's a full-service bathroom over there."

"No, that's okay. I just need a minute."

She points at the black soot all over my body. "You need to wash that away. Quickly."

I know I look like death and smell worse, but trusting strangers hasn't gotten me very far. "You don't even know me. Why would you help?"

"The greatest name man ever gave to God is Truth," she says with conviction. "You are a seeker. Thus, you are a friend to Brahman, which means you are a friend to us. Get cleaned up. Then we speak." She takes the empty Styrofoam cup and steers me toward the bathroom.

She reaches inside and flicks on a switch, leaving me in the small washroom. Before I can protest any further, she pulls the door closed behind her. My heart leaps in my chest as I wait for a click trapping me inside, but there's nothing save for her flats clipping against the linoleum.

Alone *again*.

My grip loosens on the clothing, and I struggle to set it on the back of the toilet before it falls. My reflection stares back at me in the old mirror, its glass chipped and broken in some places, much like me. My dark, wavy curls are matted to my scalp, glued in place with blood and ash. A half-coagulated wound sits over my right temple. My chin looks like its new hobby is being a punching bag.

She's right. A shower couldn't hurt.

The flowy olive-green blouse, simple drawstring pants, and a canvas messenger bag are more than I could've ever imagined. Across from the sink sits a stand-up shower with a curtain browned from years of hard water. I turn on the faucet. Air struggles to leave the pipes, causing me to nearly jump out of my skin.

Laughter erupts from my throat. I crank the hot water faucet and wait for it to produce warmth. This far into January, it takes the old copper pipes a few minutes to heat.

While I wait, I wash the grime off my face and neck before contemplating the shower. The doorknob has a simple twist lock. Nothing fancy. Getting murdered like in *Psycho* isn't my idea of a valiant death, but I can't feel this disgusting any longer. A shower it is. My fingers wrench the lock, and I collapse against the wooden door.

I spent so long dancing around Jackson, tiptoeing to avoid getting trapped in his spiderweb that my body doesn't know how to come down anymore. My oldest friend, hypervigilance, won't break it off with me. It's rewired my brain, my body—everything. I'm a skittish little squirrel who jumps at her own shadow.

Too bad the monsters under my bed are real.

I shut off the faucet and scour every square inch, down to the faded tile and ceiling panels. While there are thankfully no cameras lurking, there are no weapons either. Just a lonely soap dispenser and electric hand dryer. A trash can. A plain, boring bathroom.

I don't know whether to be disappointed or relieved. Vulnerability sucks.

It takes a minute to peel off these clothes I've been wearing for God knows how long. Weeks now? I guess the good part of dying is you no longer have to worry about tampons. No more periods. That's a win in my book.

Inside the upright shower looms all the basic toiletries, like a makeshift hotel. I step back out, taking care not to splash water on the stone floor while I search the small cabinet for a washcloth. Nestled behind the little, wooden blue door is a pile of folded rags. This must not be the first time they've hosted a stranger. Or as Chandni had called me—a Seeker—whatever that means.

I spend what feels like forever in the shower, letting the water scald my back. It stings my forehead but I don't care. A stranger in a strange place doesn't stop me from collapsing as the adrenaline finally drains from my body. The shower pours like rain, and I block out everything I can.

But that only works on the outside. There is no running from my nightmares.

Jackson, you piece of shit.

Steer-correcting after a lifetime of misery doesn't excuse what he's done. It's his fault we're in this mess in the first place. I'm such a fool. Karma, it seems, has come for the both of us.

I should've never gotten behind the wheel. One innocuous decision has rippled out in more ways than I could have ever expected. Only to find that my attempt at escaping the one man who tortured my existence failed. He has damned me in the Afterlife too.

That bastard. Even in death.

I wish Ammit would vomit him back up so she could eat him again. Narcissistic psychopaths never learn; they only use and soak up the life-force of others, draining us until they disregard us like a desiccated corpse.

I gave up on my career, my own goddamn life, and all I got

was a stupid T-shirt, as they say. I should've never driven the car that night. Never taken the keys. It was my mistake. I tried to protect him and our company. Our legacy.

But I didn't mean to you what you meant to me. That didn't matter. You were my religion, my faith. Now you're dead, and I'm left to clean up your mess.

As usual.

The moment I feel myself dozing off, I cut the water. Surveying the damage is quicker now that I'm no longer covered in filth and ash. Other than my head, jaw, and the faint bruising renewed by Zaire, I'm mostly intact. Assuming I ignore the otherworldly design encircling my wrist. I pull on the clothes and wring out my mop of curls in the sink.

Wiping the condensation from the mirror, I sop up what water I've splashed onto the green tile. I fumble out of the bathroom, dirty clothes in hand.

Chandni glances up from restocking the soda cooler. "The river cleanses all things," she says, reaching for my clothes.

When I don't budge, she leads me over to the checkout area. Snatching a plastic bag from behind the register, she holds it out for me to drop my clothes into. I do. She marches over to a large metal basin filled with burning embers and dumps the bag out. Within seconds, my clothes are ash. Chandni grabs a small jar and sprinkles oil over the flames before tossing a handful of pungent herbs and dried flowers onto the pile.

"What are you doing?" I ask.

"Warding you hopefully," Asim, the man behind the counter, explains for her.

"Warding?"

"You're not a local, are you?"

"Is it that obvious?" I say.

Chandni nods. "Oh, yes, *beti*."

"I don't really know how I got here. Wherever here is," I admit, rubbing my forehead.

"That's what the other young man said when he came through, too."

"I'm not the first?"

They both shake their heads. "But you're not like him," she assures me. "That one—he is beyond the Veil. Even Maya cannot help him now."

I nod politely and scratch my forearm. The *thing* is itching the shit out of me.

She's quickly snatches my arm. "You've been marked?"

I step back defensively, removing my wrist as I do. "If that's what you call it."

Her attention turns to the outside where it's started drizzling. The wind has picked up outside, kicking around loose items in the parking lot. The storm must be settling in for good.

Realizing this, Chandni moves behind the register near her husband and whispers something under her breath. She removes the lid of a slow cooker, fishes something out with a slotted spoon, and hastily wraps it in a cloth napkin.

"Here." She swings around the counter and thrusts the package at me. "Take this."

"What is it?"

This time, Asim answers. "*Piṇḍas*, beti. You will need them where you're headed."

"And that is?" I fidget with the ankh around my neck.

"Yamaloka." The wife points at my necklace. "Lord Yama's House."

☥

"This?" I lift my gold chain, letting the ankh swing. "It's just something I'm holding onto for somebody."

"Well, however you came into it, that amulet is a very powerful gift. The Ferryman doesn't answer to just anyone."

"You seem to know a lot about this stuff."

Asim closes the blinds behind him. "In this place, you must. Whoever gave such a gift must be very important to Lord Vishnu himself. With it, you could probably walk into Lord Yama's Hall itself."

The food resting in my palm feels heavier than his words. I try to peek, but Chandni stops me. "Wait until you leave here to eat the first one."

"Why?"

"Because their protection doesn't last forever."

The door rattles against its frame, forcing wind to whistle through the gap. Off in the distance, impossibly, a wolf or coyote howls. I chalk it up to my imagination until concern crosses both their faces; they heard it too.

"Does anyone know you're here?" Asim asks, worry faint in the corner of his eyes. "Anyone who can help you?"

"I don't think so."

"What about the person who gave you that gift?" Asim asks, pointing to Dagny's necklace. "Would they?"

I shake my head. "No, they're gone."

"Anyone you can trust?" His eyes dart around the store.

"Maybe?"

"Can you reach them?" he presses, his voice sounding more urgent.

"I can try. Is there a phone around?"

"Surely, beti," Chandni answers as the lights hum and flicker slightly. "Asim, get her the cordless."

The store owner nods and reaches for the overhead bin where they store the overstock. Retrieving the phone from its cradle, he slips it through the plastic opening. "Take it. There's a breakroom near the bathroom where you can speak undisturbed."

As I head in that direction, I start mashing buttons. Here goes nothing. *Ring . . . Ring . . .*

I inhale sharply and start preparing a backup plan.

Chandni heads to the front door, twists the lock, and flips the sign to **CLOSED**. "Be careful. There are many Asuras looking for you."

"Asuras?"

Ring.

"Vengeful spirits. Don't trust them," she says matter-of-factly. "Go around back. There's an exit that way. May Ganapati bless you."

Ring— "Hello?" A familiar voice cuts our conversation short.

"Dax?" I ask, unable to hide the relief in my voice when the line connects.

"Jesly?" He sounds far away. "Is that you?"

"Sorry to bother you . . ." I say, "I didn't know who else to call."

His smile is audible. "That's no problem. I'm just glad to know you're okay."

"Yeah," I chuff. "Me too."

"Man, I thought I'd never hear from you again," he tells me. "Thought you didn't take charity cases."

I rattle the first doorknob I come across. *Locked.* "I, uh, I've been busy."

The piercing sound of a car horn blasts through the earpiece.

He must be driving. "That's okay. How's that book I gave you?"

"I lost it," I admit, my voice wavering. "I'm sorry."

"Hey, don't worry about it," he says softly. "Why don't you tell me where you are, and I'll come get you? We can talk then."

The storm has gotten worse. It sounds like hail plummeting down. That same howling sound echoes again, this time louder. Closer. We're not imagining it. Not all three of us.

The lights flicker again. Outside the storeroom, Asim hollers something to Chandni.

"Dax? Are you still there?"

"—eah . . ." his voice cuts out. ". . . ve a bad connect . . . Where—"

The whirring of the refrigerated machines rolls to a stop as the power goes out, plunging us into complete darkness.

"It's okay," Asim hollers from the store lobby. "I'll check the generator. Beti, don't open the door for any reason."

The line hangs dead in my ear. *Now what?*

I end the call and set the handset down on the cart table nearby. Dropping into an old folding chair, I listen to the relentless assault on the roof. Between the sudden hail barreling down and the howling wind outside, I can barely hear Asim yelling at Chandni to grab their axe.

Eventually, everything falls quiet. I can no longer hear the store's patrons. The emergency exit sign flickers, a glaring beacon in the darkness. The hum of the drink coolers hasn't kicked back on. With the electricity still out, the inside temperature has plummeted rapidly. An oversized brown wool cardigan hangs over the back of the chair. I snatch it and slip my arms into it.

I shove my feet back into my running shoes. I need to get out of here and find Kane and Dagny somehow. My eyes stay glued to the sign above the exit. In the space between us, there's nothing save for the chill creeping along the linoleum.

Before I can reach for the door handle, the sign flickers again. I freeze. The metal door handle rattles. It's locked.

A muffled voice yells from outside. Asim said not to open it. What if he's right and Asuras wait outside? *Can they even open doors?*

Bang, bang, bang! Something pounds on the door.

Like a dumbass, I twist the knob and open the door. My body collides with a taller figure. One much younger than Asim. It takes a second to recognize the narrow, oval face and deep sable hair. "Dax?"

"Jesly? What the hell?" He rushes into the room, slamming the door shut behind him. He's soaking wet.

"How did you even find me?"

He looks around, bewildered. "You know? I'm not sure. One second I was talking with you, the next my truck was sitting in the parking lot." Donning his paramedic uniform, he seems visibly shaken and out of breath.

I slip the ankh pendant under my shirt. If Wonka's got one golden ticket outta Purgatory, I'd rather it stay on a need-to-know basis. If Dax is here, then he's trapped like the rest of us.

"Did you see anyone outside?" I ask. "An older man, perhaps?"

"What? No." He glances around. "You called me from here?"

"Yeah. Why?"

"The phones work?"

"They do." I scoop up the napkin of piṇḍas.

He scours the area behind me. "Jesly, nobody's been here for years. This place's a ghost town."

"What?"

He points behind me. The cramped storeroom is dusty and reeks of mold. Dry-rotted cushions molt off the chairs. Expired goods line the rusty metal shelves. All the brightness has been stripped away; the colorful goods faded from years of abandonment.

"That's impossible." I bolt to the table and grab the plastic handset; it's long since covered in dust and a thick, black grime. "I don't understand."

He pulls his keys from his jeans pocket and eyes the exit. "We should get outta here. I don't like this place."

I run my hands over my clothes. They're still the muslin ones Chandni gave me. So I didn't imagine it.

I untie the napkin to see what lingers inside. These things— these *pinḍas*—are little rice-balls, their scent rich like sesame and honey.

"What *is* that?"

"Just some food," I tell him.

Raising them to my nostrils, I can almost smell the dedication that went into creating these. Chandni advised they would protect me but only for so long. Five sit on the napkin. Without another viable choice, I pop the first one in my mouth. The ball of mush is hard to swallow and seems reluctant to go down.

Dax grimaces just watching. "Throw those out. We can find you something better."

"It's alright." I wrap the cloth napkin back around the remaining ones and stuff them into my sweater pocket. The perks of an oversized cardigan.

He grimaces. "It looks awful. Like something the dead would eat."

I laugh at the irony.

He studies me carefully before dragging the door open. The

cold rushes in and I pull my oversized sweater tighter. "I was gonna grab lunch and head over to visit my sister's grave. Say you'll come. I don't want to go alone."

"Dax, I'm not sure . . ."

"I'll pay." he adds. "Anyway, I can't leave you here in good conscience. Plus, it's only an hour before I get off."

Uneasiness tugs as I stare at the deserted store. "You sure?"

He smiles. "Yeah, come on. My boss won't mind if I take off a little early. They're just happy to have me back."

"Okay," I finally concede, his grin widening even more now. "But you're buying."

"Deal." He extends his arm. "Come, milady. Your chariot awaits."

THE ROD OF ASCLEPIUS

DAX'S CHARIOT, IT SEEMS, is a large white truck adorned with The Star of Life and the Rod of Asclepius. The word **AMBULANCE** is scrawled across the side in a huge blue letters. His ride purrs quietly in the parking lot beneath one of the gas pump awnings. He grins ear to ear when he spies his beauty.

"They cleared you for service?" I ask.

"Sure did." He mashes a button on his key fob and drags open his door. "Hop in."

The headlights cut on as he pulls us out of the lot. With the store's electricity long gone, the only remaining light is that of Luna tucked behind the blackened sky. Naively, I expect more stars out this far into the dead of winter, but then I remember where we are. It's an illusion. All of it. The firmament is nothing more than for shits and giggles.

Our route ahead is quiet and stays that way for a good thirty minutes, a difficult thing to judge when his clock is stuck at 11:11. He's so focused on the road that he hasn't noticed it's probably closer to 5 a.m. I shift in the leather seat; getting comfortable is a surprisingly arduous task given the spacious cab.

Dax taps the radio on the dashboard. Only static comes out. He pounds on the front dash panel and changes the channel. Still nothing. *So he's involved in this too. That makes four of us and I'm guessing there's more.*

"Maybe the AM works?" I offer.

A few stations later, the results are no different. Frustrated, he gives up. I don't say anything.

Dax notices my awkward attempt to get comfortable. "There's a pillow on the floorboard if you'd like." He nods behind my seat. "Help yourself."

"You sleep in here often?"

"Only when I need to. Happens more than you'd expect." With his free hand, he digs into his jacket pocket and pulls out an orange medicine bottle with a faded label, methodically steering with his knee while he twists the cap open.

"Happy to be back?" I ask cautiously.

"Sure am." He dumps a few round white pills into his mouth. "Try to get some rest. It'll be a few."

My hands rummage around the plastic floorboard and come away with a larger object than expected: a cardboard box stuffed to the brim with random odds and ends. Underneath the pillow lies a photograph featuring a younger Dagny locked in a friendly embrace with a man who I assume to be Dax as they smile for the camera. It's difficult to tell given the man's unkempt appearance and drastically lower body weight.

But it's not the blonde woman's haunted gaze that strikes me; it's the scratched-out face of the man. The printed paper violently torn, whatever made the scratches dug into the photo until I can see through to the other side.

"Find it?" Dax's voice startles me.

"Yeah. It fell under the seat," I lie and squirrel the photograph back in the box. Whoever clawed out his face, the fact remains; none of us have come out unscathed. Then my turn came.

The open fields roll by, one after another, until my exhaustion finally catches up with me, leaving me alone with my nightmares. As long as I can remember, it's been the one place I can't escape from.

Even now.

For some people, nightmares are their worst fears exemplified. For others like me, they're memories that haunt us forever.

"JACKSON, GIVE ME THE KEYS." I clutch my peacoat tighter. It's freezing outside, but he wants to argue. Like usual. "You've had way too much."

"F-fuck off, Jesss . . ." he slurs, ignoring my pleas. The rest of the dinner party has already left; it's only us now. "Stay here then. Better yet, call that pussy-eating aide of yours for a ride home."

Panic floods my veins. "What are you talking about?"

"Your Starbucks last week?"

"You're going through my receipts?" I ask in disbelief. "I bought the kid a coffee and a muffin for fixing our Lexmark and brought it back to the office like I always do."

He stumbles off the curb and digs his cigarette case out of his windbreaker. I saw you two in the copyroom downstairs.

My eyes go wide. He's delusional. "He fixed our printer."

"Yeah, I bet he fixed a bunch of stuff . . . really shined the knobs while he was at it, didn't he?" he says between drags.

"You're such an asshole," I say, half-nauseated at the thought of him leaving me downtown, but I can't let him get behind the wheel. He'll kill us or

someone else.

He grunts. "Maybe."

"You don't believe me?"

"Should I?" He takes a few more puffs before flicking the cigarette onto the asphalt. "You don't seem very invested in this partnership."

"Are you fucking insane? This is my company." I chase him around to the driver's door. He's absolutely lost it.

"Yeah, and it wouldn't be shit without me. You wouldn't be shit." He tugs on the lock, but it doesn't respond. Lunging at the car, he slams the heel of his loafer into the door, hard enough to leave a mark. To my horror, it unlocks this time.

"Jackson, you've had nearly fifteen drinks." I wedge myself between him and my Audi. "You're drunk. Get into the passenger seat. I'll drive us home."

The moment I try to wrangle the keys from his haphazard grip, his gaze turns icy. He rips open the driver's door, snatching me by my lapel with his free hand. "Get in the fucking car before I leave you here. Law sluts are a dime a dozen."

I shriek as he shoves me violently over the center console, banging my knee along the way. "Jackson, stop. You're hurting me!" My head slams into the window hard enough that it makes me pause, my vision blurring.

It's too late.

Jackson's already hit the start button on the dash and peeled out of the parking spot. In a fifteen-mph zone, he's working on sixty. The locks click, trapping us in this moment. The needle on the speedometer creeps ever higher, regardless of traffic and lights. My hands shake as I reach for the seatbelt and click it into place.

"Jackson, please stop," I beg between tears. "You're going to kill us."

"I know, Jesly. That's the point."

I close my eyes. All I can do is pray to whatever God has forsaken me. HONNNNNNNNKKKKKKKKKKKKKKKKKK!!!!!!!!!!!!!!!!

AN ANGRY CAR HORN jars me awake, jolting me upright in my seat. Dax holds a protective hand out before I slam into the windshield. "Easy, easy. It's just some jerk who thinks they own the road. You okay?"

I flip my messy hair out of my face. We're still in the ambulance. I collapse back against the seat, relieved. "Just a bad dream."

His eyes widen. "I'll say . . . Seemed more like a nightmare."

"I'm fine."

"Whatever you say," he says as the ambulance crawls off the main road into a parking lot. He fights to find an open spot but eventually shoves the truck in Park. "Ready for some tasties?"

I nod, still shaken.

The weather has gone from bad to worse, and I wouldn't be surprised if it actually snowed. Given the fact that I no longer how what's real and what's not, I'd say it's entirely possible for Dallas to end up blanketed in snow. If Purgatory doesn't have to play by the rules, maybe neither do I.

Dax nearly skips out of the truck. "This place has the best biscuits n' gravy around."

The white and red sign beams at me as I step out of the vehicle into a familiar gravel parking lot. The Original Market diner. *We're back.*

Kane. My back stiffens.

Dax notes my hesitation. "Is this alright? You didn't ask to pick."

I'm going to kill Zaire, and if Hiribaldi is still alive, him too while I'm at it. One way or another. *Somehow.*

"Of course." Feigning a smile, I say, "It's great. I was lost in my thoughts."

"I take it that's a usual thing with you?"

"Pretty much."

He nods toward the front door. "Let's get some proper food in you before you eat any more of those weird creepy balls."

I let him walk ahead. Someone's got to watch his back. What he doesn't realize is that these piṇḍas may be what's keeping me six-feet-up. I've got four more and Chandni didn't say how long they last.

The hostess glances up as we enter and seats us at a booth, eyeing my disheveled appearance. I look like I've gone six rounds in a boxing ring, but she smiles and does her job.

It's cozy near the window, so keeping an eye on the truck won't be difficult. We're the only ones in the lot at this hour.

"Morning. What can I get you two started on?" She clutches her writing pad, having already handed over the menus.

"I'll take an orange juice and a black coffee," he answers. "Jesly?"

"Just a coffee, please." I don't even act like the staff doesn't remember me.

"Absolutely," she says politely. "You guys ready to order?"

Dax smacks his stomach. "Sure am. I'll take the Ol' Number 7."

I clear my throat. "A veggie omelet and a side of toast." My hand, cut and extremely bruised, nudges the menu back at the waitress.

"Sure thing." She takes the padfolios. "It'll be out shortly."

The piṇḍas feel like rocks on my side, but I pull them closer for protection anyway. Finding out what happens if they get lost doesn't feel like the best way to spend my morning. I choose idle chatter.

"Did you learn anything more about what your sister was

messing with?"

"Maybe," he says, pursing his lips. "It's a lot more than I was expecting. I'll tell you that."

"You still think I can help?"

The corner of his mouth twitches. "Oh, definitely. Wouldn't trust it to anyone else." The waitress delivers our drinks, and he pulls the straw tab off his orange juice. "These past few weeks have really kept me busy. Work's been brutal."

"And you're happy about that?"

He nods his head emphatically. "It's been good working again. It's nice to feel like I have a purpose. You know, making a difference. But enough about me. How've you been?"

I swallow hard. "The stuff I've seen you wouldn't believe."

He snorts in his drink. "Oh, I doubt it. I've got a pretty good imagination."

"Something terrible happened. People died."

"I'm sorry," he says politely.

"I feel so responsible."

"Are you?" he asks, his serious tone catching me off guard.

My face falls.

"Kidding," he laughs, his features softening. "Do you have some kind of God-complex, Jesly?"

"What?"

"I know you're a lawyer and all, but you're not responsible for all of humanity."

No, just some.

Dax searches my face but comes away with nothing. "Ever hear of the Trolley Problem?"

"Vaguely."

His straw scrounges for the last drop of liquid. "You're driving a trolley cart when the brakes suddenly fail. Up ahead, there is a fork. To the left, you find your loved one strapped to the tracks—"

I nearly choke. "I'm sorry?"

"It's philosophical," he says. "To the right, the person who will cure cancer forever. You can't stop the train. Whichever side you choose, someone will surely die. What do you do?"

"*Neither*," I scoff. "I choose neither."

He snorts into his cup. "Sometimes there are no good choices, Jesly. Only bad ones."

I tighten the cardigan around me. "What would you do?"

"Me?" he scoffs. "I'd kill anyone if that meant saving those I love. Even now."

Silence falls over the table. Thankfully, something I don't have to worry about because our food comes out a short time later. I don't have much of an appetite, so I push it around my plate and down the coffee.

Dax notices but says nothing. After my third cup, he reaches across the table and stops my aimless spoon spinning with his hand. "You wanna tell me what happened? You look like death."

"It's a long story."

"That's why we're here," he says, waving his fork and knife. He takes another bite of his biscuits and sausage gravy.

Jackson used to like it too. *Goddamnit.* He's an ever-present poison lingering in my veins. Like cancer eroding me from the inside. Even now, the bastard's haunting me from Hell.

I hate being vulnerable, but I'm gonna need all the allies I can get. "They committed me, Dax, after you left," I begin. "Told me I was crazy—that Jackson was dead. But he wasn't—I ended up killing him myself."

He sets the fork down, mid-bite. "Jesus, Jesly."

☥

I hold my hand up. "Then they kidnapped me, killed one of the doctors from the facility, and held us captive. I'm lucky to have escaped." I leave out the part about the giant mythological beast eating dead people.

"By yourself?" he asks incredulously.

"No, no," I say. "I had some help."

He licks his lips, his voice low. "And where is this help?"

"Gone. One ran off and two got kidnapped by someone who betrayed us. He may or may not have been working with my kidnapper the whole time."

"I'm sorry, Jesly."

"Me too." I exhale and stare out the window again. It's started to snow. "That's why I called you. I needed someone I could trust."

Dax shifts back into the booth and finishes another bite. "Can't you just talk to the police? File a report?"

I shake my head. "That's not how this works."

"Isn't working with the police like your job?"

"Dax, I can't explain everything right now," I say, leaving out the details that his sister's still alive or maybe dead. Or that we all are. *Shit.* "Some details I'm still working out. From what I understand so far, it revolves around this one girl; I think she's in danger."

The lights flicker. He doesn't notice.

"Exactly why you need to go to the police, FBI, or whoever's in charge of that stuff."

"I can't," I say.

He leans in, whispering, "Listen, Jesly, I'm not going to lie. You sound kind of crazy."

"You don't think I know that?"

"You've experienced something terrible. You really need to talk to someone more qualified than me."

☥

"Dax, please. All I need is a car ride into DFW," I explain. "Can you help me or not?"

He sits back, absorbing it all. "This person who ran off? Where are they?"

"I don't know." I shrug. "She's a doctor from the inpatient hospital they shoved me in. Some complications happened and she took off."

"Complications?"

"A misunderstanding."

"Can't you call or text them?" he asks as the waitress brings the check.

"No." I finish my coffee and set the cup back on the saucer. "I don't think Dr. Kennedy wants to hear from me right now."

"Dr. *Amy* Kennedy?" he asks, surprised. "From Calgary? Quippy attitude? Really pretty? Knows her shit?"

"You've seen her?"

He nods slowly. "Sure. She's one of our ER doctors at DFW."

"You're positive?" I lunge forward. *What in the hell is she doing there?*

He looks askance, setting his credit card on the small tray. "Yeah . . . Came in yesterday. Right after I clocked in."

"Can we go?"

His brow wrinkles as he weighs the situation. "I guess. It's Tuesday. She should be working."

"Great." I nearly fly out of my seat.

He latches onto my wrist, stopping me cold. "Just gotta visit my sister's grave first," he reminds me. "Something you might want to see."

☥

WHAT DREAMS MAY COME

THE SUN HAS PEEKED over the horizon by the time we reach the cemetery. Traditional setup. Large wrought-iron gates. Ornate statues everywhere that families pay years of their salary for.

When I was little, my parents taught me it was disrespectful to step on someone's grave, so I'd say 'excuse me' and tiptoe around them in the grass. I didn't want to wake the dead. When we'd pass by car, I'd hold my breath until we'd driven past. Even at twenty-seven, I still do my best to avoid stepping onto their territory.

People foolishly think cemeteries are just places where the living mourn the dead. They are so much more. Cemeteries are the one spot where the dead can let go of the living and finally move on.

The flurries have picked up strength and blanketed the ground in fresh snow. A shock by normal Texan standards, but I'm not surprised. Not anymore. With the air as nippy as it is, I've thrown on one of Dax's spare paramedic jackets. This early, no one's here. Not even the gravediggers. We've got the place to ourselves.

The gates are always unlocked here. Perhaps the owners know something I don't. Maybe the dead getting up and leaving is exactly what they want.

We're not even through the first section when I spot a row of freshly dug graves, their lush, rich soil slowly being covered with bitter little snowflakes. Each one has a blank headstone, simple and indistinguishable from the rest of the cemetery's markers. The gravedigger must have called it quits early, probably when the ground started to freeze. Their shovel sits propped against the large building we're headed toward.

Curiosity gets the better of me, and I lift the shovel from the stone wall before setting it back. "Do they always leave graves wide open?"

Dax shrugs. "Sometimes. Come on."

He waves me around the side of the ornate mausoleum. The name *SHEPHERD* adorns the lichen-stained archway, right beneath an Egyptian ankh carved into the stone. A bronze sconce sits on either side of the large stone doorway, each one holding a half-limp bouquet of gladioli and chrysanthemums. Dax pulls them down and replaces the flowers with fresh ones from the truck.

"This place yours?" I ask incredulously. Mausoleums aren't cheap.

He nods. "My family's."

I stare at the entryway. "I thought your last name was Huxley."

"It is," he says. "My foster parents adopted me on my eighth birthday."

"I didn't know that," I say awkwardly.

"It's not common knowledge." He steps through the threshold and heads down a few stairs. "Sometimes I think if I'd never been around, Dagny would still be here."

"Dax . . ."

"No, it's okay," he concedes. "She spent more time fighting

my demons than her own."

We head deeper into the facility. It's ornate and well-maintained, save for the outside. Inside, the crypts are smooth with names lining the granite rows. At least ten generations must live here. My reflection shines back at me from the rich marble floor, distracting me from the sun peeking through the stained-glass window looming at the back.

"I thought we buried your sister."

"We did," he agrees. "But my parents wanted her body moved to the mausoleum. They made the poor old man dig her up before the ground hardened."

"Jesus . . ."

I follow him, slowly and carefully. Like if I step on the wrong thing, this place will collapse on us. I wonder how frequently he visits but don't want to ask.

I change the topic. "Was that an Egyptian ankh on the doorway outside?"

He's hunched over at a specific square on the wall, resting his hands on either side of it. "Yeah, my whole family is into that kind of stuff. Weird occult shit."

In the far corner, there's a large stone bench where guests can sit and pay their respects. "What did your sister do before she passed?" My gaze locks on the name etched in front of him. It's definitely hers.

"She was a professor of mythology and folklore at UT Dallas."

"Mythology?"

He nods, his whole chest shuddering. "Yeah . . . been into it ever since she was a kid."

"That's an interesting career choice."

"Kept her busy," he says noncommittally. "I remember when

she wrote her dissertation—all about Egypt and the Afterlife."

Of course it is. I clutch Dagny's pendant beneath my shirt. The woman knew what she was doing. I just hope I can figure it out before my time runs out. I pull my sleeve down around my wrist, taking care to make sure no part of the design is showing.

While he pays his respects, I stretch my legs. The mausoleum is simple in its construction—one way in, one way out. Dates from the last four centuries line its walls, with the earliest one I can find dating back to 1693. But it's not the polished granite or rows of the dead that get me; it's the quote overlooking the tombs that stops me in my tracks.

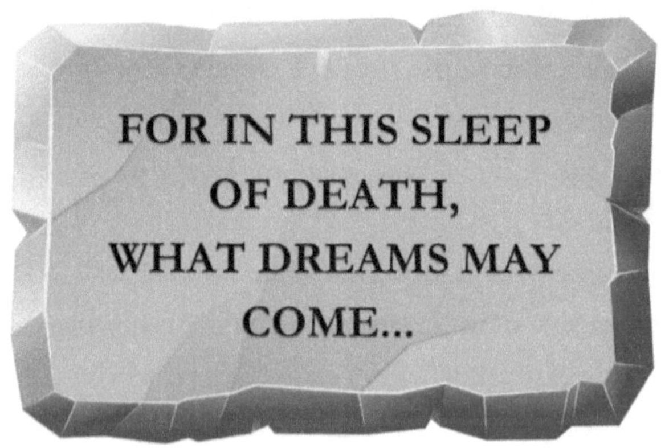

"What the—" Hiding my shock is futile; he heard me.

"Hamlet."

"Sorry?"

He points at it. "The quote. It's from *Hamlet*. You know . . . from Shakespeare?"

I nod. "Yeah, sure. High school. Why is it here, though?"

"My grandfather had it carved when Mimi passed. My sister took after her; she also loved Shakespeare," he tells me, pushing off the crypt wall. "We'd always argue at holiday dinners: who made the greatest contribution to humanity? I'd vote for Aristotle, and she'd fight me every time."

"I take it she was an avid reader," I say as we head out and he takes the lead.

"A voracious appetite," he confirms. "When she wasn't reading, she was balls-deep in research. Religion this, history that. It never stopped with her. If she didn't know it, no one did."

The sun smacks us right in the eyes, reminding me how late it already is. My pace picks up, and I let him think it's the biting chill. "Speaking of books, you said that the book you gave me was her favorite?"

He yanks open the truck door. "Yeah. She read it at least twenty times. Didn't go anywhere without it—was kinda weird."

I pull myself up into the cab. "Do you happen to know if she had another copy, maybe?"

He thinks about it while cranking the engine. "Yeah, actually. In that box in the back. Why?"

"Back in my hospital room, you told me it's about a journey to the underworld."

"Yeah. She called it a *'katabasis'.*" He turns on the dispatch radio. Unlike the main radio, this one works. Voices chirp in and out as they ticket calls for service. "Couldn't really get into it. Not my type of thing."

The calls pick up, one coming in seconds after the other. Then another. He doesn't seem to care.

"How'd you get cleared again?" I reach behind my seat and sift through the box intentionally this time. It takes some digging, but I find another copy of the book. One I cling onto for dear life. This version is dog-eared, its spine endangered and taped together. Bright colored stickers annotate the edges. This was Dagny's actual copy. I flip it open. All her research. Everything.

There has to be something in here. Something that can help.

It has to.

Dax eyes me strangely but doesn't let it distract him from the road. Safety first. "It was Ashview's hospital director. Same guy who hired me, actually." We pull out onto the long stretch of highway toward the city. "Never saw him much until Dr. Hiribaldi went AWOL. He cleared Dr. Kennedy for service too. You'd think I'd remember the guy; he's pretty unique looking."

He looks past me as we merge into the faster lane. The rising sun forces us to drop the visors. I study the novel's cover again and déjà vu hits me like a Mack truck. The figure walks along a deserted corridor, menaced by darkness. Paint peels where the walls haven't crumbled.

What the hell? I'd been warned all along—I'd been warned and didn't listen. I stuff the book in my bag and clutch it for all I've got.

"I'm sorry." She knew—Dagny *knew*. That's why she wanted me to have this. Why she found Jackson and me in the first place.

To warn us that something was coming.

And we didn't listen.

Dax pulls a bottle of water from the door and takes a swig. "All I know is they've been diverting all the Trauma Ones since I've gotten back. The ER is slammed—that's why Dr. Kennedy was called in."

I have a bad feeling about this. "This guy . . . What's he look like?"

"Middle Eastern, strong nose. Pretty normal, mostly."

There's no way. No possible way. "Mostly?" The question drags out of me like a tire on a fishing line.

"Yeah," he says, nodding. "It's that scar of his that makes him unforgettable."

My heart skips. "Does it go over his right cheek and eyebrow?"

His joy drains from his face when he sees my horror. "How did you know?"

"Because he's the one trying to kill us."

Without another word, Dax flicks on the siren and slams on the gas.

TIME STANDS STILL

NOTHING COULD'VE PREPARED me for what we find when we make it into Ashview's ER. It's not the waiting room full of sick patients or the irate family members demanding answers about the lack of service; it's the countless rows of rollaway beds that line every nook and cranny of the lobby that stop us in our tracks.

Beds that are full. Not empty.

A young registration woman wearing a blue disposable mask sits at a fold-up cart table in the entryway, furiously hacking away at a laptop. Her concentration is hyper-focused.

"Name?"

"Actually, I'm not here for treatment," I stutter awkwardly, realizing I'm still wearing Dax's paramedic jacket.

Luckily, he rushes through the electronic double doors behind me, burying his trusty companion of a pill bottle in his pocket. He had the foresight to move the ambulance before anyone caught wind of his extracurriculars.

"Rose, it's Dax," he tells the girl. "Quick question. Is Dr. Kennedy working today?"

She looks up long enough to match the voice to the speaker. "Dax, hey. Didn't you just get outta here?"

"Yeah, sorry. Something came up."

She eyes me suspiciously, more for competition than a security breach. I feign a wide smile. "I take it she's with you?" Her words hang heavily toward the end.

"Yeah," he answers. "She's catering a special breakfast for the doctors upstairs today. Just helping her offload the food into their lounge."

Dax isn't dumb but plays it well. It's a good enough lie. The doctor's lounge is a place where this chick doesn't have the rank to try to catch us. The way it's looking—she'll be stuck until lunchtime. At the earliest.

She clicks her tongue and reaches for her Styrofoam cup of water. "Okay, but save me an everything bagel, puhleeze?"

Just play along. Easy. "Sure thing. Thank you." I smile wider as she scribbles on a visitor pass and hands it over. It goes right on my chest, all smooth and stickered-like. "Delivery entrance still around back? It's been a few months since I've been here."

I glance around. Even in the worst week, wait times would be nothing like this. This is . . . unbelievable. An epidemic, almost.

"Busy day?" I ask.

"It's been like this for nearly twelve hours," she explains, side-eyeing the overrun lobby. "People coming in, not going out. It's almost like the floodgates have opened."

"It started picking up last night, but this . . ." Dax agrees. "This is something else."

I count the patients. There are at least fifty-three wedged in here, many of whom are unconscious. I play dumb, half out of curiosity, half necessity. "It's not contagious, is it?"

"Hopefully not?" she says uncertainly. "Not that they're telling us anything out here. When you see Dr. Kennedy, ask her. She might know."

One last smile. "Will do. Thanks, Rose."

People like it when you use their name; psychologists and marketers alike claim that it builds rapport and makes them trust you more. Smiling like a damned fool makes her think I'm innocuous. Harmless even.

Until I burn it all down.

She waves us through, a surprising relief.

I struggle to keep pace with Dax. He says nothing as we veer around a corner and land in the ER. He doesn't bother scanning his badge but follows another staff member in scrubs through the metal double doors. The fewer eyes on us, the better. He zips up his own paramedic jacket and buries his hands into his pockets. Now he's nothing more than a member of the team.

Past the entrance, I take off the jacket and hand it back to Dax. Left with my oversized cardigan and baggy pants, I'm the only one who looks out of place. A visitor, maybe. A patient, more likely. I rip off the nametag and pitch it into the closest wastebasket.

I need to find Amy and convince her the explosion wasn't my fault—that she got played by Zaire; we all did. Tall odds given that she wholeheartedly thinks I'm the threat. She's not likely to believe anything that comes outta my mouth. It's gonna take something a lot bigger than me.

When we finally pass through the electric double doors, I get that opportunity. The ER is awash with discordant sounds. Scrubbed bodies scurry from room to room. These halls are no less cramped. Rollaway beds line the walkways, filled with patients who could all be asleep.

☥

But I know better—not with Zaire.

Not with someone willing to trap their soon-to-be wife for all eternity. Whatever happens with these patients, I get the feeling they're not headed to Dreamland.

My stomach cramps. This is madness. I'd like to think Kane would've never agreed to help Zaire had he known what I now do.

Dax stops at this wing's main desk and tries to ignore the rush of staff bolting in and out from behind the counters. Beneath it all, heart monitors harmonize across the floor, echoing.

Beep.

Beep.

Beep.

He notices it too.

With neither security nor Amy in sight, he leans on the counter, the spare jacket wedged under his left arm. "Jenny, have you seen Dr. Kennedy lately?"

A shorter, dark-haired woman in blue scrubs turns around. Her exhaustion mirrors the rest of the staff. "Yeah, sure. She's around here somewhere." Jenny scans the dry-erase board on the wall to see which rounds are tied to Dr. Kennedy. "She's leading Rooms 1 through 6, along with the four patients in the hall in front of them. Around the corner and to the left."

"Thanks."

We take off down the hall. Based on the paper sign taped to the wing's entrance, only twenty-four rooms encompass this emergency department. Ones well past capacity. Twice that number of patients nearly burst from the seams of the lobby alone.

The staff's anxiety is easy to understand; the likelihood the department has enough equipment is non-existent. If one thing goes wrong, patients will start dropping like coins in the Sunday collection bucket.

We find Amy performing a tracheotomy on a patient tucked in the hallway. I watch in awe as she finishes and backs away, trashing her gloves with doctor finesse. It's not until she glances up from the overflowing trash can that she finds us standing there. "What the hell are you doing in my ER?"

I force a smile. "Where'd you learn that?"

"Same place as everyone else. What do you want, Jesly?" She doesn't bother stopping. There's another chart headed toward her with a scrubbed nurse chasing on her heels.

"We need to talk."

She frowns, her RBF on full display. "I'd rather not if it's all the same."

She looks over a patient outside Room 4. Unconscious and unresponsive, the only way to tell the man's alive is via the steady chirping from the monitor attached.

She flips through his chart, then studies the monitor. "What's Huxley doing here? Finally ditch your tagalong?"

"That's why we're here."

"Silly me," she grouses. "I figured my day couldn't get any worse."

"Amy, I swear . . . You need to hear this," I plead. "We're running out of time."

She lowers her disposable blue mask and points to the elderly gentleman wired to the machine. "Tell that to my patients. Dozens just showed up like this."

I stare at the man on the ventilator, his life sustained purely by the contraptions tethering him to reality. "Why?"

She shrugs. "Every tox screen and diagnostic has come back negative. Brain scans normal. They just keep coming. I have no idea. None of us do."

☥

The digital screen on the monitor reads 62/40. He's got time, but not much. It's not good—for them or for us.

"Maybe you should hear her out, Dr. Kennedy," Dax offers.

"Hear her out?" she balks, wheeling up a metal stool from nearby. "Did she tell you everything?

"She told me enough."

"Like how she tried to kill all of us?"

"Amy, please," I say. "We don't have time to stand here bickering."

"Then I suggest you leave."

"I can't," I stutter. "Lives are on the line. We need your help."

She pats the patient on the shoulder and says a quick prayer before standing. "It's amazing how you jump when it's your head on the chopping block."

"Not just mine, Amy. Yours too," I say. "I thought you wanted revenge for Henry. But you're sitting here playing doctor."

"I *am* a doctor."

Good. There's that murderous rage. Maybe now she'll listen.

"Huxley, I don't know what she's told you," she says to Dax. "But if you haven't run, she's leaving stuff out or lying. Or both."

I exhale sharply. She's possibly the most stubborn person I've ever met, and that's saying something as a lawyer.

"Can we please just talk—the three of us? Give me five minutes." I lean on the table. My whole body is exhausted, and my wrist is raring to go. "If you still don't believe me, we can go our separate ways."

"Fine." She barges through the next door her badge accepts— the breakroom. Once inside, she sets her sights on the coffee pot where an overperked carafe holds this morning's brew before rummaging the French vanilla creamer out of the tired white refrigerator. Even busy as they are, I doubt it's her first cup. She unclips her badge and drops into the chair opposite us. "You have three."

"Things happened after you left," I begin slowly. "Zaire lied."

She snorts into her Styrofoam cup. "That's funny."

"You were right not to trust him."

"Am I right not to trust you?"

I flinch. Her words are as sharp as her aim. My jaw can attest to that. "It's not the same and you know that."

She takes a swig from her coffee before setting it back down. "What I know is that you nearly murdered us."

Dax steps in. "I don't know what happened between you two—"

"I'll tell you what's happened," she cuts him off, her own moral crisis railroading ours. "God has abandoned us. That's what."

I take a deep breath and swallow hard. It takes so much energy to keep my mouth shut at times like these.

"Kane's been kidnapped," I finally tell her, leaving out the part about Dax's sister. This isn't the time. I need allies, not enemies.

Amy pops her lips. "So? What does that have to do with me, or my patients for that matter?"

"The Chasa aren't going to stop," I say. "You know that. They're after you too."

She takes another sip. "I think I'll take my odds."

"Amy, you can't be serious. There's something wrong with this place."

"Really? You don't think I know that?" Amy gets up and throws the Styrofoam cup away. "I have nearly two dozen patients out there that need me. You've had your three minutes."

"Amy, listen . . ."

☥

"No, you listen!" She slams her chair into the table, shaking the thing. "Henry is dead because of you. My kids will never see either of their parents again, and you show up asking for help? Who the hell do you think you are?"

Dax keeps his mouth shut; I'd already warned him she would be difficult. He trusts me, though God only knows his reasoning. I don't deserve it.

There's a grain of truth to Amy's words. She and I both know it. But blind rage will get her killed if not us all.

"Amy, I didn't put you here; your God did. Why don't you get off your high horse for fucking once and accept just how badly your arrogance is blinding you?" I say, looking her dead in the eye.

She's a little taller, closer to 5'8", but I won't let that stop me. I've fought scarier things in court.

"Come on, Dax," I say. "We'll do this ourselves."

She finally shuts her mouth. Having spent years at the mercy of a toxic person like Jackson, I've learned their weak points. It's the mirror that frightens a narcissist the most. The vitriol floating around the breakroom is palpable, choking.

This is Amy's mess. Not mine.

We'll find another way to save the others. Amy can wallow in her despair. The door swings closed behind us, leaving the doctor to her own devices. Excuses won't work for me anymore. I don't have that kind of time. And by the looks of the rest of the hospital, neither do the patients.

We round the second hallway. This one fares no better. It's packed and crowded, just as loud and hectic. Sadly, none of these folks really know the truth. None of them realize they're all trapped in Purgatory.

That they've died—that there's no moving on to Heaven, Hell, or wherever *The Yellow Brick Road* really leads. Those still conscious believe they're alive and living out whatever life has left to offer them. They have no idea they died somewhere along the way.

That we're all stuck here. Me included.

I've got to get them out. *Somehow.*

When Amy stumbles into the emergency exit stairwell, it's like she's a different person. The warmth has returned to her hazelnut-toned skin, the lines softened around her angled brow. Her back, a little less rigid.

"I'm sorry," she tells me. "You were right."

I've played this game before, but I'll entertain her. "About what?"

"Us. You. *Me,*" she says between breaths. For women like her, this is hard. "I shouldn't have been so angry at you. With Henry gone, I lost sight of who I was and I took it out on you. I'm sorry."

"A blind doctor heals no ills," Dax announces from the second-floor stairwell.

"Huxley's right," Amy says. "I can't heal anyone if I can't fix myself first. What do we do?"

She lets go of the hallway exit door, closing us off from the cacophony of hospital noise. Her gaze darts to the corners of the stairwell, including the spot above Dax's head. There are no cameras here. No one to overhear us.

My instincts are silent, one way or the other. I'll have to trust her for now. Dax still needs to hear the truth. *Here we go.* "Zaire's the one pulling the strings," I tell her. "Hiribaldi's just his puppet."

"I told *you.* I knew something about that fucker smelled off," Amy howls, throwing her hands up. "I had him."

"I know," I concede.

"If you would've trusted me . . . we wouldn't be in this right now. Damnit." Burying her face in her hands, she collapses against the opposite wall.

"I'm sorry, Amy. I really am," I admit, "I wanted to believe that he was innocent. It was my mistake and it cost us."

"What now?" she asks.

"The hard part." I drop in the stairwell and sit beside Dax. No sounds come from beneath us. No doors opening. We're safe for now. "Amy's right, Dax; I haven't been completely honest."

He nods soberly. "Okay . . ."

"It's about Dagny," I say, my jaw tightening. "She's still here . . . still *alive*, you could say."

"I know. I've known the whole time she's trapped," he says plainly. "Why do you think I wanted your help?"

REVELATIONS

"What?" Amy and I both balk.

How could something this important have escaped me? For me, that's my ignorance. But for Dagny's attending doctor, the shock is far more visceral. She freezes while her brain tries to compute the situation. "You've known this whole time?"

Dax nods. "I have."

"Why didn't you say anything?" I ask.

He sighs, adjusting the spare jacket in his grip. "I tried. You kept blowing me off. You aren't the only one with demons." He rips his sleeve up.

On his right forearm, the same etched design snakes its way up his tanned skin. These lines are much darker, older. Faded even. If mine are weeks old, his markings are months, at least.

I nearly tackle him. "Where did you get that?"

He pulls away. "I just woke up with it one morning. I've been trying to ask Dagny ever since. But she would never give me a straight answer. Now she's gone."

Amy eyes me warily.

"As the older brother, I'm such a fuckup." Tears bite at his eyes as he chokes back a laugh. He collapses against the wall. Broken.

"I thought she was a professor."

He nods. "She is . . . well . . . *was*. But I couldn't convince her to help me before she went missing."

A door slams shut on a lower floor. Our conversation is cut short by a wash of female voices echoing in the stairwell. The less prying ears, the better. The clanging of footsteps on the concrete stairs and hands on the metal railing echo upward. Thankfully, the staff is too loud to notice our presence. Their noise dissipates as they disappear through an exit door, leaving us alone again.

"Why?" I ask.

Dax rubs his mouth, his boyish good looks contrasted by his fast-growing stubble. "Right before summer semester, she started working 24/7 in her office. Even slept there . . . which you can imagine made my parents worry. When I confronted her, she acted like I was in the way—wouldn't listen to a word I said. Kept giving me the cold shoulder like I was invisible."

Does he really not know? This is going to take more prodding than I thought. "What do you mean *invisible*?" I ask.

He throws his hands up. "Like I wasn't there, Jesly. I don't even know what I did to piss Dags off that bad. It was like that the entire last few months we were together," he says with a sigh. "Even Mom wasn't that mad. Not at me, at least."

"Did they know what Dagny was involved in?" I ask.

"Knowing my family I'm sure they did."

"And that was?" Amy says.

"Something tied to her dissertation. Rituals and the afterlife and crap. I think that's why my mother got that necklace for her."

"A necklace?" I drop my gaze long enough to make sure Dagny's gift still rests beneath my shirt.

"An amulet, technically. My parents saw how obsessed she was becoming—thought she was onto some kind of breakthrough, so they contacted a curator who dabbled in black market antiquities."

"What kind of breakthrough?" Amy asks.

His grimace tightens. "That's the thing. She wasn't. She was under some delusion that it opened up a gate to the underworld."

I feign a smile. The air itself here feels heavy; the weight of our combined sins threatens to drown us all.

"This thing—we need to find it," Amy acknowledges. "It might help us escape."

"Out of the hospital?" he asks, his brow furrowing.

The corner of her lip twitches. "Not the hospital, Huxley."

Fear flashes over his face when Dax starts connecting the dots.

"It's not just Dagny that's trapped," I announce, the admission breaking me like water over a dam.

The fear turns to confusion, his face crunching as he tries to do the math. *It's not working.* "Wh-what are you saying?"

"She's saying we're all dead." Amy doesn't mince words. She's beginning to understand; we don't have time for sticker shock.

"Purgatory, if you want to get technical," I clarify.

"I-I . . . What . . . How?" He leans against the railing and tries to steady the rocking ship, his eyes already red.

Seeing a man cry like this makes me feel a little bad; like I'm a witness to something private. Jackson never allowed himself to be vulnerable. *Weak*, he'd call it.

"Sit down." Amy eases Dax to the ground, her professional grip steadying him.

He stares up at me, childlike and afraid. Almost like I'm oxygen after nearly drowning in a riptide. "Why didn't you tell me?"

There's no hiding the shame on my face. "I didn't know how. Dagny said—"

He jumps up. "You've seen her?"

"It's complicated," I say.

"Is she okay? Is she hurt?"

"Dax—"

"Just answer the damn question," he snaps.

I can't blame him. But I don't know which is worse: finding out his sister isn't entirely dead or that we're all trapped in Purgatory together.

One admission down, one to go.

"I-I don't know . . ." I say. "Amy was there. As a doctor, she'd know more."

She smiles, her guard lower than what it's been this whole time. Softer, weaker. Perhaps seeing your life flash before your eyes after you're already dead does that to a person.

A prison sentence no one sees coming and no one wants. Especially not those devout in their piety.

She takes a breath and steels herself. "There was an explosion," Amy explains. "One your sister rigged. Could have killed us."

"What? I thought you said that was Jesly's fault."

"For the hundredth time, I didn't do it!" I scream, my composure failing. "The whole place was ready to blow when we walked in. Rigged with explosives that *your* sister set. Not. Me."

He blinks his tears away. "Dagny wouldn't do that. She didn't have demons like I did. I'm the black sheep of the family. Not her."

"Dax . . ." I sigh.

Amy rests her hand on his shoulder.

☥

"She just wouldn't . . ." he trails off, lost.

I dig the book back out of the small bag Chandni gave me and hold the tattered thing for them to see. "Dagny knew something—something *terrible*."

He swallows hard. "What do you mean terrible?"

"It's not just us. People are dying and not passing over."

"It's like we're all stuck," Amy finishes.

He rubs his face with his hands. "That's crazy talk."

Amy snorts. "Funny how that works, isn't it?"

"I don't understand," he says. "How is that even possible?"

I shrug. "That's what we're still working on. At least we were before we got separated."

Amy raises an eyebrow. "You mean before Zaire played us for fools."

I turn back to Dax. "Do you know why your sister was forced into in-patient care?"

"Dad thought all her work had caused a breakdown—that she couldn't tell what was real or fake anymore," he breathes, the guilt washing over him.

I bite my tongue.

"Did I do this to Dag?" he asks. "Is she dead because of me?"

"Dax, she died because of a car accident," I say. "Nothing more."

"Then why was she messing with research? For what?" he asks. "Someone knew what she was doing and wanted it stopped. There's no other explanation."

My hand brushes the ankh. "I don't know about that. These things just happen."

"Stop making excuses, Jesly," he tells me. "You're too soft. Whoever did this needs to pay."

"We're dead, Huxley," Amy quips. "It's a little late for

vengeance now."

Great. Keeping him off his investigation just bumped up my to-do list. He's steadier and on his feet, albeit not by much.

I clear my throat. "There's something else we need to talk about. This may be difficult to hear, but she keeps trying to escape."

"Okay . . ." he says.

"By killing herself."

The realization hits Amy, the truth dawning on her. "She's known this whole time."

Dagny hanging herself in the dayroom. The times before it. The explosion.

"Yeah," I agree. "Zaire won't let her leave; he won't let any of us leave."

"Not if I have anything to say." Dax wipes his tears on his jacket sleeve. "This is his hospital, right? He should be here. Let's just go confront him."

"I have an idea." Dr. Kennedy rushes off like the hounds of Hell are upon her. Swinging around the corner, she makes a break for the next floor down.

Our hands clang against the railing, their echoes bouncing off the stairwell walls. We take the stairs two steps at a time until we reach the bottom-floor exit.

I reach for the metal handle, but Amy stops me. "You noticed the rush of patients when you guys first came in this morning, right?"

"Yeah," I answer. "How could we not?"

"You were wrong when you said people aren't dying," she tells us. "They are. We lost five just this morning."

She's taken us to the morgue. *Where the dead dwell.*

Dax points at the door. "Will your badge work?"

"Only one way to find out." She swipes her badge against the electronic panel. It beeps and glows red.

I sigh. "I guess that would be too easy."

Dax scours for cameras. Thankfully, still nothing. "Zaire's not gonna let us walk right in."

The doctor clicks her tongue. "Maybe not, but his head nurse came down here earlier. They're accessing it somehow." She bounds back up the stairs. "Now I understand why."

The seventh floor is bustling when we make it out of the emergency stairwell. A place normally reserved for long-term patients; these nurses tend to be less frantic. But not today; it's like everywhere else in the hospital.

"Zaire's turned this place upside down," I whisper, avoiding glances from any onlookers. Two staff members and a visitor in plain clothes, we might pass undetected. Assuming no one recognizes me. Something Amy also realizes when she diverts our path and yanks us into a nearby room.

"Where are we going?" I ask.

"Zaire's head nurse works on this floor," she whispers. "I don't know her name, but I'd recognize her anywhere. She's got an accent that's hard to miss."

Dax digs into his pocket and pulls out his trusty bottle. He drops a couple white pills into his mouth, much to the disapproval of Amy and me, before sliding it back out of sight. "Accent. Nurse. Got it. Where to?"

She lifts open the blinds to the main hallway, enough to see out. "The station on the left. She's got red hair."

"Okay . . . we get her alone, and then what?" he asks.

"Steal her badge? Question her, maybe?" I answer. "I'm a lawyer; I don't know espionage crap."

☥

"You don't need to." Amy shifts past us and grabs the doorknob. "I'll handle it. Just do what I say."

I follow her directions to a T. We're soon leaning around the corner of a wall, looking way too conspicuous. Dax realizes it also. He starts rifling through a nearby utility cart and acts like he's preparing linens.

Amy watches the nurse's station. "She's there. So is Zaire."

"What are they saying?" I mouth to her.

"Can't tell." She switches places with me and pretends to help Dax as a pair of nurses passes by, too distracted by their conversation about some Thai restaurant down the street.

Amy's right; we need to get closer. Whatever Zaire and his nurse are saying, we're too far to hear it.

The woman's face is too obscured from this spot. Younger than me and Amy, her blue scrubs dwarf her slight frame. Her bright red hair makes her stick out in a corridor of blues and greens. Their conversation finished, Zaire touches her arm and whispers something before walking off in the opposite direction.

The woman lingers, like whatever he's told her isn't what she expected. Collecting herself, she clutches her clipboard to her chest and walks down the same hallway. Her hand slowly reaches for one of the doors as she looks to either side of her before entering.

Hopefully she hasn't sensed us. Unease tugs at my insides. A feeling that only grows stronger as the door swings closed behind her.

"Let's go," Amy whispers.

In no time, we're crashing into the women's locker room. Dax, ever the gentleman, stays outside. Inside the locker room, it's quiet. And for a second, I naively think I got the wrong door—that it's just us.

It's not.

"I know you're there," her thick Irish brogue hails several aisles over. A locker slams shut, drawing us toward it.

Amy and I exchange glances, and I reach for the large metal lock on the door.

"I wouldn't do that if I were you," the woman says. "Wanna talk? Let's talk."

Of all the times I wish I'd brought a gun, now was it. I glance at my fearless companion. There's no way the respectable doctor has brought a weapon into the hospital and risked a criminal charge. The wary look in Amy's eyes says she's thinking the same thing. We creep around the aisle to find the younger redhead waiting on a bench.

Her legs are crossed, her blue leather clutch strewn across her lap. It's clear that she's not as responsible as Dr. Kennedy. A small .45 caliber pistol sits square in her grip, its blue frame blending in with her scrubs. "You're a chancy lass, aren't you, Jesly?"

"Do I know you?" I ask.

The woman ages, the lines growing around the corners of her mouth and brow. Her body softens and widens, her hair growing more faded by time. The face is replaced by a more familiar one— the same one who cared for me while I was unconscious and bedridden. The one that told me I had nothing to fear.

My stomach lurches. "*Ailbhe?*"

"Aye, doll." She grins, waving the gun in my direction. "Welcome back." Her age reverts to the younger version, her feminine curves well-defined and her scarlet hair bright and vibrant.

"How'd you do that?"

"I see you found your fella again," she says, ignoring my

question. "That's good. I've taken a real shine to the other one. Nice company, he is."

My eyes widen. "What have you done to Kane?"

"You just can't seem to keep 'em, can you?" Her bright cherry lips stretch into a wide toothy smile, full of delight as she laughs. The red taunts me like I'm a bull in Pamplona.

Amy cuts off my path before I jump the bitch. "What did you do with Kane?" she echoes.

"Nothing he didn't enjoy." Ailbhe pulls an ol' fashioned cigarette pouch from her bag. Soon, menthol fills the locker room.

"Tell us where he is," I hiss between my teeth.

"Why? What for?"

"Your life, for one," I seethe.

She laughs between puffs, and I can feel my blood pressure throbbing in my neck. I shift past Amy to the nonchalant vixen and lean in her face. "Give him back, or I'll kill you."

"You can try, but I don't think you've got the stones," she says with a sly smile. "Dr. Kennedy, what about you?"

This is the nurse who was supposed to keep me alive in the hospital. A ruse concocted by Zaire and Hiribaldi to keep me docile. Up close, I can make out the myriad colors in her irises. But it's not the color that strikes me—it's the fact that her pupils are nothing more than vertical slits. Like a cat or a fox.

I pull back, terrified. "What are you?"

"A Bean Sídhe," Ailbhe says, barely above a whisper. Her grin widens even more as she exhales smoke into my face.

"Why are you working for Zaire?" Amy steadies me as I stumble backward, coughing from the secondhand smoke. "People are dying. Don't you care?"

A flick of ashes hits the ground. "Of course not," she says.

"Humans are a blip in the universe; the Sídhe will exist long after you lot are gone."

"Then what do you want?" I ask. There's no point in arguing with a delirious mythological creature holding a gun.

"You don't have the power to give me what I want."

Another flick.

"Try me," I say. "Maybe I do, maybe I don't."

She puts the cigarette out by smudging it with the heel of her sneaker. The butt stays there as she returns to her locker and grabs something inside before slamming it shut. She shoves it in my direction, and I take it.

A picture, frayed and faded, featuring a quintessential family full of spirit. Two parents, a handful of teenagers, and a bunch of young'uns. Except this family isn't a modern one; it's much older.

Both parents don farming clothes, the boys in suspenders and trousers, and the girls match in their knee-length Sunday best. All the sisters, save for the toddler, have their hair braided with ribbons. I turn the picture over to see a list of names and a date.

1913.

"Is this your family?" I ask.

Her scowl tightens. "Aye, they were. Now I belong to the Sídhe." She stuffs the gun into her waistband, grabs a blue sweater from the bench, and pulls it around her shoulders.

Amy studies the photograph. "Is this why you're working for him?"

The locker room door creaks open. Dax pops his head in. "Everything alright?"

"Come on in," I announce.

"It is." Ailbhe buttons her sweater so that the gun isn't visible any longer or her oversized breasts. "Hey, cutie," she tells Dax as he creeps inside. She looks back at me with contempt. "He has 'em in the Donn."

Amy hands over the picture. "The *what?*"

"The place between places. Before the Otherworld."

"Your family?" I say.

"All of 'em. Even Siobhan," Ailbhe answers.

The toddler, I note from the back. *Why?*

Horror creeps over Amy's face. "How is that possible? Is this guy some kind of god?"

Ailbhe runs her tongue over her lower lip, her bright red untarnished. "No, he's just a manky dosser out for blood."

"Then why can't you stop him?"

"If I interfere, he'll send them to Annwn." Ailbhe's brow furrows at our confusion. "The Otherworld?"

"And here is better?" I lean up against the lockers. No one's willing to stick their own neck out. "Here they're stuck."

"Don't you think I know that? That I tried?"

"I think a little backup might help," I say.

"There's no one else," she says sourly.

"There's us."

"Why would you help?" she balks. "We've lied to you this whole time."

I look down at the photograph. "Because I don't have a choice."

"What about the morgue?" Amy adds.

The strange woman shakes her head, her tone grave. "That's where he keeps 'em."

"The dead?" Dax, who has been quiet this whole time, asks.

"Not just 'em. The livin' too."

"What does he want with them?"

"I don't know," Ailbhe admits. "I'm not privy to that kind of stuff. There's only one person who'd know anythin' and that's his mot." She grabs another cigarette from her pouch and lights it. Chain-smoking must be immortality's best friend.

"I'm sorry?" I ask. "His what?"

"His girl—his dame," she scoffs like it's common knowledge. "Dagny."

At the mention of his sister's name, Dax stiffens. "They're together?"

"Well, he sure seems to think so," Ailbhe says. "Presented her with an engagement band and everythin'."

My head swirls, not knowing whether Dagny is telling the truth or Zaire is. She seems dead set on wanting to escape the man claiming to keep her alive. Nothing makes sense. This rabbit hole . . . *How much further do we go?*

"Only one way to find out," Dax says, taking a deep breath. "Can you lead us down there?"

"To the morgue?" Ailbhe asks.

I clutch onto my necklace and then stop myself. Just knowing that it's there calms me. Now I get Amy's early predilection. "We're not gaining anything by standing around."

"Alright . . ." Ailbhe finally agrees after a minute. "But I don't think it's the place you're thinkin' of."

"Trust me," I say with a laugh. "I think we can handle it."

PART IV

GOING DOWN

FOR A MOMENT, I naively believe I've seen the worst of it, having scoured the upper sections of the hospital.

But I'm wrong.

So wrong.

Ailbhe leads us back down the emergency stairwell. The electronic panel flashes green when her badge passes over it, and she holds the thick metal door open. "Come on, you lot."

We cross into the morgue, a place meant for death and decay. But that's not what we find. *Not quite.* My hands scramble through the darkness for a light switch. It's a risky move, granted we don't know what's waiting.

So when my fingers eventually latch onto something solid, the dull hum of old halogens fills the room. And then there's no longer any doubt of Zaire's intentions.

In place of a cold medical lab filled with slabs of the covered dead, we find a massive sandstone cavern and countless rows of the living. Many of whom are tied to machines, some of which pump oxygen; others filter blood.

But not a single patient moves. Not an inch. They're still as statues, as if this could be called living. This is Hell, certainly.

A yawning expanse of crimson, the cavern stretches hundreds of yards in any direction. Aisle after aisle of human beings lined into neat little rows. Some still donned in their hospital gowns. Others are simply naked, exposed in all their glory and shame. For them, there's no more hiding. No more running. The world sees them for who they really are, all the way down to the ugly scars and flaccid genitalia.

"What the fuck is this?" Dax doesn't wait for permission but rushes to the closest embalming table and tests a man for a pulse. Amy follows suit.

Ailbhe stays behind. "I said you wouldn' like what you saw."

Amy moves from patient to patient. "This is madness. How could you let this happen?"

She races around the closest autopsy table to the rollaway metal cabinets nearby and starts ransacking the place. Drawer after empty drawer clang to the ground. It's like where Mars and IKEA went to have a baby and died instead.

"Amy, wait!" I chase after her. "What are you doing?"

The first cabinet produces nothing, so she tears up a second. "We have to help these people."

"You tryin' to wake the dead?" Ailbhe asks.

Amy spins around, her eyes full of vitriol. "I'm sorry? Did you just make a dead joke in a fucking tomb?"

Dax wanders from aisle to aisle. "It kind of reminds me of China's first emperor."

I follow, too horrified to touch anything. There's just so many. "What does this have to do with China?"

Dax points to the countless rows beyond him. "This crazy

emperor—Shihuang something—tried to take his entire army to the afterlife with him. Didn't work. Now it's a tourist attraction filled with thousands of terracotta warriors."

The cavern walls recess so far back that we could wander for hours and still not find an exit. I creep down one aisle before it finally clicks.

The people. The rows. The synchronized beeping of those still tethered to the machines.

"This isn't a tomb; it's a farm," I say.

"What?" Amy's forehead crunches as she looks around and sees it for herself.

They both do.

"These people—he's using them for something," I say.

Dax swallows hard. "Jesly?"

"Yeah?"

"You said that Zaire kidnapped two of your companions."

I nod.

"Was Dagny one of them?"

I nod again.

Now they're both ransacking the place.

With no telling how long the search will take, we split up. Our footsteps crunch the rocky soil as the search crosses into the couple hundredth aisle. It's a laborious process made even longer by the sheer size of this place. This cavern, even larger than the last I stumbled into, only amplifies the nagging feeling in my gut.

Something's wrong.

By the time the first shout echoes across the chamber, Dax bolts toward Dr. Kennedy like the hounds of Hell are on him. She's found something.

No. *Someone.*

Dagny.

Centered smack dab in the chamber lies an autopsy table different from the rest. Here, she rests comfortably, a red satin pillow beneath her head, her attire far more extravagant than the last time we saw her. No longer wearing the same drab patient clothes, she's dressed in something more akin to a dinner party in polite society. A long navy silk dress clings to her narrow frame, her curves slight and barely noticeable. Her breathing has slowed, her chest raising periodically. Her stringy blonde hair lays flat on the autopsy table, echoing the lack of life.

"Dags? Wake up," Dax pleads, staring down at his twin. Shaking her is useless; whatever Zaire's done to them, she's not coming out of it.

I turn to Ailbhe, horrified. "You knew about this?"

The Bean Sídhe shakes her head. "No, this is different. We should leave."

"No way." Dax rips out the wires tethering his sister to the equipment. "I'm not leaving her."

"Huxley, wait," Kennedy shouts. "We don't know what they've done to her. She could be hemolytic."

Ailbhe shoots me a warning glance and quickly starts backpedaling. Our problems are only beginning. 6Seconds later, a blaring alarm goes off, its deafening whoop seemingly blasting from all directions.

Barely able to move, I latch onto a nearby table. The sound grows until all I can do is clutch my ears and collapse to my knees. The others fare no better; they too find themselves wrenched to the rocky ground.

"Nice one, Huxley," Amy hollers beneath the table. "Ailbhe, can you turn that off?"

The Bean Sídhe shrugs.

Dax doesn't wait. He disconnects the last of the wires and tubes, and scoops Dagny into his arms. Compared to him, she seems tiny. Perhaps it's only her sunken frame, weak and exposed.

The whooping alarm echoes throughout the chamber, ricocheting off the crags until there's nothing left. Dax signals to the exit. A long stretch, but we can make it.

Movement flickers in my peripheral vision. I'm not fast enough to catch it. I miss the hooked mallet in Ailbhe's hands striking me in the temple.

Nausea surges through me as I collapse to my knees, my hands catching me too late. This dilapidated world shifts into one of flickering stars and vertigo, my body shaking.

"Oh no, you don't." Amy takes off after the wayward nurse, her military training roaring to the forefront. Not a single footstep out of place. She lunges at Ailbhe, tackling her to the ground.

For some reason, strangers are always impressed when I mention I'm a prosecutor—they tend to think I'm some valiant character woven into the heart of Dallas. But I'm no warrior.

Seeing Amy makes me certain of that; her fearlessness just makes me doubt myself even more. She's tied to the cause, through and through. She'll save them all—with or without my help.

The Bean Sídhe unleashes an otherworldly wail loud enough to nearly counter the alarm. Thrashing beneath Amy does no good. The doctor straddles Ailbhe's chest and pins her to the ground, the other woman's collar clutched in her grip.

"Why you trying to run, Ailbhe?" Amy barks between breaths. "Huh? What did you do?"

The alarm finally stops, returning the chamber to the endless quiet. Ailbhe's struggling forces Amy to adjust to keep her from escaping.

"You're goin' to die," the Bean Sídhe says, her toothy grin wide and bloody. "And so is everyone else in this place."

I wipe the sweat from my face. "Enough games, Ailbhe. What do you know?"

"He's comin' and not just 'em. His helpers too."

Somewhere in the distance, a cascade of howls rip through the chamber. One after another.

"What was that?" Dax inhales, his fear front and center, as he clutches his sister tighter. There's no separating them now.

"The Cú Sídhe," she says. "You lot call them *Hellhounds.*"

The clacking of nails scratch against the concrete, a sound that gets louder the longer we wait.

"They're His to command," she says triumphantly. "The Guardian of The Scales."

The howls we heard outside the gas station. Zaire's been watching me this entire time, and I wonder how much he really controls—how much power he's really accrued. How many deals he's made with the devil to get there.

'Whose side are you on?" Amy drags them both to their feet. "You said your family was on the line. Was that a lie too?"

Ailbhe looks away. "It's not goin' to end like you think."

"I'll be the judge of that," the doctor says.

In the time we've taken to scour the chamber, we've isolated ourselves. Our only respite looms at least a half-mile back toward the entrance. The scampering of claws continues, albeit louder than before. A nearby bark breaks our focus.

They're close.

"I'm leaving," Ailbhe announces, wrenching her shoulder out from Amy's grip and backing away from the barking.

Amy throws her hands up. "Now what?"

☥

I nod at Dagny. "How long do we have?"

The doctor feels Dagny's cheeks and forehead with the back of her hand, then the carotid artery. "Her pulse is thready. Weak. We need to get her back to the main floor."

"What about the rest?" Dax signals to the endless aisles of patients.

"What about them?" a malevolent voice echoes from nearby, evanescent and out of frame. His words seep into the room, full of disdain and condemnation.

My whole body freezes as I spin around, searching.

It's Him, as Ailbhe said. *Hiribaldi.*

The last person I want to hear from and the first one Amy's looking for: Zaire's right-hand man and master of puppets.

No more pretenses, my attending physician and kidnapper stands ready, his sinewy body covered in half-coagulated wounds. No longer wearing his doctor's coat, he's simply dressed in a tattered, black ribbed turtleneck and slacks.

Amy's eyes widen. "You—"

With her husband murdered and the likelihood of ever seeing her children again gone, Amy's rage has become a finely sharpened weapon. As she slips past me, I know I should stop her—to keep her from making a mistake she'll regret.

But I can't.

My own body shakes too uncontrollably, caught in a whirlwind of pain that swells along my forearm at the sight of my kidnapper. There's nothing I can do but clutch it tightly, grit my teeth, and wait for the chaos skirting down the tracks like a derailed train.

So when Amy snatches the Bean Sídhe by her bright red ponytail and drags a scalpel across her bare throat, I don't blame her at all.

Not anymore. I just blame myself for not doing it first.

☥

STRIKING A DEAL

I CAN'T EVEN SAY I'm shocked when Ailbhe's body crumples to the cavern floor, the moral compass of our group stepping over her to head toward her actual prey.

Dax, however, is. "What did you do?"

"She's not a person, Huxley," Amy says. "She's not even human."

"Ms. Allbrook and *Mrs. Caspar*," Hiribaldi greets us as he treads barefoot toward us, his smile wide. "So good to see you again."

The scalpel steadies in her grip. "It's *Doctor* Kennedy to you, *Kenji*. I thought I killed you . . ."

He snorts. "Foolish woman. We don't die that easily. Not even that *thing* over there." He nods at Ailbhe bleeding out. "Give it a few. She'll be crawling around like the sad sack she is before long."

"I won't make that mistake twice," Amy warns.

"Oh, I'm sure," Hiribaldi says as the source of the clacking appears. "Neither will I."

Looming on either side of him are two massive black dogs, closer to the size of Irish wolfhounds and more akin to horror than hound. *The Cú Sídhe*, Ailbhe called them.

Their jackal-like faces house large eyes that glow bright like rubies, poised in our direction. Beneath the matted, torn fur, their bodies stand eroded by time. Ribs and internal organs peek from the inside. Patiently, the wolf-like beasts sit beside their master. For how long is anyone's guess.

I swallow hard. "What's your endgame, Hiribaldi? You and Zaire."

"Me and—" he chokes. "I don't work for that interloper."

"Then who?"

"*The Scales*, and I've come to collect their quarry," he says matter-of-factly. "Ammit will be so delighted to see you both." He nods at Amy.

"Fuck you," she responds.

"Don't be so crass, *Mrs.* Caspar," he says, emphasizing her married name. "It's nothing personal. You can't fight Fate."

"You made it personal when you murdered my husband, Hiribaldi, or whoever the hell you are." The scalpel flips around in her grip so that it's poised for a knife-hand strike.

"I'm sorry you feel that way. Your husband made his own bed."

"Fuck your sorry," she says. "Do these people—these patients—understand?"

Hiribaldi caresses one of the Cú Sídhe, his fingers gliding through their mangy black fur. "They are inconsequential."

"How dare you?" she barks back. "These are human beings."

He nods. "And they will serve their purpose in time. Your friend has seen to that."

"Purpose? What purpose?" I ask.

"The Scales do not like to be broken," he says, ignoring my

question. "Your friend will pay for his transgressions. He must stop before he breaks them."

"What do you mean, *break*?" Amy asks.

He ignores us both. "The male can come out. There's no use in hiding. My hounds can smell you."

Reluctantly, Dax crawls out from his cover, his eyes wet with tears. Dagny is still unresponsive, her head and limbs draped in his grip. "What did you do to my sister?"

"Mr. Huxley, I already told your companions," Hiribaldi says. "This is Zaire's mess. Not mine."

The man scratches the chin of the closest beast. To him, we're insignificant. He's got all eternity—something the scorching pain in my arm reminds me I don't have.

You can end this, Jesly. Right here and now. It would be so easy to just let me have them all.

My chest tightens as I try to ignore the sonuvabitch. I try to stall. "If Zaire's a problem, why not stop him?"

Hiribaldi shifts his focus, amused. "To what avail? No one beats The Scales. Not him. Not even you."

"Me?" I balk. "I'm trying to get us out."

He laughs. "Good luck, child."

The slightest whistle pierces the stillness, and I don't put it together at first. It's not until the undead hounds bolt across the cavern, their snarling thirst unleashed, that the fear welling inside me breaks like a dam.

"Jesly, run!" Amy signals a cut-through in the aisles.

To the left of where Dax guards his sister, a rocky outcrop leads out of the chamber. Doable if the hounds of Hell weren't vying for an evening snack. The Cú Sídhe are unnaturally fast as they zigzag through the aisles, forcing Dax to scramble toward the bridge.

My legs burn as we push in that direction, the distance increasing. We're almost a half-mile out when Amy stops cold.

"Come on." I wave her along, but she doesn't budge. "What are you doing? We can't stop."

"I'm gonna buy you some time."

"Stop joking," I say. "We gotta go."

The corner of her lips turn upwards. "You never asked me why I ended up in Purgatory . . . why I never questioned it."

"Amy, tell me later," I plead. "We don't have time for a Catholic confession."

"There won't be a later," she says. "I was there, Jesly. The night of your car accident."

"Okay, so what?"

She won't even look at me now. "I worked in the ER before getting reassigned; that's why Ashview called me in when the hospital got overrun."

It takes everything not to grab her. "Fuck it. You were there. Doesn't matter."

The hounds are close now.

Tears line her eyes. "Yes, it does. Here. Take this," she says, holding out the knife.

"Come on—"

"Jesly, just take the damn thing."

"Amy—"

"Take it," she shouts.

Reluctantly, I do.

"You weren't driving that night."

"I'm sorry?"

"Your accident." She licks the sweat from her upper lip and

turns to me, her eyes full of absolution. "Your injuries originated from where you sat in the passenger seat. You weren't driving. You never were."

"What?" My knees buckle, and I try to latch onto something. *It wasn't a dream . . .*

"Someone paid me to doctor the write-up."

"What? Who?"

She shakes her head. "I don't know. I never saw their face. Probably paid off the cops in your witness statement too."

"I-I don't—" I stutter, my head swirling. "Why would you do that?"

"They threatened Henry, Jesly," she says. "My kids too. I'm a wife and mother first."

A snarl erupts to her right—the Cú Sídhe have caught up. She dodges its first attempt, leaving the creature a second go.

She smiles, the resolution etched into the crown of her forehead. "Sometimes good people do bad things, even when they don't want to."

"Amy—"

An enormous wall of black fur collides into her, sending them both crashing to the cavern floor. I stare in horror as she wrestles to keep its massive fangs from ripping her apart, its body weight close to a grown bodybuilder.

The battle doesn't last long.

"Jesly!" Dax yells from the far end of the sandstone bridge. He's made it across with Dagny.

My body freezes as the red-eyed beast tears into the doctor's throat, my knees giving in. A shuddering sob erupts from my throat, and I can't. I just can't. *This entire time . . .*

Jackson's tricks forced me to believe I was the one

responsible. He gaslit me until I was convinced the accident was my fault. I was never behind the wheel.

Back in the ambulance with Dax, it wasn't a dream. It was a memory—*my* memory of that night.

"Jesly, goddamnit. Come on!"

I watch helplessly as the hound destroys what's left of Amy, a woman so reticent and yet open. The lead in my veins chains me in place. Just like before, the horrifying sound echoes again and again until the world itself spins.

I wrench my eyes shut. Eventually, hands pull me to my feet and drag me along. My thrashing stops when I realize it's Dax.

"Snap out of it," he pleads. "I can't do this myself."

I nod half-heartedly. "There's another dog out there."

"I know," he says. "Let's hurry."

We make it across the outcrop, our destination unknown. All that greets us is a dead-end—a canyon wall a thousand feet high. The hounds haven't followed. Something I don't know whether to be grateful for or afraid. The second Cú Sídhe sits at the opposite end of the makeshift bridge, waiting.

I turn back to Dax, uneasy. "They've stopped chasing us. Why?"

"Who cares?" Dax lifts his focus from Dagny. Her color has grown paler since taking her off the mechanical contraption. "Let's count it as a blessing and get outta here." He scours the chamber for the exit.

"I'm not leaving," I say. "Not without Kane."

"Your guy?"

"A friend," I correct quickly.

"We'll find him," he tells me. "But Dagny needs help—*we* need help."

"Dax, look around; no one's coming. It's just you and me now."

We inch toward the far end of the chamber, this place mirroring everything else in this godforsaken hell. "I feel like I've been here before."

"How?"

"Not this chamber, perhaps, but something like it," I explain. "I wonder if these tunnels run the entire way beneath the city."

"Forget about that," he cuts me off. "But we've gotta get somewhere safe. Then we can figure out our next move."

I stare at his sister. "How can I help?"

"Don't worry," he says. "You will before this is through."

Our eyes meet.

There's something brimming beneath the surface there, but it disappears before I figure out what it is. He changes the topic. "Just get us out of here . . . Find an exit or something." He nods toward the red limestone wall, its lengthy surface running straight upwards until it disappears from sight.

I run my fingers along the stone. "Why is there a wall here?"

Dax brushes his sister's straw-colored hair from her pale face. "I wish Dags was awake. She'd know what to do."

"I only know one other person who might know how your sister got mixed up with a guy like Zaire."

"Who?"

"Kane," I say, my nails catching on a slight groove in the red stone. My fingers slide vertically along the tiny recess. It's a door. "Hey, help me out a sec."

"Find something?" He glances behind us to make sure the coast is clear. It is.

Wherever Hiribaldi went with his death dogs, they're no longer near the bridge. Hopefully, it'll be the last time we see them, but it seems unlikely. It's like Hiribaldi said; he's a man with a mission—a bounty hunter for the dead.

"Yeah." I blow into the stone and watch the line spread. "There's something here . . ."

Dax's face lights up. "Thank God."

I shrug. "If God's real, I doubt he's got anything to do with this. Come help a sec."

I can see Dax work out the mental math of whether it's safe to set Dagny down. Having carried the woman this entire time, he must border on exhaustion, but he sets her down and helps me get a grip on the wall.

It consumes almost everything I've got left. The sudden pang through my stomach reminds me I'm not altogether forsaken. I can't remember the last time I've eaten.

The thought rivets through me like a lightning bolt. I let go of the crevice, realizing its true purpose. "It's a door."

To Yamaloka.

"Really?" Dax tugs at the frame harder before stepping back to look. "Well, whatever it is, it's not budging."

I follow the crevice to where it forks to the right. Hard to discern, but it's there. "I've got an idea."

The piṇḍas.

Digging into my cardigan pocket, I pull out the last four piṇḍas and shove them in my mouth.

"Those things again?"

I shake my head. "No, not them. This," I say as I slip off my sneaker.

Please let it still be there. Digging into the hidey-hole woven into my old running shoe, I find the small, tarnished coin. Right where I left it at the start of this nightmare. *Thank God.* If I survive this,

I'll have to write the manufacturer a glowing review. Into my palm it goes as I shove my shoe back on.

Before Dax can stop me, I swallow the last bite of *piṇḍa* and dig Amy's knife out of my pocket.

"You sure about this?" he asks.

"Not really, but I don't have anything else." I spring open the knife. It drags across my left palm, stinging as blood pools to the surface. My clean hand stuffs the empty napkin back in my pocket, while the bloody one clutches onto the coin for dear life.

He notices immediately. "Where did you get that? That's a Greek obol."

"Your sister."

"Jesly, that could be dangerous. You don't know what will happen," he warns.

"Only one way to find out." Placing my hand over the crevice, I let the blood run down it. I'm no mage. No mythologist. A few weeks ago, I wouldn't even have said Heaven and Hell exist. Now I'm trying to fast-track an Uber into Hell. "Charon . . . Reaper . . . Samurai dude. Whoever you are, I summon you."

Dax gawks at me and I shrug. "Gotta make it sound good."

We scour the emptiness for any signs of life. Nothing. Minutes pass as we watch the arch bridge. No change.

Then, out of the corner of my eye, I see it. We both do.

Not an "*it*" so much as a "*them.*"

Dax stumbles backward.

Standing between us and the bridge are the three towering figures Kane and I met outside the facility's back entrance. Still masked and donning their armor, I can't tell if Oni, Skullface, and Birdbeak are happy to see us.

The piṇḍas churn in my stomach. *Please work.*

I look down. The coin is gone.

"Skullface," I shout. "I want to make a deal without your master."

"We are Chasa," it responds without missing a beat. "We answer only to The Balance."

Dax is smart to say nothing. He never saw what happened outside the underground facility. He wasn't there, and with Amy gone, it's my word against theirs.

"Then why did you go after Dagny?" I demand.

"We have our reasons," the Oni says, its disembodied voice coming from its brethren simultaneously. *Supernatural surround sound. Cool.*

My grip tightens on the open blade, letting the serrated edge dig into my flesh a little deeper. Adrenaline floods my system, forcing my careful focus. A cheap trick that works.

"And Kane? Why did you attack him?"

This time it's Birdbeak who answers, "He interfered in The Weighing."

"A Watcher cannot intervene," says Oni.

"A Watcher *watches*," Skullface tells us. "Only The Chasa have that right."

"*We* are Chasa," says Birdbeak.

These guys make my head spin. "Thank you for that enlightening mythology lesson," I say, "but people are gonna get hurt if you don't stop this."

"The Scales are balanced," Oni says, turning to leave. "We will do nothing."

Stupidly, I grab it by the thick slate-colored armor only to realize they're made from scales and flesh. Whether human or animal I don't know. "You call this *balanced?*"

I let go but try to keep a straight face as the creature looks down at me. I'm not short for a female, but it dwarfs me by comparison. It has gotta be the better part of seven feet easy. Its corporeal form is unnatural and just as unnerving.

"Human sentiment has no purpose here," Birdbeak says. "Only the—"

"The Balance. We get it," Dax blurts. "Are you helping us or not?" He glances at his sister, who has shifted to shallow, rapid breaths; we don't have long.

The three otherworldly entities mull it over. After a moment, Skullface says, "We will. The one called Jesly Allbrook follow."

"Jesly, no," Dax protests.

I wave him off. *I can do this.* Even if it means cutting a deal with these infernal creatures. Kane's worth it. "Hey Skullface."

It grunts beneath the mask.

I've amused it. *Oh, goodie.*

"For wanting a favor, you seem . . . how do you humans say it . . . *flippant?*"

"It's a new look. You should try it sometime," I quip back.

It snorts, surprisingly. I must be doing something right or something very wrong. "I need beyond this wall." I point to the large rock face. "And I want you to return, Kane."

"No," The Chasa echo in unison.

"Why are you defending Zaire? He's going to get Dagny killed," I signal to Dax's sister, where it finally dawns on the creature that she's amongst us.

"Lady Dagny?" Skullface says, its voice bordering on reverence.

"*Lady?*" I scoff.

Skullface drops to its knees, its frame bowing.

"What are you doing?"

Even I've got an arm up to block them should they attempt anything. Meaningless against a katana the size of a telephone pole, I know, but I've gotta try.

"Lady Dagny is to be Lord Zaire's queen."

"You're mistaken," I laugh. "Dagny is human."

"Irrelevant," Birdbeak tells us, his own towering form dropping to one knee. "She's been chosen." Its lifeless eyes stare at me through the mask, its elongated features unnerving.

"Preparations are underway," the Oni says.

"Dagny isn't going anywhere but home," her brother says.

"This is not up to you," Skullface declares.

Dax bows up at the creature. A stupid idea and he knows it. "Then who?"

The Oni draws his katana from the scabbard behind its right shoulder. "The Lady belongs to Lord Zaire now. Her home is Yamaloka."

All color drains from Dax's face. "I'm sorry?"

This is madness . . . Absolute madness. Dagny, what have you gotten yourself into?

"You're lying," Dax hisses. "My sister would never agree to this."

I don't want to break it to Dax that younger sisters don't always tell their older siblings everything; he's got this protective older brother thing down pat.

Albeit endearing, he should be worried; Dagny's pallor is worsening by the minute, growing more yellow. Slowly but surely, her sclera is turning a bluish tint. Her body's not getting the oxygen it needs, and soon she'll start shutting down. Amy was right. *Hem-a-something.* We've got to get Dagny back upstairs now.

Hemolytic, Amy's explanation hits me. Dagny's red blood cells are dying. At worst, it's already too late. At best, she'll need a transfusion. A Herculean task down here. The machines were only meant to keep bodies warm—not well.

"Dax?" I say, forcing him to break his Mexican standoff. "When this gate opens, get Dagny back upstairs and find help. She's hemolytic."

"I know. Where are you going to be?"

"Doing the right thing," I tell him, walking away. He's got this; he has to. I head back toward the outcrop and clutch the ankh. I just hope my trump card holds.

The three figures notice me approach, their large statures stiffening as they look me over. "How can The Chasa support Zaire?" I ask. "He doesn't respect The Balance." I nod at the scores of patients tethered to life support across the cavern. Dax was right; it is a terracotta army. "Zaire's willing to consume every single life here if it gets him what he wants."

"Humans are inconsequential," Birdbeak answers.

"Not to their loved ones," I tell The Chasa. "Help us."

Skullface shakes its head. "That is not an option."

"We're heading toward a precipice," Oni chimes in. "A new era."

I press my tongue into my cheek. It's like arguing with a brick wall. All three of them.

"How about I go out on a limb and wager it's been a while since any souls have crossed over. Am I right?" I say, taking a deep breath as I'm reminded that the seven-foot-tall figure has a sword nearly my height. "How much longer for you Chasa to admit The Balance is broken?"

Skullface blinks. "Your sense of time is meaningless to us."

"We can wait," says Birdbeak.

"Maybe." I shrug. "But I'd wager someone above you wants to know what's taking so long down here, and I'm going to assume that someone isn't Hiribaldi." *He's the middleman—the foot soldier.*

A grunt. "What is your proposal?" Skullface answers.

"Release them, return Kane, and let us through that door."

"Quite a demand." Skullface chuffs. "What do The Chasa get in return?"

This part is a little harder. I whisper it so Dax can't hear me. "When this is all over and Zaire is stopped—I'll serve whatever sentence on Kane's behalf."

The creature weighs my offer, and I know my fate is sealed. "Deal."

WELCOME BACK

THE YAWNING VOID OPPOSITE the gargantuan door is the first thing Kane sees when he appears beside us. The Chasa are gone. They've left us to our own destruction. *For now.*

I steady myself as the ground quakes again, the rocky terrain trembling as it rises to meet us, and that sinking feeling that we're running out of time is back.

Kane doesn't meet my gaze but scours the new environment, taking it all in, including our newfound entrance. "What have you done?"

"I would settle for a thank you, but whatever," I say. "We need to talk."

"Not now," he replies. "Where are we?"

"No. Me first. How long have you known what Zaire was intending?"

"Long enough."

"How long is that?" I quip. "Days? Weeks? Since you sent me back?"

"Would anything change if you knew?" He turns to study the

entryway, reading the symbols that are faintly visible. "I've told you a half-dozen times. I'm not your enemy."

I glance back at Dax, who, to his credit, simply waits for a signal on whether to trust Kane or not. The first time their paths have crossed; Dax's protective meter is at an all-time high. With Dagny incapacitated, I don't blame him.

"No, this is just business now," I say softly.

Kane flinches. *Good.* I've struck a nerve.

His secrets have cost us too much already, and I'm no closer to getting out of here than when I started. I'll escape this nightmare, even if that means dancing with the Devil himself. I might not agree with Zaire's methods, but he lays all the cards on the table. Finding Dagny's partner just topped my priority list.

Knowing I won't budge, Kane changes topics. "Where are we?"

"Don't know," I answer truthfully. "Under the hospital, maybe?"

"And Amy?"

"She's . . . gone," I say.

"What do you mean *gone*?"

I poke his chest. "No. You don't get to do that. You want answers? Try giving some."

Now I'm a dog with a bone. I'm pissed. At him. At the situation. And at myself. There's no forgiving my sins when they just keep stacking.

Kane's eyes latch on the large outcrop above our heads. The distant sound of barking snaps across the arch bridge. "A while," he finally admits. "I've known for a while."

"Not good enough." I wrench him around to face me, and we stare at each other, our bodies closer than they've been in days. There's a tightness in my chest that won't budge.

I want to trust him but don't know if I can. Not like this. It's my afterlife on the line. *Not his.*

Studying his stained face for any tell or sign of weakness, all I find is dirt lining his brow. It mixes with the dried blood caked along the edges of his temples. He's suffered a lot, and probably mostly on my behalf.

But there's something in the emptiness that belies his silence. Whatever he's keeping from me—it's enough to get us all killed. As it stands, we're useless to each other. And until I break this divide, there is no *us*.

"What does Zaire hold over you, Kane?" I whisper, tears forming. "What deal did you make with him?"

"Let it go, please. It's not that simple."

I reach for his arm. "Then make it."

"Some other time. The others come first."

I press my lips together and fight the flood of emotions washing over me. Before Kane can figure out what I've done, I wrench my eyes shut and steel my mind, hopefully shutting him out. I've never tried before, but I hope it works.

He's right. With Dagny hemolytic, we've got minutes. An hour is a pipe dream.

Moving is our only choice. And with Kane's strength, the process becomes much easier. He's able to take some of the responsibility; something Dax hesitates over at first. I finally ease up around Kane and that's good enough for Dax.

A naïve decision granted my track record. Evidence shows I'm a terrible judge of character, especially when it comes to men. Even friends.

"Any idea which way?" Dax asks him.

"No." Kane glances in my direction. "But I'm not after the exit. I know what you're going to do and I'm going with you."

☥

He doesn't wait for my rebuttal but simply walks toward the threshold, pausing right before he passes underneath. He's sweating. It's slight but noticeable. *Something's wrong.*

Kane steadies his footing before grabbing onto the sandstone recess where the wall once was. With The Chasa's help and the obol now gone, the door is left wide open.

Luring, beckoning.

"What about that?" Dax signals to the outcrop above us, where the faint echo of barking lingers.

Kane shakes his head. "They can't cross the entrance."

"The entrance to what?" he asks.

"Yamaloka," I say.

Dax still doesn't get it. Not yet.

So I add, "Hell, Dax."

And then realization finally crawls across the worn lines and increasing brown stubble. "I-I can't take Dagny there. She'll die."

"Yeah," I agree. "That's exactly what Zaire wants. Dying there means she'll live forever."

"This is crazy. Doesn't he know she'd never agree to that?" Dax eases Dagny from Kane. Her breath is growing fainter.

"I don't think he cares," Kane says plainly. "Ever since she died, he's been gathering power down here—almost like he's becoming—"

"Hades," I blurt out, remembering my Greek mythology from middle school.

"I thought Hades was a person, not a place," Dax says.

I shake my head. "It's both. The person runs the place."

"And Hades is Hell? Like the real bonafide Hell?"

"That's the way it's looking," I tell him. "Your sister's set to become the next Persephone, Queen of the Underworld."

"How is that even possible?"

"I don't know," I say in earnest.

A beat passes and Kane finally speaks again. "It raises several questions—like what happened to the old one?"

Killing a goddess must not come easy, but somehow I think we've found ourselves smack dab in its aftermath. A realization that only grows as the hope fades from Dax's face, reminding me of how utterly screwed we all are.

OLD FRIENDS

A pungent smell that borders on vulgar greets the four of us when we enter the next towering cavern. Whereas the previous chamber was massive and vacant, this new expanse is filled with thousands of pillars clawing their way skyward until they disappear into the false night. It's as if we've entered a labyrinth of columns stretching endlessly, and it doesn't take long to trip over nothing.

"Either of you have a lighter?" I say after the guys nearly bang into a large column.

"Yeah, sure." Dax nods and digs into his pocket. He pulls out a worn Zippo and hands it over.

"Great." It takes a few tries, but my fingers latch onto the striker. It's not much, but some light is better than nothing. I swing the lighter around to figure out where we are.

It's quiet. There's a slight wind that makes the flame flicker just enough to piss me off. Somewhere in the distance, rushing water echoes. If we're lucky, that current will lead back to the surface. Finding the bottom of Wonderland isn't going well.

"Which way?" I ask, lifting our pathetic little lantern.

Kane shifts his head, raising his ear toward the tunnel. He points forward. "That direction. The wind is coming from somewhere else. Anyone else have ideas?"

"Yeah. We don't split up," Dax answers. "No use wandering in the pitch black."

"Agreed," Kane says. "One wrong move and one of us walks off a cliff. Zaire's not letting you go without a fight."

"He can try," I say. "I'm not worried about Zaire; I'm worried about Hiribaldi."

The image of me injecting Jackson with the poison rushes back, and a swell of bile in my throat meets it gladly. Unlike the rest of them, *that* one is on me.

Kane eats the last of his Skittles package. "You can't stop Hiribaldi, Allbrook. The Balance won't let it happen. Zaire, though, we might have a shot."

"We're not getting any younger standing here." Dax points to our assumed exit. "You really think this way leads us outta here?"

"Only one way to find out," I suggest as Kane heads deeper into the cavern.

And I follow them into the darkness.

Here, my senses jump at the slightest noise. Our footsteps crunch pebbles beneath us. The deeper we go, the colder the air becomes. It's not long before the air stings like ice, and each breath makes it nearly impossible to keep up. I prop myself against a column and glance at my otherworldly mark.

The deep sable lines are quiet, the electric blue absent. Whatever this feeling tearing into me, my newfound alarm system is deeply quiet. Like this place.

My hands burn with the aching cold, and I blow into them. All the warmth has left, taking my internal heat source with it.

☥

I've never felt cold like this. Not even during Christmas in Northern Canada. This is worse. Far worse.

A rush of air threatens to knock me over, carrying a voice in the frozen wind. *"Jes . . ."*

A voice I'd know anywhere.

In any world.

Any dimension.

I don't move. Whatever blood remains in my veins freezes on the spot.

Dax notices my fear. He's not like Kane and me; he can't hear what we can. "Hey, you okay?"

Kane halts before passing the next column. The sudden fear on his face tells me he didn't sense anything. A fact he fixes at once. He's on me in a second, pushing past the twins to latch onto my shoulders. His grip is rough—frantic, accidentally hurting me in the process, but he's swung me aside just in time.

Because the voice isn't my imagination.

It's real and belongs to Jackson standing yards away, his pallor reminding me he's already dead. *"Hello, Love."*

'TIL DEATH DO US

"YOU DIDN'T REALLY THINK it'd be that easy, did you?" The rattle in Jackson's voice reminds me he's no longer amongst the living on the off-chance I've forgotten. The emptiness in his eyes only underscores whatever Hiribaldi and Zaire have done to him.

No irises. Only blackness, like the abyss itself.

I clutch my throat. *I can't* . . .

Kane notices my discomfort immediately. "You're supposed to be dead. You have no business here anymore."

"Listen, motherfucker," my ex says. "This is between me and my girl."

"I'm not your girl anymore, Jackson! I scream. "*We* died a long time ago."

"It doesn't have to be that way, Love," he says. "We can be together forever—for always. Like them."

Kane widens his stance, his arm barring Jackson from coming any closer. "What deal did you strike with Zaire?"

"There's nothing he has that I can't get myself," he says plainly. "He's not the only one around here with power."

"Jackson, what have you done?" I gasp in horror.

"Learned the truth. I was wrong, Love. You have no idea what's waiting for us. The possibilities, you and me."

The dead man's footsteps drag against the rocky soil, his normally lithe movements slow and languid. His skin is sunken, his pallor notwithstanding whatever trip he's been on since we last saw each other. The clothes Jackson wears are tattered and stained with more blood and filth than could ever wash clean. There's a deep blue tint to his skin, his eyebags recessed and blackened.

I naively believed I had absolved myself of my sins. Wrong again. Making it yet another problem headed my way. The tightness in my throat returns.

Kane tries to steady me, but it's not much help. "Allbrook, we've got to go." He tugs on my sleeve, but I don't move.

People are wrong about *fight or flight*; they forget there's also *freeze*. The fear lining my veins has turned my blood to lead. Now I'm nothing more than a deer stuck on a country backroad.

"Jesly, please," Kane begs, this time using my first name. "Come on."

Seeing this ride-or-die thing is my only option now. *By killing him for good.* "I can't," I tell Kane. "He and I have some unfinished business."

In life, Jackson was selfish, cruel, and broken. His delusions forced us into a moment that changed us both forever. In death, he's here—standing right in front of me.

But the afterlife doesn't discriminate. I'm dead too, or close enough to it, brought to ruin by the humanlike creature across the colonnade from us.

"You can't be serious." Whether it's my thoughts or the resolve on my face, Kane's terrified. "If this is Zaire's handiwork, you have no idea what he's capable of."

"Yeah, I do." I pull my arm from his grasp. "There's nothing Jackson can do that he hasn't already. Help the others."

Kane wants to press but doesn't. Points for him. Perhaps in some distant future where we're not all dead, we could have something together. Until that point, he's stuck with this.

"Wait, stop." Kane can't hide his fear, his voice frantic. "You're coming. End of discussion."

A scraggly cough echoes through the chamber. "Sorry to interrupt this lover's quarrel, but you might want to listen. She gets feisty when she's angry."

"Fuck you," Kane curses. It's the first time since we met, way back when he was first assigned to keep watch by the same fools dead set on hunting me. A list that grows longer by the day.

I smile half-heartedly. "It's my fault he's even here right now." I have to finish this—Kane understands that, whether he wants to admit it or not. "Jackson should be rotting in a grave somewhere, but he's here rotting our afterlife."

Kane scoffs. "His inability to let you go made him an easy target for Zaire. You're walking right into their trap."

"You don't get it. He's never going to leave me alone," I say. "Not now, not ever."

Kane's shoulders fall as he sizes up the fight. It's not one he's going to win, and he knows it; it's my choice. "I'm sorry."

"It's okay." My voice trembles as I slip my arms around him, feeling his rigid frame tense before he can tell me not to.

He doesn't fight my embrace, but he doesn't hug me back either. Every fiber of his body hums with restraint. He looks at me, his adult features now childlike with vulnerability and worry.

"You don't have to do this." His voice cracks and the sound

pierces through the thick air between us.

"You're the only one I trust to get them out." I slip the amulet over my head, press it into his hand, and curl his calloused grip around it. "Take this. Keep it safe."

Something flickers over Dax at the sight of the ankh, but it's gone as quickly as the necklace disappears into Kane's shirt pocket.

"Allbrook, just stay alive, okay?" Kane whispers softly.

"I'll do my best." I force a smile, lingering for a moment before their footsteps fade into the eternal quiet.

It doesn't take long before Jackson and I are alone again in the vast chamber, our motives starkly contrasting.

"I knew you'd choose me. You always did." Jackson holds out his hand, beckoning me. "Come, Love."

My chest pounds like a trapped bird, choking me from the inside. I have no intention of taking Jackson's hand. No desire to join him in this Machiavellian nightmare. Whether the man standing in front of me is the truest version of himself or some warped concoction that Hiribaldi and Zaire came up with, the fact remains: What I want is to kill him. Here and now.

It's the only way.

Maybe then I would've deserved this hell. But I was tricked and manipulated, gaslit and coerced until his mistakes became my own. All for nothing.

I brush my fingers against my thigh. *Good.* The switchblade from Amy is still there.

"Alone again," Jackson muses, pleased with himself. There's no bringing back any color to his pallid skin, but what emotion can writhe across his sunken features does. "You don't know how happy this makes me, Jes."

My face is already damp with tears. "We're going to end this, you and me. I'm going to kill you and that'll be it."

"You can't kill what's already dead." His smile crests from ear to ear. "But Jes . . . you're '*in transitu.*' For you, there's still time."

"This whole time you made me think it was me."

"No, Love." He inches toward me in the all-consuming blackness. "You've been sick a long time. The doctors tried their best, but you wouldn't listen."

"Stop lying."

"No, Jes. I'm not," he says sadly, stepping closer. "This was your doing . . . You killed us. I loved you—I would have followed you anywhere. I *did* follow you. But it's okay. I'm not mad. Now we'll be together no matter what. Just like you always wanted."

In the flickering shadows, I can see the old him. The one I met back in college and fell in love with. Not the monster he's become.

It's faint but there. Just like the agonizing pain shooting up my left arm. A shriek bursts from my lungs as I glance down and claw at the scorching fire; my nails dig into my sore flesh to stop it.

But I can't. Not anymore.

The snaking blue lines coil repeatedly around my wrist, one layer over the other until they take a new shape entirely. Between my ragged cries, I can make out a plastic bracelet, charred and covered in blood.

It's my hospital identification tag.

"Stop playing these fucking games!" I scream and rip the thing off my wrist.

Laughter escapes Jackson's throat. "This is why you need me, Love. See? You can't even tell what's real anymore."

"No!" I whimper and fall to my knees.

He slinks closer. "I'll take care of you, just like I was supposed to. No more work. No more clients."

☥

"Stop lying."

"I'm not, Jes. I mean it," he says. "We can go anywhere. Just the two of us."

My palms sting, and I realize I've been digging my nails into my hands. A wake-up call from my subconscious. *Thank God. I need it.* "Stop with your lies, Jackson. I was never driving. This whole time—it was you. And for what? Where did it get us?"

"Together, forever."

"You'll have to kill me first."

"That can be arranged," he replies, the mask disintegrating as something metallic shimmers in his grip.

So I'm not the only one armed for a fight. Whatever happens, I can't let Jackson get Dagny. I'm so lost in my own thoughts that I don't notice him until a sharp pain bites at my side, his blade slicing into my abdomen. *Shit.*

I break for the opposite end of the colonnade, my footsteps hitting the ground as fast as I can. It's now or never. In the quiet emptiness surrounding us, each footstep feels like a lifetime. My breath struggles to catch up, leaving only a stale sense of despair behind. It's choking—violent and visceral.

I buy what time I can by scurrying behind the next closest column. My fingers graze the sharp burning in my side and feel a gap in the fabric. It's wet. *Damn.*

Luckily, it's superficial. *Thank God.* He missed anything vital, but it doesn't calm the pounding in my chest. If I don't slow down my breathing, I'll be a sitting duck.

"What did they promise you?" I yell, struggling to keep the fear out of my voice. "What was so important you were willing to risk both our lives?"

"Nothing."

"Then why did you do it? Why did you kill us? Why couldn't you have just left?"

He simply stares at me.

"Answer me, goddamnit," I demand, my voice breaking. "Tell me why."

"You still don't get it," he says, striding toward me. "It doesn't matter why. There are no takebacks."

It's so fucking dark that I stumble backward. It's impossible to spot where I'm going. "You shouldn't be here."

"See, that's where you're wrong. Unlike you, I know where I'm supposed to be. Here . . . with you . . . forever." His voice is too loud, too close.

I spin around to find Jackson inches away, his hand outstretched, his face blank and unassuming. There is no threat; he doesn't need one. A simple gesture that means so much more.

My hand burns, itching even. I can feel it; a part of me wants to. That part I'll have to kill next. "I-I can't," I say, pulling out Amy's knife.

His face crunches in heartbreak. "You'll regret this moment," he tells me, his rotten breath hot on my skin.

"I already do," I say. "You were my biggest mistake."

Anguish and decay distort his once gorgeous all-American face. "You don't mean that."

"Yes, I do," I shriek. "Every single chance I gave you to prove me wrong, you proved me right. So fuck you when you say you love me. You don't know what love is."

"That's not true."

"Each time, each choice I gave you, *you* picked the wrong one," I seethe in anger. "Not me—*you*."

"Jes, please," he begs.

☥

Amy's blade tightens in my grasp. "You'll never feel sorry for anyone but yourself. I worshiped the ground you walked on and all you did was play me like a fool."

"I'm sorry you feel that way," he says dejectedly.

The time for absolution is gone.

He's here. I'm here.

We're doing this.

Living with him taught me a lot of things. One of them being the difference between lies and truth. The moment he realizes I'm not playing around, his whole demeanor shifts.

No more wounded schoolboy routine.

Dr. Jekyll is gone. With his piercing blue gaze and vacant expression, Mr. Hyde is all that's left.

My side screams, breaking what little concentration I have. Sending Kane back to the surface was a terrible idea, but what's done is done. He doesn't need to see this.

"Have it your way then." Jackson digs into his pocket and pulls out something small and gleaming faintly in the darkness. It's not until the faint clink of metal skips in my direction and lands near my feet that I realize it's my old engagement ring.

He stalks in my direction, any human emotion drained from his voice. "You promised 'til death do us part.' I'm just making sure you keep it, Love."

The dark abyss fills my vision as I'm heaved into the air, thrown backward in the most inhumanly way possible. The cavern becomes a whirlwind. It's a lifetime before I land on something solid. Each part of my body screams in protest as my head slams into an object, stars ricocheting through my field of view.

Jackson straddles my chest as he chokes me, his eyes filled with unconscionable rage. "Goodbye, Love."

PUNISHMENTS

I COULD PRETEND JACKSON never laid his hands on me, but that'd be a lie. Most often, fear and intimidation were the key tactics in his repertoire. He didn't need to leave marks to scare the shit out of me. That was just a bonus.

My broken nails claw at his grip around my throat, his strength even more unfettered as I writhe beneath him. The throbbing in my head makes my eardrums feel like they're going to burst. His weight pins me down, his knees digging into my upper arms. Trapped beneath his sheer muscle, I hate myself for this.

Clawing is futile when it's a hundred and eighty pounds of dead weight. There's still enough of him to be a threat. Even now. The only thing to stop him were my tears, and even then, it didn't last long—bought me a few minutes if I was lucky. Seconds more likely. It would never be enough.

I would never be enough.

Not then and not now.

"You should have listened, Love," Jackson growls beneath his breath. "It didn't have to be like this. I found it—a way to be together forever. A place where nothing can drive us apart. We can go back to how it used to be. I promise."

The whooshing noise in my head keeps me from focusing on anything else, even when a familiar presence erupts from the darkness. Hopefully rescuing me.

But I'm wrong. So wrong.

"Alders, enough." Zaire's voice cuts through the chaos, disdain dripping from his words. "I told you to find her, not kill her. Dead isn't worth shit."

Jackson doesn't let go.

He slinks closer. "I won't say it again."

"We had a deal."

"Yeah . . . well . . ." Zaire clicks his tongue. "I changed my mind."

Jackson grunts awkwardly above me, his eyes widening.

The pressure releases from my windpipe. Drops of something wet hit my cheek and my eyes lock with Jackson's.

It's blood.

I watch helplessly from below as the bright sanguine liquid erupts from his lips, slowly at first and then faster. I scramble to reorient myself out from under him, but it's no use. The man collapses on top of me, all of his weight pinning me down. He's dead for real this time.

Zaire kicks Jackson's body off me like unwanted cargo, his hand clutching something bright red and soaking wet. "Hello again, Jesly."

It takes a second to realize the thing in Zaire's grip is a human heart, like a nightmare out of *Indiana Jones,* but this is real and actually happening.

Holy fuck. I struggle not to vomit.

"That should help his guilt a little," Zaire says plainly. "He should have listened."

Something's changed, the armor gone. Zaire no longer has to pretend here. In this place, he doesn't have to hide his true self. There's no one left to judge him.

I clutch my throat. "What have you done?"

"Got rid of that fool." Zaire shoots Jackson's corpse a sidelong glance. "You're welcome. Now I need you to listen to my proposition. There's not a lot of time."

We're all mad here . . . I really am in Wonderland.

Swallowing is a struggle. On the off-chance I see tomorrow, my face will probably be an intricate pattern of blue spiderwebs, veins bursting like fireworks.

"Jesly." Zaire snaps a finger in my face.

I merely blink, frozen. Had Zaire wanted to kill me, I'd already be dead. I force my bloodshot eyes upward.

Zaire notices. "Can you understand me right now?"

I hesitate, weighing just how limited my options really are. Nodding buys me time.

"Good. I need you to find Dagny."

"Wh—" My hands fumble to scoot me back from the looming threat, and I instantly know I've gone from bad to worse.

He sighs, disappointed. "Jesly, I've already told you. Even your boy, Kane. We're all trapped here. Every. Last. One of us."

"I, uh . . ."

"She has something we need."

I choke back tears. "Where's Kane? Dax?"

"They'll be along soon enough," Zaire says, nodding to a nearby passage. "Got someone looking for them."

I already know who. *Hiribaldi.*

"You're crazy. You're both crazy," I rasp.

☥

He shrugs. "Perhaps, but it's only through madness that humans accomplish something great."

"You can't do this. Hiribaldi will kill them."

"No," Zaire tells me. "He's under orders not to."

"So was Jackson, apparently," I say. "Didn't do him a whole lotta good."

The amicability drains from Zaire's face, leaving only determination behind. In the harsh light, his features seem sharper, angrier than when I last saw him. "Stop stalling. What'll it be, Jesly?"

"You can't just trap us here," I say. "We're human beings."

"I know," he says without hesitation. "That's entirely the point."

"Someone will figure it out."

"That's fine. The more the merrier."

Commotion in the corridor interrupts us. Saved by the bell, it would seem. Hiribaldi's back. He's found them.

With another shotgun wedged between Dax's shoulder blades, the not-so-good doctor marches him through the towering colonnade, his free hand dragging Dagny's unconscious form by the ankle like a ragdoll.

So much for the help . . .

I gasp when Zaire's flashlight centers on Dax. His forehead is dripping blood, his left eye socket already blackened. His nostrils are lined with blood and his angled nose is sharper than I remember. Dirt and blood cake his shirt while his one good eye drills into Zaire.

"As you requested," Hiribaldi announces and slams the butt of the gun into the back of Dax's left knee. My friend drops in a heap beside his dying sister, the woman Zaire so desperately wanted to protect.

☥

It takes a second, my mind a contorted mess when it finally dawns on me. "Where's Kane?" There's no hiding the hysteria in my voice. "What did you do with him?"

Zaire waves to Hiribaldi, who releases a shrill whistle. My answer comes, sending the earth quaking beneath us once more. The discordant mix of pitter-pattering and scraping nails echoes down the colonnade. Once again, we stand nearly face-to-face with Hiribaldi's overgrown pet.

Ammit.

Only she's not alone.

Stuck between her flesh-riddled jaws the size of a banquet table is Kane. One fang has pierced through his right femur while the other half of her jaw has dug into his right shoulder, shattering his collarbone in the process. He's trapped, skewered between her fangs like a grilled kebab.

Nausea rushes over me as I struggle to breathe. There's a part of me that prays he's dead—that he can't feel what's about to come.

"I'm so delighted you could be here with us for this last part, Jesly," Zaire says. "I know how much you appreciate a good visual." He nods at Hiribaldi. "If you would."

"No, wait!" I shout just as another whistle echoes through the colonnade.

It's no use. Before I can rush toward him, the first bit of blood splatters the ground, and my screams fail to drown out Ammit's destruction.

Please God. No . . .

Outside of my guttering sobs, there is nothing to mask my despair. It hits me like a Mack truck. The bile in my stomach wins, and I'm left retching between my tears.

☥

"I'm so sorry," I blubber between the crunches of bone.

Zaire doesn't stop me as I drag myself to where Ammit drops what remains.

"Please . . . no," I weep and struggle to sort through the disheveled pile for something still human. Anything. Shreds of fabric and bloodied bone are all I find. I vomit again, my heartache nearly capsizing me.

There's nothing left. Even Dax looks on, horrified. Hiribaldi, on the other hand, grins like a shit-eating cat. My body surges with rage now that the adrenaline has washed out the last shred of disorientation.

"I told you," Zaire says. "You didn't listen."

"You bastard!" I say, completely surrounded. But I don't care. Not anymore. "Innocent people are dying."

A bitter laugh erupts from Zaire's throat. "Innocent? Are you really that daft?" Zaire yanks me to my feet. "For a lawyer, you're incredibly stupid. Watch." He snatches me by the hair, forcing me to stare at the pile that was once Kane.

Impossibly, it moves.

Even with nothing recognizable, the mass moves again. Something unnatural sluices and scrapes against the stone ground, and it's only seconds before bone follows suit.

"What's going on?" I ask, but Zaire ignores my question.

Our eyes stay fixed on the shifting pile in front of us. To my horror, it begins to grow as specks of white beneath the blood fuse and wire together. Soon there are tendons, sinewy muscles, and veins to carry that sanguine liquid. Our horror is magnified when flesh covers the pulsating humanlike creature and Kane's clothing appears shortly thereafter.

"What the fuck?" Dax says as Kane bolds upright with a

suffocating gasp.

Against probable laws of the universe, Kane is alive. His clothes tattered, his body bloodied, but he's in one piece.

If ever I doubted this is really Hell, I no longer do.

"See, Kane here can never die," Zaire tells me with a grin. "Some punishments run too deep."

☥

COLLAPSE

"WHAT HAVE YOU DONE?" I say, unable to keep the horror from my voice. A man got eaten alive, only to reassemble before my eyes like nothing ever happened.

"Me? I have nothing to do with this," Zaire balks. "The credit belongs to a power far greater." When he sees my vacant expression, he adds, "You really are something. Watch." Zaire grabs a disheveled Kane from the rocky soil and drags him over.

Pulling out a wicked-looking dagger, Zaire cuts through what's left of my companion's sleeve, exposing the fresh skin beneath it. Plunging it straight into Kane's arm, he rips it back out. Blood pours for several seconds and then stops. Again.

Zaire brushes away the bright red liquid, leaving only a faint scar behind. "Now do you get it?"

Kane won't meet my eyes, his body exhausted; Hiribaldi, meanwhile, borders on delirium, his amusement on display for all to see. Torturing the Watcher is sport to him.

Kane takes a ragged breath. "You should have never come back. This is exactly what he wants."

"I know," I acknowledge then turn to Zaire. "What do I need to do?"

He was expecting more of a fight. Not today. Visibly relieved, Zaire lets go of the man. "Dagny must return with us. Otherwise, none of this ever stops."

"It's true then," Dax says. "You can stop this."

Zaire kneels in front of me. "That's what I've been trying to tell you two this entire time. Nothing will ever change unless we're willing to change it ourselves."

"Change? Change what?" I ask. "What are you? Some kind of undead vigilante?"

"What I am doesn't matter—only what you do next," he tells me. "Until she returns, no one's free. Not you or those patients you care so much about. Not even your boy Kane here."

"Dagny needs treatment, Zaire," Dax blurts from where Hiribaldi still guards the paramedic.

"No," the man says simply. "She *needs* to come home."

"This is my sister you're talking about. She's not going anywhere with you. Hell or otherwise." Dax lunges toward us but freezes when Ammit makes her presence known. It's a warning anyone can understand. Especially when it comes in the form of a carnivorous Mack truck.

Zaire nods at Hiribaldi. "Handle him."

The former doctor doesn't move. "I don't take orders from you."

"That so?"

"Yeah. That so."

"We've got one shot at making this work," Zaire reminds him. "Are you with me, Kenji, or are you going to keep playing patty-cake inside God's sandbox?"

Hiribaldi says, "I think I'd rather do things my way. Ammit!"

☥

The lumbering primordial beast rises from where she's been waiting for her second course. The rocky soil beneath the columns shivers beneath the creature's massive weight.

I try to drag myself to my feet but slip in the copious blood left over from Ammit's last meal.

"Lady Ammit!" Hiribaldi roars. "Show them who the true master of the Duat is."

The creature wastes no time in scampering toward her next potential round of kebabs. Her jaunty run is every bit of business in the front and party in the back. The lightning-fast sineviness of her upper torso is cruelly and thankfully countered by the cumbersome powerhouse that is Ammit's backside. Whatever created this chimeric monster had no sympathy when it came to its construction. Ammit is too large for the colonnade. Which gives us time.

But not enough.

The ground quakes beneath us, enough that our balance fails. I slide in the blood once more, shooting fire through my left knee as we're sent crashing to our knees. *Fuck.*

Kane snatches the dagger from Zaire's distracted grip and plunges it into the zealot's lower back. "Jesly, run!"

Dax and I try again to scramble to our feet, and with a busted knee, it's quite a struggle. Ammit shifts her focus to the next closest prey. *Dagny.*

Thankfully, Kane notices and latches onto the man's sister before pulling her into a fireman's carry. She's light, but with the ground trembling with each step we take, the process is treacherous.

Ammit's tail thrashes into the first mountainous pillar, sending Dax diving against another. The towering stone plummets to the ground, rubble the size of boulders cascading all around us. The second pillar follows soon after, threatening the platform we're standing on. It's not long before the ground crumbles beneath us and Dagny falls from Kane's grip.

"Run away, Jesly. Run away and live to love another day," Zaire croons as he rushes to safety, leaving Ammit hot on our tail.

Dax doesn't move as the cavern decays around us. He just stands there, watching.

"Dax?" I shout. "Come on—"

"Allbrook, we need to get out of here." Kane tries to sling Dagny over his shoulder but can't. It's too much. His body is too weak. But he tries again. And again until he can.

I serve as cover, following behind the two of them until we reach the next pillar. I turn back around, expecting to see Dax, but he's gone.

It's just the three of us now. *Shit.*

"Where'd he go?"

Kane pops his head up, surprised. "Doesn't matter. We keep moving."

"What if Zaire's right, Kane? You just got eaten alive." I lean against the closest column. "What if that's all it takes—she goes back, this all stops?"

"You can't be serious," he chokes between steps.

"But I am."

"Now isn't the time to have a question of faith," he counters and sets Dagny down. "Even if we get out of this, The Chasa are still out there."

"About that—"

He coughs. "Listen. I don't know what price you paid to release me, but I can tell you it's too high." He digs into his chest pocket and throws the ankh necklace back at me.

I barely grab it in time and slip it around my neck. He doesn't know I've sold myself into this. *Not yet. If I play my cards right, he never will* . . .

"Allbrook, you didn't—"

Too late.

"Tell me you didn't." He frantically pulls me into his grip and shakes me hard. But before he can scold me further, the third pillar comes crashing down on top of us, destroying the platform once and for all.

The world goes crooked, like a topsy-turvy version of Hell; Kane lies above me while Dagny slides downward along the platform like the trailing end of a hellish seesaw.

"Shit!" I dive after her. My fingertips latch onto her gown.

"Jesly, no!" Kane lunges after me but struggles to keep ahold of the divot he's latched onto.

A thunderous crack snakes through the cavern floor, its chaos reverberating. A large piece of the platform gives way, falling into the growing chasm beneath us.

"Kane!" I cry out. Our fingers graze but it's not enough.

Still unconscious and unable to save herself, Dagny tumbles over the collapsing cliff's edge, with me following right behind her.

The platform finally succumbs, becoming a series of falling boulders like hail from an angry sky. No light exists where we're going. Wherever it is, I hope my deal with The Chasa still holds.

Seconds pass as we plummet into the infinite darkness, and it feels like forever before we finally succumb to solid ground.

This time, there's no question whether I'm still alive.

This time, I stumble to my feet, unbroken and unafraid.

UNDEAD GIRLS

THE AIR SMELLS STALE, earthy and ancient, as if Time itself has forgotten about it.

"Anyone? Hello?" I yell into the blackened veil, my hands fumbling across gravel and stone. A pebble moves and I fling myself in that direction. "Kane?"

He's not going to go through this nightmare again. Not for me. I dig until my nails shred and they're damp with blood and sweat. There's no energy left. Nothing to keep me moving forward except sheer will.

"Dax?" I call out, praying for a sign, but there's nothing.

No reason to expect the paramedic to answer. Ammit beelined for him on the far end of the cavern. If he's lucky, he made it out.

The likelihood that Dax has fallen here with us is slim. Wherever he disappeared to, I just hope he's okay. We don't all have some supernatural knack for surviving things that should otherwise kill us.

Eventually, my hands latch onto something human, and I claw away what rubble I can. I dig into my pocket for the lighter one last time in the hope that it's still intact.

It is.

But before I can even flick the metal lid open, the lighter tumbles from my grip. I'm left to scour the rubble once again.

"Goddamnit, come on," I cry between breaths as I rinse and repeat. My fingers latch onto the smooth metal, and I flick the striker. *Thank God*, I sigh. Whether it's the all-knowing entity or someone else, my prayers have been heard.

There's not much lighter fluid left, but it's enough. The faint light passes over the chaos and I stumble on the image of a woman's form.

It's Dagny that's here with me. Not Kane.

My hand hovers above her mouth. She's still breathing. Faint, but it's there. I raise the light higher to search where we've landed but can't even make out the platform. Wherever we are, it's hundreds of feet down.

Exhaustion finally catches up. I collapse in a heap. If I'm not careful, this place will be our tomb. Trapped, forever. I finally stop to survey our soon-to-be mausoleum.

Patches of moss cling to the jagged rock face, adding splashes of muted green to the scarred surface. Here and there, small shrubs and stunted trees defiantly sprout from precarious ledges, their gnarled roots seeking purchase in the unforgiving stone. Even the earth stands defiant in this forgotten hell.

My body aches. It's deep in my bones now.

Is this what dying truly feels like? I've been running for so long that I don't even remember what rest feels like anymore. I flick Dax's Zippo open and closed a few times before stuffing it back in my pocket. The rock wall is rough against my head, and I fight to smooth out a spot. It doesn't work.

Somewhere in the distance, more rocks settle. No, wait—*move.* My eyes snap open. "Kane?"

"No." A female coughs. "Just me."

"Dagny?" I balk, the lighter front and center in a heartbeat. "How are you awake right now?"

"There's no time to explain," she says, ignoring me. Still visibly weak, color returns to her face. She struggles to her feet, but gravity demands otherwise. "I've gotta go. I can't stay."

I inch closer. "You nearly died," I state but don't dare say the other part—the fact that I was in the car that killed her and left her to bleed out. I'm not ready. Not yet.

"Yeah," she says sourly. "I hear that's a thing. Help me outta this." She starts shoving rocks out of the way.

I'm less than ten yards out when her high-pitched scream rushes through the crevice floor and we nearly collide.

"What is it? What's wrong?" I ask.

"There's someone else," she shouts, flailing as she scurries past.

"Kane? Please God, no . . ." I drop to my knees and tear through the rocks. "Kane?"

She shrugs. "I've seen him before."

I work faster.

Eventually, I make it. Like something out of *The Wizard of Oz,* a set of boots lay beneath a mountain of rocks and boulders. Ones different from Kane's, much to my relief.

She clutches her throat. "He was working with Zaire."

Hiribaldi.

A shuddering sigh escapes my lips. *Thank God.* She's right.

I'm not entirely sure if immortality can outlast ten metric tons, but I'll take those odds. Especially when Zaire and the immortal bitch-beast are still roaming around. With Hiribaldi out of the way, it's one less thing to worry about.

I should feel relieved. But I don't. It's not over, not by a long shot. "What now?" I croak.

Dagny reaches for the slit of her floor-length gown and tugs at the hem. The fabric shreds as she rolls up the length and ties it off at her thighs. "*Now?* We get out of here."

Within seconds, she's scaling the crevice wall. She's tiny compared to me and moves like a hummingbird. Hard to see and even harder to pin down. Her bare feet dig into the side walls, making her ascension look like child's play.

I blink. "Dagny, you're not well. We need to wait for help."

She ignores my pleas and keeps going. "Look around you," she tells me. "Where do you think we are? No one's coming." Already standing on some ledge, she stares down at me triumphantly.

"That's crazy high," I argue. "There's no way."

"Suit yourself." She resumes her ascension.

I stare at the mountain of rubble and take a deep breath. If Kane is in there, I'll never forgive myself. He may be immortal, but that doesn't mean he can't be permanently trapped like Hiribaldi. Forever tortured. All for trusting the wrong person—*me.* As my mission leaves me behind, I pray I don't end up the same.

Here we go.

At this point, I'm certain that rock climbing is not in my top five skills. Like, *at all.* It takes me twice as long to traverse what Dagny already has. She's made it to the third ledge before I've even reached the first.

"How . . . are you moving . . . so quickly?" I ask between breaths. My frazzled nerves combined with the lack of air make this process that much more difficult.

"State champion in undergrad three years in a row. Comes in handy sometimes. I'll give you a hand." Latching onto the rock face, she extends a calloused hand. "Just don't look down."

"Ok." I grab her hand and use my own to pull myself to the next ledge. We use each other's body weights to ascend the chasm. I follow in her footsteps, literally, placing my feet in the grooves she finds in the jagged wall. We're nearly a hundred feet up.

"Let's catch our breath," I plead.

"Okay." Brushing her bangs out of her face with the back of her hand, Dagny collapses against the rock, her blonde hair stringy and damp with sweat. We both notice the damp chill creeping through the chamber at the same time. Rubbing her hands together, she blows between them. She returns my stare. "You obviously have questions. Ask."

"How are you conscious right now?" I repeat my question from earlier. "You've been on the verge of death for hours."

She looks around the chasm. "We're no longer in Kansas, Dorothy."

"I'm sorry?"

"I assume Zaire told you the truth?"

"That we're all trapped? Yeah." I tell her what I know.

Purgatory. The Scales. The Chasa. And now, she and Zaire.

"I've seen things, Dagny. Things I can't explain."

She scoops a couple of pebbles and chucks them over the edge, one at a time. "The fucker is delusional," she grouses. "He's obsessed with trying to keep me here. Every time I run, he finds some new way to drag me back."

"Who is he?" I ask.

"A mistake after one too many Jägerbombs."

"I'm really sorry."

☥

"No need," she says. "I knew what I was getting into."

The corner of my lip twitches. "Dax."

"I was trying to find a way to get him back."

"Did it work?"

She shakes her head. "You see where we are, right?"

I grimace. "Uh, well—"

"And he always thought I was the good twin. I didn't know my research would land me here though." Hugging her knees, she adds, "Might've just gone to bereavement therapy had I known I would get chased around forevermore."

"So you aren't some undead goddess doomed for all eternity?"

Her gaze narrows. "No? I'm just some undead girl from Odessa for all eternity." When she sees the horror on my face, she adds, "Jesus, Jesly. Lighten up. What's done is done. There's no going back."

I rub my shoulders and swallow hard. My fingers instinctively clutch the amulet. Amy was onto something.

"You still have it," she notes.

"Yeah. I kept it safe."

When I start to give it back, she waves me off. "Keep it. You still need it."

"But—"

She forces a smile. "It can't help me anymore. I can't leave. Not really."

My eyes widen. *It's true.* "Why?"

"When my brother died, I did some stupid shit. Got involved in the wrong things, made deals with the wrong people," she says, chucking the last of the pebbles over the ledge. "I ended up going down the rabbit hole far more than I intended, and it led me here." A heavy sigh escapes her lips.

☥

"But why us? Why our firm?" I say.

"We all make choices, Jesly." She points at my arm, and it takes me a second to realize she's talking about my scar . . . tattoo . . . whatever the hell it is.

And then I realize.

"It wasn't an accident," I say in disbelief. "You knew what you were doing."

Dagny bites her lip and nods slowly. "I should've never gotten you guys involved in this. Maybe one of us would still be alive."

She waits for me to process what she's just said, letting the silence creep in around us. Even if Jackson hadn't been speeding that night, she would've found a way. The woman is far more resourceful than anyone gave her credit for.

By sheer dumb luck, Jackson and I happened to be in the wrong place at the wrong time. Something that's unraveled the lives of every last one of us. Maybe Fate really does get her way sometimes.

To Dagny's relief, I eventually ask, "What are you going to do?"

"It doesn't matter. Whatever I do, Zaire will just find some loophole in the system to reincarnate me into this nightmare forever."

"How can he do that?"

"Did you happen to meet his three tagalongs? Like something out of a really bad Halloween party?"

I nod. "The Chasa."

"Yeah," she says bitterly. "They're some old Korean death gods. Turns out they're real and beholden to him somehow."

"How?"

She lumbers back to her feet. "Don't know. Zaire stole my research before I got the chance to figure it out for myself. Now, we're stuck here and he's taken it upon himself to play God."

"The cavern with the patients."

"Yeah," she confirms. "But it's not about me anymore. He's planning something far worse."

I snort. "Well, he ripped out a man's heart right in front of me, so how much worse could it get?"

"A lot. He's out for blood and likely won't stop until he gets it. He's sick. Mental." She wiggles her finger next to her temple. "His obsession with keeping me here is just the start."

My stomach drops. "What do you mean?"

"You want to help, right? Well, whatever happens next is on us both. I hope you're ready to visit Hell because that's exactly where we're headed."

VERITAS

For a moment, my breath stops. "What?"

The birdlike woman nods. "You heard me. There's only one way out—by killing Zaire."

"Kill him?" I gawk at her. "That's the entire reason we're here in the first place. I've done enough for a lifetime. Find someone else to seek vengeance in y'all's war."

"Don't you get it?" Dagny says. "It's everyone's war. Zaire won't stop until he drags the entire world into it. I don't know how he found me, but he was more than happy to chat me up about my research."

"He used you."

She nods. "Looking back, I should've realized. He was way too interested, way too eager. I just thought he was horny. I didn't realize he was *interested* in opening a portal to the Underworld."

I mull it over. "That's why he keeps you trapped."

"I know too much," she concurs. "I've *seen* too much."

"So what now?"

"We stop him before he kills anyone else."

I take a deep breath and start climbing, while Dagny passes in half the time. "So I'm gonna take it that whole thing about you two being engaged isn't a thing."

She nearly loses her grip. "Don't tell Dax I said this, but have you ever heard the tale about Diogenes?"

"Should I have?"

"He was a philosopher that supposedly went through Greece with a lantern in search of an honest man," she says as she steadies her breath and wedges her body into a tight crevice.

"And?"

"He never found one."

I sigh and scour every inch of the wall, the uneven slate and gneiss serving as footholds back to the surface. If we survive this, I'm never climbing again. My arms and shoulders scream with the ascension, reminding me that I should have spent more time in the gym and less in the meeting room. It feels like hours before we make it to an opening in the chasm.

Dagny's still unfazed by our daunting trek. "Grab my hand." She pulls me up and onto solid ground.

Finally.

Whatever's left of the cavern, it's unrecognizable.

"It looks completely different," I say, spinning around in awe.

Not looks, is. This cavern is smaller, more cramped. Here, bioluminescent vines cling to the stalactites, beckoning us in. The cool air feels heavy, tinged with an earthy heaviness that hints at something far more dangerous.

Shadows dance along the walls of the cavern, flickering in the wavering light. They aren't ours.

My stomach tightens. *We shouldn't be here.*

She brushes herself off in the faint blues and greens. Wobbly, but intact. "You hurt anywhere?"

"No, I'm good," I tell her. "You sure about this?"

"Great. It's just up ahead." She ignores my question and heads deeper into the cavern.

I use my shirt collar to rub the sweat off my forehead. "Maybe we should slow down. We have no idea what's waiting for us."

"No." She storms up to me, her jaw firm. "*You* don't know what's out there. *I* do, and I promise it's not waiting."

"You mean Ammit?"

"Worse than her," she says. "I've been studying this stuff since back in grad school. This is just the start."

"What are you saying?"

"I'm saying that if Zaire has his way, that beast will be the least of our worries. There are far worse things lurking in the dark."

The bioluminescent vines hold my attention locked. "I need to tell you something."

"Okay," she answers. "What?"

"Dax is here. He was with us before the cavern collapsed."

She doesn't even flinch.

"I'm sorry," I say.

Or acknowledge what I've said.

She just keeps moving, navigating this place at lightning speed. Her footsteps echo in the small puddles gathered here and there.

Up ahead, there's a small opening in the wall. This entire chamber is damp with moisture from the humidity buzzing around us. Crouching, she tears some of the vines before pushing into the narrow tunnel. I crawl in behind her, the tight space reminding me to breathe deeply.

It reeks of earth. What little light there was outside the tunnel disappears instantly. My stomach lurches for a moment. That ancient quiet has returned, but it's darker . . . angrier.

Get out.

Kane? I bash my head on the short ceiling. "Goddamnit."

"Come on. I can see the exit," Dagny informs me. "We're nearly there."

Squeezing through the tight crevice, she drags herself army-style. Soon she's pushed into another chamber without much effort. With her body blocking the tunnel exit, it's nearly impossible to tell where we've ended up.

"Hey, help me out of here," I say.

Hands reach back into the tunnel and latch on to my shoulders, stronger than Dagny's grasp should allow. But I'm grateful to be dragged out of the claustrophobic hell.

A wide expanse of beach surrounding a large subterranean lake awaits us. There are no glowing vines to illuminate our path this time. Not that I need them to. I can see it for myself.

The hands saving me belong to none other than Dax, alive and well. Before I make a sound, he claps his hand over my mouth and drags me behind an outcrop. Hiribaldi's shotgun hangs from his back. *Thank God.*

"Shhhh." His muscles tighten around me, holding me still. He waits for me to calm down. "Breathe, Jesly. Breathe. We don't have a lot of time."

I fight the urge to hug the guy. With Dax back, that leaves only Kane now. A rustle on the far side of the chamber distracts me. It's Zaire, and he's making a beeline straight for a hunched figure resting at the water's edge.

Dagny spins around, startled. "Hey."

He smiles. "I see you enjoyed your rest."

"I did."

"Did you find the woman?" he asks. "Hiribaldi's missing—that useless sack of dung."

"I left her in the tunnel, Zai." Dagny nods in our direction. My eyes widen in horror and Dax forces us even lower.

"Good, good. It's almost time." Zaire pulls her into a deep embrace, his body engulfing her smaller frame. "I was so worried. You scared the shit out of me."

"I told you I'd be fine," she says. "Let's just get this over with. I want to go home."

He gently strokes her cheek. "I know. I'm sorry it took so long."

Following the water's edge, he reaches a stone platform that stretches out across the water's surface. Deep within this hidden oasis, a large wooden waterwheel stands sentinel over the lake, and I get the feeling it's guarding more than just what lurks beneath.

Dagny takes a quick look back at the tunnel before following. "Do you have everything we need?" She scrambles onto the platform.

"Close." He passes her the torch. "Here, give me a hand."

He pulls a lever recessed in the stone rock face, forcing the waterwheel to move. Like a long-slumbered beast rousing from the grave, it rattles into motion, each pass clacking as it stirs the dead. "Fetch the Watcher." He signals toward a cave on the lake wall.

"Seriously?"

Zaire nods. "You want to go find Kenji?"

She stifles her breath. "No, no. It's fine. I'll do it." Dax and I helplessly watch as Dagny jumps into the water. "Shit, Zai," she shrieks. "You didn't tell me it'd be cold."

Zaire uses the torch to light a nearby sconce on the wall. "It's an underground cavern. What did you expect?"

"Hell, not this." She wades into the channel. "You'd better be right." She dives into the water and swims into the darkness.

"Mr. Huxley, if you would," Zaire yells into the shadows. "Bring our special guest."

Fear bolts down my spine as quickly as Dax's grip tightens around me like a python. I've been played. *Damnit. They're both crooked.* Dax's grip only clamps down more. All my squirming and thrashing do nothing.

He latches a hand around my ponytail, and I fail to claw his grip from my scalp as he drags me toward the lake. "Don't try and struggle. You're just going to hurt yourself," he says.

Zaire laughs at the sight of us. "Dagny won't be long. I sent her on a little mission for our other honored guest. Come now."

Dax doesn't hesitate to follow orders, using Hiribaldi's shotgun to steer my path. My eyes scour for an escape route because running is out of the question. If anything, it'll land me a shot in the back. The water it is.

"You were working with them the whole time, weren't you?" I say in disbelief.

Dax simply pushes me further into the lake.

Dagny was right. The water is like ice. It sends my already weak nerves into a frenzy. My hands struggle to catch me as I stumble into the quickly rising depth.

Zaire drags my freezing body onto the wooden platform. "Congratulations. You get to be a part of something special today, Jesly."

"Wh-where's K-Kane?" I chitter like a half-drowned cat. "What did you do with him?"

"That vermin? He'll turn up soon enough. Mr. Huxley, on the other hand, that's someone I can get behind." He hits a second lever, this one below the first. It doesn't budge.

Fuck, it's cold. My body won't stop shaking. "You bastard."

"Looks like we've got something to fix. Ladies first." Zaire points to an old, dilapidated ladder hanging against the rock face.

"Me? What for?"

"There's a control panel that needs looking into, so you're up."

"Move." Dax wedges the gun deeper between my shoulder blades, forcing me back to my feet. The wooden railing splinters beneath my grip as I avoid the part that's weak from water damage and time.

"Don't do this, Dax," I say. "This isn't you."

"You don't know the first thing about me," Dax says through gritted teeth. "Now shut it."

"We don't have all day, children," Zaire muses. "Chop, chop."

More climbing. *Great.*

My arms ache, my side screams, and I still have zero idea where Kane is. It feels like ages before we reach the top of the platform and I see what all the fuss is about.

Embedded deep in the recess of the gypsum rock face is a Victorian-era control box, ornate and bristling with levers and gears. Brass pipes twist and snake around it. Valves silent, the mechanisms are covered in a thick layer of grime. The dials and clockwork mechanisms are frozen, their labels faded, and their gauges nearly cracked.

"What now?" I ask, not forgetting the muzzle in my back.

"Fix it," Dax says dispassionately.

"How?"

"Figure out something. You always do." He hands back Amy's switchblade. How he ended up with it, I have no idea, but beggars can't be choosers.

"Don't get any funny ideas," he snaps.

☥

"I'm not." I take a deep breath, trying to steady my shaking hands. The grime-covered levers and gears look ancient, their purpose almost inscrutable. I crouch down, inspecting the brass pipes and frozen dials, searching for any sign of life.

Nothing.

I fumble through my pockets. Only the napkin remains. Switchblade first. Prying the control box takes less time than I expected as it pops open with a metallic clink. Inside, a tangled mess of gears, springs, and rudimentary electrical components greets me. Crud lines the gears, jamming them until they have completely seized.

"Clock's ticking," he tells me.

"Jesus, give me a minute," I say. "I got a B in physics, shit."

With a shotgun at my back, now is as good a time as any to start remembering. I strip the cloth into makeshift insulation and carefully try to reconnect the loose conductor. The gears remain motionless. Dax, on the other hand, paces back and forth like a caged lion.

Fuck. I spin around and look for something else. A small stone sits close-by that I might be able to use. With my hands raised innocently, I point at it. "How about that?"

He follows my line of sight, never lowering the gun. "Give it a shot."

I scoop it up and tap lightly on the gears, trying to dislodge any rust or grime. Slowly, painfully, the gears crawl back to life, protesting at their disturbed slumber.

It takes several minutes, but I continue tapping, alternating between the switchblade and the stone, chipping away at the layers of grime. Sweat drips down my face as I work, my forearm muscles burning from the effort. One more time. With a final decisive tap,

☥

the gears start to turn. The dials twitch and the valves hiss softly as they open.

"There," I say, stepping back as I slip the knife in my back pocket. "It's working."

Dax narrows his eyes at the contraption then nods. "You did it. Now get moving." He shoves the gun deeper into my back, forcing me away from the control box.

"Why are you working with them?" I question as Dagny resurfaces from the freezing pool of water hundreds of yards below. "You're doing this because of her?"

"I'm doing this because of *you*, Jesly." Dax levels the muzzle at me.

"Me?" I balk. "I thought we were friends."

"Just stop pretending for once," he says derisively. "Nobody believes your bullshit here."

"Dax, I don't understand." I inch backward, my hands raised as I peer over the edge. The platform is narrow enough that one wrong move will send me plummeting into that freezing water, and I have a sinking feeling that lightning won't strike a third time.

From this height, it could paralyze me at best. Kill, at worst. Either way, the odds aren't looking good.

The butt of the shotgun slams into my ribcage, sending me into the stone wall. We wrestle for the grip as he strikes me again, this time in the jaw.

"You're the reason she's here, Jesly! What don't you understand?" Dax bellows, his eyes brimming with tears. "It was your responsibility to keep her safe, and you failed! You're never getting out of here. I will die before that happens."

It's seconds before I say anything, running over my options. My ribs burn, the cavern pulsates in a way I know it shouldn't, and when I touch the back of my head, my fingers come away with bright crimson.

When I finally do speak, it's not what he wants to hear. "Dax, I did nothing to Dagny. We've been together the entire time."

"Really?" He rips the ankh from my throat and shoves it in my face. Slamming me into the wall again, shooting stars flood my vision. The gun digs into my flesh below my jaw, reminding me who's in control. "You maybe want to rethink that a little?"

"She gave it to me," I choke between breaths. "Just like you gave me that book of hers."

"*I* gave you that book—that coin—to lead you here," he explains. "That necklace though, Dags would've never given it up willingly. Just like she'd never work with someone as corrupt as Zaire. You've done something—played some kind of mind game on her."

"No," I argue. "You're wrong."

"None of this would've happened if not for you."

My eyes widen, and I try to put distance between us. "I'll tell you whatever you want to know. Just put the gun down."

"That's what I thought."

A hummingbird threatens to burst from my chest, my heartbeat thundering against my ribs. Each breath becomes harder to catch. "Please . . ."

"Stupid, I mean before all of this. Before the hospital. Before I failed to kill you the first time."

I blink. "The roof? That was you?"

"Yes," he agrees, his breath hot on my wet cheek. "Ever since I found out that you dragged my sister into this nightmare, I've been following you."

"Why?"

"I want to hear you say it."

"Dax, please . . . Dagny—"

"Don't even say her name." His viselike grip latches onto my long curls once again, yanking me toward the edge. "Tell me what happened that night." he demands. "I'm not going anywhere until you say it."

"It won't change anything," I cry. "You know that, right?"

"Do *you* know you're gonna die today?" The resolution in his eyes voids any doubt.

I thought I'd gained that resolve myself. Until now. Until one more friend turned against me, and I realized I was wrong.

"No one's gonna die," I blurt before I can help myself. Impulsivity is a bitch. My dumb mouth's gonna get me killed. *Just tell him.* "If you knew this the entire time, why play into this farce? Why not just finish the job in the hospital?"

"I don't have to explain myself to you."

I stabilize myself with the wall. "No? You were willing to shoot a woman in broad daylight with no explanation?"

"Stop stalling, Jesly."

"You think I'm the only one with secrets?" I pit back at him. "How did you die, Dax? Did those pills take you on one ride you couldn't get back from? How many times did Dagny have to fix your fuckups? Clean up your mess?"

"Shut your mouth," he snaps.

"No," I tell him. "I don't think I will. Grow some balls and say what you really want."

It takes him a minute to steel himself, his back straightening as he takes a deep breath. This is just as hard for him as it is for me. "Because I needed to look my sister's killer in the eye and ensure justice was served."

"Dax, I tried to persuade her to drop the case," I admit. "But Jackson—"

"Isn't. Here. Anymore," he cuts me off, the corner of his mouth twitching.

The memory of the needle in my shaking grip flashes in my mind. All the people Jackson hurt. All the terrible things he did. In the end, Zaire tossed him aside like a ragdoll and Dax's vengeance was stolen from him.

At least in his eyes.

Which makes me his only choice. Telling him Dagny did this to herself would never sit with him. She's too perfect—too innocent. *The good twin.*

"I'm not a **murderer**," I say half for him, half for myself.

"How long you gonna keep lying?" He clutches my collar and yanks me toward the edge of the platform. "You could have done something—anything. Ran for help, screamed, flagged down a cop even. But you didn't."

"That's impossible," I try to explain. "There's no way I could—"

"I want to hear you say it—that you left my sister to die. It's your fault she's like this—with *him*—so why can't you just own up to it?"

"Dax, that's not what—"

"Say it!"

"I was there," I finally admit. "I walked away. Is that what you want to hear?"

There's nothing I can say to make him see reason—nothing I can do to change the past. To him, Dagny is trapped because of me. Telling him the truth won't change anything.

He chokes back tears. "Finally some real honesty for once.

Thank you."

Too caught in the moment, he ignores my grip on his hands. But I don't. It's the only thing keeping me from plummeting into the lake a half-thousand feet below. I have one chance to get this right. "I'm so sorry," I say, my own tears already blurring my line on the shotgun.

With Amy's switchblade still nestled safely in my pocket, I let go of his grip around my shirt collar and reach for the weapon. Amy died saving me. In the end, her oath upheld.

Each of us made decisions to get here.

Each of us has only one path forward.

So when I drive the blade straight into the side of his neck, I have less than a second to make it count. The serrated teeth do that for me as I rip it back out, covering us both in his life source.

Thankfully, his grip loosens.

It just so happens to be while we both go over the edge of the towering mezzanine, the rotten wood finally giving way. Scrambling for one of the rungs of the ladder gets nowhere. My shoulder bangs against it. Adrenaline obscures the pain as we tumble helplessly downward.

We careen toward the icy water at an alarming rate, Dax's limp form mirroring mine. So much for a plan.

Here's to lightning striking . . . again.

FROM THE ASHES

DAGNY'S SCREAMS GET DROWNED out as we plunge into the freezing water. From this height, it feels like bursting through an already broken window. Like a thousand shards of glass shred what's left of me.

Beneath the surface, everything is distorted, time having lost its meaning long ago. I spend what little energy I have left to not suffocate. My leg muscles burn with each kick. My lungs mock me, reminding me that I've never been the greatest swimmer. I wish I could laugh at the irony. *Futile*, I know. I would only end up struggling in the dark water. The universe has always had such wonderful humor when it came to my life.

Dax is gone.

The shouting above the surface confirms it. That, and the sudden rush of bright red encroaching the water. Like an old-timey cartoon, I've gained firsthand experience on what happens when a moveable object meets an immovable force.

But Dax didn't have an amulet to protect him—something his beloved sister gave to me. Unfortunately, that same woman is currently screaming bloody murder.

Sour bile threatens my airway. I've got to reach the surface. *Fast.*

I can't blame God for forsaking me—I'd forsake me too. There are no words for what I expected, but this wasn't it. Never thought Dax would be my enemy. Didn't want Dagny to end up here, trapped at the hands of Zaire.

In the end, Dax did what he thought was right. But others gave up their lives for me to be here and I've failed them. I'm no hero. The first real challenge and I retreated like a coward.

From Hiribaldi. From Jackson.

The only thing that mattered was my own skin.

Both Jackson and I thought we walked away that night— foolishly believing we left her to die. But we were wrong. So wrong. All this time.

We all fight like animals in the end. Human instinct. Self-preservation at its finest. Dax was right.

I am a killer—a poison that corrupts everything around it.

This punishment is my own fitting end for treachery.

But Dr. Caspar didn't deserve it nor did Dr. Kennedy. Neither Chandni nor Asim, who are the only reason I made it through the gate in the first place.

Yamaloka. Hades.

Call it whatever, the fact remains; the Underworld wants me for one of its own. I just hope the deal I struck with The Chasa still holds. Being a reaper might not be that bad provided I find a way out of this first.

Right after I find Kane. That is . . . if I don't die first.

My shoulder writhes in agony as I fight to reach the surface. When I finally crest the water, Dagny and Zaire have already

☥

fished Dax's body out.

The amount of blood floating in the water confirms no amount of CPR will help. Dagny clings to her brother, shaking in a flood of emotions. The shrieking terror escaping Dagny's throat confirms we're no longer in Kansas.

Zaire spots me treading water and stalks across the shallow beach. "You really shouldn't have done that," he grouses as he snatches me out. "Had you died, that would've complicated things."

Unlike Dax, his grip is firm without tearing my hair out. Dagny beelines for me, her eyes filled with rage. Zaire holds her off.

"You murdered him!" she shrieks, her wailing bordering on the unnatural.

"Easy, Dags. Your brother made his own bed," Zaire tells her. Noticing Dagny's burning gaze, Zaire snaps his fingers between us. "You need to focus."

"Fine." Dagny steels her jaw.

"Perfect. It's time." He shoves me in Dagny's direction. "Check her for weapons. Everything's prepped." Zaire navigates to the platform with the wheel and lever, leaving us alone for a moment.

Dagny doesn't hesitate. She's on me in less than a second, patting me down. Her hands pass over the knife in my pocket but don't remove it. "I owe you now. Before the end of this, you'll see," she says loudly. "You're next."

I look down at the rocky shore where his body lays mangled. "I didn't want to hurt him, Dagny. He left me no choice."

"*Choice* is a funny word."

"I'm sorry."

"Remember: this is on you," she whispers.

"Ladies!" Zaire yells from the far side of the platform. "Stop conspiring and get over here."

His shouting from across the cavern makes one thing clear: he doesn't trust Dagny after all. Her vacant expression hits me like a punch to the gut. His soon-to-be queen. *'I'm just some undead girl from Odessa.'*

She's not with him at all.

She's lying. It's an act—one that Dax believed in enough to join Zaire's insane quest.

I did fuck up. "Shit."

She nods slowly as my understanding takes form. The guilt that I feel must be compounded for her. She didn't get to tell Dax the truth.

I killed him first.

"No, Zaire. Of course not," she says calmly. "I would never."

"I would hope not. It's almost time, my love," he announces. "Let's get them prepped."

"Of course." She strides dutifully in his direction.

The universe's dark humor strikes again. The only ally left is the one person I can't communicate with telepathically. Those who do have that connection with me are ones whom I have to hide from most.

So we're doing this the old-fashioned way.

"Where's Kane?" I ask as we mount the wooden dock once again.

"He's here," Zaire announces to my relief, pulling down a different lever recessed into the gypsum rock face. The wheel spins and rotates toward us, reminding me of one of those daytime gameshows. But there are no numbers on this one.

Only a bound and gagged Kane tethered to it.

My chest tightens. "What is this thing?" I ask Zaire as he stops the wheel from spinning further.

"Something irreplaceable."

My relief fades when I realize what this Inquisition-looking contraption really is—a torture device with one simple purpose: to break the victim or drown them first. But it's not the wheel part that worries me. It's the monstrosity next to it.

On the right-hand side is an old machine. Cylindrical vials that have yellowed with time loom above the contraption, each one having its own lever beneath it like some Lovecraftian switchboard. The left side of the machine is a tangle of old rubber tubes tied to early nineteenth-century needles the size of meat skewers. Between the growing rust and blood crusted on the contraption, it's a hepatitis outbreak waiting to happen.

"A while ago, you asked me who I was, and I told you it wasn't important. Do you know why?" Zaire flips the first lever, and the machine roars to life finally.

The ancient mechanical purr is lost to the discordant tottering sounds it now pushes outward, like an old train barreling down misaligned tracks, its engine knocking as it goes. All I can do is shake my head as he flips the second lever.

Slapping Kane on the face, he says, "I'm not the one you should be concerned with. It's this guy right here."

"Him? Why?" I gawk at the barely conscious man hanging from the waterwheel.

"Unlike us, Kane here has been around a long time. *Millennia*, in fact. Comes from a very special line. Might have heard of him in your good ol' Sunday Bible study."

If anyone would know, a mythologist would. But Dagny doesn't meet me in the eyes when I look at her for the truth. Not this time.

"That's nuts, Zaire," I tell them. "It's just a story."

"Have you looked around lately?" Zaire furrows his brow. "Where do you think you are? You're standing before an immortal—a member of God's own family."

I struggle to keep my mouth shut, unable to tear my eyes off the hanging man. "That's impossible."

Kane, as in *Cain*, the brother from the Abrahamic tales—the Christian Bible, the Islamic Quran, and the Jewish Torah. Son of Adam and Eve.

"It's just a myth, a legend," I say incredulously. "There's no fucking way."

"Nothing is impossible, Jesly," Zaire announces confidently. "Not even this."

There's a recoil in my body that makes me want to run. I thought Kane was like me. Human. But he's not. None of them are.

And now I fear . . . neither am I.

Not anymore.

BLOOD BOUND

EACH TIME I THINK I get somewhere, I'm put in my place—told to stay in my lane by a spiteful universe. This entire time, I've been playing a game without knowing all the rules or the odds I'm up against. Without learning who those at the table really are. And now that ignorance has come for me.

I've gotta get us out of here.

Me, Kane, and Dagny. *Somehow.*

Am I even supposed to? If this really is Cain from the stories, he murdered his own brother. Thousands of years ago. Has he been serving out his punishment ever since?

Is that my future too? And if I save him, what does that say about me? A thousand questions rattle around in my head, but I've got to focus. I take the deepest breath I can and count backward from five.

This contraption doesn't seem like it's going to win us any favors. Least of all Kane's.

"What are you going to do with him?" I ask hesitantly.

Dagny and I watch as Zaire becomes the puppet master, tying Kane to a vast number of intricate tubes and wide-mouthed needles—the stuff of nightmares.

Zaire shoves one of those terrifying hepatitis-loving needles into Kane's forearm. We both flinch. "He's going to help a lot of people, and you ladies are going to help us get there."

I scoff. "What? How?"

"Simple, really," Zaire quips. "Dagny was onto something. I couldn't have done it without her. You see, all those patients you passed upstairs? They're terminal. But our good ol' boy Kane here can give them a fighting chance."

"I don't understand."

"His blood is precious—*golden*, they call it. Divine. One of the rarest on the planet. Kane carries an immunoglobulin that will heal everyone. One drop of this and it's over. All this suffering goes away. Forever."

I finally understand what Kane really is to them. An opportunity for sickness to be eradicated from the world. Zaire doesn't seem the selfless type. "So what do you need me for?"

Zaire scrunches his nose. "Your friend over here is too worried about the blood being rejected to seize the opportunity. He needs a little convincing."

I look at Kane still dangling and helpless. "We could kill a lot of people."

"And they're dead if we do nothing," Zaire tells me. "Eternity is a long time, Jesly, and I, for one, have no intention of dying. Not today, not ever."

"But you're human."

"Exactly. The Chasa only care about one thing, and that's The Balance," Zaire says. "They've already passed their judgment on all of us."

"You honestly expect me to believe you're out to save the

world? You and Hiribaldi killed anyone who stood in your way."

"By the end of this, you'll understand what's at stake." He flips a third lever, and the machine whirs into overdrive. "Sometimes progress means taking uncomfortable risks."

"And Dr. Kennedy and Dr. Caspar?" I ask. "Is that all they were to you? Progress?"

"Exactly."

The machine pumps Kane's blood through the vials one at a time. Some sort of Victorian centrifuge, each chamber built to separate something else out until it leaves only a single vial on the right side.

A final resting chamber, one that's as thick as a half-gallon container of milk.

Jesus.

Zaire sees me trying to do the math. "It's close to two thousand patients. Maybe a little more," he explains. "We'll get a better idea once we refine his blood and synthesize a derivative."

And here I was worried about giving blood at a citywide fundraiser. *This is horrifying.* "He's not your cash cow."

"He's not human, Jesly," Zaire snaps back.

I stare at the half-conscious man dangling from the wheel. "He was once."

"You're right," he agrees. "*Once.* Now, he's just the scourge of humanity, and you want to save him."

"You can't do this. He has a choice."

"Don't be so naïve, girl. He did choose," he says. "That's what got him here in the first place. He did this for you."

"Kane?" My voice breaks.

He looks up, his head bobbing. The machine is robbing what little energy he has.

☥

"Is that true?" I ask.

It's impossible to save him when he's trying to do the same for me. I made a deal with The Chasa on his behalf—to serve them when this is all over—or wherever recruitment is in the Afterlife.

"Is it true?" I repeat, helping him out.

One blackened eye snaps open, blood-shot and laser-focused on me. "J-Jesly? What are you doing here?"

"I came for you. And Dagny."

"No," he says, almost a whimper.

I grab Zaire by the shirt. "Disconnect it. Let him go."

The vial is half-full now, the machine whirring and clanking as it drains Kane pint after pint. Much more and his body will go into shock.

"I mean it."

Dagny slaps my hand away and yanks me back. "Who do you think you are, Jesly Allbrook, in the realm of gods and men?"

"She's right," Zaire says. "Your boy chose this."

Each breath is slow and painful to watch. "Kane chose to be tortured?" I say. "You're a fucking liar, Zaire. No one would ever choose this, immortal or otherwise."

"Jesly . . ." Kane calls out.

I force a smile, tears already forming. "Save your breath. I'm going to get us out of here."

"Zaire . . ." he says slowly. ". . . is telling . . . the truth."

"Stop lying for them," I say in denial. "You don't have to do this."

"I do. You were supposed to be my last charge. The end of my sentence."

His words strike me like a bullet.

"So, I was right; this was just business then." I swallow any emotion left inside me.

☥

"Jesly, please," he begs, much to Zaire's amusement. "Don't do this."

"Tell me."

"I . . . can't . . ."

"Kane, goddamnit—"

"Yes . . . and no," he rasps. "Is that what you want to hear? It was my job to see you through to the end, be that whatever it may. But you kept running, and now our time's run out."

"So that's it?" I swallow any remaining emotion and turn to Zaire. "You've got Dagny's research. You've got what you want. Let us go."

"No way. Kane is far too precious," Zaire laughs and pulls out an ornate curved sword from his waistband. The damn thing looks like a cross between a sickle and a sword.

There's something unsettling about it. Hungry.

He signals to an upper recess. "Take Jesly to the mezzanine." But before Dagny can even drag me away, he turns to me. "I wouldn't want her to miss the finishing touches. This blade . . . This is the best part. It kills whatever it touches."

Dagny hesitates.

Zaire doesn't notice. He's too busy adjusting the hellish contraption on the wall. The far right vial is three-quarters of the way full, having slowed dramatically now that Kane has lost several pints. Both the machine and the man are struggling to keep up.

"Sure thing," she reassures Zaire.

Our footsteps dig into the rocky soil, and I only make it a few yards before she shoves me behind a large outcrop. "You aren't going to like this next part. Take this," she whispers, tossing something in my direction.

My hands fumble as I try to catch it. It's the necklace Dax

ripped from my neck. "How do you have this?" I clutch the lapis amulet for dear life. The Eye of Horus stares back at me. Watching. Judging.

She smiles wryly. "Some things need to be set right. Don't lose it again."

"Dagny, I—"

"Put it on. Now."

Reluctantly, I slip it over my head and tuck the amulet away beneath the grime of my muslin tunic.

She nods, seemingly satisfied, then heads back in their direction. "It belongs to you now."

Across the way, the machine shuts down, the cacophony of disjointed gears finally silent. It's done.

Zaire approaches Kane, satisfied. "You don't know how many lives you're saving with this."

"Stop the bullshit, Zaire," Kane wheezes. "We both know you're not trying to save anyone other than yourself. Why lie to the girl?"

"I'm not lying to anyone," he says as he sets the blade on top of the machine. "This is going to change the world." He pats the vial on the wall.

"All those people are already dead," Kane says. "I'd say that's lying."

"Hmm, maybe," Zaire chortles. "Then again, I never did have a modicum of right and wrong."

"What next? Are you going to bring them all back?" Kane asks. "Have them serve in some undead army?"

"Dear God. Millennia old, and you're still as dense as the day your mother shit you out," Zaire scoffs in disdain. "They're a bargaining tool."

The realization hits Kane. "You're trying to buy your way out of here, aren't you?"

Zaire slaps him on the face affectionately. "Now you get it. An undeniable offer for the Ferryman, and your golden blood is going to help get me there."

"Jesly's right. You've lost it," Kane says in disbelief.

"No, I told you at the start. I'm just someone willing to do something about it."

Zaire pulls a small suede cloth from his chest pocket and unravels it to retrieve a wide syringe and a rubber tube. A few seconds later, he's tied off a vein and extracts some of Kane's blood from inside the canister. Dagny and I both watch in horror as Zaire empties the syringe into his own arm.

"Goodbye, my friend." He shoves the supplies back into his chest pocket. With the task done, he closes the gap between them a little more. A cat-and-mouse game where the prey can't run. "Today begins anew." He pulls the blade back down from the makeshift shelf and spins it in his grip.

It's different. Smaller and lighter than before. Easier to manipulate. "I hope you're ready," Zaire warns.

A grin crawls across his face just as the blade plunges straight into the flesh and bone of the person in front of him. But it's not until that joy disappears like a fallen house of cards that I realize what's happened—it's not Kane who's been stabbed but Dagny.

Having blocked my vantage point, she knew I wouldn't—*couldn't*—stop her. Zaire lets out a shrieking roar as he rips the blade back out, much to Kane's and my surprise.

Dagny crumples to the ground, gasping for air like a fish out of water. "*You aren't going to like this next part.*" She planned this.

"What have you done?" Zaire rips out the tubes holding his

puppet on its strings. "You bastard."

Kane collapses on top of her. He struggles to stand; the blood is too much on the wet dock. Slipping, he comes face to face with the cold stone. Zaire snatches him up like a mother cat would do to her young, flinging him back onto the shoreline like it's nothing. I scramble out from behind the outcrop toward him. Kane's alive, but barely.

Come on. Don't die.

It's on me to get him to the surface—to get both of us back. Before I get the chance, Zaire cuts off my route. "Jesly, I've got to hand it to you. That's some talent you've got there."

"Fuck you."

"Please. Hiribaldi was right. People around you do have a knack for ending up dead," he says as Kane tries to crawl away. "Oh well. Beggars can't be choosers. Ain't that right, buddy?" He drives the short sword into the Watcher's spine, skewering him like a rat in an alleyway.

The sword withdraws and then descends again.

And then again.

I lose count between my screams.

The agony I feel is magnified each time Zaire's blade plunges into Kane. After each strike, Zaire hesitates just long enough for Kane's body to keep from healing. The moment the blade leaves his body, Kane gasps for air, clinging to life until the next onslaught.

Eventually, the blade stays and enough blood coats the rocks that I doubt it'll ever wash away.

This time, Kane doesn't wake, and I can't keep the tears from falling.

☥

RUN

WHILE I MAY NOT be an excellent swimmer, I am a half-decent runner. A fact I am incredibly grateful for. It buys me the time I need. Having watched Zaire rip away the last of my allies in horrible, inhuman ways, putting distance between us is my only good choice. So I run.

If I thought Dagny was a wildcard, Zaire's got her beat. Throwing a two-hundred-pound man like a child's toy really underscores just how out of my league I am. Going back through the tunnel Dagny and I traversed earlier isn't an option. Up it is.

The worst idea in every horror movie—the one where the chick always ends up dead. But first things first: I need a weapon. Something able to even the odds between us and fast. Amy's switchblade stopped being an option the moment we went over the edge. Diving isn't my idea of a good time.

The blade trapping Kane, on the other hand, that's a viable choice. There's something sentient about it. If I can manage to pull it back out of Kane, I might've half a spitting chance.

Maybe both of us.

Kane deserves it. After everything he's sacrificed—what he's survived. How much punishment does one sin deserve? I spent my entire career putting bad guys away. Now I'm giving up my own afterlife to save one. How times have changed. Maybe Amy was wrong and bad people are capable of redemption.

Even me.

Dagny's crumpled body lies on the platform near her brother, both giving their life to something they believed in. I can't let them down. I check to make sure the amulet is still tucked safely beneath my shirt. It is and I say a small prayer to keep it there.

If Chandni and Asim are right, this is our ticket outta here.

"Jesly . . ." Zaire howls from the other end of the chamber.

The water is still freezing, but I fling myself into it, using those precious extra seconds to circle back to the platform and ascend the wooden ladder in record time. I'm about halfway to the mezzanine when the ladder shakes.

It won't be long now. I move faster.

The next level is nothing more than a deteriorated railing and broken scaffolding. I waste no time scrambling across the narrow, dilapidated walkway. Even before the fight between Dax and me, it had seen better days. Now it'll be lucky to take another hit. Wooden shards litter the walkway. I hold my breath, moving as if it's a sheet of ice and don't dare break it.

I inch farther along to find Dax's borrowed shotgun wedged between the wall and the platform. He must have dropped it when we fell—a failure I'm willing to overlook. I yank the butt of the gun, tugging until it eventually tears free of the earth's hold.

Staring from the mezzanine, I finally understand this chamber. The waterwheel draws its power from the falls below. I peer over the railing; the ladder cranes its way until it disappears into an endless waterfall. Below us, it's only an empty abyss. I can't make out anything past the stalagmites and rows of wooden spikes several hundred yards below the scaffolding.

But it's enough.

A warning sign to the unaware, including the faintest reflection of white nestled in the spikes. Bones. A lot of them. This is where the dead go—their final resting place.

The mezzanine shakes again. Zaire bounds in my direction.

"Don't do this," I say, backing away. The shotgun levels on his chest. Seeing as how Dax never fired his weapon, there should still be two shells in the barrels. I better make them count. The wooden platform shakes, further throwing off my balance. "Let Kane and me go."

"No." He lunges at me, a smaller blade in his grip this time, just as my index finger squeezes the trigger.

Click.

He laughs when I freeze. "You didn't really think I'd give that fool a loaded gun, did you?"

I snap open the action on the gun. *Fuck.* "It's empty."

"Nice try, Jesly," he says. "Sorry to break it to you but killing me isn't going to be that easy."

The gun clicks again.

"Are you stupid, girl?" he asks. "You think shells appear out of nowhere? Not when I have them, they won't." He pulls two brass shells from his jacket pocket.

I watch as they go over the mezzanine and disappear somewhere amongst the rocks and spikes.

He takes a deep breath. "Now . . . let's get back to business."

I clutch my chest, that familiar feeling of anxiety crashing over me. God can't help me now.

☥

ABSOLUTION

Almost like I'll die if I don't get a clear, steady breath. Anxiety can take reality and turn it into a merry-go-round. My only choice is to steady myself on the railing, but vertigo sets in and my body is no longer my own.

Now it's just another enemy.

I take another breath between the chest cramps and fight the spinning chamber. Long ago, I'd visited the hospital for panic attacks, years before I'd met Jackson. There's always that slight bit of terror—that it's a heart attack and not anxiety. Stress increases anxiety, which increases stress: a self-fulfilling prophecy.

I need more time, but my body doesn't wait until I'm ready for the final onslaught.

And neither does Zaire.

Unlike Dax, I'm not skilled enough to use the shotgun with any real finesse. I get ready to swing it like a baseball bat, a horrible idea given the circumstances. I ran out of good options hours ago. I'm left with a wing and a prayer.

No therapy in the world will help me process the amount of death and carnage I've witnessed. Some sins will never wash clean no matter the penance.

At this point, surviving is a pipe dream. I'm not delusional. The likelihood I'll see the topside again is slim. I made a promise to The Chasa, and I intend to deliver.

For Kane. For Dagny.

For all those innocents who lost their lives to this asshole.

I wasn't ready before, but I am now. Even if that means killing someone. It took a while, but I've finally found my resolve. Somewhere along the way, I had lost it with Jackson.

But not anymore.

Not ever again.

"I'm glad it's you and me in the end." Zaire slinks down the mezzanine. "I'm going to kill you for what you've done. I hope you understand."

"I didn't kill her," I say. "You know that."

"Doesn't matter." Another syringe, like the one he injected himself with, slides down the underside of his wrist. Unlike the first, he doesn't need seconds to draw something into the vial— it's already prefilled. "Funny. I would've thought you'd understand by now."

"What?" I say.

"That I'm getting out."

"These people aren't your puppets," I tell him. "You can't just use them however you wish."

"No? What about you?" Zaire asks as he pushes matted curls from his eyes.

"What about me?"

"Don't you get it? You're just a piece to be manipulated—a

means to an end for The Chasa," he posits. "A tool to further their obsession with The Balance. Fuck the goddamned Balance."

"That's not true," I say.

"Did you really think everyone dying around you was mere coincidence?" His thick laughter fills the air. "You did. From the moment you were sent back, they've been using you to fill their quota."

"That's a lie."

"No, it's not," he argues. "You and Kane both. You really believed you could just make amends and everything would be okay? It's *never* going to be okay, Jesly. This is it. There are no second chances."

I clutch Dagny's necklace tightly. "No, you're wrong."

"Denying the truth won't change it. Either way, you're helping me get where I need to go. That necklace—" He points at Dagny's amulet around my neck. "How did you get that?"

"This?"

"Hand it over. Now."

Maybe he really does care about her. "What for?" I ask.

"That's my business," he barks, never averting his eyes. "Give it to me. *Please.*" His voice trails up at the end.

I've struck a pressure point. *Good.*

"Okay." I reach around my neck and unclip the chain. The amulet drops into my hands. "Say I do—what then?"

He swallows hard. "This'll be over . . . a horrible memory erased like it never happened."

The joke's on him; there's nothing to go back to. I was intending to jump for a reason. "What's so important about this stupid necklace?" I ask, taking a step closer toward the edge. My eyes scour the edge. I can make it.

He slams his hand on the railing. "You still don't get it. It's not just any necklace. With that amulet and Kane's blood, I can fix this. You freed us, Jesly. We can start over—we can move somewhere new and *be* someone new."

"No second chances," I repeat. "That's what you said, right?" I tumble the talisman between my palms, dropping it back and forth.

His jaw tightens. "You aren't listening. Starting over *is* the only path."

"Then you won't mind this." I toss the amulet and its protection over the railing, ignoring the guttural scream that bursts from Zaire. I'm forced to dodge the syringe lunging in my direction.

Whatever this glass vial holds, it's probably safe to assume I've got 50/50 odds on what it contains. A laundry list of communicable diseases passes through my head. Just one stick of a needle is all it takes and life changes forever.

Zaire doesn't seem to care. I'm guessing the dead don't have such concerns. He lunges again, this time more erratic.

I jump back just in time to avoid the needle. There's no time to figure out what's inside it. No time to turn my back.

I swing the shotgun at him again. It's no use; I'm too slow. He latches onto it and sends me reeling into the wooden scaffolding. The shotgun connects with my jaw, sending vertigo rushing back. This time it brings shooting stars with it.

He drops the gun and kicks it over the edge. "You won't be needing this anymore."

My hands clutch the railing, long enough to distract me from the slight pinch on my right side. I look down long enough to notice Zaire retract the needle and then throw the syringe over the edge.

"You'll thank me later," he says dryly.

A wave of red and black crashes over me like distorted watercolors clouding my mind. "Wh—did—" I collapse through the dilapidated wooden railing and over the mezzanine's edge.

By the grace of God or the universe, I land on something solid, ten yards or so below where I started.

It's hard to move. I can't breathe.

I tell my body to do something—anything—but it's slow to react, sluggish. Extremities still intact, my lungs finally catch up. Stale air surges back into my lungs, and I painfully roll over onto my side.

Nothing's broken, at least. That's the good news.

This far into the earth and my luck's all but run out. If it was dark before, now it's pitch black. I blink a couple of times, forcing my eyes to readjust faster. Sitting up in the darkness takes precious seconds I likely don't have to feel around. To my left, closest to the cliffside, my hands latch onto small cylindrical pebbles nearby.

The shells. My hands clutch tighter. *Please God, let them work.*

To the right, nothing but emptiness. An eternity of death via stalagmites and spike pits below. Climbing back is gonna be a bitch.

I close my eyes and fumble around. *Please tell me the gun made it in one piece.* One shred of good news. That's all I need. Just one. I've got maybe five seconds before Zaire follows. Exhausted and battered, I scour the ground.

"Jesly, stop," he coughs. He's exhausted too.

Ignore him. Just keep looking. With so many boulders and rocks, the slightly narrow path I've landed on doesn't leave a lot of room. One good solid bounce and physics would have destroyed my only chance. *Please let it be here. Please.*

My frantic prayer continues until I latch onto the frame of Dax's shotgun. "Thank God," I mumble and break open the gun to load both barrels.

This time, I know it's loaded for a fact. I rack the chamber and lean against the pile of haphazard boulders, positioning myself. I'm small enough that this gun will have more kick than I can handle on this tiny ledge. If I want to avoid falling, these shots better count. My index finger settles over the first trigger.

Steady . . .

"Hey there."

Boom! I don't hesitate to squeeze the trigger.

I look up to find Zaire in front of me—I didn't even hear him approach. He stumbles back against the boulders, his left hand outstretched to verify that it's his blood pouring out and not mine.

BOOM!

Both triggers are pulled back now.

He collapses against the railing.

"That's enough." His arm slackens to his side, blood sputtering from his lips.

"No," I reply. "It'll never be enough. Not in this world or any other. Not after what you've done."

Something in the distance catches his eye, and he's suddenly lost in thought for a moment. His glazed eyes pierce through me like I'm not even here; he's staring at something I can't see. Behind me, there's nothing but the abyss.

Wherever he is, it's no longer about me.

I don't risk lowering the gun, out of ammo or not.

"Zaire?" I call out, but he's not listening. Not anymore.

He takes one step, then another. He coughs, his chest ragged and moist.

"I found it," he says, talking past me. Out of his pocket comes the amulet I had flung over the cliff. Somewhere in the scramble, he must have picked it up. His hands cling to it tighter than anyone should. Wound around his palm, the amulet cuts into it; he doesn't even flinch.

Another step.

"Zaire?"

"Here, Dags. This is for you—" He untangles the chain and holds the pendant out, but there's no one to take it. The ankh drops onto the rocky soil at his feet. He continues walking toward the precipice.

I latch onto his shirt with both hands, dropping the gun. "Zaire, whoa. Stop. There's nothing there."

"This is what she wants," he says, his voice catatonic and empty. "I must go."

"What? No." My eyes widen, and it takes a lot more force to stop him. My feet slide in the loose soil.

He shoves me away, and I stumble, shaking as he finishes the job. I reach for him and scramble to the edge, but it doesn't work.

He falls into the darkness.

It's not until he impales himself on the rocky crags and wooden spikes hundreds of feet below that I can bring myself to look away. The impact echoes in my ears, the sound of flesh and bone becoming nothing more than a resounding thud in the shadows.

He's right; eternity is a long time.

On the off chance he doesn't bleed out, severing his spinal column will keep him paralyzed until the end of time. Something I don't wish on anyone. Not even Zaire. But I'm not stupid. I'm not rappelling down there to rescue him.

He chose his path and I, mine.

It's over.

☥

It's really over.

I retch on the craggy soil; it's yellow and disgusting. I haven't eaten in so long that I dry heave until I collapse into a heap of dirt and my own tears.

I'm alone again, but it's done. Finally.

I lay against the cliff wall, the stark silence of the place no longer terrifying. I stare up at the mezzanine and the stalactites, exhaustion finally taking over. There's no telling how long I lay there. I don't rush it. There's nothing to go back to. Only forward.

Everyone's dead. The patients. The others. Ka—

I jolt up. *Kane. Shit.*

Scaling the cliffside is just as terrifying, except Dagny isn't here to guide me. It takes several tries and near misses, but I reach the platform and drag myself back over it, my triceps bordering desperately on collapse. Having lost my shoes somewhere along the way, my bare feet smack against the stone. The sharp rocks tear at my skin as I race across the open cavern to where Kane's body is still impaled.

His face is expressionless, his body still. My feet accidentally slide in the blood. Grasping the hilt, I yank it as hard as I can, its curved blade sliding back out of him. A twisted rendition of King Arthur in the twenty-first century. The blade clangs to the ground. My bloody and bruised hands grab his face.

"Kane, can you hear me?" I brush his hair out of his eyes. *Someone . . . anyone . . . has to survive this. This can't be it.*

Nothing. There's nothing.

I'm losing my goddamn mind talking to the dead. I pull my knees against my chest.

And I pray.

And I wait.

If God exists in the Universe, it's the only option I've got left. Kane's come back once. He can do it again.

I owe him too much to leave him. He's the only reason I've made it as far as I have. My fingers coil around the amulet as tightly as Zaire's had. *Please God, don't let him die.*

Perhaps I'm being selfish. Kane's endured torture for millennia, and I want him to stay alive just for me. Or maybe it's so I can feel absolved for dragging him into this hellish nightmare. If I'm lucky, God is merciful. Maybe he'll understand why I've done what I have, or perhaps it's all a lie and there's no god after all.

That would be the easy way out. But I know that's not how it works—not after what I've seen.

God helps those who help themselves. But what about those poor souls who can't save themselves? What then?

No one is coming to save me. No one is coming to save Kane.

Whatever happens next, it's on us both.

A deep, shuddering gasp echoes behind me, the sound of life returning from the universal wellspring.

I have no idea how this process works, but right now, I honestly don't care. With the sword removed, it's clear Kane is able to heal.

"Allbrook, you stayed . . ."

Battered and bloody, but at least he recognizes me. I collapse into his arms, hugging him in a way that's visceral and animalistic. Pure survival. I cling and don't let go.

For both of us. Not this time.

For what it's worth, Kane's alive. Trapped between life and death, but he's still here.

And so am I.

It's finally quiet, the voice gone. Kane's equally tight embrace is all I've got, and that will have to do for now.

Because I'm not a mind-reader. I'm no soothsayer.

I don't know what the future holds. I expect The Chasa to come for their dues soon. But I'll be ready—I *have* to be ready.

A promise is a promise. A deal is a deal.

But some gifts, like how Kane protects me even after everything, are worth the cost.

NO REST
SIX WEEKS LATER

"HOW MUCH LONGER?" KANE'S voice reaches me from across the cemetery grounds. He leans against a large old live oak, no worse for wear. A little skinnier, sure. A little less facial hair, but he's here. *Alive.* Or as close to living as we're going to get.

I don't bother answering him. He already knows. It's just for show. My sidelong glance evokes a snort of derision from him. He doesn't approve of me leaving his sight, not even in a cemetery. Knowing what we've survived, I can't be that angry.

Ever since returning above ground, he's doubled down on his duties. His hawk-eyed approach is sweet, albeit a little aggravating sometimes. At least someone is watching my back.

While Kane's feeling almost back to normal, I feel more detached than ever. Empty. Deep in my bones. It's hard to explain.

But one thing is certain: when people pass us on the street, no one notices. It's like we don't exist.

It's because we don't, Kane told me the first time it happened. *Not anymore.*

There's a harshness in his tone; he's still mad, and I don't blame him. He didn't want this to be the way it ended—for me to join him as a Watcher. But it's my choice and he knows it.

Honestly, I'm stunned he hasn't grown tired of me yet. Maybe that's because I'm his ward—his charge to guide to the other side— a tougher job now since I won't be retiring for a very, *very* long time.

He's coming around . . . slowly. Bags of Skittles also helps.

For the past several weeks, we've visited Dagny's mausoleum and set lilies in the flower holder. I haven't tried tracking down what's left of her family. They wouldn't believe me even if I did.

Frankly, after losing both their children, visiting seems a little heartless. Catching sight of one of us doesn't usually bode well for the living. *Watchers* don't interact with the living, only the dying and the damned.

This new job title—*Watcher*—is weird. I'd rather go with the classic *Reaper*, but Kane is quick to tell me the title went out of vogue centuries ago. *Ah well. Could be worse.*

Kane taps his wrist between handfuls of candy, signaling it's time to move on. Our schedule is tight today, no matter how much my kicking and screaming delays the inevitable.

To my reluctance, we head inside. Much like the permanent reminder etched on my wrist, this place is starkly silent. With Dax gone, the mausoleum has lost what little life it held. Most likely, Dagny and Dax's parents avoid visiting. *Understandable.* The wounds are too fresh.

As we descend through the lower level and into the main chamber, the place is surprisingly well lit. Nothing seems out of the ordinary. But it's not until we reach the **SHEPHERD** family wall that a stark splash of color—yellows, pinks, and oranges— yanks my attention. Gladioli and chrysanthemums. Freshly cut and recently placed. They weren't here yesterday.

"Kane? Kane!"

The alarm in my voice brings him running. "What is it?"

I point. "Did you bring those?"

He shakes his head.

"Then who did?" I swallow the lump in my throat. Ever since we've come back, I've been endlessly thirsty, with no amount of water quenching it. Maybe it's because I'm really dead this time.

"I don't know," he says between bites, though he's thinking the same thing. "Maybe the groundskeeper swung through here." He shrugs, not wanting me to stress. Futile, but sweet.

"Come on. We've got to go. We'll be late for your first day." He heads back down the corridor but pauses when I don't follow. "Jesly, don't worry about it."

"What if . . . one of them survived?" I clutch my throat.

"Then we deal with it," he says plainly. "I've done this a long time. Whatever comes, comes. We'll handle it together."

"You promise?"

"I promise." He holds out his hand for me to grab onto.

Unlike him, I haven't healed as quickly. Faster than I probably should, given Zaire's little concoction, but not enough that I walk without injury. Kane says I'll adjust once we leave this plane. Once we return to where it all started, my memories intact.

But this time, he's coming with me. "You ready?"

I wrap my arm around his as we ascend the cobbled stairs, exiting the mausoleum. "Do I really have a choice?"

His frown is all the answer I need.

"Okay . . ." I concede and take a deep breath.

Everyone thinks death is the end of something.

It's actually just the beginning.

DEAR READER
(A.K.A. THE AUTHOR'S NOTE)

Hey there!

You survived. *Congratulations*!

Thank you so much for taking the time to read *The Place We All Go*. This novel took over two years to write, and I'll tell you what . . . it was a pain. While it had been over a decade since I had last completed a full-length novel, it wasn't the issue of being rusty that made this novel take so long. As it currently stands, I have three other books in progress as we speak.

This little guy in your hands, though, felt like I was birthing a baby, running a marathon, and pounding my head into the wall simultaneously. Needless to say, it was a lot of work. I tore it apart. Again, and again, and again. There were days I would spend all my free time just thinking about one section from a chapter, trying to make it right.

I've done my best to make this novel something amazing. I hope you loved it. I know I do. And as a fan of many genres, especially thrillers, supernatural themes, mythology, fantasy, and horror, I did my best to make this novel the adventure of a lifetime.

Diving into this genre (thriller) was new for me. While I normally write fantasy (urban or dark), I had the idea for a psychological thriller that bordered the supernatural. And so, this novel was born. And the way it looks, likely half of my permanent branding.

All of that being said, I'm so glad you got the chance to experience Jesly's world for yourself. Whether you loved it, hated it, or were just kind of meh . . . I appreciate you.

Now that you've made it this far, if it wouldn't be too much trouble, will you take the time to review the book wherever you bought your copy? That would be *so* great of you.

If you didn't already know, a review is one of the best ways you can support your indie authors, as it spreads the word and allows us to keep making entertaining content that you love. Want to take it one step further? Share on social media. Tell your coworkers. Support your indies.

So if you like dark fantasy or supernatural thrillers, I hope to see you again soon.

With Love & Light,

The Dark Mythologist

NOVEL PLAYLIST

This novel took me through a very dark period in my life where I had to learn how to heal (still ongoing) from C-PTSD and complicated grief. As other survivors of C-PTSD and complicated grief and those around them know, every day is different—some good, some bad.

As such, the music that goes with this novel is also painful, melancholic, and deeply meaningful. Most of these songs deal with grief, intimate partner violence, suicidal ideation, and the complicated human experience that is love.

The playlist, or soundtrack as you will, is highly curated and vetted and access is available on the Magick & Mythos YouTube Channel and Spotify for your listening enjoyment.

All rights are reserved to the respective artists and musicians who created these wonderful songs.

1. Isak Danielson - Religion
2. FINNEAS - Break My Heart Again
3. Two Feet - I Feel Like I'm Drowning
4. The Unlikely Candidates - Oh My Dear Lord
5. Mansionair - Easier
6. Billie Eilish - Lovely
7. Billie Eilish - Happier Than Ever
8. Gnarls Barkley - Crazy
9. Isak Danielson - Power
10. Charlotte Lawrence - Joke's On You
11. Amber Run - I Found

12. Missio - Bottom of the Deep Blue Sea
13. Low Roar - Bones (feat. Jófríður Ákadóttir)
14. Lord Huron - The Night We Met
15. Labrinth - Kill For Your Love
16. Flora Cash - You're Somebody Else
17. Labrinth - Something's Got To Give
18. The Unlikely Candidates - High Low
19. KALEO - I Can't Go On Without You
20. SYML - Mr. Sandman
21. KALEO - Save Yourself
22. Bishop Briggs - High Water
23. AURORA - A Dangerous Thing
24. Labrinth - Oblivion (ft. Sia)
25. Havana Winter - Death Wish

ABOUT THE AUTHOR

Also known as The Dark Mythologist™ across social media, M. Dylan Blair™ is a dark fantasy and supernatural thriller author who has spent time immemorial trying to answer the big questions in life. As a writer, her novels are no different.

Ever weaving the strands of Time and space together with a dash of mythology and the supernatural thrown in, Blair blends genres in her search for the truth. Driven by a passion for studying religion and mythology, she's resorted to answering her questions through fiction.

She lives in Florida with her family, their rescue lab named Scout, and two cats: Patches and Momo. You can usually find Blair with her head buried in some kind of research or chilling with a hazelnut oat latte at weird hours.

Instagram/Facebook/Threads/YouTube:
@thedarkmythologist

Goodreads & BookBub
@mdylanblair

Visit

www.magickandmythos.com

to learn about future releases, join the newsletter, special perks, gain awesome access to short stories, and more!